THE SIEGE
OF MARS

YEAR
of the
BOOK

GEORGE G. MOORE

Year of the Book
135 Glen Avenue
Glen Rock, PA 17327

ISBN: 978-1-64649-457-6 (print)
ISBN: 978-1-64649-458-3 (ebook)

Library of Congress Control Number: 2024921691

This is a work of fiction. Names, characters, businesses, places, events, and incidents are either the products of the author's imagination or used in a fictitious manner. Any resemblance to actual persons, living or dead, or actual events is purely coincidental.

Cover design: Jay Aheer

This work contains no AI-generated content.

DEDICATION

For my wife, Kelly,
and my mother-in-law, Betty,
who has patiently waited for this
sequel to *The Music of Mars*.

Acknowledgments

Many thanks to the members of Lisa's Virtual Writers Group and the Loudoun Science Fiction and Fantasy Writers—The Hourlings who helped me shape this novel to my vision.

Thanks to Kelly for her sound advice and inspiration.

For her expertise in sharpening my words, I am grateful to Demi Stevens, editor extraordinaire.

Finally, my heartfelt appreciation for readers returning for another tale in this world, and for those who are new to the adventures of Gretchen and Frank.

1 | Uninvited Guest

What is keeping Gretchen? Frank Brentford waited with two salads before him. Around him, his Mars City co-workers were chatting over their lunches about the next three weeks of plays, concerts, and recreational activities.

They wore casual clothes instead of the standard steel blue coveralls with black undershirts. After two years of constant work, their downtime was well-earned.

For the past week, maroon and brown sand swirled, increasingly obscuring everything beyond the domes. All significant operations, like mining and exploring the alien city—Bvindu Dome—had been suspended, with everyone returning here to ride out the Mars-yearly sandstorm.

When Earthers, like the auditors and inspectors who'd recently departed, first witnessed these storms, they compared them to Earth's monsoons and blizzards. Often, they struggled to reconcile hurricane-speed winds with the force of a gentle Earth breeze. When reminded of Mars' low air pressure, their confusion usually passed.

Storms of all types were another reason on Frank's already long list to never bother with Earth. Visiting his ancestral home was a backward move. His future lay elsewhere on Mars, in the Belt, and the outer solar system.

Gretchen Blake, MarsVantage's Director of Archaeology, approached. Shoulder-length black hair framed her face. As she sat opposite him, she said, "Sorry I'm late, hon. I bumped into Erin and asked about her progress toward flying the Bvindu Scout Ship."

"Tell me it involved her thoughts on its faster-than-light capability." He slid Gretchen's salad across the table, then ate a forkful of his own.

Gretchen chortled. "Since she's been grounded for the last week, she's been plowing through the documentation."

In truth, Erin and her pilots were rated to fly in no/low visibility conditions, but no Earth transports were scheduled to arrive in orbit for three more weeks—the best guess from Meteorology as to when the sandstorms would abate.

"The sooner she's comfortable flying it, the sooner we can transition. The Bvindu Marsium121 energy source will save a significant sum on shuttle fuel cells." Other benefits, like bringing the outer solar system within reach, would open intriguing doors, but such things weren't discussed publicly.

As Director of Bvindu Practical Applications, Frank evaluated whatever Gretchen and her archaeologists discovered. Some, like the cold cure, had been passed along to Fordham Industries to bring to market on Earth. Others, like the Bvindu Scout Ship and the Marsium121 energy source, were kept in-house for MarsVantage's exclusive use.

"This is new." Gretchen jutted her chin off to the right. "Chuck's heading our way."

Chuck O'Donnell, MarsVantage's CEO, approached but carried no lunch. The graying at his temples and over his ears was more pronounced than before their discovery of Bvindu Dome two years earlier. Frank considered the gray mixed into his own black hair. If his dad and grandfathers were any indication, he wouldn't go bald. Some gray hairs at forty versus no hair at all wasn't a bad trade-off.

Chuck sat cattycorner from them. "I'm glad you're taking the opportunity to relax."

"To be truthful," Gretchen said, glancing both ways, "we're taking a break from the *other* project."

"My news relates to that." Chuck leaned in closer. "I received an email from the All News Network an hour ago. A reporter will arrive on the next transport in three weeks."

"A reporter?" Frank dropped his fork into the salad. "Two and a half centuries ago, Earth people marveled at a helicopter flying on Mars. Yet, when we discovered the first hard evidence of intelligent alien life—abandoned and buried under a Martian plain—all we saw were brief reports for one day before we became punchlines for late-night personalities."

"I suspect the auditors and inspectors failed to find a rationale to strip us of everything Bvindu," Chuck pointed out.

Frank pursed his lips. "Are you joking? I've had less thorough rectal exams."

Chuck placed his forearms on the table. "Our lobbyists indicate Washington's looking for any reason to nationalize Bvindu Dome, leaving us with nothing. Without those resources, we'll be bankrupt in a decade."

Gretchen scowled. "I wonder when Washington will simply manufacture an excuse."

Frank left unsaid that additional regulations were sure to come. *Having this argument again is pointless.*

"A reporter can do what the auditors and inspectors couldn't." Gretchen flopped against the seatback, happiness draining from her face.

"Like weasel Bvindu info from our archaeology team," Chuck said. "Cozy up to anyone and everyone to hear candid assessments of our initiatives. That's just off the top of my head. Reporters have an uncanny ability to connect dots."

Gretchen's eyes narrowed as she took in Chuck. "You could've just forwarded the email. Why'd you track us down?"

"I'll forward it later." Chuck eyed Gretchen. "I ran a quick background check and found it most curious that this particular reporter was assigned to Mars."

With eyes wide, the blood drained from Gretchen's cheeks. "Oh, don't tell me..."

"James Wagoner."

Gretchen shook her head and stared at the table. "Of course it is."

"You know him?" Frank asked.

With a thousand-yard gaze, she said, "He specializes in reporting on international elections and conflicts."

Why would Earth send a war correspondent to report on alien tech? "I'm missing something."

"Hon, James Wagoner is the poster child for the less said, the better."

That last phrase arranged a few puzzle pieces into an unsettling picture. "You're not saying..."

Her expression became inscrutable. "You know him as Jimmy, my ex-husband."

2 | THE PARADOX

Frank sat on Erin Knox's right in the cockpit of her MarsVantage shuttle. They wore standard green spacesuits, sans helmets and gloves, which were stowed on their seat backs. Five-point harnesses secured them during flight maneuvers.

She looked completely at home behind the controls. Like most who spent significant time in spacesuits, she kept her brown hair short to avoid tickling her forehead or creeping into view.

They were making a side trip transporting unspecified cargo to an unofficial destination, off the record, before meeting the transport at the Orbital Transfer Point. Frank could count on Erin whenever he found himself in a jam. It was mutual, but her need for him was far less frequent.

Before they reached the OTP, he would ask her to join the Citizens in Freedom Committee. Her skills and advice would be invaluable. But it was a bigger ask than anything he'd requested, and she might decline.

Friendship only went so far, after all. His best chance of success was for her to see the secret the Committee had been keeping.

Daylight dimmed through the cockpit windows as the shuttle entered a denser region of waning sandstorms. Dust and sand struck the cockpit plastiglass, sounding like safety retaining pins falling against deck plates. He held tremendous faith in Erin's piloting skills, but flights under these conditions were unsettling.

Erin looked over and chuckled. "You aren't going to vomit on my ship, are you?"

"Not unless you do barrel rolls like you did to the inspector a month ago."

"That woman had it coming, prying into everything while looking down her nose at us the entire time."

Frank ran his hand through his hair, knocking the headset from his ear. While replacing it, he said, "Chuck received an official complaint."

"I *officially* responded by citing the requirement to avoid atmospheric instabilities, per the regs as sandstorms developed."

"You wouldn't care to describe precisely what those instabilities were."

"Maybe I exaggerated, but they're Earth's regs." She shrugged. "Isn't it time they work in our favor?"

He laughed. "*Exaggerated* is an interesting take."

Erin steadily guided the shuttle to its destination. "Anyway, we're operating well within the regs."

He gritted his teeth, taking no comfort in anything conceived by bureaucrats over a hundred million miles away, probably without ever visiting low-Earth orbit, let alone traveling in open space.

Erin volunteered, "We're high enough, so our flight path is clear. The fun starts when we arrive."

"Fun?"

"After coming here a dozen times, I'm confident saying a landing zone next to a butte is a horrible idea. The reduced visibility only makes it worse. If I miscalculate our approach, we could have a sudden, unpleasant end to the trip."

"The beacons will guide us as they have for our *four* previous trips."

"I must've lost count." Erin gave him a look that declared his need for precision wasn't appreciated. "Stranger yet, I flew by a few other times over the past year, and there were zero traces of a beacon signal."

"That *is* strange."

"You and your secrets."

She'd find out soon enough, though that knowledge might not comfort her.

After several minutes, Erin put the shuttle into a slight bank. "We're on approach, and... the beacons are active. It's like someone's there and knows we're coming."

"I vidcommed ahead."

Erin manipulated several controls and adjusted her grip on the cyclic and the collective. "We're halfway around Mars. No one lives here. Yet, we're dropping off cargo. Care to explain?"

3 | Turns Along the Path

Slightly stooped, Erin pressed the control on the front landing gear's support to retract the loading ramp. With the touch of another, she closed the cargo hatch. Finally, she secured the access panel against the swirling sand.

She turned to place the strobing anti-collision light on the shuttle's centerline to her back, then blinked away the afterimage. Regs required active landing lights in the wild for cargo transfers at temporary sites like this, even if they were unofficial or in broad daylight. If this trip went sideways, no one could credibly accuse her of unsafe practices. Filing an incomplete flight plan, sure, but not willfully breaking safety regs. One would earn her a reprimand, while the other would cost her pilot's license.

Erin joined Frank, sitting on a cargo container. "Now what? And we don't have a lot of spare time before picking up that Earther reporter."

Frank slid off the container. "He'll enjoy the view from the OTP for a few minutes after thirty days of looking at the same handful of rooms."

"We ought to start on the right foot, don't you think?"

Frank turned in the direction of the butte and headed that way. "At best, that reporter's here to undermine MarsVantage with the public. I'm betting he'll surreptitiously feed information to Washington to rein us in further. He's more spy than reporter."

"You took an extra cynical pill this morning."

"The inspectors and auditors found nothing. Now, a reporter is here to snoop around from a different angle. He'll cozy up to people, make them think he's their best friend, and pump them for information."

"Or maybe he's here to learn more about the alien city and educate everyone on Earth."

The rock face grew more distinct through the swirling dust until it was an arm's length away. Frank pushed against it as he continued rightward. "If he were here about the Bvindu wonders, wouldn't he have arrived two months after Gretchen published her paper in the archaeological journal? Not two years later? He has a hidden agenda—mark my words—and it'll work against us."

Perhaps Frank was right. He saw more of the big picture than she did. Besides, he *was* Mars' leading expert on hidden agendas.

As he pushed with his right hand, the rock face moved. She blinked a couple of times, not believing her eyes. He stuck his fingers in a nearby vertical fissure and swiveled the rock face toward them, revealing a black hatch. He pressed the topmost of two oversized buttons on the control panel to its right. It lit red, and a handful of seconds later, presumably after equalizing the air pressure, it turned green as the hatch slid aside to reveal a metal cargo lift.

"An airlock hatch and a cargo lift in the middle of nowhere?" This trip had just ventured from Frank-typical oddness to outright bizarre.

He stepped inside. After turning on his exterior helmet light, he beckoned. "Come on. The good stuff's this way."

"What are you up to now, Frank Brentford?" She stepped on the metal grating, the deck sinking a fraction as it accepted her weight. She also turned on her helmet light.

"I want to show you my secret, then we'll talk." Frank pressed the Down control. The hatch slid back in place, and the lift descended in darkness except where their helmet lights shined. "This is the entrance to what we call Shadow City. Before the caretaker departed Bvindu Dome to find his people, he handed over a Manuduction—"

"Stop. Use words that regular people understand."

He exhaled. "It's an introduction and guidance to the Bvindu technology. It has an index into the knowledge base in Bvindu Dome with summaries of select topics the caretaker believed would interest us. Plus, it contains a quick reference guide to operating various Bvindu Dome systems with links to detailed instructions."

"So that's how you got the cure for the common cold to Fordham Industries and into the FDA's regulatory pipeline so quickly."

"It's more than that—it's a technique to destroy all kinds of viruses. But that's beside the point. Gretchen has been working with the Manuduction since we struck the deal to repair Bvindu Dome's manufacturing systems for the caretaker. It references thirty original Bvindu cities spread across the planet, usually near arable soil, rivers, and natural resources when Mars was green. Except for Shadow City, the others were abandoned. The Bvindu set up this city as a backup site to Bvindu Dome."

"Backup meaning..."

"It contains a duplicate database and many of the culture's lesser treasures." Frank clasped his hands behind his back.

"And the Bvindu used this very Earth-looking cargo elevator?"

"Of course not."

The cargo lift stopped before an identical airlock hatch. Frank pushed the top button on a panel, which turned red. Several seconds later—it felt twice as long as when they'd entered the elevator—it turned green. The hatch slid aside to show a wide maroon and brown hallway.

A closer inspection revealed plastiglass holding back strata of sand. The standard overhead lights left the area above in shadow, while the floor and walls were mainly rust-colored with traces of brown and tan streaks. Every ten feet or so, broad black graphene columns and beams connected the plastiglass sheets.

Highly skilled people with excavating equipment must've created the hallway, neither of which had originated with MarsVantage. Diverting personnel and machinery would've made a conspicuous ripple in scheduling. Besides, everything would've required flights, and none of her pilots had made the trip.

Peter Konklin Interplanetary hadn't been involved. Frank would dig out this corridor by hand without a spacesuit before partnering with them.

The Pan-Asian Alliance could've created the hallway, though they'd never shown much interest in Mars. Instead, they preferred to exploit a region of the Asteroid Belt near the dwarf planet Ceres.

The prospect of Frank allying with them, or any foreign Earth government, was unthinkable. They found anything associated with Mars to be more trouble than it was worth. Moreover, according to the rumors she'd heard from the crews of Earth transports, they kowtowed to Washington's demands regarding Mars, most likely for concessions related to the Belt.

As absurd as it sounded, Frank could be in league with a criminal syndicate. It was one thing to drop off or pick up cargo, but to meet thugs sent a chill down her spine. His ass and her boot might very well meet before this trip ended.

Frank checked his suit's wrist control panel, extinguished his helmet lights, and removed his helmet. Erin checked her panel. They had nearly normal air pressure and atmosphere—seventy-eight percent nitrogen, twenty percent oxygen, and a mix of other gases.

She mirrored him by removing her helmet and shoving her gloves inside it. "We have air?"

"Friends of mine converted the butte to an entrance and tunneled to the city. They set up the entire elevator as an airlock to access it." He guided her forward.

"Sure..." Whatever Frank was involved with was enormous. Before leaving Mars City, she'd marked the reporter as the day's highlight. Frank and his secret underground city had overtaken that position.

After coming to a heavy-duty metal hatch, he directed her to a narrow hallway to their left. It arced, bringing them back to the main hallway and another hatch a minute's walking distance later.

Frank pointed to their right. "Except for cargo transfers, these hatches remain closed to prevent a hostile force from taking a straight shot into Shadow City."

"Who's invading?"

"No one, but it doesn't hurt to be prepared."

He embodied the Mars Scouts motto, *"Always prepared."* Even as a Maintenance Manager, he'd kept MarsVantage's various systems running efficiently and creatively built new ones to meet their ever-changing needs. Two years into his new position as Director of Bvindu Practical Applications hadn't changed him, only the scale of canvas he created on. That canvas might be more extensive than she'd ever imagined.

The more significant point was that he'd been hiding Shadow City for some time, so it must be part of a plan. But a plan for what?

4 | SHADOW CITY

Another narrow arcing passageway brought a familiar sight. Erin blinked, never expecting the scene before her. "This looks like the entrance into Bvindu Dome."

"This entire city is virtually its clone." Frank pointed to the black and yellow line on the floor before them. "And be careful. We can't cross the warning line."

"Because we don't have security wristbands."

"Exactly," said an approaching man in black coveralls carrying a white cloth sack. He sported the reddest of red hair and looked like he moved boulders as a hobby. He stopped on their side of the line while two others in green spacesuits pushing hand trucks, one transporting a cargo container, continued past.

Frank said, "Erin Knox, pilot and Manager of Flight Operations, this is Zared Gadsden, Master Sergeant, Space Force, retired."

The stranger shook her hand firmly and peered intently into her eyes. Thugs weren't usually freshly shaved with military-length hair. Still, retired military turning to crime wasn't unheard of, though it was stereotypical for a mercenary.

"Pleased to meet you in person, Frank." After Zared exchanged a handshake with Frank, he reached into the sack and passed each an apple. "Everyone calls me Red. What do you think about these?"

Erin bit into the fruit. Unlike the apples imported from Earth or those grown by MarsVantage's botanists, Red's was crisp and luscious. She wiped the juices from her mouth with the back of her hand. "It's just like the ones I had as a kid before my family moved here."

"That's incredible," Frank added. "I had no idea apples could be so delicious."

Red beamed. "We're experimenting with other fruits. And vegetables, too. The Bvindu farming techniques are revolutionary."

Not surprising, Frank had withheld this secret city and its farming from Washington. The bureaucrats only learned what was absolutely necessary. Yet, none of this was common knowledge back at Mars City.

She looked down the street, bordered by buildings on each side, seeing nothing unusual. "How many farmers are here?"

"A little over a hundred," Red replied.

The farmers outnumbered those in Mars City two to one. What crime syndicate dealt in fruits and vegetables?

"How many people live here?" she asked.

Frank answered, "A few thousand."

"Why? How?"

"All good questions." Red stood a bit taller. "We came here because Shadow City offers what the United States—and Earth, in general—lacks. Freedom to reap the benefits of our efforts. Freedom to live how we choose, without know-nothing know-it-alls imposing regs supposedly for our benefit, but often contrary to commonsense. Time and again, people here proclaim they're the happiest they've ever been."

Erin's organized crime theory went up in smoke.

"Change is upon us." Frank frowned. "All signs indicate Washington aims to rein MarsVantage in more."

He'd just confirmed what she'd suspected. For a week before the sandstorms, she hadn't been able to move without running into an inspector asking an annoying question. Once, one had waited outside a washroom pod in Bvindu Dome to ask *more* questions.

As bad as it'd been, she had little room to complain. By all accounts, others had more intrusive experiences.

Red exhaled. "SF adopted a saying that originated in the twentieth century, 'Once is happenstance. Twice is a coincidence. Three times is enemy action.' The government views MarsVantage self-sufficiency as a threat, so they'll insist on restrictions, more taxes, regs, and the like. And that's your best-case scenario."

"What's the worst case?" Erin asked.

"Paranoid politicians confiscate the Bvindu tech, by force if MarsVantage won't knuckle under. My money's on that play. They hide their fear well, but it's there, driving their actions."

His harsh assessment wasn't news to Frank who always saw a couple of moves ahead.

"We brought the Bvindu comm equipment," Frank continued, ignoring Red's statement. "You'll be able to communicate with me without fear of detection. Can you believe one of the inspectors stumbled on to transmissions over the regular frequencies and inquired?"

"They were looking for anything to justify further restrictions," Red said.

"No doubt." For a moment, Frank half-grinned with mischief in his eyes. "We blamed the nearby Interplanetary construction crews working on their new dome."

"Good cover story," Red said. "We're bringing in your cargo and leaving a container holding a couple of bushels from our latest apple harvest. Enjoy. It also includes a datacard detailing everything we did farming-wise, noting the Bvindu data we followed. Have your farmers pay special attention to the soil reclamation section. There's also a lot of data on the other topics you asked about. Let me know if you want to run field tests."

"Thanks. It's a remote contingency."

"It's not as remote as you think, Frank. Remember, if it comes to force, SF is trained to break things and kill people."

Erin shivered. Frank was involved in something that could result in hostilities with Space Force. That was bigger than the government splitting MarsVantage away from Interplanetary fifteen years earlier. It sounded like he was downplaying hostilities for some reason, which was unlike him. Usually, he accounted for the worst-case scenario first.

"I'll get back to you." Frank pulled out his datapad and glanced at it. "We need to move out. We have to pick up a reporter... so he can actively work against us."

5 | THE CRUX OF THE MATTER

A little after seven, Senator Maura Severino strolled into her fifth-floor office suite of the Old Hart Building in Washington, DC. Her red-soled heels squeezed her feet, a reminder of the fleeting freedom that sandals had afforded while on vacation.

Her executive assistant, Brielle Porizkova, rose from behind her desk and followed the senator into the main office, as was her habit. "Good morning, Maura."

"The office looks fantastic. You had the carpets cleaned and the furniture polished." Every detail was elegant, from the Persian rug to the traditional furnishings—a cherry wood desk and credenza with a matching bookcase, mini-conference table, and wet bar.

This is the office of a United States senator.

After placing her datapad on the desk, Maura stowed her purse and laid her leather tote on the credenza. She sank into her high-back leather chair.

"You looked well-rested," Brielle politely observed.

Streaks of gray had overtaken her assistant's natural brown hair yet somehow provided an air of elegance. Though Brielle hovered around retirement age, her features were of a fit fifty-year-old. She had to have had a nip and tuck at some point.

Maura wasn't as fortunate. Dye was necessary, much like the lotions and creams that kept age at bay. She was losing the battle, and the laser scalpel loomed in her future. She pushed that unsettling thought away.

"The break was refreshing. Next time, you have to join me on the island. No holocams, and the seafood was beyond compare."

"I'd like that. I haven't had decent crab cakes in longer than I can remember. I tried faux-crabmeat once and wouldn't feed it to my cat."

"Crabs are available in Barney's back room, right?"

Barney's was an upscale retailer of clothes, shoes, and accessories. Its basement, which those in the know euphemistically called the back room, held the best quality perishables and black market goods this side of the Mississippi. Produce from the grocer, based on an individual's NutriAccount food allotment, paled compared to Barney's flavorful selection. Of course, illegal items like chocolate, potato chips, tobacco products, sushi, and so much more were available, too. One only needed a prestigious name and anonymous cash.

"I don't know anyone who can prepare them."

Maura sighed. "That's an unfortunate byproduct of the Nutrition and Fitness Service categorizing all seafood as unhealthy."

"They lumped crabs in with cholesterol-laden seafood like shrimp and lobster. No amount of facts will change their minds."

"Bureaucracy moves at its own pace, but internationally, well-prepared seafood is readily available. I mean it—plan on joining me for winter break. We'll eat well."

"I appreciate it." Brielle met Maura's eyes for a moment. "Your day's schedule is finalized. First up is Mr. Konklin in eighteen minutes."

He was the CEO of the eponymously named Peter Konklin Interplanetary and a vital part of her evolving plan. His experience with the Marsees would be invaluable in acquiring Bvindu technology, and ensuring their radical ideas remained suppressed. All for the good of the country.

Like most C-suite executives, Peter was arrogant enough to believe he ran the world, and she'd never disabused him of the notion. He was a most valuable and willing tool. She'd get what she needed, and he'd get what he desired most—MarsVantage. *Everyone wins, especially me.*

Maura glanced at the schedule on her datapad. "Peter and I will run long. Please reschedule my eight o'clock to tomorrow. Their issue isn't urgent."

"Very good." Brielle gave a curt nod. "I'll bring the breakfast selection in shortly."

"From Barney's?"

"Naturally. The oranges are delightful today. I squeezed them, and the juice is on ice. I'm sure Mr. Konklin will approve."

Brielle expertly tracked Maura's associates' preferences, not once letting her down. "Excellent. Everything needs to be just so."

Nearly at the door, Brielle turned and said, "Before I forget, I uploaded a gossip item about the outfit you wore yesterday."

"Good or bad?"

"Elegant and impeccably fashionable."

"We can ride good press like that straight into the White House as long as we get the Marsees under control."

"I agree." Brielle left to attend to breakfast.

Maura read the blurb and examined the picture. The photographer captured her from a good angle in a favorable light. Regardless of planning, luck always played a role, and it was with her.

Next, she reread the executive summary from the Space Transportation Safety Ministry report on MarsVantage's operation. She could state in one sentence what the civil servants had done in two pages—their operation complied with all regulatory practices, in several cases exceeding standards.

That wouldn't advance her agenda.

A report on MarsVantage's productivity illuminated a concern. The most recent two-year period indicated the Marsee ore exports were down ten percent, yet mining increased five percent. Plus, they'd expanded manufacturing capabilities substantially with Bvindu Dome's facilities.

Maura's mind wandered to the widely circulated unofficial report from the auditor, Ivan Valdis. Culture on Mars was nonexistent. Amateur musicians—solo artists or small bands—performed in restaurant courts or parks, much like the miscreants in the subways and on street corners. The Marsees' monthly parties included these people and added amateur productions of classic and contemporary plays. Pleasant enough, but still amateurish.

Earth holovids were the closest approximation to culture. Though fine on occasion, they couldn't hold a candle to the opera, ballet, symphonies, or Broadway. *Why does anyone choose to visit, let alone live there?* She shuddered.

Brielle placed the breakfast selection on the wet bar in the corner. "Mr. Konklin is here for your seven-thirty."

"Hold on." Maura grabbed a mirror from her top desk drawer. Her teeth were lipstick-free. Her eyeliner and mascara were impeccable. Not a hair was out of place. She replaced the mirror and closed the drawer. "Have him come in and ensure we're not disturbed."

A moment after Brielle exited, Peter entered, smartly attired, as usual, this time in a midnight blue Italian suit with a yellow silk tie. Maura led him to the breakfast setup. Each added a spoonful of fresh fruit on china plates with a red rose pattern along the gold leaf edge. After preparing bagels with cream cheese, they faced one another at the mini-conference table in the corner and ate.

Maura set the gold-plated fork beside her dish, which held a few pieces of melon and a half-eaten bagel. "Peter, we have a Marsee problem. I'm concerned about the lack of oversight regarding the Bvindu tech. I can't decide if they're hopelessly bewildered or somehow perpetrating the biggest deception since the Trojan Horse. If it's the latter, we need to stop them before they become a power. Plus, the president and State Department's talks with other nations regarding tech sharing are faltering. It's difficult to dictate a sharing agreement when we don't have the product."

"How can I assist?"

That was progress—no complaints from him about the government breaking MarsVantage away from Interplanetary fifteen years back.

She sipped her orange juice, which was just as delicious as Brielle had advertised. "What's Reed and Newton's status?"

John Reed and Heather Newton had been assigned to Interplanetary's Mars operation to covertly gather intelligence on MarsVantage. Though Peter would deny it, he'd ordered them to prevent the Marsees from getting anything of value—by any means necessary. That was before anyone knew about alien technology. They'd failed and, worse, gotten caught.

"Upon arriving home, they met with my legal team and disappeared. We had a sighting in Brazil about eighteen months ago but nothing came of it. Wherever they are, whatever they're doing, they're keeping their heads down."

Funny how he'd omitted that someone had tried to murder them within hours of meeting with Interplanetary management.

Maura met his eyes. "So long as that doesn't change. We can't have damning facts revealed by a trial."

Peter sipped his juice. "Going forward, Interplanetary won't interfere in Marsee matters. We're holding off sending construction crews until the Bvindu situation stabilizes."

Though unexpected, that decision helped—the fewer pieces in play, the better. "They're on the way to becoming financially independent. According to the inspectors, the Bvindu power generator produces Mars City's energy.

"Though unconfirmed, we believe the solar array is entirely non-operational. My construction crews watched the Marsees cannibalize it for parts."

Maura's frustration found form in a long sigh. "And they purchased no additional fuel cells for sandstorm season."

"Their fuel cell contracts are now on a quarter-to-quarter basis," Peter offered.

Inspectors should've flagged that. *What else have they missed?* She felt a frown and relaxed so as not to crease her face.

"My suppliers keep me informed—unofficially, of course." Peter winked. "Anyway, the Marsees are missing out on bulk pricing by not contracting yearly or multi-yearly. That suggests they plan to retrofit their ground transport and shuttle fleets with Bvindu power generators, or transition to pure Bvindu vehicles."

She made a mental note of this unwelcome information. "We're seeing a small but noticeable drop in their discretionary imports."

"I've heard the same. The Marsee independence streak only grew after the airlock accident."

Maura sipped her juice again. "They don't believe our government helps and protects its citizens. Earth has the best minds, and I've worked extensively with them. The Marsees refuse to acknowledge that *I'm* the Mars expert. I worked among the regulators for years and understand every detail regarding living and working on Mars.

"When bodies are strewn across the landscape, people will be outraged, blaming the government for not preventing what was easily foreseeable. Like the aftermath of the airlock accident, quite a few upstarts will ride a tragedy to political victory, usurping seats from my established and knowledgeable colleagues who paid their dues."

Peter swallowed the last bite of his bagel. "The Marsees could succeed."

Maura laughed to cover her concern that Marsee success would undermine everything she'd worked for. "Impossible. Can a bunch of miners and glorified repair people understand and utilize advanced alien technology? They'll be lucky if they only blow up Bvindu Dome."

"You're overlooking the archaeology team."

"Led by a junior person."

"Gretchen Blake, you mean."

"The same Gretchen Blake whom the preeminent archaeologist of our time, Dr. Hawthorne, blackballed because she embraced absurd theories based on scant evidence while working on his project in Antarctica."

Peter inclined his head a moment. "She did find Bvindu Dome and decipher the cave symbols."

"Did she? She refuses to explain the symbols' meaning."

"And she found the caretaker's message, which she also deciphered."

Maura asked, "You believe her?"

"I saw the first reports about Bvindu Dome's discovery in the news. They accurately summarized Gretchen Blake's paper in the *Journal of Archaeology*."

"You read that?"

"Of course, I'd like to know what's going on with my former company. The news media and pundits muddied the water afterwards. It's one thing for them to speculate that Interplanetary built Bvindu Dome back in the day—which we didn't—or that Marsees built it. I'm ninety-nine point nine percent sure *they* didn't. But they ventured into conspiracy theories and outright delusions. Then late-night comedians and entertainment holos picked up the baton."

"You're right. They went too far. I already spoke with a few people about it." She waved her hand as if brushing away a crumb from the table. "The Marsees haven't helped themselves by not producing anything for two years."

Peter raised his hand head-high and opened it. "I agree they provided little, but dismissing the cure for the common cold is foolish. Once the FDA approves the medication, millions of registered voters will benefit. I know you're not foolish, so what's your concern?"

Sheer random dumb luck had carried the Marsees this far. If they somehow managed not to kill themselves, the Earth-bound citizens might believe they could live without the government's help. Chaos would ensue, and her friends and colleagues would be on the outside looking in, unable to utilize their superior knowledge and wisdom for the public good. She consciously adjusted her posture and dragged up a smile. "Only the Marsees' safety, of course."

"Of course." Peter's tone indicated his lack of belief in his own words. He tilted his head and raised an eyebrow. "You may have some unexpected help. Scuttlebutt has it that one of Blake's archaeologists is feeding Dr. Hawthorne information. His reputation took a hit when he couldn't reproduce Blake's work. It seems he made some arrangements."

"That assumes Blake accurately reported her work. Dr. Hawthorne believes she's withholding information."

Peter sat back and placed his hands in his lap. "About the Bvindu data she worked with, probably not. Everything I've seen suggests she's savvy, though perhaps a touch idealistic. Getting Hawthorne to validate her findings would only add to her reputation. Playing games with the data would utterly destroy her, and she knows it. Dismissing her is a mistake."

"Your analysis has merit, but it's difficult to believe the best mind in the field is stumped. The simpler answer is that Blake has withheld crucial information or fabricated certain details."

"Dr. Hawthorne receives National Science Ministry grants, which Congress controls. Perhaps he may see the benefit of passing along anything he learns."

"Peter, that's an outstanding idea."

"How else can I help?"

"Let me know if you learn anything about the Marsees' affairs."

"You'll be my first vidcomm."

"One last thing. Promise me that when the opportunity presents itself, you'll publicly embrace the National Science Ministry as a landing spot for Bvindu technology. I'm sure a public-private partnership would benefit the entire country."

"Consider it done." He placed his hands in his lap. "How will you get the Marsees to go along?"

"Space Force gets a lot of funding."

He leaned closer. "What *are* you planning?"

"A couple of things—one will bear fruit. Next up involves Brielle. She has a contact high-up in MarsVantage."

Surprise crossed Peter's face.

"You don't think I hired her just for her exceptional administrative skills?"

6 | ANOTHER FAVOR

Frank had mentally braced for an interrogation as soon as he and Erin left Shadow City, but she remained stubbornly silent. As they attained orbit, the hairs on the back of his neck stood up. "When are you going to ask your questions?"

"Why would I have questions about delivering cargo halfway across Mars to where no people should be?" She adjusted several controls and ticked the collective forward. Without taking her focus from the control panel and the cockpit window, she added, "Without any invoices or bills of lading, I might add. And then eat fresh apples in a secret buried alien city while discussing a possible Space Force assault. Why would *anyone* question that?"

"You took your sarcasm pills today."

She sighed and looked over. "You're cooking up something. Again. Will you let me in on what's going on, or was I just a tourist at Shadow City's entrance?"

"A good part of this trip was preparation for what I need to ask. You saw a part of the secret—now I'll tell you the rest. No more half-answers or diversions."

Inwardly, he chuckled at the surprise on her face. *It's been a while since I was able to do that.*

"I expected more of an argument."

"It's early." He rubbed his eyes. "Let's agree that you wore me down and move forward."

"Sure."

"But before we dive in, let's get one matter out of the way. I'd like you to befriend the reporter."

"Another favor?" She swept her right hand before the cockpit window. "This flight counts as a big one. I got up at *two-thirty* for you."

"Let's be honest. It's the latest on a long list of favors."

"Besides my regular flight duties, I'm scheduling pilots to offload the transport. And I'm working on the new Bvindu Scout Ship. Where am I supposed to find time to babysit a reporter? Can't you or Gretchen do it?"

This reminded him that he needed to discuss an aspect of the James situation with Gretchen again while there was still time. To the matter at hand, he said, "I trust you to feed him all the juicy, meaningless MarsVantage rumors and keep our important initiatives like Shadow City to yourself."

"Odds are, you're looking for trouble where none exists. If this reporter plays it straight, you and Gretchen owe me a nice dinner. With some of the fresh veggies Red mentioned."

"We'd enjoy that." Odds were, Erin wasn't getting that meal. While the reporter would attempt to leverage his prior relationship with Gretchen and fail spectacularly, he'd betray MarsVantage as sure as the sun rose in the East. It was a matter of *how* and *when,* not *if.*

"I'll do it." Her eyes gleamed with devilry. "What should I say if he asks about the caretaker?"

Frank brought his hands to his face and rubbed his forehead. "You saw what the pundits said?"

"Earth commentators and their guest interviewees couldn't weave enough outlandish scenarios. Some of them have a bright future writing fiction."

"Oh, God." He exhaled loudly.

"One interviewee did suggest you were a Bvindu god. My favorite scenario was that you, as a Bvindu yourself, hypnotized Gretchen to take you home to Bvindu Dome." She added in a monotone, "You will obey me."

"Yes, yes." He sighed. "We saw it all. I preferred the pundits who called us liars to those trying to make us look foolish. Have you noticed, by the way, that when they started using 'Marsee' in a denigrating way, we began calling ourselves 'Marsians?' It was like it happened overnight."

She snorted. "My pilots were pissed and got together to make it their mission to start the 'Marsian' trend, not only here, but also back on Earth when speaking with friends and family. Several sent complaints to the media. Plus, they ensured Marsian was used abundantly in official reports and correspondence."

So that's where it came from... Frank had heard it in several conversations and adopted it. "Would you believe I suggested that Gretchen remove all caretaker references from her paper? Only you, me, and her interacted with him. No one would've noticed the omission, and her paper would've been just as strong."

Erin countered, "Salvage laws are stronger than your oral agreement with him."

"We filed that paperwork, too. Anyway, Gretchen thought mentioning the caretaker would confer an air of moral authority to keep Bvindu Dome. Our repairs to the caretaker's manufacturing facilities equated to sweat equity and capital investment. The old spaceship you delivered for him to retrofit and find his people represents more capital investment. To some, her reasons carry a lot of weight."

Erin pushed the collective forward. The stars jumped ever so slightly through the cockpit window. "Gretchen owes you one. Those commentators kicked you in the pants."

"As it turns out, I may owe *her* one. The media quickly transitioned from the Bvindu Dome discovery to caretaker delusions and other absurd theories. Regardless, without the caretaker, the media may've focused more on the discovery."

"What's wrong with that?" Erin asked.

"With the caretaker consuming the public's attention, little oxygen was left for reasonable questions and answers. The distraction allowed us time to formulate and execute our plans. We got the cold cure out quickly, hoping it would fascinate the public and placate the politicians."

"Pretty sure that tactic failed."

He inclined his head. "We needed a show of good faith. Without a rationale for how we got it so quickly, it could've backfired, scaring the politicians into making a major move before we were prepared."

"You think they're looking for an excuse to take us over?"

"They're looking for any reason to strip the Bvindu tech from us and put it somewhere safe like the National Science Ministry."

Erin turned to look him in the eye. "And we'd be back to where we started."

"Actually, worse. Without Bvindu power, we'd be forced to purchase fuel cells to supply all of our energy. Our solar array is useless since we scavenged all the power regulators and cabling to connect to the Bvindu power."

"Please tell me you have a plan. One that involves Shadow City."

That was the perfect segue as Deimos came into view off to starboard. "Indeed. The strategy is to deny Washington any reason to loot the Bvindu tech."

"This sounds involved." She yawned. "Can I get the short version?"

He laughed. "You're funny for someone running on short rest. You were never this humorous when we dated."

"We never had picnics in alien cities in the middle of nowhere, either."

Frank shifted against the harness to relieve a burgeoning cramp in his leg. "Let's start with our ace in the hole, Shadow City. As you saw, we have farming initiatives and construction projects that use its manufacturing capability. It's also warehousing forbidden equipment like fuel cell refuelers. Eventually, we'll run shuttles and tractors for a fraction of the cost."

"How did all of that get underground without anyone knowing?"

"Gretchen learned of Shadow City in the Manuduction. With my concurrence, she informed the Knowledge Keeper Order, who built the airlock and tunnel. Members with all types of skills have been quietly arriving from Earth on transports for months. Mind you, there are no official records of *those* trips.

"Order members created several Bvindu-related controversies on Earth, including my favorite—a new religion, The Devotees of the Glorious Bvindu Spider. I was surprised how easily the media took the bait, though comedians led that drive."

"For a minute, I suspected you were allied with a crime syndicate." Though she didn't laugh out loud, her shoulders bounced up and down. "When did the Order start taking overt action?"

Most people would've dismissed him as a fool for believing in the Knowledge Keeper Order, let alone belonging to it. Its members had a reputation for oddness to cover their activities when discovered.

Frank said, "The Order's thinking has evolved from simply accumulating and maintaining our history and knowledge. They've begun taking proactive steps to produce a soft landing when the government crumbles under the weight of the citizens' reliance on its inefficient services. We're providing a location, and they're providing skilled personnel. Shadow City is a key part of our self-sufficiency effort."

"What's the Order get? Assuming their prediction is correct, everything'll still crash around their ears."

Always the skeptic.

When he'd dated Erin, they'd discussed the Order. He'd never gotten her to buy off on the government's collapse, and nothing had changed.

"Self-sufficiency insulates us to a great degree from the chaos that'll come to the US." He took a clipped breath while glancing at the starfield. "There will be riots when NutriAccount monthly allowances aren't reset, and by law, no grocer will deliver food. Other disruptions will eventually occur. The Order will guide the people to a better way, one without government involvement in everyday matters. When that day comes, we'll have the resources to help the US."

Erin adjusted course with a nudge against the cyclic. "How does any of this involve me, apart from your need for a ride every so often?"

"I promise I'll answer, but for the moment, let's bookmark that."

She cocked an eyebrow. "Do you remember me being overly patient?"

"Most of our co-workers want self-sufficiency to improve their economic lives. However, the stark truth is without Bvindu tech, Washington pulling the taxes, fees, and regs strings harder only shifts forward the date of MarsVantage's bankruptcy."

She blinked several times. "I never heard that."

"Several major systems in the older domes, like the Air Generator/Filter/Reclamation system in Dome 1, are coming to the end of their useful lives. Replacing them with Earth components installed by certified engineers would be incredibly expensive at two months' travel salary plus time on-site."

"But if you use uncertified Bvindu tech," Erin observed, "Washington will collectively crap a brick the size of Phobos."

"Maintenance sees the issues. Finance sees the budget problem. The money we're saving on fuel cells hasn't offset purchasing all rights to the land Bvindu Dome resides on. Only a handful of us know the dire financial situation. We plan to sever ties with the US after achieving self-sufficiency."

She stared straight ahead for several seconds. "Given those facts, we'll have no choice. Otherwise, MarsVantage goes bankrupt and Konklin buys it, probably at a discount."

"It'll be a race between me resigning and him firing me. While sitting comfortably on Earth, he already prioritized shipping his Mars management luxuries instead of airlock replacement seals. That decision directly led to the accident that killed Lori and twenty-two of our friends and co-workers."

"I remember. You were a great couple." Erin adjusted her harness and wiggled against the seat back.

He recalled their first date. The candlelight, meal, and conversation had been like a dream, something unique, never to be replicated. He pulled out his datapad from his suit's thigh pocket and glanced at the time. After swallowing hard and clearing his throat, he asked, "What's our ETA?"

"I've been riding the throttle as hard as I dare. We shouldn't be more than ten minutes late."

"That's better than I figured. Good job." He replaced his datapad. "Like I said, only a handful of us know our endgame."

"That's where Red's prediction comes into play."

"We need to continue moving under the radar," Frank opined. "If Washington suspects we're breaking away, they'll send Space Force."

"Once we're self-sufficient and go independent, they'll send Space Force anyway, right?"

"True." He swiped his hand across his mouth. "That's in two years, give or take. At that point, we'll be able to defend Mars City, Bvindu Dome, and Shadow City. That's the data Red analyzed. If we do it right, Space Force won't even reach Mars orbit. That's where you come in."

"To do what? I'm just a pilot."

"Sure." He bobbed his head in agreement. "I'm just a maintenance manager, Chuck's just a businessman, and Gretchen's just an archaeologist. We're part of the Citizens in Freedom Committee and want you to join. Your perspective and expertise will be invaluable for us to remain under the radar and achieve our goals."

Her lips parted to say something when Frank added, "Before you answer, I promised you the full story. I couldn't live with myself if you agreed without knowing everything. Once you know, though, the future will never look the same again."

7 | INVITATION TO THE FUTURE

"I don't like the sound of that." Erin glared at him before turning her attention to the shuttle's controls. "You should've taken 'Yes' for an answer."

Frank wished the pulse thudding in his ears would subside. He had to be honest without scaring her off. "There's more at stake. We absolutely have to retain control of the Bvindu tech... or destroy it as a last resort."

"Destroy it? After everything we've been through? What's gotten into you?"

He raised his hand and took a deep breath. "Right now, in the beams of the Master Control Center's ceiling are dozens of demolition explosives. If activated, the floors holding the Bvindu data storage systems will crash into the Master Control Center. Without that, Bvindu Dome is useless."

"A portion of the supplies from the Order were demexes, huh?"

"Mining couldn't cover up reallocating so many."

Erin rubbed her eyes. "What would make you contemplate this?"

"It goes back to the caretaker. You remember his appearance?"

"How could I forget a four-armed gray metal sphere towering over me?"

"That was a mobile unit. Two more are back in the Master Control Center. He inhabited its computer system to watch over the entire city, and transferred himself into one when he needed to visit someplace physically. He originally had a flesh-and-blood body similar to ours—well, with additional arms."

Erin adjusted course again before glancing over. "The Bvindu can transfer their consciousness into a computer?"

"And then *back* into a body, one grown from the original DNA at an accelerated rate."

"That's... incredible."

"Gretchen and I thought so, too, for a minute." Frank interlaced his fingers and set his hands in his lap. "What would corrupt, greedy politicians and the unscrupulous rich do to achieve practical immortality?"

"They'd pay a lot."

"And they'd eliminate anyone and destroy anything in their way... just like Konklin got rid of Arnold and Sam already." They had been MarsVantage employees moonlighting as Interplanetary spies before he and Gretchen caught them. "The Interplanetary employees, John Reed and Heather Newton, are in hiding after getting entangled in mysterious circumstances in New York City."

"I saw none of that in the news," Erin said.

"Of course you didn't. The Order passed it along."

"Damn. I always knew Konklin was slithery, but that's downright despicable."

"The elitists would murder hundreds, even thousands if necessary. All to live forever, ruling over their lessers, as that's how they view ordinary people. You see that, right?"

"I wouldn't put anything past Konklin." She exhaled. "Tell me that's all."

Frank rubbed his eyes. "Regular people unable to afford the process would fight for it. Then, the elitists would ruthlessly clamp down. The technology on its own is beneficial, but combined with the dark side of human nature, a tyranny on a scale never before seen is inevitable."

"My God, Frank. What have you done?"

He sighed. "Gretchen and I hoped for disease cures—especially cancer—and next-level technology for energy production, construction, and new means of space travel. But the immortality process is Pandora's Box, and we can't ever crack the lid."

"Please tell me that's it."

Frank brushed his hair from his forehead, not disturbing his headset. "That's the whole story. Help us guide MarsVantage to self-sufficiency. Help us profitably use the constructive tech and suppress the destructive."

Erin stared ahead. "My first instinct is to go find saints and philosophers..."

He'd given his best explanation, no matter how imperfectly, and conveyed the offer. Anything more would be tantamount to pressuring her, and he refused to do that.

As the OTP and transport appeared on the horizon, Erin said, "If Washington goes for the Bvindu tech, we'll be in a difficult spot. Red's prediction of a Space Force confrontation could come to pass. And other countries may have their sights set on what they imagine Bvindu tech could hold. I hope the Committee considered that."

Frank resisted the urge to respond. She was thinking out loud, processing the bombshell he'd dropped. While the Committee needed her help, he wanted a reasoned decision, not a knee-jerk reaction. *Waiting is the hardest part.*

She set her jaw. "I'd rather have a hand on the controls than be a helpless passenger. Count me in."

8 | Some Still Dream

Gretchen carried a bottle of water and strolled into her third-floor office in a building inside Dome 4. Her stomach twinged again—she'd have to pick up more ginger tablets. She sipped water and pushed the distraction from her mind. Work needed to be done, and time ran short.

After sitting at her desk with her back to the wall display showing a map of Bvindu Dome, she woke the computer and checked her messages. Nothing was pressing. She chuckled at an email from the Housing Ministry in Washington acknowledging she no longer lived in its jurisdiction on-planet. Two years after transmitting her Quit Occupation notice, a faceless bureaucrat finally processed it and presumably reassigned her apartment.

Should I be sad that it took two whole years for someone else to live in my apartment, or happy that it only took two years?

She walked past a storage cabinet to the conference table, which held six seats—two on each side plus one on each end—and activated its holo display. After placing her thumb on the ID sensor and requesting her latest project, she announced her passphrase, "Some still dream."

Her stomach twinged again. She looked down and whispered, "Little Jelly Bean, calm down. You have eight months to go, and I still have to tell Daddy... Soon, when matters settle... Everything will be fine. We'll make sure of it."

The holo displayed a maintenance engineer painting a cargo container with a substance that looked similar to hot liquid tar, which the Bvindu called Spectrum Erasure Overlay. Once it dried, hand-sized sections across its inky black surface shimmered, brightening to dark gray occasionally. The effect prevented her from focusing on any specific spot for more than a second.

Then, the maintenance engineer sealed a transmitter and a heat lamp inside. His receiver never picked up the broadcast, and readings in the infrared wavelength range were negligible, less than the room's readings. They'd run more tests to confirm the Bvindu's documentation that the coating absorbed the wavelengths of the electromagnetic spectrum.

Frank entered, juggling a coffee while pushing a cargo container on a hand truck he parked by the wall. "Hi, hon. I brought presents."

"Terrific. I have one of my own."

He joined her by the conference table and gave her a peck on the lips before taking a seat beside her. She replayed the holo.

"That's interesting," Frank said. "I half-expected the coating was necessary for FTL travel."

According to the Manuduction, the Bvindu had cracked traveling great distances in short time frames using a variation of Heim Theory. If circumstances were different, she'd suggest assisting the scientists in the Socialist States of Australia who'd been diligently working on the theory only to continue to disprove it. As matters stood, the Committee had unanimously agreed that any tech that could be used against MarsVantage had to remain in-house.

Gretchen took a gulp of water. "A reference in the coating specifications pointed to the Bvindu's search that ended with Mars. They painted their ships to go unnoticed by intelligent life when exploring worlds at night. They brought that practice forward when they left a dying Mars on their quest for a new inhabitable world."

Frank stared into space as he observed, "It opens several possibilities for us."

"I'll get you an eye patch, and you can be the first Marsian space pirate."

He laughed. "Anyone who calls me Graying Beard will walk the plank."

She chuckled. "Gray hair isn't the end of the world."

"It's a reminder that many of my goals remain unfulfilled."

"We're making progress. Once Erin gives the go-ahead and the Spectrum Erasure Overlay is applied to the Bvindu Scout Ship, we're in the air. The Belt and outer planets will be seconds away. Jupiter is an unlimited resource to refill our fuel cells."

"You're right." He took a sip of coffee. "The reason we couldn't do it is the reg that only exists as a hindrance."

"Tractor and shuttle retrofits with Marsium121 power generators are unnecessary." She shifted to face him. "Self-sufficiency is within our reach so long as Washington doesn't surprise us."

"I don't want to argue again. I concede they could take drastic measures, and we're preparing for it."

So far, he'd only approached those preparations as an academic exercise. He placed far too much faith in the politicians' actions over the past fifteen years as a predictor of future plans.

Washington was making a move, and it wouldn't be another trivial regulation. It'd probably be modeled on the recently implemented mining regulations that required miners to spend no more than sixty days on-site during any ninety-day period. That was if Washington didn't nationalize Bvindu Dome outright. Frank's plan to attain self-sufficiency discreetly was all but moot. If only he could see it...

"Red sent his analysis of the Bvindu's defensive capabilities and our options to utilize them," Frank continued. "I'll go through it today. And he sent freshly grown apples."

That sounded great if Gretchen's stomach cooperated. She replied to his main point, "No one wants to deal with the worst-case scenario, but I'd rather be prepared and not need it."

"You're right," he said with a lack of enthusiasm. "By the way, I scheduled a James meeting for mid-morning tomorrow."

"It's going to be a long day. Chuck set a Committee meeting for 6:00 A.M. before our archaeology coordination meeting."

Frank took another sip of coffee and looked her in the eye. "Besides Chuck, no one knows that James is your ex. You should let the Committee know before it comes out."

"I don't want to answer a lot of questions. We have work to do. He's my past—I'm not heading in that direction."

Frank took her hand. "Good. Take that weapon from him before he tries to sow distrust among us."

9 | Breaking News

Gretchen sat at her office desk, double-checking the manifest for their trip to Bvindu Dome in two days' time. A knock came from the doorway.

Her friend and project supervisor, Ashley, asked, "Do you have a minute?"

"I have two." Gretchen waved her in.

Ashley sat in the visitor's chair. "The tractors are mostly loaded. The Marsee engineers rigged up cargo racks on their roofs. They're excited it won't interfere with deploying the solar panels when empty."

That'd been a rare slip. Marsians now loathed that pejorative. As far as Gretchen could tell, Ashley enjoyed the work—which set her apart from many on Earth. But still, she never embraced life on Mars.

Ashley continued, "We can take four additional containers per tractor. I'm thinking of FieldMeals. Do you have any thoughts?"

"Let's add another water purifier, too." The Bvindu had tapped into an underground reservoir, but numerous minerals and compounds contaminated it, making it unfit for consumption until filtered.

"Good idea." Ashley made a note on her datapad. "I want to add another data core. The statuary is coming up, and we'll take plenty of holovids and other scans."

"Better to have it on hand when we need it than to wait for a resupply run." Gretchen leaned back and exhaled. "On a different subject, the reporter arrived, and we can expect him to join us in Bvindu Dome."

"Terrific," Ashley replied with a sarcastic edge. "I hope we get someone who knows the difference between a shovel and a brush."

"You needn't worry about that. They sent Jimmy."

Ashley's jaw dropped for a moment. "You mean *your* Jimmy?"

He hadn't been hers for over two years. "One and the same."

"He knows the basics of archaeology, sure, but how will he cover Bvindu civilization and technology? He's not exactly a polymath."

"Makes me think he's here for other reasons. Like all the secret tech we're hoarding, according to a news holovid I saw recently."

"Ha. I saw Eleanor Klein's opinion piece, too. We haven't found much of practical interest yet, but secretly hoarding tech is delusional."

Gretchen sniffed. "No one on Earth will acknowledge that I'm sending everything through a translation process. Plus, they conveniently forget we provided a cure to the common cold, which is the foundation for addressing other viral diseases."

"Patience is in short supply back home." Ashley's shoulders scrunched against her neck. "What else is new?"

"Tell the team about the reporter. They're to answer his questions truthfully." The archaeologists knew nothing that could hurt MarsVantage.

"Got it." Ashley leaned forward. "Have you considered that he may want to restart your relationship?"

Gretchen shook her head. "That would be the most bizarre thing ever, and I met a four-armed alien."

10 | MANIPULATION

At the computer in the living room of Frank and Gretchen's quarters in Dome 4, he simulated the software he'd modified. No matter the command—Open or Close—the door opened one foot and froze. Bypassing the safety interlock protocols had been the most challenging part of the exercise, and this last test had finally proven he'd succeeded.

After leaning back and taking a deep breath, he made a reminder on his datapad to check the Order's progress in getting the software source code for other critical systems. They'd need it by the time they declared independence. Washington would most likely impose an embargo on all goods coming to Mars, including vendor patches.

He created an install package for his modifications and crafted a post-install script that opened all the garage bay airlocks and emergency bulkheads throughout the city. If he ever executed it, every dome would be opened to Mars. He transferred the package to the staging server without scheduling the installation.

Red had analyzed MarsVantage's situation from a military perspective and provided several recommendations. In the event of a worst-case scenario—a Space Force takeover—he suggested forcing an evacuation to Bvindu Dome while making Mars City uninhabitable. The idea was pretty good since it denied Space Force a foothold on Mars and halved what would need to be defended.

Frank planned to utilize Bvindu Dome's protection systems. They'd probably still work after all these centuries—the other Bvindu equipment had. He couldn't envision needing this plan so long as the company moved discreetly.

He turned off the computer and went to the bedroom, where he doffed his coveralls and slid into bed beside Gretchen. "I finished a contingency plan. Before Chuck's meeting, I'll install a remoting device in the Operations computer systems."

"It's interfaced with Bvindu comm tech, right?"

"Oh, yeah. If we have to use it, we don't want anyone intercepting or blocking our commands."

"It could come in handy. You should see this. It's an All News Network holovid." She leaned over and shared her datapad. She selected a link, fast-forwarded the video, and touched play.

It showed a woman helping two young children with homework at a kitchen table, while the reporter's voice narrated, "...you have it. Six months ago, Joan McMillan was married for nearly fifteen years when her husband non-renewed their marriage contract. Subsequently, he went missing, but she still receives a monthly child support payment."

The image cut to a young reporter with long blonde hair and impeccable makeup standing before a peaceful suburban house. "Joan's case isn't an isolated incident. Twenty-seven others have disappeared in New Jersey and at least three hundred across the country. Some are single, others married. In a handful of cases, entire families vanished.

"Evidence suggests something unusual is happening, and I'll continue investigating. This is Ami Hunter, All News Network, New York Bureau."

"Okay," Gretchen said, "here it comes."

In a studio, a newsreader with black curly hair and a square chin said, "Thanks for that report, Ami. To end our broadcast tonight, we caught up with Senator Maura Severino, returning to DC for the start of the Senate's legislative session. We asked her what's next for Mars."

The screen displayed Senator Severino in full politician mode. "We still have a lot of data to evaluate. While we note a minor drop in exports these past two years, we're primarily concerned about the safety of MarsVantage personnel, especially those working and living in Bvindu Dome. We appreciate the dangers our fellow brothers and sisters undertake and insist they never experience another accident like the one with the airlock fifteen years ago. Once we sift through the details within the inspectors' reports, we'll better understand what next steps may be needed.

Regardless, we'll do everything to ensure the safety of our fellow citizens laboring under the difficult and dangerous conditions on Mars."

Gretchen closed the screen and set the datapad on the nightstand. "I'll bet Severino already decided the next step."

"She mentioned safety, so I'd bet on stricter regs." The interview confirmed Frank's expectations—more regs, but not a takeover of alien technology.

"She's subtly manipulating public opinion while planting the seeds of dangerous conditions. Down the road, she can point to anything, and the public will be receptive, even restricting our use of Bvindu Dome."

Those sorts of restrictions would slow archaeological progress, but those efforts were secondary. Working with Bvindu data could just as easily be done from Mars City. Finishing the scout ship was mostly an automated affair. They could adjust. Frank squeezed her hand. "Your astute analysis is why you're on track to becoming a top-tier Knowledge Keeper."

11 | Reading the Tea Leaves

In Dome 2, Frank entered Chuck's inner office, which had a feature he would've liked. The small table that held breakfast would make a nice work area for a side project. Of course, it would never fit in his own office.

The Samuel Adams quote in black lettering on the white wall behind Chuck's desk always drew Frank's eye.

> *If ye love wealth better than liberty, the tranquility of servitude better than the animating contest of freedom, go home from us in peace. We ask not your counsels or arms. Crouch down and lick the hands which feed you. May your chains set lightly upon you, and may posterity forget that ye were our countrymen.*

Anyone entering this office could understand Chuck's mindset before one word was uttered.

At the breakfast selection, Frank chose scrambled eggs, toast, and apple slices, along with a cup of coffee. By its enticing aroma, he suspected the beans had originated on Earth.

The window blinds were drawn to not tempt curious eyes from neighboring buildings. Unusual off-hours activity tended to get noticed, and with a reporter in their midst, such events eventually would reach his ear.

Frank sat next to Gretchen at the conference table. The egg's aroma teased his nose. "Are you sure you don't want some apple slices? Erin says they're as good as Earth's."

She wrinkled her nose and sipped water. "Apples and breakfast don't mix, especially at six in the morning. Toast and what passes for scrambled eggs will be fine."

June Hudson, Director of Energy Production, and Alan Greene, Director of Security, joined them, each carrying a plate loaded with food. Chuck took his place at the head of the table, setting his plate and orange juice before him. One seat remained open for the newest member, whose version of being on time in all things except flying looked much like being a little late.

While everyone was enjoying their first bites of breakfast, Erin burst through the door, her short brown hair still wet. She grabbed a cup of coffee and took a sip. "Oh, Earth coffee. This can't be good."

"What makes you think it's bad news?" Gretchen asked.

"Nothing good happens at a 6:00 A.M. meeting, and Earth coffee is a way to take the sting out of it."

"Good morning to you, too." Chuck extended a hand to the empty chair.

"These early morning wake-ups have got to stop. Two days in a row. I need my beauty sleep."

Snickers came from around the table. Erin took a seat on the other side of Gretchen.

"Welcome to the Citizens in Freedom Committee, Erin," Chuck said. "Let's get right to it. What are your impressions of the reporter?"

Erin brought a finger to her lips while swallowing a gulp of coffee. "No tough questions yet. He's friendly enough, but he uses chitchat to elicit information."

"He's quite good at that," Gretchen affirmed.

"You met already?" Erin sipped her coffee. "I thought I kept him occupied yesterday."

Gretchen leaned in and placed her hands on either side of her plate. "We may as well get it on the table. Jimmy... James is my ex-husband."

Silence engulfed the room as all eyes turned to Gretchen.

"I had a life *before* coming to Mars."

"Of course," June acknowledged, "but what are the odds our Earther reporter would be your ex?"

"Astronomically high, against." Frank pushed his hand through his hair. "James built his career reporting on international elections and wars."

Alan swallowed. "We had co-workers covertly undermining us—spying on us—for years that we sent packing, and now we have a known spy in plain sight."

Frank ate a forkful of eggs. He added a dash of black pepper to provide a degree of flavor. Neither debating nor complaining was productive. They had to manage the reporter's presence. "He's no different than the auditors and inspectors. The government will get whatever he learns directly from him or through a contact at the All News Network."

"In a few hours, Frank and I'll meet with him and lay down the ground rules," Gretchen declared. "If he breaks them, he'll be on the next transport to Earth."

June asked, "Will the ground rules be enough to protect us?"

"He won't be able to twist our words," Frank said. "The rest is up to us."

Chuck announced, "All employees were notified of the interview condition by email before this meeting."

"We'll invite him to Bvindu Dome tomorrow," Gretchen said, "and I'm sure he'll accept."

"Is that a good idea?" Alan asked. "Unlike inspectors, reporters tend to sneak around."

"He didn't spend a month cooped up on a spaceship not to see Bvindu Dome." Gretchen ate a bite of toast and took a mouthful of water.

"James doesn't know the right questions to ask." Frank shifted as he leaned an elbow on the table in front of his plate. "The inspectors were harder to placate, but they ignored most of the goodies to focus on the dome's spaceworthiness."

"The stability of the dome appeared to be the easiest excuse to restrict access," Gretchen reasoned. "Their report on the sample of the dome material indicates it's stronger than plastiglass and graphene beams. Washington has no leg to stand on to prevent us from occupying Bvindu Dome full-time."

Erin's eyebrows drew together. "If it's stronger than our materials, how did the Baulnsville colonists break it a hundred years ago?"

Many from Mars' first colony had been caught in the breach and killed. The subsequent rescue attempt claimed the rest of the colony. After meeting the caretaker, he and Gretchen had finally learned the colonists' fate.

"The caretaker determined a manufacturing defect weakened the material thirty percent in the section the colonists were excavating," Gretchen explained. "A terrible case of bad luck. Anywhere else, and they never would've breached Bvindu Dome."

"I'll wager that dome is safer than Mars City, even considering it's been around for two hundred and fifty centuries." Chuck sat back, looking satisfied. "We purchased full rights to the land and pointed out that, by rule, the dome ought to be considered a natural formation."

Erin snorted. "Because *humans* didn't build it. Brilliant!"

"Don't be surprised if Washington doesn't change the law to eliminate *that* loophole." Frank mirrored Chuck's action. "Last night, Gretchen found an All News Network holovid where Senator Severino hinted at safety concerns."

"That's the government's default rationale," Chuck said. "I'm surprised she isn't complaining that our exports were down ten percent. If trends continue—and they will—they'll be down twenty-five percent or more by our next sandstorm season, two years from now."

"Hold on." Erin raised her hand. "Didn't Washington alter the miners' work rules last year? A while back, I had to make an emergency run to pick up a handful about to exceed their sixty-day limit in the wild."

Alan chuckled. "Your trip fixed a scheduling snafu. It wouldn't be out of character for a politician to complain about the results of a change they themselves implemented."

Chuck stroked his chin with a thumb and forefinger. "The miners used to work for up to ninety days on a five-day on, two-day off schedule. Now, they work sixty days straight and get a month back here. Sure, the new reg reduced work hours, but the miners and their families are happier."

June said, "The ones I spoke with would rather work when they're on-site. Sitting around for two days a week feels like squandered time."

"Indeed." Chuck gulped orange juice. "What the politicians are noticing most is the ore we're diverting to Bvindu Dome for manufacturing. I prefer our exports remain steady, but we need those materials for the Bvindu Scout Ship more than any goodwill gained by maintaining export levels."

"And our imports are also down." June's face registered a new alertness. "Thanks to the Bvindu power generator, we're importing forty percent fewer fuel cells. Our Mars City farming improves with each day. Shadow City farming is coming online to the point where they can begin supplying us with food soon. Washington will eventually notice reduced food imports."

They probably already have. Frank ate another forkful of eggs. The reduced ore shipments were a nuisance to Earth manufacturers, and politicians couldn't care less about Mars importing fewer goods, except it pointed to less dependence on Earth.

There was the issue—Washington wanted to keep MarsVantage on a leash. Bvindu Dome had thrown a monkey wrench into the works. Anything they did would be to neutralize advantages Bvindu Dome gave MarsVantage.

Chuck said, "I submitted my written testimony to the Offworld Commerce Committee. Thank you and the other department heads for your input. My in-person testimony is scheduled for tomorrow morning via vidcomm."

Erin refilled her coffee at the breakfast table. "I can't recall anyone from MarsVantage ever testifying before a congressional committee."

"No one has," June stated.

Deep furrows appeared on Chuck's forehead. "After Senator Byron died mid-term, New Jersey's governor selected Maura Severino from the Mars Economic Improvement Commission to finish the term. While sitting on the commission, she advocated for many new regs and pursued tighter interpretations of them, which caused us to sue in several instances."

Erin returned to the conference table as Gretchen said, "In short, she dislikes how we handle our business—she knows best."

June sat straight and rested her elbows on the table. "Is it worth continuing this ridiculous charade, or should we finally take our future into our own hands and declare independence now?"

12 | CONNECTED DOTS

Frank nearly spewed his coffee onto the conference table. June had always been aggressive, but this suggestion was out of proportion.

"Our situation is problematic." Worry lines creased Chuck's forehead. "Maintaining our relationship with the US is still beneficial."

Half-hearted murmurs rose around the conference table.

On Mars, people worked hard for all they had, while in the States, the government sustained the populace. Ordinary Earthbound citizens existed, rarely thriving. Frank was beginning to agree with a cynical saying he'd heard recently, "Fat and happy people keep reelecting leaders who hand out the benefits."

"I must point out," Alan said, "when we declare independence, we also need to be concerned about the Pan-Asian Alliance, the European Union of Socialist States, and the Socialist States of Australia, just to name a few."

"Not to mention a handful of mega-corporations and numerous crime syndicates," Chuck added.

Frank glanced in Chuck's direction. "According to the Order, the other nations are negotiating a tech-sharing agreement with Washington, so I don't expect any overt action from them yet. The crime syndicates and corporations will probably allow the government to do the heavy lifting and steal the tech when it hits Earth."

Frank pushed his empty plate away, leaned his elbows on the table, and added, "Washington's the issue. They won't waltz in and take the Bvindu tech—there's no legal precedent for that. So long as we continue to move discreetly, politicians will have no reason to change course."

Though Chuck's face remained unperturbed, he inclined forward ever so slightly. "New Jersey's governor appointing Severino to complete Senator Byron's term was likely at the president's behest. It provides insight into the government's thinking."

"Keep in mind, the senate contorted itself by swapping a handful of committee assignments," Alan added, "so she's not only on Offworld Commerce but also chairing it."

"That woman has never seen a reg she didn't like." Frank sipped his coffee. "Taxes, fees, and regs will be the government's tool, and we should respond as they expect, through complaints or legal challenges."

June leaned back in the chair and flopped her hands in her lap. "And we circle back to my point. Why play their game?"

Chuck set his empty OJ glass beyond his plate. "We can get by without the US, but there's a steep price. Thirty to thirty-five percent of our employees will resign and return to Earth. Those who stay will lose access to Earthbound family, friends, and all US goods. Expect Washington to strong-arm other countries to isolate us. We'll have no allies left on Earth, in orbit, or on the Moon—which means no official shipments. The Knowledge Keeper Order can help, but more off-the-record shipments invite detection and interdiction. Should that happen, we'll starve. Going independent has to be for something bigger than hurt ego or another fee."

"I'd break away over another fee," June said firmly. "On fuel cells, Washington taxes the fuel, imposes a fee for safety inspections, and adds export and administrative fees over and above the shipping costs. Then, after we expend the cell, we have to ship it back to Earth instead of refilling it ourselves. We pay a decontamination fee, a refurbishment fee, a reclamation fee, and an import fee. Enough's enough—we could manufacture and fill our own fuel cells for a fraction of the cost. Washington insists it's unsafe, but that's just an excuse to bleed us of cash."

"No one disagrees. But breaking away prematurely would bring a slew of serious problems." Frank leaned into the table. "We have a new related concern. The Order informed me last night that a Space Force destroyer abandoned the Earth-Moon rectilinear orbit patrol a week ago. Its trajectory could place them here twenty-three days from now."

"Or their destination could be the Asteroid Belt," Alan suggested. "A couple of US startups are trying to make a go at mining operations."

"I'm surprised the government hasn't encouraged that more," June said. "The PAA is synonymous with Belt mining right now. All the other countries' efforts combined are a fraction of the PAA's presence."

Frank said, "The Knowledge Keepers couldn't get the destroyer's orders, but my bet is that it's coming to our doorstep to intimidate us."

"Exactly." Chuck framed his plate with his hands. "We've never had a Space Force vessel in orbit, let alone a destroyer, and no Marsian has been asked to testify before Congress. We're in uncharted territory. We need to prepare for independence and the worst-case scenario of a Space Force attack."

Frank exhaled. "Suppose we go independent today without any provocation. Our co-workers will squarely blame us for every hardship afterward. Two years from now, our difficulties will be far less. Timing is everything."

Gretchen's eyes turned hard. "If we misread Washington's intentions, it'll be at our peril."

"The only way I'll agree to independence," Frank insisted, "is if Washington attempts to loot Bvindu tech. At that point, our co-workers will more willingly accept difficulties."

Chuck stood, his fingertips pressing on the tabletop. "After we secured the power generation cavern, we could've declared victory then and ignored the message within that led to Bvindu Dome. We didn't. Instead, we used cash intended for other programs to purchase full land rights and start our race toward self-sufficiency and independence. We either go independent, or Konklin will eventually buy us at a bankruptcy auction."

Everyone stared at Chuck.

"Frank raises a valuable point—declaring independence serves us best when we're ready. Unless there's an objection, we're not relitigating that decision." Chuck paused for a comment that never came. "The question is one of timing. We should stay the course unless our use of Bvindu tech is compromised. The hearing is the natural place for Severino to make an announcement. It's also a fantastic forum for a response."

Frank relaxed into the chair back. "I wholeheartedly agree. If she goes for everything Bvindu, then do it."

"Considering the Space Force destroyer and the hearing, Washington is moving toward a takeover. If so, I vote to declare independence." Gretchen leaned back and placed her hands on her belly.

Erin glanced around the conference table. "I trust your judgment, Chuck."

Alan and June also agreed.

There was no better person to testify before the Senate committee. Chuck's leadership and judgment had positioned MarsVantage better than anyone ever predicted. If Chuck were to announce independence, he'd have unequivocal provocation.

A few minutes later, the meeting broke up. Erin, June, and Alan departed.

"Chuck, I know we're set to meet with Lorah now," Gretchen said, "but can Frank and I have a moment in private?"

Without betraying his thoughts, Chuck gave a quick nod as he looked at Frank. "Sure, I'll chat with Lorah."

After the door closed behind him, Gretchen squarely faced Frank. "What's going on? Washington's intent is clear, *and* your hesitancy is noticeable to everyone. If we aren't as prepared as possible, we lose. Not just Bvindu Dome, but our freedom. Once we declare independence, we become secessionists. After the first shot is fired, we're rebels. Our fate is to win, die, or spend the rest of our lives in prison... if we're not hanged."

Her words were like a slap. "The rest of you sound like a government takeover is a *fait accompli*, not a mere possibility," Frank countered. "If their suspicions come to pass, things will get ugly awfully fast. And worse, it sounds like the others *want* it to happen."

"Want? No. Do you think it's a coincidence that Interplanetary didn't send personnel or shuttles on the transport to complete the construction of their dome?"

"Are you saying Interplanetary doesn't want to be in the middle of a shooting war?"

Gretchen blinked twice. "I wasn't thinking in those terms. Until *now*. Only that they assume they're getting Mars City back. Why rush to finish another dome far enough away to be inconvenient?"

Under ordinary circumstances, he'd consider it cynical, bordering on conspiracy theory. But with Space Force on the way, maybe cynicism equated to enemy strategy. "That's an intriguing take..."

"You know what else is intriguing? Your denial of the danger staring us in the face."

Gretchen's insights had often been invaluable, but this time, she was uncharacteristically off-base. "Mars is filled with danger. We face it daily and handle it."

"Except for a government takeover. In this *one* area, you're blind." She leaned in and placed her palms on the table. "How many signals does Washington have to send? You take pride in connecting the dots—for God's sake, do it now!"

He rubbed his eyes and sighed. The truth *was* staring him in the face. He'd just refused to look at it. "You're right—all of you. As soon as we declare independence, Washington's next move is unknown. And then I'm no longer in control of the situation."

Gretchen took his hand. "No one expects you to control the situation. That's like... guaranteeing an outcome. Did you feel you were guaranteeing we'd get the Marsium121?"

"Yes, and we survived Interplanetary's murder attempt in the cave because of my preparation."

Gretchen closed her eyes and slowly shook her head. "Okay. So, were you in control when we confronted Sam for being an Interplanetary spy? When he tackled me to the ground and tore my spacesuit?"

"Well..."

"Well?" she asked with accusation in her eyes. "We're far beyond 'well.'"

"You're right—I wasn't in control, and I almost lost you."

"Because a person you knew for years surprised you. These politicians—people you don't know—*will* surprise us. If you don't recognize that, if you don't accept that, then we'll lose everything. Not only do we need to prepare for the worst, but we also need options and alternatives. Now is the time to do what you do best."

Frank's gut tightened. Trying to deny the obvious wouldn't change what was to come.

"We need to prepare for Space Force like our lives depend on it..." Gretchen declared. "Because they do."

13 | Unexpected News

Lorah Charendoff toweled off her brown hair and pulled it into a ponytail with a scrunchie. Once it dried, she'd let it fall around her face. It was the best style without involving a curling iron, and she wasn't bothering.

After brushing her teeth, she went to the bedroom and dressed in standard MarsVantage coveralls. She slid her datapad into her thigh pocket and secured her ID and NutriAccount card in her inside chest pocket.

Who knew what would come next, but she'd still be able to eat if the reporter managed to piss off the restaurant owners more than the inspectors and auditors already had.

She hurried through the living room and the short hallway. After opening the closet door, she detached her bike from the wall and exited. She walked it past three doors and leaned it against the wall.

A handful of seconds after pressing the announcement chime, Ashley opened the door, her long, wet blonde hair looking browner. She bid Lorah hello and led her to the kitchen.

Ashley's living room was like all the others except for the golden Inca statue on the end table. The foot-tall female figurine was a replica of the first artifact Ashley had found, the original, of course, safely displayed in a museum. A while back, Ashley had confided that it always accompanied her on projects as a good luck charm.

Lorah sat at the table while Ashley attended to the stove.

"Do you want eggs?"

"No thanks, it's too early."

"Once we hit Bvindu Dome, we'll eat FieldMeals for a week or so until support personnel arrive."

"Good point, Ash. I'll take a little."

Ashley set a plate, fork, and a cup of water in front of Lorah and sat down across from her.

Lorah ate a forkful. Not bad, considering there wasn't one iota of real egg in them. The government had banned them over cholesterol concerns, if she remembered correctly.

The *faux*-eggs couldn't hold a candle to the real thing, which was readily available in most black market outlets for people in the know who were willing to indulge for a price. She hadn't had any since coming to Mars as Fordham Industries liaison. Though Mr. Fordham paid her well enough, she wasn't springing to smuggle eggs.

"What's your day look like?" Lorah asked.

"Tying up a boatload of loose ends before we head to Bvindu Dome tomorrow." Ashley sipped her water. "Are you ready for your secret meeting?"

Lorah exhaled. "Not much to prepare for, and it's hardly a secret."

"It's happening at seven in the morning, and I'm excluded."

"If you like, you can take my place for this scheduled waste of time. Gretchen will no doubt outline what you'll be exploring for the next few months and discuss at a high level what Bvindu data she's investigating. I'll ask about additional tech, even weapons. But I know the answers already—there'll be no additional Bvindu tech to share."

"Terrific, like the world needs more weapons. Does Fordham Industries even manufacture weapons?"

"Not at all, but I'd like to give him something."

Ashley finished her breakfast and put the fork and plate in the washer. "How's Fordham taking our lack of progress?"

"Curiously well—he never presses me about it." Lorah had another forkful of eggs. "I give him status updates. Sometimes, he asks questions. Usually, we chitchat. Yet, the cold cure is years from hitting the market and making money. Still, he's happy—to the point of never uttering a critical comment about anything related to MarsVantage or the Bvindu."

"Kinda odd for a businessperson."

That's an understatement. "Every time I speak with him, I think this is the day his patience runs out, he cancels the contract, and recalls me."

"You're in a tough spot." Ashley returned to her seat and ran her hands through her wet hair. "Perhaps there's a way to speed things up. You could suggest to Gretchen that she shares the Bvindu database to help research the statues. I'll pass along anything I think will interest you."

Interesting... Ashley's request was reasonable and practical. It also was manipulative, and a hidden agenda warning flashed in the back of Lorah's mind. Lorah pushed that intrusion aside. "Knowing a Bvindu won a battle or brokered peace somewhere doesn't help me."

Ashley rested her elbows on the table. "I expect we'll find plenty of those sorts of statues. Back on Earth, they erected them on sites where people made historical discoveries, too. I expect we'll encounter those, too. We can save so much time if I access the database directly."

"I'll suggest it." Lorah consciously flashed an easy smile to take the sting out of her next statement. "But I doubt Gretchen will go for it. She'll provide you with translated portions as she always does."

"You're probably right. I feel like I'm riding a bicycle with training wheels." Ashley's shoulders slumped. "You know, she used to trust me. Then Dr. Hawthorne blackballed her, and James, the reporter who just arrived, non-renewed their marriage contract. She closed herself off—I'm surprised she ever let Frank in."

"Hold on, you mean the reporter from Chuck's email is Gretchen's ex-husband?"

"Small world, huh? He must have naked pictures of someone because he knows almost nothing about archaeology and less about science and tech."

Something's going on. Washington's making a move.

"That doesn't make sense," Lorah said in a neutral tone to cover her suspicions.

Ashley gave a knowing look from across the table. "Unless James is trying to win Gretchen back."

"Hmm. I'll bet Frank will have a thing or two to say about that." More nefarious scenarios flashed through Lorah's mind.

"It's gonna get interesting."

Before Lorah could reply, her datapad squawked. She retrieved it and pulled open the screen—it was a reminder about the coordination meeting. "I have to get going."

"I'll meet you for a late supper."

"Message me." Lorah exited and walked the bike to the Interdome Accessway, where she rode from Dome 4 to Dome 2, ending at MarsVantage Headquarters. Its name was written in gold with a solid red circle straddling the "V" above the front door, distinguishing it from the other nearby buildings.

She deposited her bike in a nearly vacant parking area and walked the five flights of stairs since MarsVantage annoyingly refused to run elevators. She entered Chuck's outer office and sat, allowing her heartrate to settle. After a few minutes, June Hudson, Alan Greene, and Erin Knox exited the inner office and walked past her.

Ashley had almost been right. *There was a secret meeting. But it already happened.*

14 | LEGERDEMAIN

Gretchen's stomach growled as she pushed several datachips into her office desk drawer atop the unopened chocolate bar smuggled from an Earth black market. After locking the drawer, she sipped water. While the ginger tablets were helping with the nausea, the upcoming meeting with James left her stomach rumbling with acid.

She scanned her office anew. The touchscreen occupying half the wall behind her desk displayed a map of Bvindu Dome. It showed nothing sensitive, but she switched it off, leaving a black void against the off-white wall.

From the corner of her desk, she snatched the spike-like shard of Marsium121. As she took it to the storage cabinet, it caught the light to show a dull rainbow within. She placed it on a shelf and grabbed an ordinary rock, which she put on the desk's corner.

James gets no freebies.

She set up a tripod and holocam at one end of the conference table. When the announcement chime sounded, she approached the table's head.

Normally, Gretchen preferred to keep her office door open when she worked, but this morning, she wanted James to need her permission to enter. If he were as bright as he believed, he would surely treat that tactic as a warning.

"Come in."

After the door slid aside, Erin entered with Gretchen's ex-husband in tow. Although he'd blended in with rebels in war zones and diplomats at cocktail receptions, he stood out by tugging at the collar of his black undershirt beneath the MarsVantage steel blue coveralls.

He'd put on some weight around the middle. His fondness for bourbon and black market cheesecake must be as strong as ever.

"Gretchen, allow me to introduce James Wagoner from the All News Network. James, Gretchen Blake, our Director of Archaeology," Erin said, playing dumb perfectly.

Gretchen extended her hand and firmly shook with James. In return, she received the fashionable feeble grip employed by Earthers. "James and I are already acquainted."

"Oh, I didn't realize." Erin's façade of surprise could have fooled anybody.

"I don't have much reason to talk about my ex-husband."

"Ex-husband?" Erin faced him with an amused expression. "James, you haven't leveled with me."

His shoulders bobbed, and he donned his "Oh, gosh" mask, which Gretchen had witnessed a handful of times to skirt potential awkwardness or bypass outright trouble. "It's not a subject that comes up in everyday conversation."

"Hmm, I suppose not. I gotta go—I have to take an OTP run." Erin departed, leaving the door open.

Gretchen directed James to a seat at the conference table, and she took the chair at its head.

"That Erin's a firecracker," James observed, making an unaccustomedly poor attempt at small talk.

"You have no idea." She turned right to face him square on. "You could've vidcommed to tell me you were coming to Mars. Or sent an email. Perhaps a quick message."

He leaned on the table with both elbows. "Our split wasn't overly amicable."

Is that the polite way of saying you blindsided me? "An email announcing the non-renewal of our marriage contract has that effect."

He leaned back in the chair. "I was in Kuristan—you were in Antarctica. Legal requirements are what they are."

"It's a shame you never brought it up when we were together before we left for our assignments."

For the longest time, she'd blamed herself for the breakup because she'd put her career first. The truth was, he'd done the same. While their time together was wonderful, they'd spent more of their marriage happily apart. *I should've noticed the warnings...*

She'd grown from the experience, better understanding her needs and desires to wring the most from life. That knowledge prepared her to remain on Mars and grow close to Frank. *The adventure of a lifetime awaits as we raise our children, watching them mature and learn, embarking on their future. Assuming we get past the Washington hurdle.*

Frank rushed in and closed the door. On her left, he reached across the table, and firmly shook James' hand. As he sat, he looked her way and asked, "Have you covered our conditions?"

Gretchen said, "No, James just arrived."

"Conditions?"

"Conditions," Gretchen stressed as she activated the holocam from her datapad. "MarsVantage's management knows exactly who you *were* to me. They're also familiar with your resumé. Unless we're recording too, everything we say is off the record—on background, as journalists say. Should you, your editors, or your producers play games with our statements, we'll release our full version and refuse further interviews. You'll agree to these conditions, or no MarsVantage employee will submit to an interview."

"You have the wrong idea." James pulled a holocam the size of his palm and his datapad from his coverall pockets. After setting both on the table, he opened the datapad's screen. He pressed several controls to activate the holocam, which rose and positioned itself slightly behind and above his left shoulder. "As you wish—I agree to your terms. I'll consider everything said to be background information unless the MarsVantage employee is also recording. Otherwise, I'll use no quotes. You have my assurance that my broadcast packages have the most professional quality control. You'll be quoted accurately and in context."

"Keep in mind I have friends on Earth who look out for Marsian news stories." Frank stared James in the eyes. "I'll know soon enough if you break your word."

"We've gotten off on the wrong foot." James sagged into the chairback, crossing his legs, and setting his hand in his lap. "I don't understand why you think I'll slant my stories against you and the company."

"Experience." Frank crossed his arms and leaned back in the chair.

Gretchen couldn't agree more. The media nonsense over the caretaker popped to mind. Never before had it been so clear that personalities, pundits, and entire news organizations—reporters, producers, and editors—had agendas. Their stories and opinions created the illusion of truth while being misleading at best or propaganda at worst.

Here sits their representative.

"I'll change your mind before I leave."

Doubtful. "Why don't we get on with it? Frank and I have much to do before leaving for Bvindu Dome at dawn tomorrow."

James referred to his datapad. "I thought we'd touch on various topics and go in-depth later. Gretchen, in your paper announcing the Bvindu discovery, you indicated that a holo message in the power-generating cavern pointed to Bvindu Dome. Several notable scientists, including Dr. Hawthorne, evaluated your recording of that holo and determined the dome's location by the images displayed but failed to understand how you interpreted those images as an invitation. Can you fill in the missing pieces?"

"I can." She wasn't duped by James' attempt to use his knowledge of her to his advantage. During their time as a couple, she'd expressed her loathing for others who discounted her abilities, and he'd laid a golden opportunity at her feet to prove Hawthorne wrong while demonstrating that she was just as bright and capable.

She straightened and squared herself to James. "However, I will not. Our discovery of Bvindu Dome was a blip in the news, leaving aside the rampant speculation and, frankly, the mocking by media personalities, including late-night comedians. I interpreted the symbols on the cave wall to gain access to the power-generating cavern. I then translated the holo's message contained within. Yet, Dr. Hawthorne and a handful of his colleagues failed to replicate my work, which made news for days. Hawthorne even had the gall to conduct a conference workshop about a year ago detailing my alleged mistakes."

"He did, and it made numerous broadcasts, too. Why don't you tell me where he went wrong? I guarantee it'll make the news," James said, attempting to mollify her.

"I included scans of the cave symbols and my recording of the cavern holo with my paper. I expected Dr. Hawthorne and his colleagues to replicate my work without my assistance using the same exact data I had. Besides having more resources, they claim to possess superior intellects. If those assertions are correct, recreating my conclusions ought to be trivial. Don't you think?"

As much as she'd love to highlight Hawthorne's error, doing so would be counterproductive. That would be handing Washington the key to translating Bvindu.

"Dr. Hawthorne suggests you altered the recording to make reconstructing your work impossible, thus embarrassing him, as revenge for him blackballing you. How do you respond to his accusation of professional fraud and ethics violations?"

15 | Opportunity Thrives in Turmoil

In one of Dome 4's small parks, Lorah strolled among a sparse stand of redbud trees. The subtle aroma of wildflowers found her. She continued, and the distinctive odor of rust overpowered everything else. As she turned, a green field with patches of red soil peeking through small plants came into view.

Farmers had taken lifeless dirt from outside and prepped it with water, fewer nutrients than she'd expected, and alfalfa seeds. Plants were growing nearly as well as on Earth. Once matured, they'd be plowed under to create arable soil. Afterward, tomatoes were scheduled to be planted. If successful, the farmers would harvest the plants and transport the soil to the upper portion of the dome where production farming occurred. Then, the process would begin again with a different fruit or vegetable, with any advancements applied for future plantings.

The Marsians had made strides in supporting themselves. Yet, Gretchen's announcement at that morning's meeting sounded like they were embracing the status quo. It must've had something to do with the prior meeting that'd let out while she waited.

Upon entering the transition station at the end of the path, the door behind her closed, and the one before her opened. Lorah stepped down to the dome's deck. Using this facility to enter and exit the park allowed Marsians to enclose spaces containing their experimental farming plots to monitor and regulate the environment.

She made her way a couple of blocks to her office. After sitting behind her desk, she pulled open the bottom right drawer and reached behind it. She grasped her Knowledge Keeper datapad from the floor.

Most people ignored the space beneath the bottommost desk drawer when the drawer stack extended to the floor. Instead, they used one of the many wall maintenance panels, where everyone would look first.

After logging into the MarsVantage communication network, she opened a connection to the Earth network via the minute Morris-Thorne wormholes, which provided instantaneous communication. She navigated to the Knowledge Keeper portal, and a message, *'Awaiting encryption handshake,'* appeared on-screen. After she connected the datapad, she applied her thumb to its screen and uttered her passphrase, "Course Correction." With her credentials key released, the portal displayed the Order's main menu.

She chose to search the Knowledge Keeper database, and on her third attempt, it yielded the reason for MarsVantage's change in direction. The Senate Offworld Commerce Committee had called Mr. O'Donnell to testify the next day. If that wasn't justification enough, a Space Force destroyer was coming this way.

Everything's falling apart.

Lorah searched for information on James Wagoner. The Order knew he was Gretchen's ex-husband and was on Mars—Frank had reported his scheduled arrival weeks ago. Lorah submitted an update about her meeting and chided the Order for not alerting her about the reporter, Mr. O'Donnell's testimony, or the destroyer's apparent arrival.

For this assignment, the Order shielded her reports from Frank, so her status as a Knowledge Keeper remained secret from everyone on Mars. She disliked the subterfuge, but the Order wished for an outsider's perspective about the Bvindu technology and MarsVantage, so much so that they'd negotiated with Mr. Fordham for her to become his liaison to MarsVantage. Why they had done so had never been explained.

What he received in return was also a mystery. He wasn't making money on this venture yet and probably wouldn't for years. *The wealthy don't get rich by having investments that don't pay off. And they certainly don't remain rich by squandering money. What's his payoff?*

Eventually Mr. Fordham's patience would run out, causing him to cancel the contract and dismiss her. Another job would come along, but something important was happening. Perhaps she could guide it in the right direction.

She disconnected her Knowledge Keeper datapad and returned it to its hiding place. Afterward, she vidcommed Mr. Fordham on Earth. While the connection was quick, she stared at a stylized golden "FI" logo for seconds that dragged on.

The screen changed to show him, silver hair and all, sitting at a desk in his home office with a remote Colorado forest beyond the window behind him. His compound, which held three mansions and a handful of outbuildings, was located on nearly three dozen acres.

He was one of the few in the United States with the persistence and the money to build a private home. He'd hired a consulting team to slog through a decade of red tape before beginning construction. Rumor held that over half of the project's cost had been related to getting the first shovel in the ground.

She had visited once, facing him after his security team caught her trespassing. Instead of weaving an outrageous tale for the police, that encounter had sparked conversations and some sort of agreement between him and the Order's regents.

"Lorah, it's good to see you again."

"Good morning. Unfortunately, events have taken an unwelcome turn. MarsVantage has decided to pause exploring the Bvindu knowledge base in favor of understanding the statuary."

He leaned back into the chair, steepled his fingers, and beamed, the dimple on his cheek gaining prominence. "Good."

"Sir, perhaps I wasn't clear—"

"MarsVantage sees the writing on the wall. The government is finally making its move on everything Bvindu." Mr. Fordham leaned in. "Chuck's taking a defensive position."

"Or... they're not handing Washington anything on a silver platter when they give in."

"Surrender? That's not in Chuck or Frank's DNA. Do you believe the Marsians have been spinning their wheels for two years, or have they been preparing for the inevitable?"

"They *definitely* know more than what they're saying."

"I should hope so." He perked up. "Besides this, is everything else going well?"

"You're not recalling me?"

"Not unless Chuck cancels our contract, and he won't. It'd be a bad look at an inconvenient time." He looked down and appeared to type. "Today is as good a time as any for this. I'm sending you a file on a side channel containing vital information should events unfold as I expect. Look it over and give it to Chuck or Frank at the right time."

"When is that?"

"That's for you to decide. I have faith in your judgment. Soon, you'll have to choose between Earth and Mars. I'm not pressuring you to stay, and I recommend you don't allow the Order to, either."

"Why?"

"If you don't know, that means the Knowledge Keepers don't know. Interesting..." Mr. Fordham shifted in his chair. "Do you think the politicians aren't anxious that free-thinking civilians control a treasure trove of next-level knowledge—probably advanced weapons? Do you think these same politicians aren't worried about their positions and lifestyle?"

"When you put it like that... It'd be a different story if Mr. Konklin still ran MarsVantage."

"If Konklin still ran MarsVantage, he wouldn't have found Bvindu Dome because he wouldn't have been inundated with a decade and a half of burdensome regulations."

The Order, including Frank's reports, believed the regs' overarching purpose was to hinder MarsVantage as an effort for the government to correct the mistake of breaking them away from Interplanetary. They believed Washington intended to drive the company into a precarious financial position so it could be purchased by a trusted Earth business like Interplanetary, thus bringing it back under control. Regulators, and perhaps Konklin himself, could dispel any lingering safety concerns after all these years.

Gretchen's discovery had scuttled the elites' plan.

Mr. Fordham continued, "Naturally, greed is a factor—they're politicians, after all—but they have a larger fundamental concern. The elites' reaction to Gretchen's paper from twenty months ago was telling. There wasn't an onslaught of reporters heading to

Mars to substantiate her claims. Multiple scientists ignored the opportunity to work with alien knowledge and tech."

"I expected the opposite, frankly. Transports should've been full of people eager to dive in. Instead, Gretchen was begging for scientists."

"The key to understanding is to give events the proper weight. Lacking that and a few juicy tidbits I learned, the apathy is confusing."

Lorah blinked. "Apathy—that's the word."

Mr. Fordham gave an approving nod. "The politicians learned their lesson from the Airlock Accident. That public outcry caught them flatfooted. In their panic, they split MarsVantage from Interplanetary but created a difficult-to-control wild card. There will be *no* public outcry this time—it's the entire point of their actions over the last two years."

Lorah tilted her head to one side. "The conspiracy is huge. It's not just politicians. The media's involved. But besides the news, there are the late-night personalities and entertainment holos. A stage play, *My Favorite Bvindu*, opened in Chicago, and it skewers the Marsians."

Mr. Fordham placed both hands on the desk and leaned forward. "Answers to who, how, and why are needed. The why is easy—the fear of losing power and existing as nobodies within a system they created and perpetuated, leaving their greed and egos unsatisfied. It doesn't matter if the person is a lowly staff writer in Hollywood, a news executive in New York, or a politician in DC."

"A lot of favors, outright bribes, or both must be involved."

His brows drew together. "If you look through a conventional lens, you'll never solve the mystery. We know the why—let's tackle the who. Until recently, I figured President Dohbyn was pulling the strings. He's been vocal about Mars for years, and a couple of his cabinet officers despise the Marsians, an attitude which rolls downhill to their various agencies."

"He has decades of experience and the clout," Lorah acknowledged, "but he'll be indebted to so many. Sounds like a bad deal. The last two years of his presidency will be nothing but repaying favors."

Mr. Fordham's shoulders relaxed, and he exhaled easily. "I've come to believe there's a hidden hand at work, namely Senator Severino. Dohbyn's not merely relying on her for advice—she's pushing the agenda. A dozen House and Senate committees perform oversight of MarsVantage—I mistakenly dismissed their members in favor of the president. Because Severino called Chuck to testify before Offworld Commerce, I looked closer, and the pieces have fallen into place."

Perhaps they did for him... "She's only been in office for three years. She couldn't have accumulated that much influence."

If Mr. Fordham grinned more, his face would break. "Bear with me—she's the who. The how is so exquisitely beautiful and *simple*. She started by giving voice to staffers, representatives, senators, and even the president's fears lurking in the back of their minds. She then made a suggestion here and planted an idea there. My sources say they believe she helped them save their positions. Instead of Severino owing favors, she's *accumulating* them. It's a masterclass in manipulation... Right now, a Bvindu nationalization law is written. Congress is waiting for a rationale they can sell to the public."

Oh, dear Lord. How did the Order miss this?

"Lorah, can you now guess how the media fell in line to shade its coverage to the accepted government position?"

"Severino and the other politicians, perhaps their staff—certainly administration officials—played on the pliable media executives and on-air personalities' fears. Perhaps coercion for any who resisted."

"You got it in one. The IRS is a great club. There are others. I know of one case where a top news executive was so scared he sent multiple edicts to his producers and talent, threatening firings if his wishes weren't followed. Word spread among the media organizations—news and entertainment—even into popular music."

This theory has one flaw. "How could all these discussions occur between Gretchen publishing her paper and the first news report? There was just no time."

"MarsVantage bought all rights to the land Bvindu Dome's on immediately after its discovery to ensure Konklin didn't beat them to it. That was months before Gretchen's paper and her request for scientists. The elites had more than enough time to develop a strategy and execute their tactics."

MarsVantage's exploration report, which was part of the rights purchase from the Exploration and Mineral Rights Office, would have had the same documentation that Gretchen used in her paper. Withholding information would incur severe penalties—loss of the rights, fines, and possibly prison time.

Lorah concluded, "It worked. The public gobbled up the media's misrepresentations and outright fantasies."

"One hurdle stands before the politicians nationalizing everything Bvindu, a rationale. And they've been diligently searching for one. If luck worked in their favor, MarsVantage would've corrected every untruth, giving the elites vital information. Instead, the Marsians smartly remained quiet. Gretchen never even explained how to translate the Bvindu language because she knows what the elites could do with that knowledge."

A realization struck Lorah. The Order hadn't made concessions for her to be Mr. Fordham's representative—it was probably the opposite. If he couldn't intimidate her during their first meeting, he must be betting on her staying, even with tensions running high.

Her presence on Mars had less to do with her liaison duties but more to do with Mr. Fordham's other agenda. Whatever that was.

"Lorah, are you still with me?"

"My apologies, sir. An insight struck me. So the Marsians remained mum. Enter the inspectors and auditors to find the rationale?"

"If they could've, everything Bvindu would've been nationalized within a week. It's the reporter's turn now, and he's more dangerous as his inquiries aren't constrained."

"I knew something was off—the timing and his former relationship with Gretchen are dead giveaways."

"Absolutely. As a heads up, be wary of everyone who arrived post-discovery, especially the archaeologists. I wouldn't be shocked if one or two are in cahoots with Dr. Hawthorne, who I suspect is on someone's speed dial in Washington. I haven't locked that down yet."

All the archaeologists had struck her as skilled and professional, certainly not suspicious. However, Ashley's request for help convincing Gretchen to open the Bvindu database was troubling, especially now.

Mr. Fordham leaned back in his chair. "Let me ask... given my reputation as... let's say, a nonconformist, you're not skeptical about my conclusions?"

Any public oddness had struck her as a diversion, similar to what some Order members had done to hide their affiliations. Like all the others, today's conversation was entirely reasonable and rational. "Sir, your conclusions fit the facts, and the motivations fit the players. Excluding our initial encounter, you've been straight with me. Plus, what would you get by lying to me?"

"Nothing at all... The world is filled with oddness, but it tends to make sense with the proper perspective. For instance, you should know I have a purpose whenever you hear something weird about me. You heard about the shuttle incident at my landing pad?" She confirmed with a nod as he continued, "An NSM official asked if I was attempting to contact the Bvindu. Perhaps to bring them to Earth."

"How do you know where they are? Did Gretchen tell you?"

"Nothing like that." He absently waved his hand. "I picked a star that scientists think may have a habitable planet and arranged the entire gaudy show, including a leak about it, so that the NSM *would* question me. Their questions confirmed their fears."

"Losing their positions to exercise power," Lorah stated matter-of-factly.

"The politicians will continue doing what they always do, what their predecessors did for centuries... Coercion and control to maintain their positions. To that end, MarsVantage will be offered a partnership with the National Science Ministry."

Lorah snorted. "The NSM is like a black hole. All the Bvindu data would go in with none returning to MarsVantage."

"Indeed. Chuck'll decline that offer. It's a ploy to appear fair and reasonable. Once the nationalization bill becomes law—it will, one way or another—Space Force will occupy Bvindu Dome to prevent the Marsians from looting it. Then, the NSM team takes possession. Notice MarsVantage loses either way. Only the reason—a partnership, an egregious MarsVantage problem, or a flimsy rationale concocted by nameless staffers and administrators—differs. For the past fifteen years, the basis of every government action related to Mars has been to control them. Until the Bvindu discovery, they believed time was on their side, so slowly squeezing them was fine. Time is *not* on Washington's side anymore."

"The Marsians won't allow the government to strip Bvindu Dome from them."

"They can pose legal challenges, but the government plans to walk in and take possession. Even if MarsVantage prevails in court, the government has copies of everything. With far greater resources, they'll capitalize on the Bvindu first, leaving MarsVantage with little or nothing."

Lorah slumped in her chair. Space Force would encounter a nasty surprise in Bvindu Dome, but Mr. Fordham wasn't entitled to that information.

He continued, "I put the odds of Chuck declaring Marsian independence at seventy-thirty in favor."

"Washington won't stand for that. They'll go after the Marsians in addition to occupying Bvindu Dome. How are they going to defend themselves, throw rocks?"

Mr. Fordham reached off-screen and took a sip from a water glass. "We're back to my question. Have the Marsians been spinning their wheels?"

Lorah inhaled as she straightened. "You think they have something up their sleeve."

"No." Mr. Fordham settled back in his chair. "I think they have *multiple* somethings up their sleeve. The ruling elites make a mistake by giving them no credit."

The first thought that crossed Lorah's mind was that she had to update the Order again. Then, the weight of the situation fully hit her. "I could be sitting on the front line of a shooting war."

"Yes, and I'll understand if you wish to return home."

"Or I have a front-row seat to history in the making," she speculated.

"It's possible you could play a role, perhaps help alongside the Marsian Knowledge Keeper."

Lorah kept her expression neutral. Mr. Fordham wasn't an Order member, only an ally, and he wasn't entitled to know if MarsVantage had an Order member or who they might be.

He continued, "Events are in motion. No individual, company, or secret organization can stop them. But in turmoil, opportunity thrives for those who seek it.

"One last thing, if Chuck or Frank asks, feel free to share any of today's discussion. I suspect they haven't figured out that Severino's the puppetmaster."

"I will."

He disconnected, and she stared at the blank vidcomm screen. What should have been unimaginable in twenty-third-century America was playing out before her eyes. The politicians felt entitled to rule, and fear and greed propelled them to legislate everything Bvindu away from the Marsians while duping the public in the process. As usual, Washington expected compliance and couldn't conceive of Marsians fighting back.

The politicians might've been better off acting two years earlier and putting their efforts into managing the public's complaints. They must've weighed the risks and rewards. Mr. Fordham had been correct in saying that Washington gave little credit to the Marsians, which played into their considerations. *Faulty data in, faulty data out.*

She opened the file Mr. Fordham had transmitted. Upon finishing, one fact was clear—he'd thought ahead to help the Marsians. He was backing up his analysis with money and action.

For a single moment, she pondered returning home but dismissed it. Her instinct said that her future lay on Mars. *Truly positive change for humanity could spring from here.*

Little would happen if the Order didn't step up with relevant information. They should've alerted her about the reporter. They should've volunteered his connection to Gretchen. And the Space Force destroyer? Important details were falling through the cracks.

She opened her right bottom desk drawer again.

16 | Answers Without Context

Gretchen forced her face to remain impassive at the charge James had leveled.

Though perturbed by her former mentor's assertions of unprofessionalism, she was unsurprised that Hawthorne and the Earther scientists hadn't replicated her work with the holo. The key had been the audio that played so fast it sounded like low-level hiss. She'd almost missed it, initially believing it had been a failure of the original projector. Hawthorne, armed with confirmation bias, hadn't connected the hiss to the images' rapid progression, instead believing deception.

Frank sat straighter. "We recorded the holo we found playing from a projector the caretaker fused to the cavern's deck. A copy of that recording and recordings of the cave's symbols were submitted to the Exploration and Mineral Rights Office as part of our application for full land rights to Bvindu Dome. Any alterations, once discovered, would be interpreted as fraud, and we'd forfeit the rights. There are only downsides for us to play games with the recording."

She placed her hands, palm down, on the table. "An assertion of data alteration is an excuse for Dr. Hawthorne's failure. He and his colleagues didn't *disprove* me but rather exposed their own incompetence. Set aside their excuses and accusations—no one can erase the fact there's a buried alien city east over the horizon, and I found it."

When she'd been married to James, he'd mentioned he would occasionally begin interviews with a pointed question or two to throw the interviewee off-balance. All of her and Frank's practice with mock questions had been effective. June, Alan, and Chuck had taken expected questions, put the worst possible spin on them, and then she and Frank had practiced answering.

Inside knowledge works both ways, buddy-boy.

James' face betrayed nothing, but he fidgeted in the chair nonetheless. "Since your announcement, several religions dedicated to the Bvindu sprouted up. A few minor ones say you and Frank are their prophets. Do you have any comments for those followers?"

"We only found what was left behind." Frank blew away James's chance to characterize them as delusional.

"To this day," Gretchen said, "people question the existence of the caretaker, yet the idea of alien prophets has gained traction. Strange what people latch on to."

James' eyes widened like he was about to win a poker pot. "Many find it difficult to believe that a person, even an alien, still lived after two hundred thousand years."

He swallowed the bait!

Gretchen replied evenly, "I heard that."

"I couldn't miss it, but I also noticed people never asked how. They simply assumed we lied. In fact, several jokes based on our," Frank made air quotes with his fingers, "*supposed lies* received plenty of laughs at our expense."

Gretchen leaned back, crossed her legs, and placed her left hand on the table. "The caretaker lived in Bvindu Dome's master computer system. He transferred himself into a mobile unit when he had to visit locations physically."

James' attention lingered on her hands until he finally met her eyes. "You mean he was an AI?"

"He was intelligent and didn't have a corporeal body."

"That completely alters the conversation." James touched his datapad screen a few times. "I'd like to devote an entire interview to that later. On to another topic. We've seen several odd phenomena, like people constructing bizarre monuments to the Bvindu. Another religion, The Devotees of the Glorious Bvindu Spider, created what looked like a massive black arachnid. What do you think is driving that?"

The Knowledge Keeper who conceived the Glorious Bvindu Spider ought to be awarded a medal. It'd led everyone, including James, to question the wrong things.

Frank stared blankly at James. "Since the beginning of recorded history, some people have had a tenuous grasp of reality. These days, various media outlets amplify their message to attract viewers and readers."

Without the words "odd" and "bizarre," James' question was straightforward. As it stood, James had tried to link MarsVantage to nutjobs. Again.

Gretchen rubbed her eyes. "We're not psychologists, but these instances suggest people seek a deeper meaning. Some lose themselves to alcohol and drugs. Others work hard to find an indifferent world that cares little about ability, commitment, and success but is impressed by inconsequential things like titles or associations with important people.

"With the need for meaning unfulfilled, some look elsewhere. In a way, it reminds me of the cargo cults of the twentieth century."

James asked, "Cargo cults?"

"A long time ago, during the Second World War, some natives on remote Pacific islands encountered airplanes—specifically, military airplanes—for the first time. Pallets of supplies like food, medicine, ammo, or anything else were offloaded or even parachuted to the ground. Sometimes, food, medicine, and clothing were shared. After the forces withdrew, some natives constructed replicas of airfields, control towers, and airplanes to entice the strangers to return."

"The similarity is lost on me."

"The fringe you describe may want to embrace the Bvindu to have meaning in their lives. The things you bring up may be their way to summon them back," Gretchen explained. The story's flimsy connection to James' point should muddy the water enough to separate the Marsians from the antics on Earth.

"One of the most well-known fringe personalities is Miles Fordham," James said, not losing any momentum. "A few nights before I boarded the transport, a shuttle disappeared from his private landing pad in Colorado."

Frank tilted his head. "It took off? Who cares?"

"No, it disappeared. The landing pad was surrounded by seven twenty-foot pillars with lines and circles etched onto their sides, similar to those from the cave. As a National Science Ministry task force closed in, a display erupted that one witness described as, and I quote, 'fireworks mixed with a complex laser display.' When it was over, all traces of the shuttle were gone."

"Flashy," Gretchen said, rolling her eyes to punctuate her words. The Order had reported the incident, but unfortunately, they had provided nothing regarding Fordham's motivations. One thing was clear—the symbols might look like Bvindu writing, but they were gibberish.

Frank raised an eyebrow. "I wonder what Mr. Fordham was trying to accomplish."

"To open a trans-dimensional portal to Tau Ceti f and investigate its habitability," James said evenly.

The Order had communicated that the shuttle everyone had seen was actually a next-level hologram, and its disappearance had been Fordham merely switching off the generator during the fireworks display. His stagecraft had spawned a stream of questions about trans-dimensional portals, a technology that was a figment of his fertile imagination.

"Mr. Fordham's a brilliant business person, but he's also a known eccentric," Frank allowed.

"Many say he's half-insane," James offered.

"Poor people are insane," Frank countered. "The rich are eccentric."

"Eccentric or lunatic—he's a MarsVantage partner in bringing Bvindu-based products to market on Earth." James played his trump card. "Did he get the Tau Ceti f information from anyone in MarsVantage? Did he get specifications for a trans-dimensional portal from MarsVantage? Is he bringing the Bvindu to Earth?"

By asking those questions, James had placed them in a tricky position. Should they defend Fordham, they'd utterly discredit themselves, and their credibility on Earth was already suspect. Yet, they could alienate a valuable business partner if they hung him out to dry.

Gretchen squared her shoulders against the seatback. "We care only that Mr. Fordham brings any tech we release to market. I haven't seen a reference to trans-dimensional portal technology in the Bvindu data, and astronomical data is a low priority. When

I get to it, not only will I have to translate the Bvindu text, but I also must correlate their star references to ours. That effort will be huge."

"Remember, James, we consulted with the caretaker before his departure about the Bvindu cure for the common cold. If we hadn't, it'd take years to get where we're at now." Frank's datapad beeped. He retrieved it from his thigh pocket and extended the screen. "I have to leave. One of the tractors is acting up. James, good to chat with you. We'll sit down again soon."

After Frank rushed out, Gretchen faced James. "We're returning to Bvindu Dome tomorrow. You're welcome to join us to see everything yourself, including the Bvindu ship under construction."

"Excellent. I'll give the audience their first look at Bvindu structures and tech. It'll be a must-see event." James deactivated the camera via his datapad. It returned to where it started on the table. "I suppose that's enough for now."

"You have enough for a piece?"

"No. This was more to get a lay of the land. We'll do additional sit-downs over the coming weeks."

What would he pursue? He certainly didn't get the reaction he was fishing for. "How long do you plan on staying?"

"A minimum of two months. The network wants stories on MarsVantage and the Bvindu, plus in-depth profiles on you, Frank, and Chuck."

"I don't know that I care to do a profile."

"You'll do fine." As James pocketed the camera and datapad, he asked, "I saw the ring—when did you remarry?"

She glanced at her left hand. "After I returned from Bvindu Dome to ride out the sandstorms a little over a month ago."

He looked her in the eye. "Congratulations. Who is he?"

With every ounce of willpower she possessed, she kept her expression neutral. "You were sitting across from him."

"Frank?" Surprise rumpled his face. "You married a *Marsee*?"

"Ever since you *Earthers* started using that term disparagingly, we've moved away from it, and I know this fact has made it back to Earth." She pulled her shoulders back. "The only term more debasing to us is *Martian*, which makes us sound like a poorly written and executed black-and-white 2-D vid. You wouldn't use derogatory terms for people's origins, races, or religions, yet you feel comfortable saying Marsee to my face. You'll find us *Marsians* won't be eager to answer questions if you act smug and dismissive, which is nothing more than good old-fashioned prejudice mixed with arrogance and condescension. None of those qualities are endearing."

"I didn't mean anything by it."

"Perhaps you even believe that. Many archaeology undergraduates conflate primitive with dumb. Those who succeed learn that primitive means our earliest ancestors had to be smart to survive—in some ways smarter than most alive today."

He shook his head. "What's that have to do with anything?"

Gretchen's pulse quickened. "You think because we don't have all the comforts of Earth, or the art, history, and entertainment, that we're less. Less worthy, *less bright*. On Earth, you can be dumb as a box of rocks and live to an old age. Every day, Mars will try to kill you five different ways before breakfast if you get complacent. The smart and prepared survive and thrive. Think about it, but do so elsewhere. You're dismissed."

17 | THE UNSTOPPABLE FORCE

Gretchen popped into the kitchen. "Frank, a woman from Earth named Brielle who claims to be your mother is on the vidcomm."

"Huh, it's not my birthday," he said in a monotone. Even then, her vidcomms had been perfunctory, made out of obligation, not emanating from genuine feelings. "You should listen in. Stay off to the side, though."

He laid a fist full of uncooked spaghetti on the counter near the pot of water heating on the stovetop. With slow, deliberate steps, he mentally steeled himself for the upcoming conversation, eventually sitting before the screen in the living room.

Mother wore a fashionable off-white top. Behind her lay a few skyscrapers, presumably those of Washington, DC. "What's the problem, Mother?"

"You look well, Frankie."

"Thanks."

"Who's the woman that answered?"

"She's my wife, Gretchen."

"Congratulations, son." A perfunctory smile formed but failed to extend to her eyes. "I take it that's Gretchen Blake, the archaeologist who discovered everything."

"Yes, Mother." He shifted in the chair, trying and failing to find a comfortable position. "Enough of the small talk. It's nearly supper time, and I'm hungry. What's on your mind?"

"Do you know who I work for?"

"Some government agency?"

"That was a couple of years ago. I'm Senator Maura Severino's executive assistant."

This can't be good. Frank exhaled. "Your boss is obsessed."

"Frankie, this isn't the time for name-calling. Though the senator would never admit it, she believes you, MarsVantage, and the Bvindu will steal her position and status."

"If politicians and bureaucrats would take a more hands-off approach, everyone would be happier and more productive." He leaned closer to the holocam. "And sending a reporter immediately after the inspectors and auditors is simply ridiculous."

"Frankie, no one in the government *sent* the reporter."

"Mother, the timing's so transparent that denying it only reduces your credibility."

Her face was set like stone, just as she'd done while he was growing up when facts had proven inconvenient. "Politicians don't force stories onto the media. They work together harmoniously, sometimes pointing out interesting stories, to achieve the overarching goal of exercising power. For the good of the people, of course."

The ruling elitists always claimed their endeavors were for the people's good, but power, wealth, and prestige continuously flowed toward them, not the ordinary people. "The universe contains fascinating riches. Who exercises power in one country on a distant Earth is mundane and doesn't interest us."

"Now's the time to partner with the National Science Ministry. I'm sure grant money can be arranged."

"For what purpose?"

"Experts can help catalog the artifacts and analyze the data properly. More importantly, the optics would be invaluable."

Appearance and control. Typical of Mother. But science and MarsVantage employees' welfare, not so much. He pushed his hand through his hair. "All archaeological activities are performed to the highest standards, and Earth has no Bvindu experts. They're right here. You spoke with two of them."

She gave a patient smile, much like he'd seen daily until she abandoned him and Dad. Only now, it looked phonier. "Without a partnership allowing more insight into the Bvindu data, Senator Severino and her allies will continue to press."

"We have no desire to involve the NSM because the type of partnership you suggest sounds like a takeover."

"Please reconsider," Mother said, a faint pleading tone in her voice. "Space Force is on the way to Mars. Unless you cooperate, Bvindu Dome will be nationalized, and Space Force Guardians will take possession until the NSM sends a delegation. You'll be left on the outside, looking in."

Gretchen's expectations had just been confirmed. Moving discreetly had been a failed strategy from the moment of conception. Nothing MarsVantage had done or could do would blunt the ruling elite's greed and lust for power.

"Either way, we'll still be on the outside, looking in. A partnership would only prolong the process. Our answer is no." A thought struck Frank—*probe for information.* "Besides, your boss is new to the senate—she doesn't have the kind of pull to accomplish what you suggest."

Mother shook her head slowly. "President Dohbyn is an empty suit. He's pleasant enough—good hair, a strong chin, and a sparkling smile—everything the public needs from their president. But the blowing wind determines his policies. Where Mars is concerned, Senator Severino controls that wind and owns his and his advisers' ears. She wants everything Bvindu, which means he wants it. And *he* has the pull to make it happen."

"You want me to hand over everything we worked so hard for? Everything we nearly died for? In exchange for what? Crumbs?"

"Accept the partnership, and leave Mars behind—*come home*—and put your hands and mind to something meaningful."

Years had passed since she'd tried to talk him into going to Earth, but this was the first time she'd used a scare tactic. "People like your boss spend a lifetime chasing power, glory, and fame, never realizing they're pursuing an illusion. There's never enough power to quench that thirst. Or glory or fame. On a more practical note, I'm not spending a trip to Earth and another three months under ever-increasing gravity performing circuit training to achieve a goal that holds zero interest."

"Kaitlin and I underwent the treatment, and we've never been happier."

"I'm glad for you—really, I am."

Mother sighed. "You're placing yourself directly in the path of the unstoppable force."

"Mother, the government irresponsibly wields its power with onerous laws and oppressive regs. Our safety hasn't been a consideration for years. The NSM would be the opposite of helpful. Should Space Force step foot in Bvindu Dome, they'll be uninvited and unwelcome invaders."

* * *

In silence, Frank ate spaghetti across from Gretchen at the small table in their kitchen. His thoughts were occupied with that call. Had Mother actually been worried about his safety? Or manipulating him? Frank didn't know the answers.

He did know that Washington planned to get what it wanted by imposing its will. MarsVantage could make it easy by agreeing to an NSM partnership, or Washington could concoct a few more lies for an ambivalent populous before Space Force took control of Bvindu Dome.

Washington was so used to having the upper hand that they couldn't conceive a third choice existed. His and Gretchen's efforts to hold the Bvindu data close had tipped the odds in MarsVantage's favor. Best of all, when Space Force arrived, they'd actually assist MarsVantage with a sticky problem.

Halfway through the meal, Gretchen asked, "Do you want to talk about it?"

"Not really."

"Ah." She sat up straighter. "I'll rephrase. You have to alert the Committee because of the implications regarding Bvindu Dome. You need to talk to me because family is also involved."

"Everyone has a mother."

"That's axiomatic, not an explanation." She glowered, staring him down.

"*Mother* and James are alike in one regard. The less spoken about, the better." He methodically set his fork on the plate and wiped his mouth with the napkin from his lap, placing it to one side. "But you have a point. She abandoned Dad and me and took Kaitlin to Earth when I was sixteen. Once they settled, Dad transmitted the marriage contract non-renewal, well ahead of the ninety-day deadline for those with children."

"Kaitlin is..."

"My sister. She's a year and a half older. We haven't spoken since Dad's passing."

"Why'd your mom go back?"

"She felt that our operation on Mars was becoming dangerous."

After Gretchen swallowed a bite of garlic bread, she asked, "That was well before the Airlock Accident. Were things that bad?"

"At the time, we experienced intermittent shortages. Nothing serious. We had a mining cave-in but rescued everyone. Danger was an excuse... She missed Earth's social calendar. Our monthly parties, concerts, and plays don't hold a candle to the menu of activities she could do on Earth, any given day."

Gretchen looked at her plate and slowly breathed out. "It could've been both, you know."

"Maybe." *It wasn't.* As Frank had grown older, the truth had become more apparent—Mother was selfish. He ate a forkful of spaghetti.

"The timing of the vidcomm is interesting."

"So it's not just me." He placed the napkin back on his lap. "A reporter's among us. We're returning to Bvindu Dome, and the hearing's tomorrow. My *mother* vidcomms, saying Space Force is on the way to take over and provides an out. I'd bet everything that if I were to agree to the NSM partnership, the hearing would be a perfunctory walk in the park, and Space Force would be conducting a training exercise, probably in the Belt like Alan suggested."

"Your mom may be concerned for your well-being. That vidcomm could've been a warning."

Gretchen gave Mother the benefit of the doubt that she'd failed to earn.

"Or Senator Severino could've been off-camera directing the conversation."

18 | The Calm Before the Storm

"If I didn't know better, I'd swear we were in an airplane hangar or a warehouse receiving dock." James stopped inside Dome 4B's garage bay to record the scene with his holocam.

As far as Frank was concerned, the reporter could record the bay until the sun turned into a red giant. Frank and the rest of his team, Gretchen, Ashley, and Lorah, continued toward their tractor. Three other groups of archaeologists in green spacesuits, sans helmets and gloves, were already scurrying around their tractors, loading last-minute cargo. Together, they'd be the first to reoccupy Bvindu Dome.

Heavy footfalls grew louder from behind. James asked, "You mean we're *driving* to Bvindu Dome?"

Listening to his complaints would make the trip intolerable. Frank leaned toward Gretchen, who had already turned to confront James.

She stepped directly into his path. "If you don't want to ride, you can always remain here or walk. A shuttle isn't among the choices. That's expensive and inefficient. Are we clear?"

James looked abashed as he glanced first toward Ashley and Lorah, then back to Gretchen. "Clear."

"Good." She turned back and whispered to Frank, "Even my most pampered archaeologists fresh off the transport from Earth never moaned about riding in a tractor."

Frank had expected her to keep her ex at arm's length, but not like this. "Weren't you rough on him, especially in front of the others?"

Gretchen's features hardened. "He gets what he gets. After you left our meeting, he made a highly offensive comment."

"What was it?"

"That doesn't matter. I'm calling him out for any transgression." She frowned and inhaled. "Don't look like that—the most anyone could expect from me was politeness."

Frank asked, "Can we get to that?"

"If James can keep his Earther entitlement to himself."

"You need to cut him some slack," Frank suggested.

She put on a phony façade of cheeriness. "The jackass' air vest connector is dangling. Call for a spacesuit check before boarding. I'll take him *aside* and correct it. See, I'm flexible and willing to compromise."

All of a sudden, Gretchen has peculiar definitions of flexibility and compromise.

Once everyone reached the tractor's rear, Frank stopped the group and fulfilled Gretchen's request. He donned his helmet and gloves. The mechanical odor of air vest air filled his nostrils. His wrist panel displayed a positive seal and eleven hours of air and power.

Lorah twisted her helmet in place, then affixed her gloves, followed by Ashley. Gretchen sealed into her suit while watching James from the corner of her eye. He struggled to lock the helmet. After pulling on his gloves, he accessed the control panel on his left wrist. It immediately displayed a red warning.

She approached and yanked his left arm to see his control panel. With her finger, she stabbed it a few times, resetting the integrity test. She showed him the air vest's connector and let it drop. James bit his lip and fumbled with it until securing the connection on his third attempt.

To her credit, she'd corrected the issue privately, though in a rather curt manner. *That interaction surely wasn't making the news.*

Gretchen said over the standard communication frequency, "Tractor One crew, report status."

Everyone indicated success.

"Excellent. Test complete," Frank said as he doffed his gloves and removed his helmet. The others followed his example. He pulled out his datapad and started to record. "Gretchen will give a brief tractor refresher. I'm recording, so James, feel free to use this in a broadcast."

84

"We're taking a tractor to Bvindu Dome. Normally, it's a six-hour trip." Gretchen looked over to Frank.

"This is the first outing since the sandstorms. We can expect drifted sand in places that may slow us down. We'll travel in spacesuits but without wearing helmets or gloves We'll seal in, however, if someone needs to leave the tractor."

James asked, "What circumstances would cause that?"

"Mechanical issue. Perhaps getting mired in drifted sand." Frank couldn't believe he had to explain the obvious. "That's unlikely. And we won't be trailering any supplies because our route's driving conditions are unknown."

Gretchen said, "These tractors differ from Earth's autocabs and autobuses. There is no automation using a Global Positioning Network. Frank will drive, and Ashley or I will take over if he needs a break."

"Are all of you certified to drive vehicles?" James asked. "Aside from the military units I was embedded with, I don't know anyone who can drive."

Frank shifted his weight. This quick briefing was anything but. "All the archaeologists and about ninety percent of MarsVantage employees are certified. All employees participate in exploratory missions, looking for promising mining opportunities or signs of water, so driving is a useful skill on Mars."

"The cargo area is filled with containers, mostly FieldMeals. We also have new equipment and our personal effects." Gretchen pointed to the roof. "Our engineers added cargo racks, so we're hauling extra supplies."

Ashley and Lorah exchanged glances. They must be bored out of their skulls having to hear about the basics.

Frank picked up the briefing baton. "You'll have to enter through the front doors and squeeze between the seats to access your spots. James, you're behind Gretchen on the starboard side. Ashley and Lorah, you're sitting behind me on the port side."

Frank walked to the driver's side and opened the door, allowing Ashley and Lorah to enter and take their seats against the bulkhead. With his holocam back in his spacesuit, James crawled through Gretchen's door and took his seat. Meanwhile, the other three crews, each containing four or five archaeologists plus a driver, had already mounted their tractors.

Frank settled behind the controls and cinched his harness before donning his headset. "Buckle in and earsets on."

He ran an integrity test of the tractor—the pressure was constant. He toggled the comms to External. "Control, this is Frank Brentford. The Bvindu Dome caravan is ready to depart."

"You're next in the queue, Frank. Mining Team 3 departed Dome 7 and is picking up Main Street now."

"How long, Control?"

"About ten minutes."

"Copy that. Ten minutes."

The other tractor drivers acknowledged the delay. Frank toggled the comms back to Internal/Monitor External.

It didn't take two seconds before James asked, "What does that mean?"

Gretchen answered, "There's a mining team about to pick up Main Street. That's the primary road north. Control doesn't want us bunching up, so we'll wait a few minutes."

"Road?" James asked. "I didn't know you paved any roads."

"Nothing's paved," Gretchen said. "It's a well-worn path. Nearly every tractor going into the wild rides Main Street to Waypoint 1. From there, they head to their destinations."

"Got it." James stuffed his gloves in the helmet and placed them between his feet. "Sounds like a remote area of Brazil I visited on assignment. At least there won't be any snakes here."

Except for you. Frank secured his helmet and gloves between his and Gretchen's seats. She placed her gear behind his. He leaned over to her, putting his hand over the earset's mic. "Is the ID equipment handy?"

She mimicked his move. "It'll be unloaded first. Once we arrive, I'll need five minutes to set up. You know, I could outfit us while we wait for clearance."

"It's tempting, but now's not the time to break procedure."

James asked, "Do the water tankers arrive later?"

"This is on background," Gretchen said.

"Of course. I'm not recording."

"Like each dome in Mars City, Bvindu Dome has an array of storage tanks. Fortunately, water is abundant in this region, but it's subterranean, so specialized mining crews acquire and transport it to us. While our reclamation systems are efficient, they're not perfect. Plus, our farming initiatives require plenty of water, and it's not recycled."

James asked, "You said *acquire*. What does that mean?"

"Sometimes, it's as simple as pumping it out," Gretchen said. "Other times, the water is frozen and must be excavated like ore."

"Interesting, thanks." James turned to Ashley. "What'll you be doing at Bvindu Dome?"

"We're cataloging residential living spaces, then moving on to an area filled with statuary."

"Isn't a house a house?"

Gretchen leaned over to Frank, covered her mic, and whispered, "He knows better than that."

"Many think so, but it's the opposite, really," Ashley said with an energy she reserved for archaeology. "You'd draw different conclusions from the houses of a vid star, a lawyer, and an aerospace engineer, right?"

"Sure. When I was just starting out, I interviewed a musician with a dedicated room for creating his music. He had several— what did he call them... gold records on the wall. He said they were awards from his publisher for hitting certain sales numbers."

Ashley said, "So you can't make broad statements about a culture from one sample. It's a fallacy of composition to argue what's true of the parts is true of the whole."

James had demonstrated advanced interpersonal skills with Ashley. He engaged her, prompting her to speak as a subject matter expert. Then, he'd bought into her perspective. Most likely, he'd continue to act like a novice over the days and weeks to come to finagle all the information he desired from her.

"Then there's a layer of the individual's mastery of their craft," Ashley said. "Let's take our vid star, for instance. A major star may earn many awards and keep them in storage. I heard of someone from the days of two-dimensional vids who kept her Academy Award in the bathroom. Yet, a mediocre performer may keep an obscure award front and center on the mantle."

"How does that factor into your conclusions?"

"Part of the evaluation has to determine what's typical versus extraordinary." Ashley leaned forward. "After all these centuries, Albert Einstein is considered a great scientist, whose current peers still strive to prove—or disprove—some of his theories."

"Sure," James said with curiosity in his voice.

Ashley continued, "But some of his ordinary habits would have you think him a dullard. He painted his front door red so that he could find his own house."

James laughed. "That can't be true."

"There's evidence pointing that way. He pondered so much that he didn't want to have to think about where he lived."

Gretchen rolled her eyes, and Frank scratched his upper lip to conceal amusement. Perhaps James' management had sent him based on his talent to put people at ease in addition to his connection to Gretchen.

"I never expected to learn about a long-dead scientist. Would it be okay if I tag along when you explore the residences?"

Ashley answered, "As long as you stay out of the way, it's fine with me. Gretchen?"

"That's a great idea."

Frank couldn't imagine investigating living quarters alongside Ashley would occupy James for long. He'd eventually want to tour the Master Control Center. Frank disliked the idea of showing him inside, but a guided tour under close supervision would reveal only what Frank wished him to see.

James asked, "What's the most interesting thing you found so far?"

"Interest is in the eye of the beholder," Ashley said. "I'll give you puzzling—every building's outside walls slope inward by exactly one degree. We didn't notice it at first, but several team members mentioned something feeling off. Anyway, once you know what to look for, you can't miss it."

"Why'd the Bvindu engineer their structures like that?"

Ashley said, "We haven't found the answer yet."

"I'll check it out," James said. "Lorah, you're Fordham Industries' liaison to MarsVantage? My understanding is that this is his pet project."

"That's correct."

"Is Mr. Fordham concerned about the lack of marketable Bvindu products?"

"I'm not privy to Mr. Fordham's emotional state."

"It'll take years for the cold cure to gain approval. What else is he hoping to market?"

"Everything," Lorah evenly said.

Gretchen added, "We're still evaluating the opportunities."

"Mr. Fordham must be patient."

"There's a time for everything," she said, "including patience."

Lorah was certainly not succumbing to James' charms. Frank had never heard her say a word of gossip or voice a complaint about Fordham. Nor had she passed along any doubts or concerns he might have over the availability of marketable products. The likelihood that James would break that streak was virtually nil.

He hadn't reacquired the conversational initiative before Frank received the signal from Control. After the other caravan drivers confirmed they were ready, Frank alerted the personnel in the garage bay that they were preparing to depart. A few seconds later, he received the all-clear signal. He acknowledged it and pressed the Hatch Open button. In response, the bay emptied of atmosphere, and the large door slid aside.

He led the other three tractors in the caravan from the garage bay. The transition from industrial gray to red was like flipping a switch. Traces of brown and even a streak of yellow here and there passed by as Frank guided their tractor forward.

Off to the left in the distance, Interplanetary's partially constructed dome stood. A range of the Maelstrom Mountains towered over it. An inspector had called them *menacing*—Frank always thought of them as fierce defenders, protecting Mars City from the brunt of the sandstorms' effects. He turned right and set out to pick up Main Street. Once on it, he applied full power on the straightaway.

Nearly an hour into the trip, Gretchen announced, "Heads up, Frank. Two o'clock. It looks like a dust devil."

"Got it."

"What's up?" James asked from between Gretchen and Frank, arms on their seat backs.

Gretchen ordered, "Get back in your seat and buckle in."

After he obeyed, Gretchen explained, "It's a dust devil, just like on Earth."

"I'd like to record this. Can someone else record it, too?"

Ashley pulled her datapad from her thigh pocket. "I will."

James pulled his holocam and datapad from his spacesuit. He pressed several controls to position the holocam between the seats, pointing out the windshield. "Is it dangerous?"

"It can be," Frank said.

"But not like you think," Gretchen added, looking Frank's way. "We've all seen vids of debris swirling in tornadoes on Earth. Now imagine that on a smaller scale, like several yards wide, maybe a half mile tall minus any debris."

"Okay... Can it pull us from the ground, flip us over?"

As Frank concentrated on the dust devil creeping closer, he replied, "No. The winds are moving fast and churning up a lot of dust. With the low gravity and thin atmosphere, we won't feel it."

"Then what's the concern?" James asked.

"Visibility. People instinctively slow in low visibility. We can't have a pile-up with the other tractors, so we'll perform a structured stop."

"Structured stop?"

Gretchen turned around to face James. "Watch."

Frank toggled the comms to External. "Tractor Four, this is Tractor One. We spotted a dust devil on a possible intercept course."

"*Roger that. We see it, too. What's the plan?*"

"Structured stop. Go now, Tractor Four."

"*Stopping.*"

Gretchen brought her right fist up to her shoulder. She tapped her thigh with it and extended her index finger. Again, she brought her hand up to her shoulder and tapped her thigh, now displaying two extended fingers. She continued until four fingers were extended. With her left hand, she patted Frank's thigh.

"Tractor Three, stop now."

"*Stopping.*"

Gretchen performed the same sequence again. Another tap. "Tractor Two, stop now."

"Stopping."

Four seconds later, she tapped his thigh again.

"Tractor One stopping now." Frank released the accelerator and gently applied the brake. "Report any issues."

All of the caravan's tractors confirmed no problems. They waited. The dust devil zigged, appearing as if it were going to pass to port. Then it zagged. It grew and engulfed the tractor. Dust and sand pinged against the plastiglass in swirling streaks of red and brown.

Frank gestured to the windshield. "Other than low visibility, everything's fine. In the days of NASA, they used to maneuver their rovers and helicopters into the paths of dust devils to clear the solar panels of accumulated dust."

After several seconds, the view cleared. Tractor Four reported that the dust devil had moved past their position a minute later. Frank moved the tractor forward.

After a second, Frank said, "Tractor Two, start now."

"Underway."

Frank did the same for the other two tractors. "All tractors tighten up the spacing to normal at your discretion."

James announced, "What a display of teamwork and coordination, manually operating heavy equipment. It'll get people's attention."

Frank stared at the red landscape speeding by, considering the ride so far. Positive PR would be appreciated. Even if it happened, it wouldn't last for long. James' purpose was to expose the unsavory side of MarsVantage. Positive comments in the moment couldn't erase his long-term goal.

19 | THEATER FOR THE MASSES

At the conference table in Chuck's office, he sat dressed in one of three conservative suits reserved for formal events. His datapad and a cup of water sat before him. Beyond them was a holo of the Senate Offworld Commerce Committee. Its central portion showed the committee members in a semi-circle. His visage sat in the lower left corner, with the lower right corner reserved for a close-up of the questioner.

"I yield my time to Chairperson Severino," Senator O'Brien said.

Chuck concentrated on maintaining a pleasant appearance. The hearing had been surreal—every committee member from the chairperson's party had yielded their time to her, despite politicians adoring the spotlight as much as hearing their own voices. Something was in the offing—Senator Severino was banking a lot of time to ask questions when her turn came.

The parties were all-important for the elected officials, their staff, and the bureaucracy. Over the centuries, their positions had shifted like tides on the beach. Yet, one truth remained constant. There was no problem too small that Washington couldn't address by smothering it with money and regulations.

While Earthbound citizens found these circumstances natural and rarely posed questions, Marsians viewed the government solving their problems as nonsensical. It was incapable of repairing the oxygenators, irrigating farmland, or providing power. Nor was it going to grow crops or mine minerals. Rather than implementing solutions, the government often hindered or outright thwarted practical solutions.

Chairperson Severino looked off to the side. "You have the floor, Senator Freeman."

"Thank you, Madam Chairperson." A healthy mix of gray in his beard and hair gave the senator the appearance of someone two decades older than the forty-five his profile indicated. "We shed a lot of light on the results of audits and inspections, which are part of the public record. My reading is that the inspections were exemplary, and the audits found everything in order."

Chuck's datapad softly chimed, and the notification light blinked. Unless the dome had been breached, whoever messaged him would have to wait. He had to give the hearing his complete attention.

He returned his gaze to the holo. Severino opened her datapad and, a second later, frowned.

Senator Freeman continued, "I'm curious about the events after Mr. Brentford and Ms. Blake discovered Bvindu Dome before returning to Mars City. I read the incident report and your self-reported violations. You tallied three traveling at night over unfamiliar territory *on foot*. Another traveling at night over unfamiliar territory by vehicle. Why did you confront the Interplanetary spy in Bvindu Dome?"

"These events occurred two years ago," Senator O'Brien interrupted. "They were reported, and MarsVantage was appropriately fined. Is there new territory to cover here?"

Senator Severino banged the gavel three times. "Senator O'Brien, you are out of order. This is Senator Freeman's time. Mr. O'Donnell, please answer the question."

Senator Freeman's question was an opportunity to get the truth on the record for the public to hear. He slyly grinned.

Chuck straightened. "My team desired incontrovertible proof that Sam De Angelo was working covertly for Interplanetary so that we could rid ourselves of the cancer in our midst. Up to that point, he had a sterling reputation among his co-workers and management."

"Don't you think the recorded conversation of him coordinating his action with an Interplanetary employee was enough proof?"

"If I may be blunt, Senator, no. For the past several years, MarsVantage hasn't received any benefit of the doubt regarding anything, either officially or in the media. We had to catch him in the act."

"I understand. Still, it wasn't like Mr. De Angelo could shove the city in his pocket and walk off with it."

Chuck took a sip of water. "My team wasn't sure what information he could glean, and on Mars, information is as valuable as air. Overriding all other considerations, the caretaker warned Mr. Brentford and Ms. Blake that the automated systems would handle intruders, and he wouldn't override them if Mr. De Angelo approached any critical areas. Mr. Brentford and Ms. Blake refused to allow him to die needlessly."

Senator Freeman opened his arms like he was releasing the truth. "So you balanced competing priorities to achieve an acceptable outcome?"

"Senator, I was willing to pay the fines to save his life."

"Thank you, Mr. O'Donnell. Not many people face such life-and-death decisions. While sitting in a comfortable chair and second-guessing your team's actions is easy, I won't do so."

"Senator Freeman, your time has expired," Senator Severino announced, holding her datapad. "We'll adjourn the hearing for today. Mr. O'Donnell, we invite you to return on Tuesday next week to continue your testimony. Thank you for taking the time to speak with us today."

The transmission ended as she banged the gavel. It was only mid-afternoon, but hearings had been known to run until dinner time. Something was afoot.

He grabbed his datapad and extended the screen to check on the message, which was from Frank. He read it once, then read it again. Undoubtedly, Severino received a similar report, probably from the All News Network, which explained why she'd ended the hearing early.

Severino would use this newfound tragedy in Bvindu Dome against them. Guaranteed. "Damn."

20 | THEATER FOR ONE

F rank guided the tractor down the slope that he, Gretchen, and his former maintenance team had excavated two years earlier. Areas of drifted sand from the recent storm shifted beneath the treads. A vision of them sliding uncontrollably into the airlock's doors flashed to mind. He eased off the accelerator to regain traction.

At the bottom, he stopped before the garage airlock. A reddish-brown patina of dust clung to its normally-white doors. He pushed the Open Garage Airlock button. Nothing happened.

Gretchen asked, "Everything okay?"

"We must be getting some electromagnetic interference from the dust." He put the tractor into gear and pulled closer to the hatch.

Gretchen covered the mic and leaned in. "Any closer, and the remote command failure will be the least of our problems."

He shielded the mic. "I'd rather not have James' first impression of Bvindu Dome be a problem."

The airlock door slid aside in response to another transmission. Dirt and sand shifted inward as the garage bay's interior illuminated. He drove in, stopping when the fluorescent yellow tennis ball hanging from the ceiling touched the tractor's front, the drawn-on smiley face greeting him. The green light was lit on the upper set of lights. The lower set had the red one lit.

He pressed the Close Garage Bay Door button, undid his harness, then twisted and fixated on James. "We built a small garage bay airlock on Bvindu Dome's entrance for our convenience. There are two pairs of red/green lights. The upper pair beside the arrow pointing toward the ceiling indicates the status of the dome. It's green, so the dome has a proper atmosphere and pressure."

Gretchen gave him two pats on the knee.

He continued, "The bottom pair with the arrow pointing toward the deck indicates the status inside this bay. It's green now, so we can get to work. You need to be aware that the safety interlocks prevent the outer and inner doors to Bvindu Dome from opening simultaneously. Nothing prevents the inner doors from opening if Bvindu Dome isn't pressurized. We haven't interfaced with the dome's systems yet."

Gretchen said, "Before we get to work, take note of the warning signs under the lights here and before a black and yellow caution line in the hallway beyond."

The sign read:

Danger
Severe bodily injury may occur
Proper identification required beyond this point

Gretchen narrowed her eyes in James' direction. "You must always wear a wristband so the Bvindu intruder protection systems recognize you. If your band breaks, do not move. Vidcomm for help."

"You haven't disabled the Bvindu security systems?"

"That's exactly what we're saying." Frank fixed his gaze on James. "Without that wristband, Bvindu Dome is lethal. I don't want to deal with dead bodies on the deck. Are we clear, James?"

"As water."

"Good. Let's unload the cargo. The identification equipment first."

James took his cue from his fellow passengers, leaving his spacesuit gloves and helmet inside. He assisted in unloading the tractor. An unexpected gesture, but guaranteed to generate goodwill. Except from Gretchen, if the contempt on her face was any measure.

She corralled a cargo container and opened it. With the ID kit in hand, she headed toward the hatch leading to Bvindu Dome. She stepped onto the ramp that easily allowed cargo on hand trucks to navigate the hatch's lip. Once through, she disappeared.

Several seconds later, Bvindu Dome's main entrance lighting sprang to life.

Meanwhile, everyone else unloaded the cargo containers and placed them against the garage bay wall shared by the personnel airlock. Gretchen reappeared with a handful of wristbands and affixed them to Ashley, Lorah, and James.

Lastly, she approached Frank, wrapping the plastic band loosely around his right wrist. After inserting both ends into the fuser, she melted them together. It was snug but not too tight. The slight odor of melted plastic found his nose.

He asked loud enough for all to hear, "Gretchen, is the flumolator working?"

"Yes."

"And is the interlocking granistan joint giving off any hedenine interference?"

"None."

"Excellent."

Ashley and Lorah exchanged looks but thankfully remained silent. Neither he nor Gretchen had briefed them on this little fiction for James' benefit. As expected, he paid rapt attention.

Frank continued, "The hemolac levels?"

"All normal."

"Good. We're ready to proceed."

Gretchen took Frank's wrist, stepped closer, and whispered in monotone, "We have a problem inside. You need to see."

Frank traversed the ramp to the hatch's threshold with her close behind.

She said at normal volume for others to hear, "During the dust storms, we had a trespasser."

Just beyond the black and yellow caution line, a figure in a white spacesuit lay unmoving on the ground between buildings lining what he always considered was a roadway. When MarsVantage had departed a month ago, they'd left no one behind, certainly no one in a white spacesuit.

The trespasser was dead, probably for some time—the Bvindu security system would've ensured it. This poor soul should've paid attention to the warnings, but instead gambled and lost. *What a shame.*

Hopefully, they hadn't suffered.

The rest of his tractormates crowded the hatch's opening.

"Oh, God," Lorah exclaimed. "Is he dead?"

Frank raised his hand. Grief had to wait. The moment called for leadership. "Everyone, take a breath. We will help them in a calm and orderly manner. Ashley, get a medkit."

"Frank, he's dead," Ashley pronounced.

"Maybe, but we'll render aid if we can. Now, go. Datapads out and start recording. Everyone will need to file a witness statement."

Lorah implored, "Ash, hurry up."

Gretchen stared at the body, her face like stone. "Do you think it's Interplanetary again?"

"I doubt it—that's a white spacesuit." By rule, all personnel working in space wore white spacesuits, while everyone stationed on Mars wore green. He scratched his chin. "It's probably someone associated with Belt mining."

"Perhaps the PAA isn't satisfied with the data-sharing negotiations after all," Gretchen said.

By the time Ashley handed over the medkit to Gretchen, James had his holocam hovering over his left shoulder. He asked, "What's the next step?"

"Ashley, Lorah, stay here. Follow us, James." Frank touched Gretchen's arm. "Start recording on your datapad."

After Frank retrieved his datapad and pressed Record, he placed it face-up on the hand truck parked against a bulkhead next to Gretchen's worktable holding the ID band creation equipment. The report to a handful of Washington regulatory bodies would have five perspectives of their actions with overlapping holovid evidence. *No one will be able to accuse us of covering up this incident.*

He pushed the hand truck toward the body, glancing over his shoulder to ensure James was following instructions. Gretchen was nearby, keeping an eye on him, too.

After crossing the warning line, they stopped at the body. Frank parked the hand truck off to one side. He grabbed his datapad and crouched down next to Gretchen, who was on one knee. While holding datapads, they rolled the body onto its back.

Gretchen gasped.

The bloated face in the helmet confirmed Frank's assumption.

Frank recorded the body's length, starting with the boots covered in red dust. PAA patches adorned the air vest and the arms of the spacesuit. He pressed the control pad on the trespasser's left arm. After a couple of seconds, it lit at half brightness. With the air vest's power long exhausted or outright destroyed, the panel's battery backup had taken over.

Chinese characters that Frank couldn't understand were displayed. Everything pointed to the Pan-Asian Alliance.

"It appears we have three air vest punctures, which likely compromised it." Frank pulled at the air vest. "Directly beneath are three spacesuit punctures and yellow leak sealant. There's no decomposition odor, so the punctures were sealed. It appears the lungs and heart were hit from a steep downward angle. The damage is almost certainly from the Bvindu security system. Blood droplets on the inside of the faceplate and the lack of blood on the deck support this conclusion. The face is bloated, and rigor mortis isn't present, suggesting several days have elapsed since the incident."

James said, "That terminology sounds more like a conversation doctors and nurses would have than a former maintenance manager."

James clearly lacked everyday knowledge of Mars and MarsVantage's operations. Not surprising, much of that information was unavailable, but if he truly were interested in learning, he would've phrased his observation as a question.

"All MarsVantage employees are trained in first aid," Frank explained. "Many, including myself and most of the miners, are certified medics. In the wild, we can't wait for doctors to arrive to handle a medical emergency."

Gretchen pushed herself upright. "Back to the issue at hand, James. There's nothing we can do. The trespasser was probably dead before hitting the deck. Hopefully, they didn't suffer."

Frank rose, closed his eyes, and bowed his head for several seconds. *Dear Lord, this unfortunate person made a mistake but keep his soul close.*

"Those look like scorch marks," James noted after Frank lifted his head.

Gretchen replied, "The intruder system uses focused, high-energy pulses."

James' eyes widened. "That's next-level technology. Earth has nothing like it. You allow lethal measures to continue to be employed?"

Frank pointed to the wall. "We have signage at all of the excavated entrances. Not only are we concerned about theft, but we're also worried about allowing potentially dangerous Bvindu tech to slip into the world. Gretchen and I don't want to be responsible for the aftermath."

James looked at the body again. "Is there dangerous Bvindu tech?"

"Aside from the security system, we don't know," Gretchen admitted. "We haven't reviewed everything, but we're taking a better-safe-than-sorry approach."

Her statement was the truth, as James must be thinking about offensive weapons. Gretchen hadn't found any references to them in the Manuduction. Defensive weapons were a different matter.

After laying his datapad on the ground, Frank took hold of the trespasser's arms. "Gretchen, get the man's legs..."

She set her datapad aside, and they transferred the body to the hand truck. Afterward, they each retrieved their datapads. Frank placed his on top of the body and guided the hand truck toward the airlock.

As sad as the trespasser's untimely passing was, it would be an excuse for the full weight of Washington to come crashing down. The small shred of hope Frank held onto had evaporated the moment he'd seen the body.

Within hours, Washington would have justification to take Bvindu Dome. The trespasser might have company if the government forced the issue by employing violence.

As they closed on the ramp, Lorah wiped her eyes before she and Ashley retreated into the garage bay. Frank pushed the hand truck up the ramp and down by the cargo containers.

"Please save your recordings. We'll get instructions on where to send them along with our written reports. Lorah and Ashley, please start transferring our cargo inside. I need to report to Chuck. When I'm done, Gretchen and I will locate the trespasser's spaceship."

James said, "I'll file a breaking news alert. Then, I'd like to join the search."

Gretchen glanced toward Frank. He didn't have to ask to know she disliked that idea, but he had no good reason to exclude him. "Fine. We leave in fifteen minutes."

21 | No Further Incursions

Inside the tractor, Frank backed out of the garage bay. He cut the wheel until the vehicle was parallel to the hatch. He pulled forward and climbed the slope to level ground, where he stopped with a bit of a jolt beside the other three tractors of the caravan. *This is not how I wanted today to go.*

Gretchen provided the waiting archaeologists an update while James looked on from behind her. Surprise and shock came from the archaeologists in the rest of the caravan. Gretchen concluded by saying, "Go about the entry procedure as normal. Ashley will create your ID bands. Tractor Two, you're a go for the garage bay. Take it slow. There's quite a bit of loose sand."

Frank grabbed his helmet with gloves inside. "Suit up and run an integrity check."

"Can we take a few seconds to answer a couple of questions?" James requested.

Gretchen wrinkled her brow. "I thought you filed your report already."

"I filed a breaking news alert, just bare-boned facts with a promise of further details. It took longer to connect to the comm network and transmit than to write."

That explained how James had already been waiting when Frank finished his message to Chuck. Frank had included everything he knew and suspected, as well as the immediate plan to move forward.

"Nevertheless," Gretchen said, "we have a lot to do. Replying to questions with obvious answers is a waste of time."

Frank pulled his datapad from his spacesuit's thigh pocket and pressed Record. Perhaps they could salvage something from the situation. "We have a few minutes to spare, especially if we can shed light on this unfortunate tragedy. Perhaps we can even prevent future deaths."

Gretchen shot him a side-eye glare. She'd tell him about it if this interview blew up in their faces. At least once.

Meanwhile, surprise crossed James' face as he activated his camera and positioned it just above his left shoulder. "Thanks for agreeing to answer a few questions. What's MarsVantage's procedure for handling deaths in Bvindu Dome?"

"We never had a death in Bvindu Dome," Frank answered, "so there's no established process. However, company policy is to transport the departed's remains to Earth or bury them with honor in our graveyard outside Dome 6. All according to the deceased or the next of kin's wishes."

"You're preparing to search for the deceased's ship. Why is that important?"

"It could help determine the *trespasser's* identity. Right now, headquarters is notifying the State Department. Presumably, they'll contact their PAA counterpart. If we can identify the deceased, perhaps we can expedite matters." Frank cleared his throat. "We can't discount that the trespasser wasn't alone. He could've arrived in a shuttle with others. First, we'll find the ship, then we'll have a better idea of what to expect."

"There was only one body. Where would others be?"

"They could've driven monoriders—"

"Excuse me, monoriders?"

"Think of it as a powered bicycle with wide tires designed to ride atop the sand."

"Got it."

Frank continued, "So they could've driven a monorider to one of the other excavated entrances. If we believe there are unaccounted-for people, we'll bring in search teams from Mars City to find them. I don't want the archaeologists stumbling across them. They didn't sign up for that."

James swiveled the camera to Gretchen. "Would that be a problem for your archaeology team?"

"No one wants to come across a dead body. But if someone's injured and miraculously still alive, we need to locate and help them."

"We're going to seal into our spacesuits and perform a search on foot." Frank grabbed his helmet with gloves inside, intending to end the questioning.

"Wouldn't it be quicker in a tractor?" James asked. "Or is cost a factor?"

Frank suppressed the urge to comment on James' unnecessary baiting. "My hope is that we only have one trespasser. His spaceship should be obvious. However, if the trespasser traveled *here* by monorider from a spaceship that landed elsewhere, we have to look for signs of anything unusual, which can easily be missed from within a tractor. Unfortunately, the sandstorm would have erased tracks and boot prints. We'll go slow, on foot, and stay attentive."

"I see." James conceded the point without signaling whether he believed it. "I'm sure the audience back home will appreciate your perspectives."

Frank attached his helmet and gloves to the spacesuit and ran an integrity check from his wrist control panel.

Gretchen did the same. James was last but gave a thumbs up a few seconds later.

Frank handed Gretchen an air vest harness designed to hold a datapad to document whatever the wearer faced. MarsVantage had never bothered with them until the Earther inspectors had arrived and pried into everything. Documenting the ground search for a foreign spaceship would put them to great use. Plus, it kept their hands free, which aided balance on uneven terrain.

They donned and adjusted the harnesses and datapads. Frank relished the idea of a reporter, whose purpose was to hinder MarsVantage's cause, actually documenting them following good practices and procedures. *Not that any of this will matter—the dead trespasser will garner all the attention.*

Frank purged the tractor's atmosphere, and Gretchen dismounted. He did likewise as Tractor Two entered the airlock. Gretchen joined him a few seconds later, with James and his holocam trailing a step behind.

Aside from the MarsVantage caravan, no other vehicles were in sight, which wasn't overly surprising as no one noticed anything during their arrival. Several large dirt mounds, two to three times as tall as him, littered the landscape from when they'd excavated Bvindu Dome's entrance two years earlier. Those could easily conceal a shuttle from sight.

"Where do we start?" James asked.

Gretchen replied, "Our trespasser didn't just materialize in the city, so he walked here from a spaceship or monorider. That means it ought to be close."

"How do you think he got to Mars?"

"His spacesuit had PAA patches," Gretchen cited, "so he probably worked in the Belt. When Mars is favorably positioned, their ore transports use it for a gravity assist. It saves a few days of travel and a significant amount of fuel."

Frank glanced around. "Let's begin our search off to my right. We would've noticed a spaceship left of here when driving in. Behind me is the dome beneath the sand plain, and straight ahead is also flat sand to the Maelstrom Mountains. I don't see anything in those directions. These mounds from excavating the entrance could conceal a shuttle from view."

After glancing around, James concurred, "Makes sense."

"Gretchen, head about one hundred yards toward the mountains. James and I will stay here."

"Give me a minute."

As she set off, James asked, "What can I do?"

"We're going to proceed to that mound. Gretchen expands our search area."

"We can cover more ground if we separate."

Without taking his eyes from Gretchen's receding form, Frank said, "We're not bopping around Earth. Mars is dangerous. If you rip your suit in a fall, you can die. As long as you're my responsibility, we'll take every safety precaution."

"What about Gretchen?"

"She's experienced and knows the protocols. She has my full confidence." Frank imagined her satisfaction in hearing his praise. "You must stay with me, no more than six feet away. Are we clear?"

"Yes."

"Gretchen, that's far enough." Frank pressed several settings on the control panel on his left wrist. "I set an alert tone to sound every minute. When you hear it, stop and find your partners. If you don't see both, speak up."

"Got it, Frank." Gretchen raised her hand in the air.

He stared at James.

"Yeah, got it..."

"Okay, start walking east. Be careful of larger stones and rocks. They'll shift underfoot." At the sound of the tone, Frank stopped and peered over his right shoulder. James looked in Gretchen's direction. Frank turned and picked out Gretchen's green spacesuit against the rusty brown background of Maelstrom Mountains in the distance.

They continued scanning the landscape. Every so often, Frank took extra glances at Gretchen. He approached the towering dirt mound. "James, we'll proceed clockwise around the hill. Gretchen must always be able to see us."

"I suppose climbing it and getting a bird's-eye view is out of the question."

Is this a test? Impatience? Fear? Frank confirmed, "Except for miners, no one would climb it. It's too dangerous."

"Got it. We go around."

A few minutes later, Gretchen pointed farther ahead. "I found the spaceship. It's on the other side of the mound you're transiting. A few more paces and you'll see it."

Frank stopped. "Good work. Join us, and we'll go together."

"Can't she just meet us at the spaceship?" James asked.

Frank replied, "The regs allow for separation only until we locate the target. We must rejoin as soon as possible, so we stay put until she arrives."

"Don't you find the regs constraining?"

"Constraint isn't the issue—safety is. Every second, Mars tries to kill you. Let down your guard, and you may not live to try again. In this case, the sooner we're together, the safer we all are, even if only marginally."

If James used that quote in a report, it'd play well back on Earth. Odds were, he'd ignore it because it didn't fit the elites' narrative.

"Was safety top of mind when you and Gretchen walked here at *night* to confront the person you accused of spying?"

"We aim to minimize risk so we can work and live here as safely as possible," Frank responded. "That's as true today as it was that night. For someone who's covered armed conflict, I'd think you'd understand the concept."

"I'm a reporter. I ask questions."

Still some distance away, Gretchen chimed in, "Believe me, James, we know. We certainly didn't want the spy, Sam, to compromise our discovery. Far more important is that we didn't want him dead like this PAA trespasser."

She met up and stared at the reporter-slash-spy.

Frank credited James for having the guts to ask a hard question. Perhaps he thought the trespasser would distract them into revealing something. He had been wrong. Worse for him, he'd advertised whose side he was on, not that it was news.

Frank led them around the mound until a single-person miner explorer pod stood before them. It sported a PAA flag of five white stars—one at each corner with the last in the center—on a field of red.

"This pod probably originated from an ore transport ship. At least we know we found everyone." Frank unzipped a thigh pocket and withdrew a locator beacon. After extending its legs, he planted it firmly near the landing skid. He activated it, then unfolded a pair of solar panels, each the size of a playing card.

"Why deploy a locator beacon?" James asked.

"When we return to Bvindu Dome, I'll report the beacon's frequency. I don't know if Space Force wants the explorer pod or if the PAA will retrieve it, but it has no home with MarsVantage. And I'm not acting as a tour guide, especially not for spies and thieves."

Frank tried the hatch control, and it opened. A layer of red dust covered the inside from when the trespasser disembarked during the dust storm.

James asked, "It's not locked?"

"Who was going to steal it out here?" Gretchen scoffed.

"When not in use, it's stowed in a hangar. I'd be surprised if it even has a locking mechanism." Frank withdrew a handwritten note from his other thigh pocket encased in a clear plastic bag and placed it on the deck inside the hatch. "James, get a clear shot of this."

James directed the camera to the note Frank had composed after messaging Chuck.

Attempt no further incursions into Bvindu Dome.
The intruder defense systems are active, accurate,
and deadly.

22 | HUMAN NATURE

"Thank you for the information. I won't forget it," Senator Maura Severino said.

"It's my pleasure, Senator," a managing editor at the All News Network said before Maura disconnected the vidcomm.

She rose from her desk, went to her office's mini-bar, and poured two fingers of whiskey. After a sip, she savored a hint of vanilla and the burning in her throat.

The unexpected news from Mars handed her a lever so big she could move the planet. Luck had broken her way again.

Tuesday, I take a giant step toward 1600 Pennsylvania Avenue.

She called to the outer office, "Brielle, work is over. Come in for a drink."

Her assistant sauntered in. "Seven and seven, please."

Maura poured the cold whiskey over ice. Next came the clear soda from Barney's. Because of a wellness push by Congress to lower medical costs in the mid-twenty-first century, all carbonated beverages had been legislated away, so its black market popularity had soared.

Instead of the traditional lime, Brielle preferred a lemon wedge. While lemons were perfectly legal, Barney's had the best quality. Ruining the drink with mediocre garnish made no sense after going to the trouble of procuring soda.

She passed the glass to Brielle and sat with her at the small table. "Have you seen the news from Mars?"

"I couldn't miss it." Brielle sipped her drink. "The story leads the hour, every hour."

"The president and his team don't know any more than the newscasts." State, Commerce, and Defense were burning the back channels with the PAA for information. So far, nothing had come from those efforts. "How do you think I should play it?"

Brielle took a long sip. "Luck handed you a winning hand. The Marsees believe they own the moral high ground, but failing to disable the Bvindu security procedures was reckless. Trust me, *that* decision was based on the expense of purchasing Washington-approved security equipment. And now a person is dead because of it."

Maura leaned back into the chair. "Reckless... I hadn't considered that angle. I was thinking that their greed was so overwhelming that human lives were meaningless. But recklessness is better... simpler. You know, I'm beginning to think this is fate, destiny even."

"It allows you to implement the correct policy." Brielle finished her drink and went to the mini-bar.

Upon her return with another drink, Maura raised her glass in a salute. "To protecting the Marsees from themselves and the Bvindu."

After the clink of glasses, Maura continued, "Do you know why Frank dismissed the NSM partnership?"

"He's his father's son." Brielle frowned and took another sip.

"Which means..."

"He's so stubborn that if you told him he could drink anything except milk, milk would be all he'd consume."

"An NSM partnership is the perfect compromise. The Marsees can reasonably profit, and we ensure nothing dangerous is unleashed." Any destructive tech could be transferred to government control, where expert wisdom and judgment could safeguard it. More importantly, the NSM would know precisely what Bvindu tech MarsVantage was pursuing. "The Marsees are children who found matches. They're going to burn themselves."

"Or burn down the entire house."

"They won't be satisfied until they rule Washington, then Earth as a whole," Maura said to probe Brielle's understanding of the Marsees' intentions.

A slight frown crossed her assistant's lips. "Marsees never showed interest in governance except to loudly complain about the supposed unfairness of Washington's rules and laws. They aren't stepping up to rule for ruling's sake."

Maura finished her whiskey, setting the glass before her. "Should the cold cure ever come to market, the people will look to the Marsees for more. They built a Bvindu spaceship instead of buying more ships from Earth. It must be better—if they can fly to Earth in a week or two, rather than four, they can start their own shipping company. What additional tech is waiting? It could be enough for them to become self-sufficient. Or worse, give our citizens the idea that government is unnecessary."

"Perhaps, but the people are satisfied for the most part," Brielle said. "Making such a drastic change isn't likely."

"What will happen ten or twenty years from now? Human history is the story of war and conquest. The Marsees will be no different, especially wielding advanced Bvindu tech. They'll come here and eliminate all social programs like full housing and NutriAccounts. Centuries of careful planning and social engineering will be erased in a blink of an eye.

"Compete for living quarters... Eat anything, no matter how unhealthful, in any amount... Oh, they'll offer education, but ultimately, they'll allow people to make self-destructive choices. Imagine people living—and dying—in the streets. Malnutrition. The health care system overwhelmed by preventable diseases. Plus, a score of other problems running rampant. All because the Marsees distrust government."

Brielle opened her mouth for a second but shook her head. "I was about to say they wouldn't change anything that works well, but that's untrue. On principle, they'll eliminate everything with a large government footprint."

"They'd drag us back to the dark ages."

Brielle took a gulp of her drink. "They'll bring chaos to us all. We have to get control over the Bvindu tech before they master it and use it against us."

Maura beamed, savoring the success. Brielle was still part of the team. *She'll help me rein in MarsVantage, which will pave my way to the White House.*

23 | A New Discovery

The next morning, in Lorah's fifth-floor quarters three blocks from the Master Control Center, she reached for her Knowledge Keeper datapad hidden in a thigh pocket of a pair of coveralls hanging in her closet of what everyone had agreed was a Bvindu bedroom. She sat behind a table holding a computer and a vidcomm and connected the datapad to the computer, then connected to Earth.

After logging into the Order's system, she caught up on recent events, focusing on an analysis of Mr. O'Donnell's testimony before the Senate Offworld Commerce Committee the previous day. No wonder the coverage had been scant—no news had been made.

From an inside-politics perspective, Senator Severino's party had performed an unexpected ploy that even the most hardened Washington pundits had never seen, yet they remained mute. *The fix was in.*

Why not schedule Chuck's follow-on testimony for today? The Senate was in session, after all. Instead, Senator Severino pushed it the whole way out until Tuesday of the following week.

Five days from now, Senator Severino will use the PAA employee's death as the rationale to nationalize Bvindu Dome. She doesn't want the weekend to distract the public from the news.

Staying on Mars was becoming more real by the second. She'd give up a lot, though. Mainly her sister, Ella. The time they'd spent together in Colorado had been the best. Ella's pull with the Nutrition and Fitness Service had cut through the bureaucracy when her NutriAccount grocery allocation hadn't reset at the start of the month. Until speaking with Mr. Fordham, she'd expected to see Ella in a few years, but that might never happen.

After disconnecting and hiding the datapad under clean socks, she departed her quarters carrying a backpack holding two FieldMeals for lunch. She stepped onto the lift at the end of the hall, which was reminiscent of a cargo elevator. The door closed by sliding upward from the floor. She moved to the lift's rear, and it descended.

A group of circle and line symbols at waist level near the entrance disappeared every couple of seconds. When only two groups remained, she stepped forward. The second to last group disappeared, and the lift stopped. The door slid down, and she exited into the building's atrium. She retrieved Ashley's assignment on the computer against the wall, which looked out of place among the wavy sculptures that were presumably Bvindu decorations.

Outside, she mounted a Bvindu cargo mover and guided it through the dome's boulevards, reaching a dark zone. An instant later, the mover's lights came on automatically as she eased off the throttle.

Her palms became sweaty, manually controlling the cargo mover through the black void. Though she'd done so countless times, the discomfort hadn't eased with only seeing directly in front of her. *Frank and Gretchen really should illuminate the entire dome.*

Several seconds later, she returned to a lighted area and maneuvered to the building Ashley was processing. She headed inside to find it was much like her own apartment building. She pulled her datapad from her coveralls thigh pocket and messaged Ashley.

in the atrium

A few seconds later, Ashley replied.

go to the second floor
first apartment on your right

Lorah found Ashley on her hands and knees in the living area, examining an obsidian cube large enough to hold a basketball. "What is that?"

"Something interesting at last. The Bvindu furniture faces it like a holovid projector."

Lorah knelt and inspected the cube closer. It didn't simply rest on the floor—it fit into a recessed receptacle. For a moment, she pictured the scene without the cube.

"The receptacle. I've seen it before. Not in another apartment. Somewhere else..."

"I've processed so many apartments I've lost track." Ashley leaned in, inspecting the base closer. "My initial scans indicate the cube is a dense storage device around a processor array."

"If it were built on Earth, what could it be?"

"A dedicated processing module?" Ashley brushed her hair back onto her shoulder as she bit her lower lip. "Perhaps holding data on the exabyte level."

Factoring in how advanced the Bvindu were, that estimation was likely on the low side, probably by a lot. Could it hold data on the yottabyte level? Regardless, the cube had incredible storage for its size. There was a market for high-capacity, low-footprint storage. *Would Frank license it for manufacture?*

Even if he were predisposed, it'd never happen—the situation was about to come to a head.

What had the cube held, and where had it been? The other one hadn't been on the floor. It was on a table... Elevated, not a table. Lorah touched Ashley's hand. "I just remembered where the other receptacle is."

24 | THE TRUTH SHOWS THE WAY

Frank sat beside Gretchen in the Master Control Center of Bvindu Dome, not far from where the trespasser had been discovered. Directly before him lay the Bvindu control panel. Its top half held a holo display. A touch interface panel—typically displaying a menu on the left, leaving the rest of the panel for the selected topic's haptic controls—comprised the bottom half. Every time he'd used it, the experience had been awkward, as if writing with his left hand. Gretchen, though, worked it like an expert.

Beyond lay row upon row of waist-high cabinets. A blue glow emanated from their long sides, a physical manifestation of the control systems' operations, many of which were automated.

Next to the Bvindu control panel, a table held a stand-alone computer and a vidcomm. Gretchen connected to Chuck's office, where June and Alan had gathered with him.

Everyone exchanged pleasantries before Chuck asked, "Have you seen James' report about our trespasser?"

Gretchen shook her head.

Frank said, "We've been settling in. I verified two facts about the trespasser, though. The Bvindu Asteroid Defense System monitors on Phobos and Deimos captured the PAA ore transport convoy approaching and leaving Mars space—sending alerts here. Neither detected the explorer pod, probably because it departed a transport within the moons' orbits. Second, the internal sensors captured the trespasser's entry twenty-two days ago, during the height of the dust storm. For what it's worth, he looked directly at the sign before crossing the caution line."

"I think I speak for everyone when I say I would've preferred that he heeded the warning. He couldn't access anything worthwhile, correct?" Chuck asked.

"That's right," Gretchen affirmed. "He could've looked at most of what the archaeologists already explored, but he wasn't getting in here or the inner workings of the Manufacturing Section."

Frank shook his head. "If it weren't for us returning to Mars City to ride out the sandstorms and Mars being well-positioned for a gravity assist maneuver, he never would've made it to the caution line."

"In that regard, luck wasn't on our side." Chuck took a sip of water. "Anyway, back to my point—I saw two versions of James' report, a streamlined segment that lasted one minute and a five-minute extended piece. He played it straight. No innuendos. No half-truths. In the extended report, he included on-screen quotes from both of you. Good job, by the way."

Alan asked, "Does that mean he's not a plant?"

"He needs to be watered daily," Gretchen said with a healthy dose of cynicism.

"Senator Severino will use the PAA trespasser in the next hearing," Chuck said, "to justify taking control of Bvindu Dome. She couldn't have asked for a better reason. She has a couple of uninterrupted hours to lay out the groundwork."

"She won't need all that time. Her attack will be straightforward." A touch of sadness found Gretchen's features.

"Mixed with a lie or two perpetuated by the media," Alan said as he thrust his chin forward, "people won't think twice about unfairness or government overreach. By the time the courts hear our first argument, we'll have lost everything."

June crossed her arms. "So, we're breaking away on Tuesday."

"All signs point to Washington asserting control over everything Bvindu." Chuck laid his hands against the table. "This is our last chance for second thoughts. Do we declare our independence when they claim ownership?"

In unison, everyone said, "Yes."

"We have to enact our plan." Chuck straightened his shoulders. "We need Red on-site. Erin is pre-flighting her shuttle to ferry the trespasser's body to the OTP for the transport's turnaround trip to Earth as soon as the tractor arrives. I'll have her pick him up afterward."

A few hours earlier, the PAA had sent a terse message to the State Department, which they passed on to MarsVantage. The trespasser was named Xi Zhai, who they alleged was a defector. Since a defector would've landed outside Mars City, he must've been a spy. Regardless, they wanted his remains.

Frank raised his hand. "With James here, Red can't join us. He looks like Space Force, even in the dark."

"I've seen James wandering about, taking in the sights. Red's presence would provide a vital clue about our capabilities and intentions." Gretchen tapped her foot against the chair leg. "You know he'd report it."

Frank added, "Chuck, you should also know that James made inroads with Ashley. Everything she knows, we have to assume he'll know... and shortly afterward, Washington will know."

"What about Lorah?"

Gretchen replied, "She hasn't given him the time of day."

"Huh, I would've expected the opposite." Chuck glanced downward, probably at his datapad. "We'll wait on Red. Do what you can to justify evicting James. Make it plausible—we don't want to advertise that something's in the offing."

"We'll see what we can do," Gretchen said. "So far, he's been a model guest."

"The logistics to transfer personnel and supplies to Bvindu Dome are ready," June said, bringing the conversation back to topic. "We'll use all of our tractors, trailers, and shuttles for two weeks. It'll be expensive but doable. More time would be better."

"Start sending food deliveries and other supplies by tractor," Chuck ordered. "If anyone asks questions, say I'm planning a large exploration mission, so we're resupplying early."

"The employee access privilege changes are ready for those we're sending back to Earth," Alan announced. "As soon as you declare independence, I'll implement them and stand ready to make changes for those who choose to leave."

Chuck leaned forward, his expression somber. "I'll update Erin when she returns. I'll also light a fire under her—we need to get the scout ship in the air."

25 | Theories Without All of the Facts

While still in the Master Control Center, Gretchen finished reading a message from Ashley, who'd found a dangerous clue. Along with Lorah, they'd jumped to an understandable, yet incorrect, conclusion.

Gretchen retrieved the medical center's survey file on her datapad. It noted the transparent cylinder, but held nothing—not even speculation—regarding its purpose. Now, Ashley and Lorah believed it was part of creating new AIs.

According to the Bvindu database, the cylinder's ceiling contained twenty-one sensors. The elderly or severely injured Bvindu underwent a procedure where each lead was placed on a specific location of their heads. Their essence was transferred into a Consciousness Cube, which was then given to the family to interact with until a cloned body could be grown at a highly accelerated rate. When the new body matured, the family returned with the cube, and the consciousness was transferred. Every Bvindu had undergone the process multiple times.

When the archaeology team explored this building about a year ago, she'd translated its purpose from the Bvindu database as Being Repair facility. The archaeological team called it a medical center for convenience and not to confuse it with equipment repair complexes. Later translations based on more Bvindu language samples had translated the building as a hospital. Withholding that information looked like a genius move that helped Ashley assume the Bvindu were AIs in mechanical bodies.

The caretaker having resided in the Master Control Center's computer, and upon necessity, inhabiting a mobile unit, was an outlier, not the norm as Ashley had assumed. She had good reason, considering Gretchen had only shared this information with Committee members.

The details of the Bvindu consciousness transfer process resided in the Master Control Center's information systems. Access was restricted to only those providing a Bvindu voice command to open the building's door. As an extra precaution, Frank implemented the security protocol that'd protected her workshop two years earlier. That protocol had never been tripped, and security monitors recorded no failed access attempts.

Soon, Washington would declare everything Bvindu theirs and have Space Force secure it. Declaring something was easy, but no matter what, the Bvindu technology would never leave her control.

I'll destroy it first.

Gretchen took a cargo mover to the medical center and found Ashley and Lorah. Like them, she pointed her hand light toward the floor. The reflection created enough illumination to see many of the lab's details and everyone's faces comfortably.

When more people occupied the dome and the Manufacturing Section was running at capacity, they'd restart the other power generators, which would solve the lighting situation. Until such time, Frank was concerned that producing more Marsium121 power than utilized could somehow damage the three power-generating caverns.

Ashley showed Gretchen a recording of a cube in residential quarters and explained how she and Lorah came to be in the medical center. "It appears this is how the Bvindu created offspring. An individual AI in a mechanical body enters the tube and attaches the sensors. Their cognitive constructs, not memories or experiences, are copied into the cube, which the Bvindu then takes home, interacts with, and instructs. When the new entity is sufficiently trained—you could call it conscious or alive—the Bvindu returns the cube and implants it into a new mechanical body."

They had concocted a surprisingly self-consistent theory, better than any lie Gretchen had considered to disguise the immortality process. She inspected the tube again. "That tube is too small for the body I saw the caretaker inhabit."

Lorah suggested, "Perhaps his unit was for harsher environments. You said the caretaker had to repair the dome after the Baulnsville explorers breached it. The Bvindu probably had more streamlined suits for everyday use."

"This explains how the caretaker could be thousands of years old," Ashley reasoned. "The Bvindu are replicating artificial intelligences."

"It does explain that." For the sake of appearance, Gretchen pulled out her datapad and made a note regarding AI references in the Bvindu database. "Ashley, have the archaeologists look for an everyday activity suit. In fact, return to the living quarters containing the cube and see if one's there. There's one problem with the theory, though—the cube is inactive in the living quarters."

"I'd expect it here after a transfer occurred." Lorah shifted her weight Gretchen's way. "The Bvindu wouldn't have abandoned a partially trained AI, would they?"

"Nothing suggests that type of behavior." Gretchen made another note about abandoned AI consciousnesses. "For all we know, the cube was stored in the apartment to get it out of the way."

"That's a great point." Ashley looked toward the glass cylinder. "We may be imparting meaning on an insignificant action."

Ashley and Lorah never questioned the assumptions at the heart of their theory, making it easy to hide the truth. "We note the existence and our theory as just that. We'll look for more data to confirm or disprove it."

"Agreed." Ashley's shoulders relaxed as she turned toward Lorah. "We're going to have lunch. You want to join us?"

"No, thanks," Gretchen replied. "I think I'll poke around a bit. It's been a while since I've been in the field."

After they departed, Gretchen closely inspected the room, finding nothing pointing toward the practical immortality process. Her breath eased out. *The secret's safe.*

26 | Imagination Driver

After lunch, Lorah returned to her Bvindu quarters, where she vidcommed Miles Fordham. His assistant put her through immediately.

Mr. Fordham was taking his seat as the video feed turned on. "What happened?"

His attention never wavered as she described the find. When she finished, his eyes sparkled like he'd heard an amusing anecdote. "It's curious that Ashley assumed AIs..."

Two centuries earlier, the promise of AI had begun to be more than a dream of science-fiction lovers. These days, they'd advanced to handling public transportation reliably, but goal-setting and desire—the essence of consciousness—eluded them. The promise of solving society's ills lay just beyond their reach.

He resumed, "Other possibilities come to mind."

Lorah made a note on her datapad. "Like what?"

"Consider why an artificially created being would need to enter a tube and affix multiple sensors when an interface port would be more efficient."

"Now that you point that out, there had to be two dozen connectors. I didn't inspect them in detail, but they appeared to affix to a surface, not plug in." She looked squarely at the vidcomm. "What do *you* think we found?"

"It could be as simple as a biometric scanning device to provide profiles for the automated security system to consider safe. I can't imagine Bvindu wearing wristbands. But that's unimportant in the end."

What a curious connection of disparate facts. It was so off the wall that it could very well be true.

Mr. Fordham leaned back into the chair. "I'm curious if Gretchen will explore Ashley's theory... or other possibilities. And if she does, will she report any results?"

"It sounds like you don't think she will."

"Setting aside my doubts for a moment, advanced AIs could truly optimize water distribution, energy production, and farmland utilization. Perhaps they could fine-tune weather prediction to where modification is practical."

Mr. Fordham's analysis predicted AIs as a license to print money. And he'd have a piece of it all. He'd permanently pass Konklin on the wealthiest people list.

"If our assumptions turn out to be true..." Lorah said evenly, Mr. Fordham's doubts erasing her enthusiasm.

"And MarsVantage wants to monetize them." Mr. Fordham clenched his jaw. "I doubt either is the case. But, oh, to dream..."

They concluded the conversation with routine matters. Afterward, Lorah closed her datapad and took a deep breath. Mr. Fordham had been more indifferent than ever over a lucrative opportunity. He clearly had non-monetary interests. *What is going on?*

She considered updating the Order but decided against it. Mr. Fordham had been correct—the discovery only looked like AI on the surface. Peeking beneath cast doubt, so she'd wait.

Upon exiting her quarters, she strolled a couple of blocks toward the Planning Huddle Area. The archaeologists had erected several tables and a computer network in the alley between the Master Control Center and the neighboring building. Every morning, they mapped out their day's activities, and in the evening, they met to recount accomplishments. In between, it held a welcome change of scenery.

Upon arriving, she found James working on a portable computer. He looked up and waved her over.

She sat on his left. "What're you doing?"

He adjusted his screen to provide her with a better view. "I'm working on a what-we-know-now package about the Bvindu. Just a background piece."

"Isn't that old news?"

"With new visuals." His eyes remained fixed on the screen. "Producers drool over interesting video, and the public eats it up."

"But the facts are the same."

"Great images can make a mediocre story good. I just recorded Erin's landing and the platform descending from the dome top to the ground. It's some of my best camera work."

He knew the job, which made sense—no one would send a newbie alone into the field—but he looked down on his audience.

Lorah crossed her legs and placed her hands in her lap. "Erin was here?"

"She delivered a load of supplies from the OTP." He continued working on the computer. "We got to talk for a couple of minutes while they were off-loaded. She'll return in a bit after another run."

"Ah. I expect she'll work on the new spaceship."

James ignored the computer and looked Lorah in the eye. "It looks ready to go to me."

"I thought it was ready months ago, but Erin insists on understanding its innermost workings and performing simulator training before she'll even think about flying the real thing."

He leaned back and crossed his arms. "Huh. Pilots are particular about their ships, but she's procrastinating."

Lorah canted her head back and forth while considering the idea. "I figure she doesn't want to crash immediately after take-off."

"I plan to interview her about it..."

"I'll be interested in what she says. Everything I've heard so far has been generalities. It's hard to judge if it's ready to bring to Mr. Fordham's attention."

James's eyes filled with compassion. "Your assignment must be tough. From what I can tell, the Marsees aren't leaping to monetize Bvindu tech. For a group of people who complain about living a spartan existence, they aren't capitalizing on their best opportunities."

Aside from using the tasteless term, his conversational gambit was as smooth as ice. Whether she gossiped about the Marsians or backed up his statement with examples of overlooked opportunities, he'd gather valuable information. *I'll give him a different conversational path.*

"Beats me. I do know they aren't stupid. They *must* have a vision of their future, where their current actions make perfect sense."

He leaned forward. The look on his face suggested he was pondering a completely new idea. "*That's* insightful. I'll consider it more."

"If you learn anything, I'd love it if you fill me in." Fair was fair. James was attempting to pry information from her—she could do the same.

"No problem." He put on an innocent expression. "Perhaps you can give me a new perspective on a story I'm tracking down in my spare time. Have you heard about the people disappearing? It's been going on for a year and a half."

The Knowledge Keepers knew of the issue but surprisingly had no details, not that she'd tell James anything. "I saw news reports recently. Weird, right?"

"Yeah. My gut's screaming there's something huge happening right under our noses, and everyone's missing it. It's a little silly, but I half-expected them to be in Mars City or here."

"Everyone would have noticed that. Anyway, haven't you been beaten to the punch?"

"The people-missing story's been broken, sure. Any second-rate back-bencher can luck into that. A good reporter digs to discover the story within the story... Where are the people, and why are they there? *That* would take my career to another level."

He looks down on his colleagues, too. What a guy.

After several seconds of acting as if Lorah were considering the situation, she mused, "Good fake identities cost money, and how are they getting jobs? That'd involve access to the HR Acquisition Network to forge education, job experience, and references."

"That can't be done?"

Lorah consciously shook her head. "Here and there, a handful of people. Maybe. The reports I saw pointed to hundreds missing—entire families in some instances. That sounds like an underlying organization or even a conspiracy."

His eyes enlivened as his gaze locked onto her. "Yes, it does. As I said, that story would take my career to another level—I wouldn't have to go to some godforsaken third-world hellhole to report on two unsavory sides slaughtering each other."

She moved closer, and James mirrored her move. She lowered her voice. "My sister, Ella, works for the Housing Ministry. Not long ago, she mentioned that three low- to mid-level employees abruptly stopped coming into her office in Grand Junction, Colorado. Until then, they largely went unnoticed but were apparently vital in keeping everything running smoothly."

James planted his back into the chair. "That's not the first time I've heard of that."

"One was Ella's close friend, so she stopped by her apartment, which she had visited many times. Even watering the plants when her friend vacationed."

"What did Ella find?"

"Everything looked normal at first glance, but..."

He leaned closer, hope etched across his face. "But what?"

"A suitcase and some clothes were missing."

James blinked rapidly. "She took a trip?"

"Without using any of her vacation time. She'd accumulated nearly twenty days."

"That's odd. No one passes up free money."

Lorah inclined her head for a beat. "Also, she didn't have any canned food in the kitchen."

"If you're traveling, there's no sense using your food allowance on groceries."

"Spoken by someone who travels more than stays home. Most people use any extra food allowances on canned goods so they can splurge in the future and still not go hungry. Her friend's cupboards were empty. She either took it with her, or she knew she wouldn't need extra food in the future."

James pulled out his datapad and made some notes. "No one picked up on that."

Lorah touched James' hand. "Ella's friend left behind her passport, ID, and NutriAccount cards."

"There it is." He inhaled deeply, straightening against the chairback. "She couldn't go anywhere unless she assumed a new identity. The real questions are, why'd these people disappear, what're they doing, and where are they doing it?"

27 | THREAT TO EARTH

Frank stopped by the Planning Huddle Area and picked up two FieldMeals for a late supper. According to Gretchen, the archaeologists, who were old hats at providing their own infrastructure, had created this depot as well as one like it in their current work area. They also had strategically placed common shower facilities near the buildings serving as quarters and set up a cafeteria nearby. In a week, it'd be fully operational with staff. Freshly prepared food would be a welcome change.

After he placed the containers in the cargo mover's bed, he drove a few blocks to his quarters. He skipped the lift and took the stairs. Every step required diligence since their height was slightly greater than standard. At the top, he fumbled one-handed for his datapad and played the Open tones. The door descended in response.

In the kitchen, he set the FieldMeals on the table, kissed Gretchen on the cheek, and sat across from her. He and the engineers had yet to determine how the Bvindu used the area. By its location, it was where a kitchen should be, so they'd placed a refrigerator, a food prep unit, and a table and chairs in it.

Gretchen pulled the heating tabs on both FieldMeals. "You wouldn't believe what Ashley and Lorah found today."

He had skipped the day's wrap-up in favor of a quick logistics meeting with Erin. *Figures something good was found.*

She related the story and finished with, "And they landed on AIs without any prodding. We couldn't have gotten a bigger break."

"We dodged a bullet, for sure. What do you make of the Consciousness Cube in the living quarters?"

"The caretaker's operations logs indicate he left a dozen throughout the city so he could transfer quickly."

"Do you know why?"

She glanced at the FieldMeals. "As a last resort in case the Master Control Center was severely compromised. He'd transfer to one of the cubes in the least damaged area and await the Bvindu's return."

The heating indicator turned green, and Frank opened the FieldMeals. Steam carried the tantalizing aroma of roasted vegetables and meatloaf. Of course, *meat* was a euphemism for an engineered substance that looked, smelled, and tasted like beef, so he'd been told—he'd never had the real thing.

Frank took a couple of bites. A hot meal after a day of cereal and cold-cut FieldMeals was welcome. "Out of earshot of James, Erin confided that she's satisfied with the Bvindu Scout Ship. The question is, when do we apply the Spectrum Overlay Erasure coating?"

"Not while James is around." Gretchen swallowed a bite of her meatloaf. "We need to get him out of Bvindu Dome, preferably off Mars."

Frank was about to ask if she had any ideas when their vidcomm chimed. He rose and peeked into the living area to see the ID. He sat before it. "Hon, you should sit in on this."

She pulled over her kitchen chair and settled in next to him as he completed the connection. "Mother, you're the last person I expected to hear from."

"I hoped never to make this call."

"You're not in the habit of calling at all," Frank pointedly said. "We're very busy. What do you want?"

Mother inhaled. "The senator's legislative staff is putting the final touches on a bill that will pass Congress with little debate and less opposition. It'll nationalize all alien technology. Space Force will secure Bvindu Dome until an NSM task force and Peter Konklin Interplanetary can take charge for the good of the people."

"Regardless of the outcome of the next hearing?"

"You and Mr. O'Donnell made MarsVantage's position clear. The hearings have no bearing on the bill."

Nothing MarsVantage did or said would change anything. *The fix was in.* "What moral authority underlies the government stealing our property?"

"Alien technology is dangerous, either inherently or through ignorance. In the hands of mere business people—not scientific experts—it's an existential threat to public safety."

As Gretchen leaned forward, Frank gently laid his hand on her wrist. "Mother, that's the excuse of every petty tyrant throughout history. Underlying it is that you're afraid we'll accumulate power at the expense of the Washington elite."

"Son, nationalization will occur unless you invite a partnership with the National Science Ministry. These are your choices. You never had another."

"Both are unacceptable. We will not submit. We have no interest in Earth affairs, but we're eager to keep what we worked hard for."

"You're as stubborn as your father."

What Mother called stubbornness, Frank called determination, a quality that had delivered an alien city. A wave of satisfaction washed over him. "Thank you, Mother."

"That wasn't a compliment." She narrowed her eyes. "Wise up. The government holds all the cards, from military force to the very food you eat. What will you do when your imports don't arrive? View the situation with clear eyes. You have no choice."

"You're playing silly games on a corner of a small stage. Our future lies in the larger universe. Goodbye, Mother." Frank disconnected the vidcomm.

Gretchen shook her head. "Did you notice how we're only *business people*, but they're ready to hand Bvindu Dome to Peter Konklin?"

"He's not a mere business person, is he?"

Confusion crossed her face. "Of course he is."

"Ah, he's a *connected* business person. He knows the right people and thinks the right way." Frank tapped his nose twice. "The critical difference is that he'll go in whatever direction the government points."

28 | THE INTERVIEW

Erin exited the shower, stepping into the cramped changing area in the hygiene pod. Little was better than the simple joy of warm water flowing over every inch of her body and clean hair from flowery shampoo. After performing her morning ablutions, she stowed the toiletry kit in her assigned locker and took a Bvindu people mover toward the Manufacturing Section.

Quickly, she entered the dark zone and drove on with the same serenity as when piloting, unbothered by seeing only a portion of the street in the cargo mover's light. A time later, she entered the Manufacturing Section's lighted zone and drove to its far side, where she parked next to a Bvindu control panel. After dismounting, she faced the Bvindu Scout Ship. Its white hull with silver accents glistened in the transition area between the Manufacturing Section and the landing pad.

The bow was conventional, holding an extended cockpit for three—a pilot, navigator, and sensor analyst. On the port side amidships, a hatch was set into the hull, allowing the sensor analyst to deploy satellites from the cargo area three times larger than her shuttle's.

The stern contained a tail assembly to stabilize atmospheric travel but lacked the engine nozzles of human-designed spaceships. The Heim Theory generator for faster-than-light travel, the Gravitational Force Adapters for sub-lightspeed travel, and a Marsium121 power generator nestled together within.

She walked to the hatch and pulled her datapad from her thigh pocket. After playing the Open tones, the hatch slid into the ship's underside. It lacked a ramp, so she pulled herself aboard. Once past the sensor analyst station, she settled into the pilot's position on the port side.

The original controls were designed for a four-handed pilot. At Frank's prompting, the caretaker had altered the design, so some controls were actuated via feet like human spacecraft.

Frank and Gretchen had entrusted her with the scout ship's specs and operating instructions, details of which were on par with her shuttle's blueprints, operations guidebook, and repair manual. She'd received more Bvindu data than anyone else, including the archaeologists, and that'd been before Frank had talked her into joining the Committee.

On several occasions, he and Gretchen had implied that they'd participated in detailed discussions with the caretaker while MarsVantage maintenance teams repaired the Manufacturing Section. Those discussions better have included city operations and defenses in detail. The emergency Committee meeting they'd convened the previous night about Frank's mother's vidcomm had confirmed their situation was circling the drain.

Trouble is coming.

She activated the pilot's console with the help of her datapad translating the gauges, readouts, and control symbols to English. Ship power transitioned from standby to flight-prep mode, with flight-standard available at five seconds' notice.

After manually testing the hatch separating the pilot and co-pilot stations from the sensor analyst's position, she placed the flight and propulsion systems into a thorough diagnostic. Then, she wirelessly connected her datapad to capture the results for analysis and set it in a convenient cubbyhole the Bvindu designated to hold various tools.

Frank's idea to retrofit her shuttle fleet with Marsium121 power generators was pointless when the Manufacturing Section could create more Bvindu ships with a larger cargo bay. *Assuming this one doesn't crash and burn on its maiden flight.*

"Erin, you in there?"

She rose and walked a couple of steps to peer into the cargo bay. James' head appeared in the hatch. "Over here. Come on up."

He pulled himself up and brushed off his coveralls. "So this is a Bvindu ship. Do you mind if I record?"

James wasn't about to see anything Washington's inspectors hadn't already. "Go ahead. My datapad is not handy, so my statements will need to be on background."

"Of course. We can shoot some footage and then have a proper interview to discuss it later." From his coveralls leg pockets, he produced a holocam and datapad. Upon activating the holocam with a few presses on his datapad, it positioned itself above his shoulder and a bit behind.

"Let me show you around." She directed him to the pilot's seat. "Sit but don't touch anything. I have a diagnostic running."

He wiggled into the seat. "These controls are similar to Earth ships."

"The Bvindu were like us, and spaceflight is the same, so the solutions are the same. Check this out, though." She reached over his shoulder and toggled a control.

"Wow!" James looked all around—above, below, and side to side. The cockpit's hull had become transparent, allowing a view of their cargo movers, lighting panel, and landing pad. "It reminds me of a helicopter, but why have a single band of windows?"

"Bvindu data indicates windows, especially large ones, are less structurally sound than the hull. They created a way to have the best of both worlds—a spaceworthy ship and excellent visibility."

He faced her. "Why have windows at all?"

"I never saw the rationale. My guess it's in the event the tech fails."

"Prudent. What's this station?" He pointed to his right.

Erin stood behind the navigator's station. "Co-pilot. That's how the Bvindu think of it. I look at it more of a navigator's position because it lacks maneuvering controls."

"It takes two to fly the ship?"

"Strictly speaking, no. From what I can tell, it's just more convenient. I'll know more when I get airborne."

"When will you do that? I'll make a story out of it." Hope washed across his face.

Having a reporter for the first flight of a new spacecraft wasn't high on her priority list. A slight but real chance of crashing the damn thing existed. The Committee wouldn't want Washington to know about that, so those tests would wait until he left. "That's tough to tell. The Bvindu proscribe a strict testing regimen."

"I can imagine. I reported on an aircraft harness upgrade a few years back. The manufacturer conducted tests under typical operating conditions. Then, they tested harnesses after exposure to negative one hundred degrees and positive one hundred and fifty degrees. To get the government's certification, they wasted over a hundred harnesses. Then, to maintain it, they chose ten at random every month and performed the same tests." James' eyebrows furrowed. "There aren't any harnesses with these seats."

"And the ship doesn't have standard anti-collision beacons or many other features required for flight certification."

"You're going to fly it anyway?"

She placed her hand on the navigator's seat back. "Technically, this ship is considered an experimental craft. I think of it as a proof of concept. If I avoid drilling a hole in Mars, *and* it performs as advertised, we'll bring it up to the regs. My list of needed upgrades is seventy-two items long and counting."

"And you're going to fly it anyway. I'm impressed." Everything about him exuded sincerity, which brought to mind Giraudoux's quote, "The secret of success is sincerity. Once you can fake that, you've got it made."

"That's the job. The news holovids make it sound like we're up here with a treasure trove of fantastic toys, capriciously denying Earth everything. There's so much that goes into every technological advance that, looking in from the outside, makes progress seem nonexistent. In reality, we learn something every single day."

"Perhaps if you hired more specialists to help?"

"The archaeology team would easily like to double in size, but no one else from Earth cares to rise to the challenge. I want to hire two more pilots. No interest on Earth. I'm training eager Marsian students, though."

"Good for you." He awkwardly extracted himself from the seat and gestured with his chin toward the hatch. "I have a question about the hull."

She headed toward it with him following, his holocam trailing along. There, he jumped down and headed aft. She did the same.

He played the curious newbie so well that it was impossible to tell what direction his questioning would take. "There are no engines. What propels the ship?"

James was observant and intelligent. And affable and cute. She understood why Gretchen had married him. If what he presented were his true self, she'd ask him out. But his crafted persona had one purpose—to get the story, not reveal the truth or enlighten the public, but push the desired narrative of the Washington elites. *Damn, I'm starting to think like Frank...*

He'd interpret playing dumb for the lie it was, and she'd lose all the credibility she'd accrued. The trick was to answer truthfully but not in a particularly illuminating way, which was as difficult as threading a needle while wearing mittens.

"The power generator is similar to the dome's," Erin revealed.

"You mean Marsium121."

"Yep."

He focused all his attention on her. "Where did you mine it?"

She attempted to feign embarrassment, though she couldn't get her cheeks to heat up on command. "I guess that involves Bvindu data I'm not entitled to."

"I see. Have you figured out how it produces energy? Or how the ship's propulsion works?"

His question confirmed Earth still hadn't determined how Marsium121 acted as an energy source. The Committee would love that news. She answered, "Beats me about the power. The propulsion system leverages a new aspect of physics."

"That sounds exciting. How's it work?"

"I'm not a physicist, but it involves the gravitational force and its interaction with the other fundamental forces. A while back, Frank laid it out at a high level. The technique looked at the forces from a new perspective. I can't explain it."

He gave what Gretchen had called his "Oh, gosh" look. "That's okay. It'd go over my head. I'll get Frank to step through it for my viewers later."

"The result is no conventional thrusters or exhaust. It's exciting, but it's *so* different."

"Seriously, this is where Earth's expertise can help." He glanced at the ship and spread his arms wide. "You have so much opportunity to tap, but very few with the ability. MarsVantage has had to concentrate on practical aspects of living, leaving precious little time for theoretical topics."

"But will Earth help us or help itself?"

"Does it have to be one or the other?"

"In my mind, no, but Washington has repeatedly steamrolled us. Each time, they've greatly benefited, but not us. MarsVantage has the expertise, and we have every Bvindu expert in the solar system." She shoved her hands in her pockets, satisfied the truth was in the spotlight.

James grabbed for the holocam with one hand and deactivated it with the thumb of his other hand via his datapad. "I shouldn't say anything, but I keep my ear to the ground. Regardless of your excellent points, the government is eager to learn what you know as well as what you have."

29 | REVELATIONS AMONG FRIENDS

W*hat a way to start the day*, Frank thought as he sat before the living room's holovid, watching a newscast while finishing a fried egg and cheese muffin FieldMeal. James had showed Erin on the holovid, but she hadn't forwarded her version of the interview. Unless she'd forgotten—and those odds were slim—there wasn't one.

James had shattered their interview agreement. *On the plus side, now I have the excuse we need to ship him home.*

Frank took a sip of coffee and replayed the holovid. The section where James narrated over a slow pan of the Bvindu Scout Ship came, "As you can see, there's no facility for engine exhaust in the ship's design. I asked MarsVantage's top pilot and flight operations manager, Erin Knox, about it."

This was where James showed his true colors.

Standing beside the scout ship, Erin said, "The propulsion system leverages a new aspect of physics."

James narrated, "When asked for details, she disclosed that it involves the gravitational force and its interaction with the other fundamental forces."

James appeared on camera before the backdrop of Bvindu Dome buildings. "Pilots have a working knowledge of their ship's systems and a fundamental understanding of the principles it utilizes, which leaves unanswered questions. How does the interaction among the fundamental forces of nature work, how do they create propulsion, and when will MarsVantage share this groundbreaking discovery and technology with Earth experts for examination and testing?"

Most assuredly, James must've toiled to twist his report around Erin's quotes, taken out of context.

Frank took another sip of coffee and reclined against the chair back. The James problem had neatly resolved itself with minimal damage. He'd trade this story to send James packing any day.

The quarters' door descended, and Gretchen entered. "You won't believe what that bastard did."

Erin followed, looking like she'd bitten into a lemon. The door rose behind her.

Frank swiveled his chair to face them. "James published a story about the scout ship that included a couple of juicy quotes. How close am I?"

Meanwhile, Gretchen grabbed a chair from the kitchen and placed it in the living area. She sat while Erin took a spot on the couch.

"I'm sorry, Frank. I explicitly said that our conversation was on background, and he confirmed. I guess you don't owe me dinner after all."

Gretchen gulped down a breath. "Dinner?"

Frank waved his hand like he was brushing a crumb from a table. "I bet a dinner with fresh Shadow City vegetables if James played it straight. Nothing would've made me happier than paying off, but you were destined to lose."

"How can you two smile?" Erin asked. "Earth knows the Bvindu unified the forces, and that's the foundation of how the sub-light and FTL engines work."

Frank brought his palms to chest level. "Washington already believes we're withholding information—James only confirmed it."

"I thought I was clever by sharing vague insights, but that report has zero context. I feel like I disclosed a state secret."

Gretchen leaned forward. "I'm convinced that he knew the shape of the story before saying a word to you. He used snippets of your statements to construct a piece to advance the elites' agenda. The underlying issue is that he's not a journalist—he's a propagandist. None of us can change that."

"Scientists have been trying to unify the universal forces for centuries," Frank declared. "They aren't solving that conundrum anytime soon. Not without the underlying Bvindu data, which we haven't really looked at yet."

"Erin, can you fly him to the transport in thirty minutes?" Gretchen asked.

Erin glanced at her datapad. "It pulled out an hour ago."

Gretchen smacked her knees. "Then we send him to Mars City."

"Support personnel are tractoring in later today with more supplies. James can ride back tomorrow on the return trip." Frank stood.

"Good enough." After standing, Gretchen tugged her coveralls sleeves and straightened like a ramrod. "*I* get to tell him."

"Perhaps I should do it." Frank didn't need Gretchen's hostility to take form.

"He twisted my words into a pretzel," Erin pointed out as she stood. "I'm more than happy to deliver the message."

"He's here because of me," Gretchen insisted. "*I'll* correct the situation."

30 | No More Games

On the street, Gretchen pulled her datapad from her coveralls' thigh pocket. She extended the screen, and her finger hovered over the button to call James.

She inhaled and exhaled three times, deep and purposeful. The desire to rip his arms from his body and beat him about the head and shoulders remained. She repeated the breathing exercise, allowing the urge to pass.

She didn't need to be a mind reader to know Frank and Erin thought she'd assault James like she had done to Arnold when he tried to steal her work. They had a point, though she'd never admit it. Seeing James leave with his tail between his legs would be satisfying enough.

What has gotten into him? His reporting was always fair...

Or had it been? How much had she known besides broadcasts, his behind-the-scenes tales, and those of his cohorts? Had they relayed the truth or perpetuated the elites' narrative?

Events, big and small, dating back to her teen years, sprang into question. How much had the media misled or outright lied? She'd never know.

A few seconds after she pressed the button, James answered. "Yes?"

"Where are you?"

"The Planning Huddle Area."

"Stay there. I'll join you shortly." She disconnected, pocketed the datapad, and marched the entire way to burn off her anger.

James was alone and stood as she entered.

She stopped before him. "I saw your latest report."

"I'd like a follow-up story with you and Frank."

"There will be no more stories." She crossed her arms. "Oh, don't give that surprised look. You broke our agreement.

MarsVantage wasn't recording the interview, and you quoted Erin anyway."

He matched her stance by also crossing his arms. "She was unprepared, and I was under time constraints."

"Oh, so you heard unvoiced exceptions to our conditions? It's Erin's fault, and you're the victim?"

"I never cared for your sarcasm."

She stepped closer and jammed her hands in her pockets... for his protection. "Erin told me all about your conversation. Your editing implied we know far more than we're letting on."

"MarsVantage is utilizing a physics breakthrough. Was Erin wrong?"

"No."

"Is it true that pilots fly only technology they're comfortable and familiar with?"

"Expertly done. Bravo on providing a false impression that Erin's comfort level is high. And you squeezed in a bonus by implying we're comfortable with the physics breakthrough."

James smirked, his first genuine display of emotion since he'd arrived on Mars. "Your complaints are more telling than anything Erin said. Makes me suspect you know more than you're letting on."

You're right. Her response, thinking it was an endgame, had been a mistake. His statement had been a chess move, in part, to elicit a reaction. "Interpret my statement however you wish. Before alerting your handler, you should keep something in mind. Gravitational attractions work in a precise way. So much so that you can launch an object from Earth and land it on Mars within a mile or two of the target. If you perform a couple of course corrections, you could land it in a target zone the size of a baseball diamond. No one knows *why* gravity works, only *how* it does. Erin's goal is not to understand *why* the physics work. Instead, she's striving to learn *how* the ship's systems work with physics.

"More importantly, I don't like being played. All of MarsVantage has been wary of you since your arrival. We regarded every word you've said as manipulation, and our suspicions—no, *expectations*—have been realized."

"You act like a Marsee... Like you were born here." He pointed to the floor. "Your—their—inherent distrust of all things Washington, and Earth for that matter, has led to the untenable position they find themselves in. Fighting Washington's authority at every turn has consequences."

"Five hundred years ago, Hamilton wrote something that is just as true today as it was then—'Unjust authority confers no obligation of obedience.'"

He flared his nostrils. "What the hell happened to you?"

Is he joking? "What happened to me? Two strangers tried to murder me over this, and they haven't seen a courtroom yet. That's just for starters."

"Well, Sam De Angelo stupidly died cleaning his apartment by combining ammonia and bleach." Contempt formed on James' face. "No sense trying the dead."

"Sounds damn hinky. Anyway, on the plus side, I discovered an alien civilization and spent two years doing what I love. Along the way, my eyes were opened. Washington is supposed to govern, not rule. Until I came to Mars, I was like most—I never understood the difference.

"Now, Washington expects us to eagerly hand over the Bvindu data simply because they want it. According to scuttlebutt, they'll pass a law to steal it when Space Force arrives. That tyrannical power grab is a bitter pill to swallow. That's what happened to me."

"Oh, it's *Gretchen's* turn to be the victim."

"If I allow Washington to have our prize or allow you to continue working here, you'd be correct. We knew you were playing games from the beginning." *Did you believe your charisma could hide your agenda?* "I'll clue you in on something. People don't like being manipulated. Often, they walk away. Sometimes, they play their own game. We dumb, ignorant *Marsees* did both, and you, the superior, civilized elite, never suspected."

"What the hell does that mean?"

"We got what we expected and what we needed from you. You showed your true colors. Now, we're walking away." She stepped back. "You are *persona non grata*. Your privileges to Bvindu

Dome are revoked. Tomorrow, you will be on a tractor back to Mars City. As we speak, Frank is notifying all personnel that no MarsVantage matters will be discussed with you under a penalty up to and including termination. After that, you *will* be on the next transport to Earth. Until then, feel free to transmit all the reports you like without our input."

James' eyes widened. "I'll appeal to Chuck!"

"Who do you think authorized this? You'll either go on your own, or I'll help you. I would *so* much like to. Ask Arnold Janssen. I broke his nose."

"Can't—he's dead. Suicide by cyanide."

"It's convenient how Interplanetary's spies are all either dead or missing. *There's* a story worth telling, but you won't because it doesn't fit your overlords' agenda."

"That's not my assignment."

"The problem is, it's *no one's* assignment."

He frowned. "Getting kicked out of Bvindu Dome is bad PR."

"Ha! We expected nothing else." She stepped close, patted his chest, and firmly said, "Get your gear packed, buddy-boy. You leave at dawn."

He sulked out of the Planning Huddle Area, and she sat in the nearest chair, her hands trembling. She closed her eyes and took deep, even breaths.

Washington has only one play left—Space Force. Will our preparations be enough?

31 | THE BEAR AND THE HONEYPOT

An annoying din roused Frank from a deep sleep. After the momentary disorientation passed, the noise resolved into an alarm. He sat up, snatched the datapad from the nightstand, and read the alert. The alarm volume halved—Gretchen's datapad still played it.

He shook her shoulder. "Wake up, hon. We have a problem."

She sat upright and grabbed her device as he donned his coveralls and boots. "Well, shit."

She dressed, bouncing to get her feet out of the coveralls' legs. "You know who this is."

"No doubt." Frank reached under the bed and grabbed a shock-tab gun and holster, which he strapped to his waist. He'd last handled it purposefully two years earlier while stranded in a dark cave in the Maelstrom Mountains. "James is making one last try."

"He won't get anything. If he does, he can't do anything with it—nothing's translated."

"I still don't like the raw data going public." Frank rubbed the sleep from his eyes. "We have to deal with James once and for all. I need to focus on facing Space Force. If the timing's off just a little, we're..."

"Screwed is the word you're searching for."

He sighed. "Yes."

"If you didn't have doubts, I'd worry." She finished pulling on her boots and followed him to the front door. "Space Force isn't our immediate problem—James is. We should've had Erin fly his sorry ass to Mars City instead of waiting until this morning."

"Hindsight and all that."

They took a few flights of steps, which were quicker than the lift, and exited the building.

Gretchen sat in the cargo area of the Bvindu cargo mover. "Why do people working against us keep using the same tactics?"

"Maybe we should publish a list, so they can try something interesting." Frank stepped on the back of a cargo mover. He pushed the throttle forward, covering the two blocks to the Master Control Center in less than a minute.

At the closed door by a sign that announced, '*Authorized Personnel Only*,' Frank stopped Gretchen when she reached for her datapad. "Hon, we both know James is inside. He's trapped. You can't confront him like you did with Arnold."

She sighed. "I don't go around punching everyone who wrongs me."

"Arnold tried to steal our work, and James is replaying the script. Plus, James is—"

"Stop there. If I had embraced my feelings for him, you would've found him on the floor to start our first meeting." Gretchen pulled out her datapad. "Besides his unsavory schemes, I'm annoyed he's been here only four days and already figured out how to enter the Master Control Center. He must've recorded one of us entering at some point, and I don't know how he did it."

Frank wondered the same, not that it mattered now. "After seeing the body in the entryway, you'd think he'd be more cautious."

She shook her head. "Whatever he was promised must be worth the risk. He says I've changed, and I have—for the better—but so has he... for the worse."

Frank proposed a plan that garnered her agreement. They crouched on either side of the entryway. She pressed the datapad control to sound the familiar tones of the Open command. In response, the door descended.

Crouched down, she entered and scooted right. Frank crossed the threshold, heading left. He input the code, 10289, on the keypad lying on the floor.

When MarsVantage had taken control of Bvindu Dome, he'd installed a grid of invisible laser sensors around the interior door frame. If someone entered and failed to provide a code within thirty seconds, it would transmit a notification to his and

Gretchen's datapads. Tonight, James had activated that security protocol for the first time.

The door rose automatically behind him. Gretchen peered over the rows of waist-high cabinets displaying electric blue sparks traversing their faces. She moved up an aisle while he did likewise about ten feet away. They closed in on James, near a corner where the Bvindu control console resided before two dark gray Bvindu mobile units, each with four arms and two legs, attached to a large sphere with a smaller sphere atop it.

As they converged, James looked up from MarsVantage's computer sitting to the left of the Bvindu control console and vidcomm. He stood and backed away with his hands up.

His holocam wasn't active. He must not have been planning to broadcast trespassing and burglary.

"Is that a shock-tab gun, Frank?"

"What gun?" He caressed the rough texture of the grip. "Gretchen, you see a gun?"

"I only see a lying spy."

James took a step back. "There's no need to shoot. I took one of those once. I nearly bit through my tongue."

"Yeah, yeah." Gretchen knelt and retrieved zip ties from a storage container against the wall. After standing, she said, "The last time I heard that story, you bit the inside of your cheek."

James glared at her while Frank approached and pushed a chair before him. "Sit."

Rather than obeying, James looked at it.

Now behind him, Gretchen placed a hand on his shoulder. "Sit, or you'll wake up in the chair... Either way, you're in the chair."

James looked at Frank.

"Frank's not your problem. Now, sit."

James turned to her and paused for a heartbeat. He must've noticed the determination in Gretchen's eyes, understood what it meant, and wisely chose to comply.

After securing his wrists to the chair's arms, Gretchen bound his ankles to its legs. Then, she yanked his holocam and datapad from his thigh pockets and deposited them atop the vidcomm, pulling their datachips and pocketing them. "These are confiscated."

He stared at her hip pocket. "That's the property of All News Network."

"Not anymore." Gretchen patted them. "These chips contain stolen MarsVantage proprietary information. Any other data storage devices we find among your belongings are likewise confiscated. You'll be issued blank replacements when you reach Mars City."

Frank stepped within arms' reach of James and Gretchen. "The last time we encountered spies, they tried to kill us. An impartial reporter—should such a mythical creature exist—wouldn't have created that propaganda piece I watched yesterday morning."

"You remind me of the fable of Truth and Falsehood." Pity covered Gretchen's face. "They were swimming in a river. Falsehood exits first, puts on Truth's clothes, and walks away. Your lies are wrapped in a thin veneer of truth, which disgusts me."

"I always hated your cute little anecdotes," James spat out. "It's as if you think you have special access to knowledge."

"I appreciate knowledge. By the way, Truth exits the river, refuses to don Falsehood's clothing, and proudly walks naked." She leaned over, coming to nose to nose. "Now you can be annoyed by the entire story."

Gretchen backed away as Frank said, "Your agenda offends me. In fact, the illusion of truth you peddle offends me. You and the rest of the ruling elite want something for doing absolutely nothing. Most of our fellow citizens—and honestly, at this point, we're treated more like subjects—think nothing of it. Except Marsians—we despise it."

"Frank, MarsVantage needs to accept its role in the grand scheme," James countered. "The government and the people have an inherent interest in what happens here. You are answerable to them, which Mr. O'Donnell will do again in a few days. And most importantly, you need Washington more than they need you."

Gretchen turned from the computer. "He didn't gain access."

"You broke in and tried to access our computer, without a cracking program running on your datapad?" Frank asked. "You really aren't good at this."

"You've changed, James." Gretchen's face turned hard. "You did me a *huge* favor by not renewing our marriage contract. I'm forever grateful."

Frank vidcommed Erin. After several long seconds, she appeared disheveled on-screen. "This better be good. Do you know what time it is?"

"The bear is stuck in the honeypot."

32 | WISHFUL THINKING

Outside the Master Control Center, Frank ended a vidcomm with Red by retracting the screen and pocketing his datapad. Erin pulled up on a cargo mover.

Her wet hair was slicked back. She rubbed her eyes and asked, "Why'd you declare an emergency at oh-dark-hundred?"

"Or, as normal people say, 1:30 A.M.," Frank retorted. "Gretchen's packing up James' quarters and will meet us at your shuttle. I need you to fly him to Mars City. Right now. Alan is waiting for you at Pad Seven Alpha. Make sure you get James' ID band when you land. Cut it into multiple pieces and return them to me or Gretchen."

"He's already scheduled for the tractor just after sunrise. You woke me for a couple of hours difference?"

Frank recounted James' treachery. "He is no longer a biased journalist. He's a proven spy. You'll find him tied to a chair inside."

She stepped closer and glanced in both directions. "Gretchen didn't hit him, right?"

"Don't let her hear that." Frank looked around for good measure. "She's miffed I brought it up."

"If people tried to steal my work, I'd get physical, too. No apologies."

A couple of occasions sprang to mind when Erin had applied a percussive maintenance technique to a shuttle component with whatever tool was in hand. "Just so we're clear, I expect James to arrive at Mars City uninjured."

"I don't know if I should be happy that you believe I'd extract a little revenge or angry that you think I'd attack him just because he twisted my words." The expression on her face shifted to one of consideration. "Perhaps, a broken bone—"

"Erin! That won't help."

"I know." She smirked. "A few aggressive flying maneuvers. That happens when a pilot gets played for a fool."

Frank smacked the side of his head with his palm. "I'm having difficulty hearing. Must have water in my ears."

"There'll be no evidence. Just his word versus mine."

"Really, my hearing's on the fritz. After dropping James off, pick up Red. The beacons are active. He's expecting you."

33 | PLAN, IMPLEMENTED

As Frank neared the landing pad the next day, he parked the cargo mover beside another and stepped off. Gretchen parked to his right and joined him.

The landing pad was seeing regular use for the first time since MarsVantage occupied Bvindu Dome. In response, Gretchen had activated the overhead lighting for the area, and none of the archaeologists asked a single question. Life without James was good.

Over her shoulder, pinprick-sized lights of cargo movers carrying Red and his team of retired Space Force guardians shined in the distance. Within minutes, they'd arrive to offload a shuttle containing more supplies from Shadow City.

Yesterday in the Master Control Center, Red's team had retrofitted the area behind the Bvindu control console, replacing the caretaker's two mobile units with military stations to create a tactical alcove. Frank had been impressed at their coordination, precision, and professionalism.

While waiting, Frank took in the expanse, which was a rarity for anyone on Mars without a spacesuit. It smelled of... openness, not organic like Mars City's farms or recycled like anywhere else. Just different, in some ineffable way.

He stood near one of the eight enormous pillars supporting the landing pad currently at dome level, looking upon the spaceship staging area, which was now empty. He had returned the Bvindu Scout Ship to the nearest building in the Manufacturing Section to receive the Spectrum Erasure Overlay coating. The three-story portal encompassing most of the building's face was open, ready to allow the scout ship to exit from the Manufacturing Section one last time.

Gretchen pointed toward it. "She looks ominous now that she's painted."

Black and dark gray patches faded and brightened across the ship's hull, giving the impression of motion. No matter how hard he tried, he couldn't focus on anything specific. "It's like a phantom."

"I doubt anyone will see it in space unless they know where to look."

"We'll find out soon enough."

Her jaw muscles clenched. "You're not planning on tagging along with Erin, are you?"

"Of course."

She took his hand. "It's a bad idea to put multiple leaders in danger."

"Hon, if the test goes well, we're going to Earth. It's a two-person job. I loaded the cargo after Erin whisked James away yesterday."

"And if the test doesn't go well?"

"Then we'll need to be rescued."

Gretchen frowned. "Assuming you don't disintegrate, implode, or end up in the middle of the sun."

"Washington is forcing us onto a dangerous path, which means accepting more risk. If this ship doesn't work, our options will be limited, and our chances for success reduced."

She sighed and hugged him tightly. "You're right. I hate that the government pushed us to this point."

Red and his team of four Space Force retirees parked their cargo movers. They dismounted and approached. Even wearing MarsVantage coveralls, everything from their strides to their haircuts radiated military. *If only one of them had long hair or a mustache...*

"Everyone," Red announced, "I know yesterday was hectic. We have a minute, so let's make proper introductions."

Without any direction, his team stood shoulder to shoulder. He started with the leftmost person. "This is Dylan Baker. His specialty is piloting gunships. Next is Tony Rizzoli, one of the best sharpshooters to serve. Here we have Jorge Rodriguez, also a gunship pilot. And Henrietta Rockford—"

"Everyone calls me Hank."

In a single moment, Frank's assumptions clashed with reality. His eyes had glossed over Red's team members to the point of never noticing details. Her voice was definitely feminine, and with a closer look, her features matched.

"As I was about to say—everyone calls her *Hank*. The only sharpshooter to keep up with Rizzo."

Tony Rizzoli pushed his chest forward and winked.

Frank and Gretchen greeted them.

Red continued, "And here are Frank Brentford and Gretchen Blake, the discoverers of the Bvindu. Gretchen has been working with the Bvindu equipment, and Frank is our liaison with MarsVantage. Is there anything you'd like to add?"

Frank took a step forward. "We expect Washington will push us beyond the point of no return in a few hours. Once that happens, we'll transfer people with strong Earth ties to Mars City. Afterward, we'll be able to work in the open."

He glanced in Gretchen's direction, who stepped beside him. "Ah, yes. As I mentioned yesterday, you need to avoid the archaeologists. We don't want them to mention your presence should any choose to leave. Remember, if asked, you're maintenance engineers working on a special project for Frank and can't discuss the details."

"We got it," Red affirmed.

A deep, barely audible thrum emanated under the landing pad's pillars. Overhead, purple strobe lights burst to life on the underside of the transitional airlock doors.

Erin had arrived, and the landing pad retracted into the transitional airlock. It would equalize the air pressure once the Mars-facing hatch doors were closed and sealed.

A minute later, the lights stopped, and the city-facing doors opened, allowing the landing pad to descend and settle at deck level with a distinctive *tha-dunk*. Erin's shuttle perched on a sliver of its surface.

A staleness wafted about like air discharged from a bicycle tire. Though the odor was unpleasant, MarsVantage had lucked out with the Bvindu engineering. They couldn't have used the landing platform without the transitional airlock. Presumably,

Mars conditions had deteriorated so much that the Bvindu had needed the airlock as much as the Marsians now did.

The shuttle's cargo hatch opened, and the loading ramp descended. When it touched the ground, Erin strolled down and joined everyone. "Here's your latest shipment from Shadow City."

"Thanks," Red said through an easy smile. "We're looking forward to having the rest of our equipment to prevail against Space Force."

"Damn right, Master Sergeant!" Hank said.

Red gave her a curt nod. "Overnight, I learned some disturbing news. The inbound destroyer is the *Baffin*."

His team muttered, mostly under their breaths, but one expletive was distinct.

Gretchen looked from Frank to Red. "What does that mean?"

"Do you remember the *Icarus* Incident?" Red asked.

"I do." Erin raised her hand shoulder-high. "About ten years ago. Space Force retook the *Icarus* from pirates."

Red added, "Pirates hijacked it on the Earth/Moon run. Major Steele shadowed the ship, watching the bridge. At one point, the pirates met there. She surmised the entire pirate crew was present and opened fire on the bridge. Long story short, the decompression killed all but one of the pirates, the captain, and a crew member."

"That's horrible." Gretchen's face contorted in horror.

"Major Steele retook the ship with no injuries to her team or damage to her ship. SF promoted her to light colonel shortly afterward. Five years ago, she became a full colonel. Pirate incidents between the Earth and the Moon are virtually non-existent now. She's commanding the *Baffin*, and SF reassigned it to Mars. Washington means business."

"We always knew our road was difficult," Frank concluded.

"Mars is a high-profile item for Washington. SF sent a commander predisposed to action."

"What does that mean?" Gretchen asked. "This Colonel Steele will just carry out her orders, right?"

"Not understanding individuals is the quickest path to failure." Red spent a moment taking in Gretchen's confused expression. "At the beginning of the American Civil War, General

Scott planned to seize control of the Mississippi River, blockade the coast, and wait out the South by depriving them of resources. Several generals requested troops and supplies but refused to engage the Confederates. General Meade forced the Confederates to retreat from Gettysburg but failed to pursue."

"I'm missing something," Gretchen said.

"Each general interpreted their orders differently and acted to pursue that interpretation. General Grant accomplished Lincoln's goal of uniting the states by defeating the Confederacy. Steele is in the Grant mold. Her orders are to take custody of Bvindu Dome. She'll happily capture us—or kill us—if we're in the way."

"Make no mistake," Frank said, "we're in the way. Our only advantage is that Space Force is in the dark regarding our capabilities."

Red and his team stood straighter. Hank elbowed Rodriguez. Gretchen looked concerned.

Erin faced Frank. "Can you coordinate the cargo offload? I need a bio break and to get a bite to eat before our test flight."

"Not a problem."

"Thanks." She disappeared behind the shuttle.

Red stepped forward. "Hey, Frank, we do this all the time. Trust me. You and Rizzo get in the cargo bay."

Frank climbed the cargo ramp, curious about what was to come. Meanwhile, Rizzo eschewed the ramp and pulled himself up effortlessly, demonstrating that he hadn't allowed retirement to dull his conditioning.

Red continued, "Gretchen, I need you to direct where we place the containers. You'll grab my coveralls back and pull me where I must go. Give me a double pat when we arrive."

After Rizzo retracted the ramp, Red placed Rodriguez and Baker facing one another on the deck next to the cargo bay while he and Hank faced a few steps away.

Frank bent low and placed his hands against the cold, heavy-duty container, mirroring Rizzo's actions.

He ordered, "Go."

Together, they pushed it to the mouth of the cargo hold.

Rizzo announced for all to hear, "Pass!"

"Catch!" Rodriguez and Baker said in unison. They allowed the container's momentum to pull them toward Red and Hank. "Pass!"

"Catch!"

Gretchen's eyes flashed surprise, but she quickly grabbed Red's coveralls and guided him to the cargo movers, where she tapped his shoulder.

After the container settled to the mover's bed, Red said, "Let's move it, people. We ain't union getting paid by the hour."

They repeated the process for all of the containers. By the end, Frank had broken a sweat and was breathing hard while the retired Space Force guardians looked like they'd walked in the park.

Red flipped the latches on either side of the last container and removed the lid. "Ten minutes. Water and a quick FieldMeal. Then we move our equipment to the warehouse."

Gretchen took Frank aside. "Do you think we'll have to fight Space Force?"

Red's Civil War example must've made her nervous. "You made me face up to a possible conflict. You were more right than you knew. I don't want a fight, but we're at a crossroads. If we lose, everyone loses. Humanity loses. We have sixteen more days to create a favorable battleground."

34 | Bvindu Scout Ship

Frank watched Gretchen and Red's team depart on the cargo movers holding the storage containers. Erin, appearing refreshed, strolled up in her spacesuit.

"Let's see what our new ship can do." She led the way left around the landing pad to a dual-level console designed for the Bvindu's four hands. After passing along her helmet and gloves to Frank, she inspected a piece of paper attached to the edge of the lower console and touched several controls. The shuttle levitated about a foot off the landing pad, moving through the transition area and into the shadows on the way to the Raw Materials Entrance.

"How do you know how to do this?"

"Your wife gave me the instructions along with the scout ship information. Though I have to say, the Bvindu symbols are anything but intuitive."

"I'm thankful that their senses are similar to ours." He ran his hand through his hair. "Imagine trying to deal with information in ultraviolet wavelengths. As it stands, we almost didn't realize how quickly they process audio-visual information."

With a few more control presses, the scout ship emerged from the last building of the Manufacturing Section, slowly transiting to the landing pad.

Eventually, it settled into position. Erin led Frank to the hatch and played tones from her datapad to open it. She pulled herself up, and Frank passed along her helmet and gloves. After he joined her, she said, "You need a spacesuit."

"I stowed one with the remoras."

"Get changed while I do the flight prep." She headed to the cockpit.

He shed his outerwear and donned the green spacesuit, including boots and an air vest. Once he tucked the gloves inside the helmet, he walked past the sensor analyst's station to take the navigator's seat, resting his helmet in his lap.

He looked over as Erin worked the ship's controls. "What's with all the stickers?"

"We're changing the captions on the console to English for the next ship we build. I can't remember all these Bvindu symbols. I also created this cheat pad on my leg, so I can flip to the appropriate page for whichever menu of the touchscreen I'm using."

The console looked like a kid's craft project. He hadn't considered the control labels when talking with the caretaker. "You're ready for this, right? You *can* fly this thing?"

She met his gaze. "I can understand the readouts now. I'm confident in basic actions. The more I fly her, the easier it'll be to perform complex maneuvers."

That wasn't the full-throated "of course" he'd hoped for. "Basic maneuvers are enough."

"Just relax for a few minutes while I finish flight prep."

Frank closed his eyes, taking advantage of the downtime.

* * *

Sometime later, Erin smacked Frank's arm. "We're about to make history, and you're sleeping?"

"Not anymore." Frank rubbed his eyes. She was just annoyed that he rested while she worked. "Are we ready?"

"*I* am."

The catnap had helped—he was ready for the challenge ahead. "Let's get on with it."

"Seal up your spacesuit, and hold on tight. If we don't explode, I don't want sudden accelerations or decelerations to injure you."

We should've installed harnesses. He did as she'd ordered. The control panel on his left arm confirmed spacesuit integrity.

After verifying her suit was sealed, Erin pressed one last button and gripped the cyclic and collective.

The landing pad lifted the scout ship. The buildings fell away, leaving only far-off shadows. The shuttle paused in the transitional airlock. Eventually, the dome's thick, translucent edge passed by. At last, Erin guided the ship airborne.

An invisible restraint gripped him tight to the seat around the tops of his legs and across his chest. Apparently, physical harnesses weren't needed. He pondered the technology involved and how it could work but came up empty.

"Head away from Mars City," Frank said. They'd witnessed the caretaker engage the faster-than-light engine, which created a display that looked like a circular rainbow. "We don't want anyone to see the light show."

The Maelstrom Mountains shifted to port, and the scout ship continued level flight. After a time, the landscape receded, leaving only a reddish-orange splat of color, which faded, revealing a star-filled blackness of low Mars orbit.

Erin said, "Sub-lightspeed is more responsive than my shuttle. I like it. We're going to perform a short jump. If all goes well, we'll proceed to phase two."

"Are you sure we're ready?"

She stared at him through the helmet's clear visor for several seconds. "What's on your mind?"

"Washington is forcing us to move faster than expected. We're relying on a lot of untested Bvindu tech to protect and support ourselves. We'll be in a bind if this doesn't work."

"There's an old saying I once heard—you go to war with the army you have, not the one you wish you had. I could fly around for another hour, and we'll learn nothing more. We *have* to test the FTL engine."

She was right. "Let's find out where we stand."

"Here we go..."

The scout ship shuddered. A faint, high-pitch whine emanated from aft. A deep red filled the cockpit window, though not for long—it transformed into orange.

A rainbow of colors appeared, like flying through light emerging from a prism. Stars against an inky black background appeared at last as a wave of nausea crashed over him.

As quick as it had come on, it departed.

"Did you feel that?" Erin asked.

"Uh-huh. You okay?"

"We didn't explode. Everything else is negotiable."

The stars rotated until a red crescent about the size of his bent pinky finger scrolled into view. He'd never been this far from Mars.

"All levels read as expected." Erin pointed to a bar on a gauge that was ninety percent filled. "That's our energy reserve. We can jump immediately."

It increased as he examined it. "Sure. My stomach's ready."

"No barfing in your suit. Hold on. Next stop, Earth orbit."

Again, the whine, the colors, the nausea.

Erin banked the scout ship—blue and white filled the window. She activated the cockpit's transparent mode, making the forward half of the cockpit's hull clear. She whispered, "Frank, *this* is Earth."

Thick white clouds drifted over green landmasses and blue oceans.

The seat's restraints faded away. For moments on end, he took it all in. "Pictures and holos don't do it justice. It's a shame that greed and power lust push us further away."

"You often said that Earth holds nothing of interest. If Washington treated us as equals, you'd feel differently about Earth and its natural wonders."

Perhaps she was correct. In that fantasy, he might undergo gravity treatment to witness them firsthand. "We must live and work in the world as it exists."

"Mark my words. Someday Washington and Mars will see eye to eye." She pressed a pedal and shifted the collective. "I'm coming around to the nearest target satellite. It's military. Get into position."

He rose, passed the sensor analyst station, and stood in the cargo bay. Six small containers, arranged in two rows, awaited. Each contained a remora, a cube-like device he'd created to attach to a broadcast satellite, allowing him to take control and override broadcasts meant for Earth.

The best part of the Bvindu comm tech was that it used quantum entanglement, which Earth scientists had barely proven in theory. All MarsVantage communications using this tech would be undetectable by Earthers.

"We're here. I'm keeping the cockpit hatch open in case you need help."

The Order had provided the locations of three military and three commercial satellites for the remoras. MarsVantage was guaranteed the opportunity to send a single message and already knew its contents. After that, no one knew how many more messages they'd be able to transmit before Space Force got wise.

Frank attached the carabiner of the tether line to a loop on his spacesuit's waist. He anchored the other end to a convenient tie-down. Although the scout ship generated its own gravity, a safety precaution was prudent should he manage to fall out of the hatch.

From his thigh pocket, he withdrew his datapad. He faced the hatch and compared the controls on its right to his datapad's instructions. He pressed several buttons, and the cargo bay depressurized. Afterward, the hatch descended into the scout ship's underside, revealing swirling whites against blue with patches of green and yellow.

After unlatching the lid from a container labeled with an "M," he withdrew the remora and stepped evenly to the hatch. He'd never live it down if Erin caught him dangling outside after stumbling.

With both hands, he pushed the remora toward the satellite to his right and below, a fair distance away. He used his datapad to maneuver it. As it closed the distance, he activated its grapple. Seconds later, it attached. A self-test verified the remora was fully functional.

He activated the failsafe. If the remora became detached or were opened, a small charge would destroy its innards. Washington wasn't getting the quantum communications technology.

Frank closed the scout ship's hatch but kept the inside a vacuum. "One down. Any indication that we were noticed?"

"Space Force command frequencies indicate no alerts."

They were encrypted, but the Knowledge Keeper Order had provided the keys, allowing Erin to monitor the chatter.

With the Spectrum Erasure Overlay, radiation didn't emanate from their ship, nor was it detectable by standard instrumentation.

The only way Earthers would know they were there was if someone below saw the ship eclipse a star or someone above noticed the ship's silhouette against the planet.

"Good. Next satellite."

Erin said, "The nearest one is commercial. On our way."

During the trip, he opened a cargo container marked with a "C." According to the Order, the commercial remoras were assigned to Fordham Industries satellites with Fordham's approval, so detection and removal by him weren't a concern.

Whether Space Force destroyed the satellite, removed the remora, or ignored it wasn't critical as long as their first message got transmitted.

The *Baffin*'s actions upon arriving at Mars were the concern. *If they try an invasion, a lot of blood will be shed.*

35 | Zugzwang

Like the previous week, Chuck readied to testify before the Senate Offworld Commerce Committee. The authority conferred by the Citizens in Freedom Committee weighed heavily today. His suit jacket lay uncomfortably on his shoulders. It tugged oddly, no matter how he adjusted his shirt or tie. Since activating the holocam, he'd forced himself not to fidget.

This was Chuck's moment. In an odd way, he had the easy task. What came after the hearing would challenge the Committee and all of MarsVantage. *Tough times lay ahead.*

As the appointed time approached, senators in ones and twos took their seats while their aides perched against the wall behind them. Last was Senator Severino. Unlike the previous hearing, her shoulder-length blonde hair was stylishly arranged in a traditional updo. A maroon jacket over a button-down cream top complemented her muted makeup. All in all, she presented the image of a formidable professional.

While an aide whispered in her ear, Chuck reached for a datapad and located the Must-Depart list and a prerecorded message to all MarsVantage employees. He'd need them soon.

The aide stepped away from Senator Severino, who then took in the committee members. She gaveled the hearing into session. After some general pleasantries, she said, "Mr. O'Donnell, thank you again for your time. Please remember that you are still under oath."

"Understood, Senator."

"I'll begin with the unfortunate incident where your team discovered the body of a PAA worker."

He forced himself to remain stoic.

She continued, "Was it a MarsVantage security system or a Bvindu system that killed the PAA citizen?"

"First off, on behalf of myself and all of MarsVantage, we express our sincere condolences to the PAA citizen and his family, friends, and colleagues. To answer your question, the Bvindu security system detected an unidentified presence that had moved beyond two written hazard warnings and a yellow and black hazard line. The security system functioned as the Bvindu programmed it millennia ago."

The senator had skipped over how the trespasser broke into the dome, so Chuck wouldn't have to lie about the cracking program for every PAA-manufactured airlock on the trespasser's datapad. *What Washington doesn't know, can't be used against us.*

"Intruding merits a death sentence?"

"Not at all. Unfortunately, the PAA spy disregarded multiple warnings, and no authorized personnel were there to prevent it."

She looked directly at him, which entailed looking into the holocam in the hearing chamber. It was an effective technique. "Do you have control over the Bvindu security system?"

"We haven't come across the instructions to disengage it. One theory is that the caretaker wanted his cultural treasures protected, so he didn't provide those instructions." That wasn't a lie... It was more of a half-truth. A heading for the security instructions was in the Manuduction, but Gretchen never read about disabling the intruder detections system. *Perhaps it's a quarter-truth.*

She gracefully placed a hand on the tabletop in front of her. "Cultural treasures or not, do you realize that we have an international incident because of this?"

"Indeed. A foreign company with direct ties to a foreign government attempted to perpetrate industrial espionage."

"The PAA filed a formal complaint with the World Nations Organization and us. Other nations have expressed concerns about misuse of the Bvindu equipment and data. Are you certain no malfunctions occurred?" She consulted a datapad. "Were the hemolac levels correct? Was there any hedenine interference? Was the flumolator working properly?"

Not that confirmation was necessary, but the absurd terminology used in James' presence had quickly traveled a great distance to find Senator Severino. Odds were that James hadn't been speaking directly with the senator or her staff. More likely, someone in his line of authority had been communicating with one of her subordinates. "Senator, someone is putting you on. None of those things exist."

"I have it on good authority that your personnel discussed such matters. Do you deny it? Before you answer, remember you are under oath."

There was her trap. She must expect him to deny those ridiculous words were ever spoken. She overlooked an option—the truth. "MarsVantage personnel did discuss those things. I understand an interlocking granistan joint was also part of the conversation. Still, those things only exist in the imagination of a couple of trusted employees and the recollections of a handful of people privy to the conversation."

"And why would your employees discuss meaningless things?"

To recover, she'd asked a question for which she didn't already know the answer. His response needed to generate the best PR possible, not rub her face in her misstep. Should today be the day he and the Committee anticipated, history would judge his every action and word.

He cleared his throat. "A reporter decided to join us after an ordinary sandstorm—not after the Airlock Accident, not after the discovery of an ancient alien city, not even when a swarm of inspectors and auditors descended. The timing is curious, considering nothing is overly newsworthy at this point.

"We suspected this reporter wouldn't be objective, given his assignment history and prior relationship with our Director of Archaeology. So, we seeded several small items to see when and where they might appear."

The senator's cheeks reddened, and she frowned ever so slightly. "As you mentioned the auditors and inspectors you recently hosted, let's discuss them briefly. I was concerned to read that they were mistreated regarding meals. Can you explain?"

A masterful attempt to place me on the defensive. "I believe you're referring to our restaurants and grocers requiring their NutriAccount cards."

"Precisely."

He forced a smile and exhaled easily. The impression he made was as important as his words. "I wouldn't equate presenting NutriAccount cards with mistreatment since millions of citizens do so daily. After all, NutriAccounts are the hallmark of the government's concern for its citizens' wellbeing.

"The auditors and inspectors demanded the most inconsequential details regarding safety, health, and finances. Our vendors, who operate as semi-autonomous subsidiaries of MarsVantage, contacted their counterparts in Earth orbit and on the Moon. Never had the others experienced such intrusive inspections. In light of that fact, our vendors banded together and decided to strictly adhere to every regulation."

"Those beyond Earth aren't held to a NutriAccount," Senator Severino said in a slow, even tone.

"The law states that the presentation and processing of a NutriAccount card is *not* required. Since our vendors were being treated differently, by being held to the strictest standards and interpretation of the regs, they rightfully reasoned that those doing so would expect to be held to an equally high level of compliance."

While her face betrayed nothing now, the slight quiver of her hand laying down one datapad and picking up another told a different story. The hearing must not be proceeding as she'd planned.

Now wasn't the time to celebrate his victories. She still held all the cards.

"Mr. O'Donnell, you've been working with the Bvindu data for over two years, and your progress is imperceptible. Why don't you bring on Earth experts?"

The Bvindu data was the ultimate Catch Twenty-two. Exploiting its immediate commercial value meant selling, licensing, or leasing to Earth interests. The breakthroughs and advancements, while lucrative, could and likely would be used against MarsVantage, placing them in a worse position.

Severino had based her question on the easy assumption—MarsVantage was too incompetent to evaluate and utilize the

Bvindu tech. She failed to consider that MarsVantage saw her game for what it was... Or she didn't care.

"MarsVantage made multiple posts to the HR Acquisition Network and found suitable candidates. Aside from the archaeologists, everyone ignored our vidcomms or refused the opportunity. Regardless, we have the foremost Bvindu experts. No one's translating and evaluating the Bvindu data any faster."

"You're referring to Gretchen Blake, of course." The corners of Severino's lips upturned a tick. "The same person who Dr. Hawthorne—our foremost archaeologist and her one-time project supervisor—rated as substandard. I'm speaking of people like him with real expertise, credentials, and accomplishments. The type of person who'll refrain from taking reckless chances... like allowing the Bvindu security systems to remain active."

Chuck took a sip of water. The elitist conceit of relying on reputation and credentials was on full display. "Dr. Hawthorne's education is impressive, and he's led numerous expeditions, making groundbreaking discoveries, primarily at the beginning of his career. Yet, how he handles others' discoveries alarms me. A true scientist wouldn't have dismissed a colleague's theories out of hand as he has done. That's not science, and such behavior doesn't meet MarsVantage standards."

Chuck settled back in the chair and concluded, "I'm thrilled with my team, their caution, and most of all, their results."

"Yet, we're unsatisfied with your progress."

"Science doesn't work on corporate timetables. Or political."

Senator Severino's face remained impassive. "The Offworld Commerce Committee's opinion is that MarsVantage needs help from the National Science Foundation. The administration is in agreement."

"I fail to see the rush or the benefit to MarsVantage. We earned the right to work with Bvindu data. When the common cold treatment gains FDA approval, millions of people every year will be appreciative, and that'll be a huge advancement for humanity."

"You stumbled over the Bvindu technology while searching for an energy source. You didn't create the science."

"Sir Alexander Fleming discovered penicillin by mistake. Should we not use antibiotics because they weren't purposefully discovered? Not only did MarsVantage put in the effort that led us to the Bvindu, but we also held multiple discussions with the caretaker to guard and utilize the tech safely," Chuck said evenly.

Senator Severino narrowed her eyes. "The idea of a caretaker wraps up your claims nicely. You allege he inhabited the city for hundreds of thousands of years, which on its face is impossible."

"You succinctly summarized what the media has been broadcasting. For two years, everyone assumed we were lying while many treated the caretaker as a punchline, yet no one asked how it could be true."

She stared at Chuck for seconds that dragged on. Instinct urged him to fill the silence. His intellect knew the tactic, understood it, and battled it.

Senator Severino finally asked, "Very well. So how did the caretaker live for so long?"

This was a dangerous area, and Chuck's words had to be carefully measured. "He lived within the city's computer control system. When needed, he transferred himself to a mobile unit, which was how my team interacted with him."

She interlaced her fingers and placed her hands on the table. "You have access to the ability to create sophisticated artificial intelligences, yet we've seen nothing."

He'd diverted the senator onto the unprofitable avenue the archaeologists had created. Because James hadn't broadcasted an AI report, she must have heard about it through a back channel. "It's an unproven theory less than a week old. If confirmed, it'd mean that a Bvindu is needed to create a new one. Warnings concerning unhinged or uncontrollable AIs date back three centuries. As with all things, safety is our foremost concern."

"Are you stating that you are working on this project?"

"The initiatives we pursue are confidential. When we come to market, we will ensure that any product is safe and complies with all rules, regulations, and laws."

She took on the bearing of a confident politician. "We're concerned about your lack of transparency in everything Bvindu, glacial progress with the Bvindu data, and most of all, recklessly employing deadly measures without proper safeguards and oversight. We'll have legislation on the president's desk within a week to nationalize all alien technology. Space Force will secure Bvindu Dome, and the National Science Ministry will oversee its ongoing development."

It is done.

These hearings had never been about revealing the truth. The outcome had been predetermined, even before he'd transmitted his sworn written testimony, most of which hadn't been covered in a public setting. It had all been theater, optics, and narrative to manipulate the public.

While offering Gretchen the Director of Archaeology position, he'd mentioned that MarsVantage needed to retain possession of Bvindu Dome in the face of a board member attempting a power play. Two years later, the situation persisted—this time, the threat came from without, not within.

"If you insist on this drastic measure, MarsVantage will take equally drastic action."

"This committee and the United States do not take kindly to threats."

"I apologize if my statement sounded like a threat. That wasn't my intention. When MarsVantage was part of Interplanetary, Washington cared little for its activities. Until the Airlock Accident.

"We wished only to get the required supplies to perform timely maintenance. Instead, Washington split us away from Interplanetary and added oppressive regulations—many bordering on illogical nonsense—accompanied by intrusive regulators. Now, you intend to loot the Bvindu tech you've done nothing to earn. We did everything by the book, including purchasing the land rights and filing salvage claims."

"Mr. O'Donnell, MarsVantage has done *nothing* to earn the technology. Stumbling across it doesn't count," Severino said in a firm tone.

"You have no precedent for such action, and as of today, no law permits such action. Since the Interplanetary split, the media gleefully twisted every unusual or unexpected find into Marsees seeing Martians behind every rock. To the point, we became a punchline."

"Which is why the law will be passed and signed."

Chuck straightened and leaned forward ever so slightly. "Had there been a law on the books, we would not have investigated beyond the Marsium121. There would've been no reward for the risk."

Severino, her eyes wide, leaned in, not toward the camera but to her holo display.

Chuck continued, "While you faced no danger attending cocktail parties dressed in gowns and tuxedos, unconcerned over where your next breath would come from, we took the risks. You rubbed elbows with the rich and famous, laughing it up with the media while we toiled to advance our interests."

Every senator sat stone-faced, focused intently on their holo displays. They must've anticipated Chuck to rail over the unfairness but ultimately knuckle under. *I'll gladly shatter those expectations.*

Chuck purposely looked into his holocam. "As of today, Mars is no longer part of the United States. Earth interests are no longer welcome here. The employees of MarsVantage are now citizens in the Mars Republic."

36 | THE FUTURE BEGINS

Chuck stared at the wall beyond the conference table. He considered Severino's comment *vis-à-vis* finding the technology rather than making the scientific discoveries. She'd exposed the weak part of MarsVantage's case and masterfully glossed over the fact that everyone on Earth had done precisely nothing.

Not that the elites—politicians, staffers, bureaucrats, reporters, entertainers, and hangers-on—cared. They propagated a narrative, and most citizens, distracted with their everyday lives, didn't give matters a second thought. The elites cared for the Marsians only as much as they could derive power and riches. They reasoned that since they held the levers, they were entitled to the Bvindu tech.

But Mars Republic wasn't ceding the Bvindu tech to Washington. That decision would have consequences.

Space Force could use force when they realized the Republic wouldn't roll over. Probably, they would.

Success now depended on Frank and the Committee's preparations. No matter how well done, pain was coming to them all.

From Chuck's datapad, he uploaded the Must-Depart List and the Independence Video to MarsVantage's communication system. He directed both to every MarsVantage datapad. He commanded all emergency screens to display the video message immediately. His last command was to transmit the video to the US State Department and numerous media outlets on Earth, assuming Washington hadn't shut down the comms on the Earth side of the communication wormholes.

A video of Chuck, dressed in a suit, standing in front of his desk played on the screen beside his office door.

* * *

Lorah was investigating AI concepts on her computer when a message from Mr. O'Donnell appeared on her datapad. She played the video.

"MarsVantage employees, neighbors, and friends, the United States government announced its intention to nationalize the Bvindu technology. Government derives its authority from the citizens for their benefit. However, these days, the citizens and their interests are secondary to politicians and bureaucrats' insatiable greed, boundless lust for power, and unquenchable thirst for control.

"Year upon year, they chisel away rights and freedoms to achieve their singular goal. They forget we are not subjects but citizens. Should we acquiesce further, we'll be no better than serfs. Today, I announced that MarsVantage and its employees no longer recognize the authority of the United States. We will provide new guards for our future security and prosperity."

Lorah paused the video. Once Mr. Fordham had pulled back the curtain to reveal Senator Severino's machinations, this moment had become inevitable. Sadly, the poor deceased PAA worker had only accelerated matters. Had Senator Severino considered Mars declaring independence?

She exhaled—the possibility would never have occurred to her. She was the type of person who rose by manipulating the rules. Thinking outside of the box wasn't her strong suit.

Mr. O'Donnell must have a plan. It better be good because Space Force wouldn't stop at threats.

After resuming the video, Mr. O'Donnell continued, "Let me be clear—MarsVantage employees bargained with the Bvindu caretaker for access to his technology and the artifacts within Bvindu Dome. As agreed, we executed our responsibilities, and MarsVantage now administers Bvindu Dome on an ongoing basis. No one on Earth was a party to our treaty.

"MarsVantage followed every Washington law and regulation related to Bvindu Dome. We purchased Full rights, not Exploratory rights, from the Exploration and Mineral Rights Office. Yet, the government intends to enact a law after the fact to take what they had no part in earning, and do so without any compensation. We, the employees of MarsVantage, refuse to sanction this action.

"I understand many have strong ties to Earth. You are, of course, free to leave. Whatever you choose, you will have to live with the decision. If you go, you won't be able to return anytime for the foreseeable future. Likewise, if you stay, Earth will be out of reach.

"Also, I published a list of personnel who must return to Earth. This decision is no reflection on abilities. I endorse every one of you in your next pursuit. However, we must have the personnel to meet the challenges ahead.

"A Space Force destroyer is due to arrive in two weeks. Everyone on the list, plus those who wish to leave, will transfer to that vessel.

"Afterward, the Mars Republic will accept no ships until the US government formally recognizes us as an independent nation. Any spaceship that approaches within half a light-minute will be deemed hostile, confronted, and forced to turn back or be destroyed.

"For those departing Mars, make your preparations. I expect you'll be able to take little with you. For that, I sincerely apologize.

"We are a free people. We are the Mars Republic."

Apparently, Mr. O'Donnell had thought ahead. How he planned on having a Space Force destroyer transport his unwanted employees was an open question. Space Force was tasked with several missions, none of which would include acting like a ferry service. *I really want to see how he pulls that off.*

Lorah looked at the Must-Depart list and unsurprisingly found her name. Her known skill set didn't help MarsVantage with the Earth market closed. Arguing with him would only secure her a bunk on the Space Force destroyer. Frank was the person who could change Mr. O'Donnell's mind.

She grabbed her datapad to arrange a meeting when a message from Ashley appeared.

archs meeting my quarters 1 hr
come sit in

Lorah slumped into the chair. After a long breath, she searched the Must-Depart list again and found none of the archaeologists listed.

Would Gretchen attend the meeting? After a few seconds' consideration, Lorah suspected the answer would be no. The natural meeting spot would be the Planning Huddle Area, yet they were squeezing into Ashley's quarters. Lorah shook her head as her stomach roiled—something was going on with the archaeologists.

37 | AGENDAS REVEALED

Outside Ashley's quarters, Lorah heard an energetic din from within. She thought an argument was in process until laughter erupted. The door slid down to reveal Ashley.

"Lorah, come in. I thought you weren't going to make it."

"Sorry, I'm late." She stepped inside, and the door returned. "I was trying to reach Mr. Fordham but couldn't get past his assistant."

As Ashley led her to the living area, she said, "I suspect there's a whole lot of people unavailable right now."

All of the archaeologists—except Gretchen—sat on the floor in a circle. Ashley took the open spot while Lorah sat on the couch pushed against the wall.

The chatter was really three or four individual discussions. This meeting was more like a cocktail party, though without any drinks.

"Okay, everyone," Ashley said.

The others quieted and gave her their attention.

"I spoke to several of you already. It's clear the Marsees have lost their minds. We're not on the Must-Depart list—they think we're going to continue doing research. That will quickly go by the wayside because everyone will be too busy starving to death. I say we transfer to Mars City, wait for Space Force, and leave this Republic nonsense behind us."

The lack of food was an interesting excuse. Lorah had spent enough time with Mr. O'Donnell to know he hadn't capriciously declared independence. He must've thought through the issue and solved it, probably with Frank's help. Something else was going on. Otherwise, this could've been an email, not a secret meeting.

A young man with a buzz cut, Gino, sat in front of Lorah and raised his hand. "No question, their food production won't support everyone. Dr. Hawthorne gave me reassurances of a soft landing after this project. I can't get hold of him. Returning to Earth with a Marsee taint isn't overly appealing."

That was the most he'd ever said in Lorah's presence. The others grumbled in agreement.

Ashley pushed her palms on the floor. "I've been in regular communication with Dr. Hawthorne since taking this assignment. He's been in contact with the NSM, and a sizeable grant is in the works. We'll double or triple the archaeologists on-site plus receive dedicated resources like tractors and shuttles, including pilots."

Ashley confirmed Lorah's fears. Her request for help accessing the Bvindu database had nothing to do with making the archaeologists' work more efficient or even helping Lorah with Mr. Fordham. Ashley was playing both sides against the middle to advance her own career. *She hid it so well...*

"How will you enter the Master Control Center and understand the Bvindu database?" Lorah asked. Someone would bring it up—it might as well be her.

"Frank and Gretchen exiled the reporter for breaking in," Ashley replied. "I'm sure he'll tell us." She thrust her shoulders back. "Understanding the Bvindu database is simple—we'll go to the cavern and inspect the invitation holo ourselves. I'm certain that we, along with Dr. Hawthorne and the best minds on Earth, will be able to replicate Gretchen's work with a pristine version."

Those on the floor chattered among themselves. Apparently, the archaeologists sided with Dr. Hawthorne in believing Gretchen had altered the recording. Modifying it, though, held a huge professional downside. So much so, it was hard to imagine.

No, the Bvindu messages must be complete—Dr. Hawthorne and his colleagues must've overlooked something. Most likely, Ashley would hit the same wall.

Ashley looked among the archaeologists. "I propose we return to Mars City. Once Space Force takes control of Bvindu Dome—including disabling the damn intruder system—we can return under the auspices of Dr. Hawthorne and the NSM. Then we crack everything Bvindu and return to Earth to lead any project we want. Who's with me?"

Hands darted in the air, even Gino's, though he was last.

"Excellent. Let's get packed. Once we're in Mars City, we can plan out how to work this project properly."

While the archaeologists chatted among themselves, Lorah was torn about convincing Ashley to stay. Her heart urged her to try, but her mind insisted it was a fruitless effort. She recalled her Knowledge Keeper mentor, Seraphina, explaining that facts would never change opinions arrived at by emotion. While that concept was fundamental in determining when someone could be disposed to becoming an Order ally or even a Knowledge Keeper, it could also be applied here.

The truth was Ashley's words and actions proved she was thoroughly entrenched with the elites. The meeting already demonstrated that she valued her place within the corrupt system and the position she could eventually attain. By working with Dr. Hawthorne behind Gretchen's back, she'd proven that she'd compromise any principle to advance.

Lorah's mind won the contest. Her words were for ears ready to hear unpopular truths and minds eager to forge unimagined paths. Unfortunately, that didn't describe Ashley.

After the last archaeologist left, Ashley sat on the couch beside Lorah. Her eyes sparkled with ambition. "I'd like you to stay with us. This is a big job, requiring a massive coordination effort. You're good with logistics—you'll have a couple of assistants, I'm sure."

"Thanks. I'd love to see all the Bvindu's secrets, but I can't."

Ashley recoiled. "You aren't going to join the Marsees, are you?"

"I'm on the Must-Depart list—they don't have any use for me. No, I'm going home. I miss my sister. I can't imagine never seeing her again." Lorah hated to lie, but she wasn't starting an argument where no one could win.

Ashley patted Lorah's hand. "I get that. I'm going to miss you."

"Me, too." Lorah forced a grin. "Perhaps the decision makers will quickly come to their senses and reach an equitable compromise."

"Seems unlikely. Not anytime soon, anyway."

"True." Lorah stood and Ashley mirrored her a moment later. "I wish you the best. Keep me updated on everything you find."

"Thanks, I will."

They hugged, and Lorah left, taking the steps down one floor to her quarters. Once inside, she crawled onto the bed and closed her eyes, breathing evenly. Her best friend on Mars had just revealed that she embraced everything Lorah despised about the States.

Gretchen mustn't be aware of Ashley's collusion with Dr. Hawthorne. If so, Ashley would've been back on Earth already. Gretchen had gotten lucky that she hadn't provided direct access to the Bvindu data. *How'll she react when she finds out?*

Another breath, in and out. Lorah settled on a fundamental truth—some things were out of her control. She sat up and exhaled.

But what she could affect, she would.

She rose and sat in front of her computer to write a report for the Order. They needed to know everything—the archaeologists, Dr. Hawthorne, the National Science Ministry, and MarsVantage's machinations, especially with the Must-Depart list.

Sometime later, her stomach growled. Hours had passed unnoticed—it was time for dinner. She grabbed a Ham and Cheese FieldMeal from the kitchen and returned to her desk, reviewing the update while she ate. After making corrections and amplifications, she connected her Knowledge Keeper datapad and initiated a connection to Earth's data network.

She yawned as it failed. Two more attempts and nothing changed. An error appeared when she vidcommed Mr. Fordham. Even the entertainment channels were offline. Washington must've shut down the comms.

"Looks like my update will have to wait," she muttered to herself.

After hiding the Knowledge Keeper datapad, she picked up her other one and began typing a message to Frank. Before sending it, she had second thoughts.

When she spoke with Frank, she needed to have her wits about her. Revealing she was a Knowledge Keeper would require answers to difficult questions about spying. If she struck the proper tone, she might be able to stay. Otherwise, she was heading back to Earth for sure.

Tomorrow. First thing, when I'm fresh.

She closed her eyes and sighed. Everything was going to Hell. Independence would affect everyone somehow. Those returning to Earth would leave behind friends, and everyone who stayed would forego Earth friends and family. Conceivably, Marsian families could be divided.

Lorah's heart sank.

A lot of people are paying a high price for Senator Severino's greed.

38 | TRUTH GIFT WRAPPED IN PROPAGANDA

With Frank at Gretchen's side, she entered the Master Control Center. She traversed an aisle between processing cabinets while he attended to the keypad code.

She headed toward the back wall, which now held a new set of consoles with Red tending to one of the workstations.

"How's the progress?" she asked.

"We finished setting up the tactical console and three remote cockpits for the drones. When the loyalists leave, we'll install sensor equipment on the plain outside to keep track of the theater of operations. We're using Bvindu comm tech, so Space Force won't detect any transmissions."

Frank caught up. "What'd you find, Red?"

Red directed them to a vidcomm beside the Bvindu command console, opposite the tactical alcove. "Washington shut down the infrared laser receivers on the Earth side of the wormholes. Our transmissions are going nowhere. That's a tough break. However, they still allow us to receive certain broadcasts. We captured this impromptu press conference after the hearing. Politicians are drawn to holocams and microphones like moths to flames, but Senator Severino set a new record."

Red touched a few controls, and the press conference in the Capitol Building Rotunda began with Severino stepping into view.

"Ah, yeah... Hello, everyone. I have nothing prepared, but I'll provide my initial impressions." Severino glanced down, frowned, and exhaled before looking into the camera. "The Marsees are selfish. They refuse to share the benefits that—to be perfectly frank—they lucked into. Without the requisite expertise, they'll never properly utilize the next-level technology for our collective benefit. Without the requisite wisdom, they'll endanger themselves."

Reporters erupted with questions. She pointed off-camera.

A female voice asked, "Can Mars declare independence on a whim? Will you just let them go?"

"Those questions are better asked of the State Department and President Dohbyn. At the very least, there are consequences to such a move. The Marsees import a substantial percentage of food. Without that, I'm afraid they'll starve, and we'll have a humanitarian crisis."

Red pressed a control to stop the playback. "That was prior to the broadcast of Chuck's message. This was a few hours later."

He pressed several controls again. A different recording played this time.

Severino sat in a chair opposite the premier personality of the All News Network, Brock Simons. He smiled, highlighting his perfect teeth and chiseled square chin. "Earlier today, MarsVantage unexpectedly declared its independence from the United States. In our ongoing coverage of the Crisis on Mars, I'm joined by Senator Maura Severino, the Senate Offworld Commerce Committee chairperson and former Mars Economic Improvement Commission member. Welcome, Senator."

She wore a stylish midnight blue pantsuit with a simple white top underneath. Her blonde hair was down, brushing her shoulders. She looked at ease as the most momentous event of a generation unfolded around her. "I'm always glad to visit, Brock, though I wish it were under different circumstances."

"Indeed. The question on everyone's mind is, can MarsVantage sever relations with the United States and claim the entire planet as its own?"

Severino crossed her legs and placed her hands on her topmost leg. "The short answer is no. Florida can't declare itself a sovereign nation, and neither can the Marsees. Claiming an entire planet is without precedent."

"President Dohbyn consulted with you this afternoon. Can you share what his next moves may look like?"

"I attended a classified intelligence briefing with the president and his team. Naturally, I can't divulge specifics, but what I saw has shaken me. Reports suggest the disappearances over the last year or so relate to the Marsees. Approximately four to five thousand men, women, and children are believed to be living and training in a remote part of the globe with the intent of being the Marsees' ground forces here on Earth."

"Children, too? That's unthinkable."

"To you and me, but there are many instances where entire families have disappeared."

"While disturbing, how could five or even ten thousand people take over the whole government?"

The senator pushed a wisp of blonde hair behind her ear. "There's evidence that they may have inside help from people in sensitive government positions. A group of loyal government investigators started new background checks this afternoon. They're working tirelessly around the clock to identify and address any vulnerabilities. It's our highest priority.

"Likewise, physical measures were implemented earlier. Our communication networks no longer accept Mars feeds. There are reports the Marsees have access to advanced Bvindu artificial intelligences. Imagine them training an AI to disable power and communication networks, and then transferring it into our systems. What if they target our ground and air traffic control?"

The close-up of Brock's shocked expression emphasized the point. It might've even been genuine. "What steps are being taken to address the root of this problem?"

Senator Severino uncrossed her legs and leaned ever so slightly toward Brock. "President Dohbyn already has a Space Force destroyer *en route*. Our brave guardians will take custody of the Bvindu data before the Marsees can weaponize it against us."

Red stopped the vid. "Notice how her concerns changed in a matter of hours."

"I noticed recent information that James was privy to made its way to Washington," Frank said, "and the elites connected several data points in astonishing ways."

Gretchen snorted. "How can anyone believe that steaming pile of manure?"

"A flash poll stated that seventy-four percent of all people have a somewhat or very unfavorable view of MarsVantage." Red turned to her. "Note that no one is saying the Mars Republic—it's MarsVantage. That's a subtle shaping of opinion. Regardless, our unfavorables will rise to eighty or eighty-five percent a week from now."

Frank asked, "How'd you get poll results?"

"We can still receive select news broadcast channels. Washington is executing the PsyOps section of their battlefield playbook point by point."

Given Severino's interview and a sycophantic media to perpetuate her paranoia, Space Force would have multiple options upon arrival.

Gretchen asked, "Have we bitten off more than we can chew?"

"Washington's lies are accomplishing exactly what they want." Red pointed between her eyes. "Messing with your head."

"You think Space Force will attempt to take Bvindu Dome by force?"

"Not as an invasion. Not at first," Red reasoned. "Instead, they'll start with a blockade to prevent resupply. Most likely, inbound shipments have already been rerouted back to Earth or the Moon. They'll also interdict shipments between Mars City and here."

"That's one reason we're abandoning Mars City," Frank stated. "I spoke with Welles, one of our best mining supervisors. He should be here the day after tomorrow. He'll dig out our defenses."

Red gave a lone nod of acknowledgment and forged ahead. "We can't accept shipments from Shadow City, either. If SF realizes it's there, we'll be fighting on two fronts."

"So, they can wait us out?" Gretchen asked.

"We have enough water stored for four months of consumption and oxygen production." Frank shoved his hands in his pockets. "We have only ten days' worth of food, though."

"They won't wait us out," Red announced. "It's not Steele's style. She'll force the issue."

Gretchen's stomach tightened. She'd intended to understand the Bvindu civilization and use its technology for MarsVantage's benefit. She wasn't a soldier, yet she and her co-workers would likely have to fight to keep the discovery.

Not only had MarsVantage earned the right to use the technology, but they also had a responsibility to conceal the dangerous portions from those who'd pervert it. *The future could become so messy that there may be no winners.*

Frank said, "We have fifteen days. We're going to make Colonel Steele exercise muscles she rarely uses."

"What are we facing if we don't confound Steele?" Gretchen asked.

For a moment, Red's lips pressed together tightly. "The *Baffin* is equipped with the latest and greatest Strike Phantom Gunships, the G7 version four. It's about the size of Erin's shuttle but more maneuverable. Besides a pilot and co-pilot, it can transport six guardians. It deploys two alternating rapid-fire fifty-millimeter guns capable of producing bursts at just under one hundred rounds per second. It also sports four air-to-air SwiftFire missiles.

"The *Baffin* itself can transport a brigade of about five thousand soldiers. The good news is that my sources tell me only two regiments of guardian ground forces are aboard."

"How many are in a regiment?" Gretchen asked.

"About a thousand."

"What Red and I planned is meant to thwart Space Force by keeping them occupied with other matters," Frank added. "We stay here, safe because we're sitting in the middle of their prize."

"Our goal is to minimize casualties." Red attempted to blunt any misgivings he must believe she held. "We'll bruise Steele's ego, which I'll take great pleasure in, but that's far different from indiscriminately spilling blood. Once that happens, ending the killing becomes difficult. People still slaughter one another over centuries-old grievances, after all. We aim to force SF back to Earth with the loyalists currently living here."

"That's what winning looks like," Frank said. "Afterward, we convince them that Mars isn't worth the trouble."

Space Force's arrival had occupied her thoughts while others had considered factors beyond that. She asked, "How are we going to do that?"

Frank's cheeks reddened. "I haven't quite worked that all out yet."

Hearing this admission was like saying he was going outside without a spacesuit. The Frank she knew *always* had a contingency plan. "Okay... Let's all come up with ideas. I don't want to live in a constant state of war."

"No one does," Red agreed. "My team will monitor Earth's broadcasts. That propaganda will provide insight into their thought process, especially since they constantly need to mold public opinion. Propaganda is a blade without a handle. It cuts the wielder, too. Sometimes worse."

"Good, we'll take all the help we can get," Gretchen said.

"One thing to remember—we know our opponent, and they underestimate us. We have the advantage."

While true, they weren't soldiers, but stating that wouldn't make her feel any better. "What's in this cargo container?"

"We just completed tests on Bvindu comm units," Red replied. "They need to be integrated into all shuttles and tractors. Hank's installing them in the spacesuits that she's already in the process of modifying, and we should be able to get our datapads upgraded before SF arrives."

Gretchen asked, "Hank's modifying spacesuits?"

"The regs specify Mars suits are green." Red frowned. "SF, however, has red, brown, and black camo suits for Mars. Yeah, they've been preparing for years. So, we're applying makeshift camo to ours. I don't want to hand SF any easy targets."

Red's team was addressing the smallest of details. *Perhaps we have decent odds of getting through this mess without deaths.*

Red added, "We'll also modify our vidcomm to receive and decode SF's frequencies."

"Good," Gretchen said. "We're going to need training on all of this equipment."

"When the rest of the Committee arrives two days from now, we'll start. Tomorrow, we'll get shock-tab gun training for those already here."

"Guns? I never fired one." She had held a VLF gun for several minutes when the Interplanetary employee attempted to kill her and Frank. *Not that* that *counts.*

Red said, "In a worst-case scenario, you'll want to defend yourself."

"Excellent," Frank replied. "I'd rather have the gun and not need it than need one and not have it."

39 | UNKNOWN UNKNOWNS

Frank sat in the kitchen area of his Bvindu quarters. After pouring maple syrup on hot pancakes, he took a bite.

A message arrived from Lorah.

we need to talk asap

She was up early. Did she want to cut a deal for Fordham? Remain on Mars? Why had she waited until this morning to talk?

He poured another cup of coffee and took a sip. The day was too young to deal with her without caffeine. He messaged back.

Meet me at the Planning Huddle Area in 15 min

After finishing breakfast, he departed his quarters, took the lift to the first floor, and mounted a cargo mover. When he arrived, he took the nearest seat in the vacant area and reviewed reports on his datapad.

The one he wished to see most was absent. Alan hadn't published an update yet on personnel who'd chosen to return to Earth.

Lorah pulled up faster than necessary. Or safe. She hopped down from her cargo mover. A short march later, she sat directly opposite him. Her datapad was in hand. "Why are you sending me back to Earth?"

"Nothing personal, Lorah." To mask the annoyance of a pointless argument, he put on a pleasant air. "Earth markets no longer exist for us. There's nothing here for Fordham Industries, so there's no need for a liaison. You get to go home. If I remember correctly, you have a sister on Earth. You can visit her."

"And I miss her, too, but I don't make life decisions based on whether I'm close to Ella." She sighed and shook her head, then met his eyes. "The knowledge I keep is true."

Frank's shoulders tensed. *This can't be happening.*

She continued, "I note the lies for what they are. I seek and safeguard knowledge for prosperity, so humanity will never lose its knowledge, its history, or its essence. *I* do so for a time when we'll need it the most."

Frank's heart sank. Somehow, she knew the Knowledge Keepers Oath. On rare occasions, outsiders had learned of the Order, though he'd never encountered it. "Lorah, I don't know what you're talking about."

She tilted her head. "I saw your expression. You recognized the Oath. I'm with the Order, and I know you are, too."

For a moment, he had no response. With everything going on, he was unprepared for another Knowledge Keeper to be hiding in his midst. He recovered the best he could. "The Order *clearly* did not want me to know about you, and they must've directed you not to disclose your affiliation. I'll have *that* conversation with them later."

"Those were my instructions. I was told that certain regents wished to have a more objective evaluation of the Bvindu tech. For the record, I disagreed with them."

Up to now, Frank had shared high-level items with the Order. *They must be dissatisfied.* "Have you seen any of my reports?"

"Yes."

"Why hasn't Fordham pulled out of the agreement?"

She furled her brow. "He was pleased with the cold cure but never pressed for more results. I think he's cut a deal with the Order."

"Interesting. The Order's take is that he wants to swap out unfriendly government bureaucrats and representatives for friendly ones, but not fundamentally change anything."

Lorah's cheeks reddened. "That's my report. Since I wrote it, I've spoken with him quite a bit. I'm convinced that his goal isn't exclusively to advantage himself. Though, like the Order, he's big on manipulating perceptions."

A better phrase would be managing perceptions. The question was, what perception exactly was he managing? *Another topic to discuss with the Order.*

Frank vidcommed Gretchen on his datapad. "I need you in the Planning Huddle Area."

"I'm getting things set up for the personnel transfers. Is it urgent?"

"We have..." Frank looked at Lorah, then added, "...a wrinkle."

40 | WHAT WAS LOST

With Lorah sitting in the freight bed, Gretchen guided the cargo mover to the garage bay airlock and contemplated why the Order had slipped another member among them. That answer was sure to be troubling.

Lorah looked over her shoulder and asked, "You're an Order member, too?"

"Yes."

"How long?"

"A little over two years."

"I only knew about Frank," Lorah admitted.

"The Order should've told all of us a lot more. Or perhaps not sneaked around behind our backs at all."

"I couldn't agree more."

After parking, Gretchen stepped off and stumbled as her vision dimmed. Lorah took her arm, holding her upright. The cargo mover came into focus a couple of seconds later.

Don't fall!

"Are you okay? You look pale."

"Ah, yeah... It's been a busy few days." Gretchen straightened with no dizziness. "Don't tell me you're a doctor, too?"

"I've worked a lot of jobs, but my medical experience ends at applying band-aids. I'll take the first aid course at some point." Lorah touched Gretchen's arm and looked her in the eye. "Seriously, though, you should get examined."

"I already have. I just need to eat consistently and get more rest." Ordinarily, those instructions wouldn't be much of an issue, but these were extraordinary times. At least she took the vitamins the doctor had prescribed.

Please let it go. I don't want to lie, and I don't wish for Little Jelly Bean to distract anyone from the task at hand.

Lorah remained close by as they strolled to and sat behind the ID band table. Gretchen took a swig from a half-full bottle of water.

"That's better." Gretchen raised her left hand and cut her wristband with scissors from the table. "Not that it matters, but the silver insert within the band is similar to what the caretaker's mobile unit contained, so the defense system wouldn't destroy it. Everyone leaving gets their wristband removed. No exceptions. Notice where I cut. On one of three wide silver portions in the transparent band, not the narrow connective pieces."

"What's the difference?"

"The defensive systems read the wide portions. Cutting one disables the whole thing without the possibility of repair." She tossed the used band in a plastic bin under the table.

After grabbing a band strip and the sealer from a small table under the main one, she handed over the sealer to Lorah. Gretchen wrapped the strip with one hand around her left wrist, pulling it snug but not too tight. "Insert each end into the sealer and press the green button."

Lorah did as instructed. A slight odor of burnt plastic emerged.

Gretchen examined the band affixed to her wrist. "Excellent. There's a second sealer under there. We'll get busy in an hour when the first tractor caravan arrives with those remaining with the Republic."

"It'll barely be light. Isn't traveling at night against..."

"The regs? That was yesterday. Literally."

Lorah turned full on to her. "It sounds like you're throwing everything Earth out the window."

"Perhaps I was too flip. Our most experienced drivers are bringing the first group here. They've traveled the route many times, and we also have guidance beacons deployed."

"Still, it's a big change."

"Agreed. Regardless of the regs Earth imposed, living on Mars has always been about managing risks. Right now, our biggest risk is a Space Force invasion."

Ashley arrived, stopped her cargo mover about ten feet away, and stood beside it. Confusion came to her face, but it quickly left.

Gretchen said, "Space Force is fourteen days out. A million things need to be done to face them on a field tilted in our favor. Still, we have time, so go catch up with your friend."

Lorah's expression held sadness and disappointment in ever-changing proportions. "Ash isn't here to see me."

A chill traveled up Gretchen's spine. Ashley's arrival and Lorah's demeanor portended bad news.

"Gretchen, do you have a minute? In private."

Lorah studiously examined the sealer.

Ashley's face betrayed no emotion. With each step Gretchen took, she imagined bad and worse possibilities.

"What's going on?"

Ashley pursed her lips. "I owe it to you to say this in person. I'm not staying on. Neither are any of the archaeologists. None of us want anything to do with a rebellion."

This was the worst possibility of all. Gretchen reached out, but Ashley stepped back. Gretchen allowed her arm to fall to her side. "We're not overthrowing Washington, but we're not allowing their boundless greed to trample over us, either."

"You could've relieved suffering on Earth. Everyone suspects there's more in the medical files than a cure for the common cold. How about the free energy that powers this city? You talk about Washington's greed, yet you act just like them."

"Anything we provide, Washington will use for its own purposes, not for the citizens, and probably *against* us. Is it greed not to hand the hangman the rope for your noose?" *I'm starting to sound like Frank now.*

Ashley stared at Gretchen.

Though a friend, Ashley was thoroughly of Earth in her attitudes and outlook. Her decision wasn't entirely unexpected, but it was disappointing. "Leaving now means never working with Bvindu data again."

"I'll be back once Space Force takes control of Bvindu Dome. Then, I'll be part of a proper expedition, and we'll learn everything. And I'll lead the project."

Had the NSM already reached out to Ashley? Or was it the other way around? Worse, had she been colluding with

Hawthorne all along? That would explain her eagerness to access the Bvindu data directly. In the end, those answers didn't matter.

"The caretaker entrusted Bvindu Dome to Frank and me." Gretchen stood straighter, her shoulders drawing together. "We won't allow it to fall into anyone else's hands."

Ashley planted her hands on her hips. "What are you saying?"

"If we fall, Washington's prize will be ash."

"Unbelievable." Ashley crossed her arms. "You're stubborn enough to destroy the most important find ever rather than let others in. You'll never change. If you would've apologized to Dr. Hawthorne or kept your mouth shut in the first place, you would've never ended up in this backwater place."

To Ashley's credit, she'd never questioned Gretchen's capability or resolve. "It was Hawthorne who didn't respect truth, knowledge, and intellectual honesty. We're standing up for a principle that most have forgotten or forsaken. We want the freedom to determine our future, not one the government assigns us."

Ashley turned away and stepped on the cargo mover.

"Come back in five hours," Gretchen announced. "I'll put you and the other archaeologists in the first tractor caravan returning to Mars City."

As Ashley sped off, Gretchen returned to the table and finished her water in one long gulp.

Lorah asked, "Ashley's still leaving?"

"Yep."

"I thought maybe you'd get through to her. You've known her longer."

"Her belief system has little in common with mine. She can't see beyond what authority shows." Gretchen squeezed Lorah's hand. "You know, it's funny. When I first arrived, Frank and I butted heads because he treated me as a typical Earther like Ashley. Only after I showed him differently did we begin working as partners. The archaeologists, including Ashley, never got that far."

"That's why you held back on direct Bvindu data access," Lorah observed.

"That's a large part of it."

Lorah inhaled and held her breath for a moment. "Your caution paid off. Yesterday, Ashley confirmed that she's been speaking with Dr. Hawthorne on a regular basis. She's planning to lead a fully staffed and equipped expedition under NSM auspices. I'm sorry, Gretchen."

"Don't be. I'd rather know." Gretchen placed her hand on her belly. Little Jellybean would be raised with honesty and integrity as bedrock values. "Have no doubt, if Ashley ever steps foot in Bvindu Dome again, she'll be exploring rubble, but that's not going to happen. What Ashley doesn't know could fill volumes. We *will* confront Space Force and prevail."

41 | VISIONS OF CHAOS

Senator Maura Severino perused the latest Marsee intelligence estimate as she sat before a half-eaten breakfast on a small table in her office. For these unprecedented circumstances, President Dohbyn had authorized her for full access. He wanted a PR win for the mid-term elections to enlarge their party's majorities in both houses and further his agenda.

Front and center was the Marsees' lack of expertise and experience. That deficiency should allow Space Force to secure Bvindu Dome quickly.

Movement out of the corner of her eye was Brielle showing Peter Konklin to the breakfast bar. Although she'd arranged it on short notice, the orange juice was still sweet, the bacon crispy, and the scrambled eggs fluffy. She exited, shutting the door behind her.

"Good morning, Maura." Peter sat opposite her at the table and ate a few forkfuls of fresh eggs.

"Good morning. Chuck surprised me with his testimony yesterday. Did you see it?"

"I planned my day around it." Peter's fork clinked as he rested it on the plate. "I couldn't believe my ears. Initially. Then I wondered about his plan. For instance, how will they engage Space Force?"

Maura took a bite of a bagel, which was fresh and soft, and the cream cheese was even better than usual. "That's exactly why I asked you here today. Do they have access to missiles? For asteroid deflection, perhaps?"

"We never had that capability when Interplanetary administered Mars City. In case of a dangerous asteroid, we would've called upon Space Force." He shifted in the chair. "Ground-to-air missiles are hard to smuggle within legitimate shipments, and we'd know if unannounced ships were docking at the OTP."

He made good points. With Interplanetary erecting a new dome close to Mars City, the construction crews were perfectly positioned to observe Marsee efforts. Peter had undoubtedly ensured his people reported everything.

She asked, "What about guns, small arms, rifles, shoulder-launched weapons?"

"Officially, none. However, Frank Brentford has a shock-tab gun. That comes straight from John Reed looking down its barrel two years ago. I wouldn't be surprised if a few dozen more floated around. Rifles, maybe. Anything more powerful is doubtful because, again, they're harder to smuggle."

As he ate more eggs, she allowed, "That's what I expected. This should be a milk run for Space Force."

He shook his head and swallowed. "Assuming the opponent has less information or is less capable than you is a classic error. O'Donnell is cautious. He's anticipating an attack, and he'll be prepared."

The analysts were awaiting anything she could glean from Peter's experience. So far, their estimates were more guesswork than fact. They deserved a re-read, though. "Facts don't lie. They can't out-gun Space Force. O'Donnell is bluffing."

"You're right in one sense. Space Force can level Bvindu Dome, and I doubt O'Donnell could stop them."

"That doesn't do us any good."

"O'Donnell's counting on that." Peter sipped his orange juice. "He knows you want the tech, and wiping out the people won't play well with the public."

"Our polling indicates strong support for the takeover." She ate the last of her eggs.

Peter rubbed his eyes and flopped his hands into his lap. "I can get a majority to agree to anything. Pollsters specialize in shading the questions to their client's desires. Several of my supervisors, on a *very* informal basis, took the pulse of their workers. The overall sentiment is the government's move against the Marsees is unfair."

"We'll easily sway those people into thinking right." Business people dismissed polling for reasons that equally apply to their precious focus groups and market research, yet they stake millions of dollars on them. Peter's reservations were nothing more than bias.

"There's more at stake here than controlling Bvindu Dome," he offered. "It's a matter of *how* you gain control. How are you going to sell the use of force to the public? They may have a slight distaste for an administrative takeover, but no amount of manipulation will erase civilian deaths."

"We won't have to use force." That was so typical of Peter—a head-on confrontation. The Marsee problem needed finesse. Mars City was designed to be dependent. Space Force could exploit that.

"Then, you're counting on surrender. You can invade Mars City with little resistance. Bvindu Dome is a different matter. The PAA corpse proved that, so you'll have to starve them out. It'll take weeks if not months. That's not going to play well with the voters."

"How'll they know? We disconnected Marsee transmissions. We control the flow of information."

"Maura, stop and breathe, please. The truth has a way of getting out. It may not happen next week, year, or decade. Perhaps it'll happen after you've passed. But it *will* happen, and history will be an unforgiving judge.

"Have you considered O'Donnell may've arranged for food resupply or alternate means of communication? I can't say it enough—how you take Bvindu Dome matters. You don't want to merely get away with it. You want to project the bearing of a statesperson. That's an accomplishment that you can ride into the Oval Office."

Good point. Giving the appearance of serving the public—*saving* the public—was the fuel she needed. "Peter, thank you. Let me ponder that further."

Peter exhaled. "Good. The only way I get MarsVantage back is for Space Force to prevail with good PR, which brings me to another point. My intuition is screaming that we fell into a trap."

"A trap? The inspectors and auditors verified the Marsees haven't created any weapons. They only have a fleet of unarmed shuttles and one unarmed Bvindu spaceship. The fools don't even want to fly it. Our reporter friend confirmed that. Once Space Force arrives, they'll have tactical control of Mars."

After a sip, Peter gently set his orange juice on the table. "I read the same reports. The top people in MarsVantage were Interplanetary employees before the split. We only hire bright and creative people."

"What's your point?"

"O'Donnell likely had answers to the food and defense issues long before his testimony."

"He assumes Space Force is little more than an autobus eager to ferry unwanted people back to Earth." She took a large gulp of orange juice. "That's O'Donnell's fantasyland."

Peter leaned in. "My team's analysis indicates at least twenty-five percent of the Marsees will return to Earth, perhaps as many as half. When Interplanetary was in charge, some looked at a Mars City position as a short-term stepping stone to return to Earth with a sizable bank account and better position. After the split, no one on Earth would hire them. O'Donnell's rebellion is a golden opportunity for these people to leave with public sympathy. He has a plan to get them off Mars. If for no other reason than concerns over sabotage."

"Good. Fewer rebels for Space Force to deal with."

His eyes widened. "Mars needs a certain amount of genetic diversity, skill diversity, and skill depth, or their fledgling republic will fail. Baulnsville died because of a single accident. O'Donnell figured this out already. I know him—you can count on it."

One of the briefing papers had mentioned viability. Over the centuries, several variations of the viability rule had been proposed. The administration's analysts cited the one-thousand/ten-thousand version. Under one thousand people, short-term viability was jeopardized. The ten-thousand number suggested a minimum for genetic diversity to avoid inbreeding and loss of people and associated skills due to accidents and old age. Once O'Donnell sheds the unwanted employees, he would still be above the short-term number.

"I'm not concerned about fifty years from now."

Peter leaned back. "Neither is Dohbyn or Space Force, and that's my greater point. O'Donnell and his radicals have considered all of these issues—more, I bet—*and* they have a plan. I guarantee they *know* how to achieve it, and it won't simply be a matter of having babies. They *know* how to defend two locations. My biggest piece of advice is to determine what O'Donnell already knows before you find yourself boxed into a corner."

"Do you really believe the Marsees can outwit Earth's best minds?"

Peter folded his hands in his lap. "Earth's best minds never spent one day living under the conditions Marsees think of as normal. That practical experience is more valuable than every advanced degree of your brain trust."

42 | BEHIND THE SCENES

Erin parked beside another cargo mover outside the Master Control Center. At the entryway, she played the tones Gretchen had provided, and the door sank a moment later. She stepped inside and entered the code on the nearby keypad.

Frank stood facing the back wall near several Earth-made consoles, which seemed to multiply every time she visited.

She joined him. "Hey, do you have a minute?"

He faced her. "Ah, sure. I can always come back to this."

"I didn't want to put my concern in a message or on comms. I took my shuttle's fuel cells for recharge and found Lorah overseeing the process. Wasn't she on the Must-Depart list?"

"And you asked her how she managed to stay."

"You know me so well. She said you saw the benefit of her presence."

"And she didn't elaborate."

"No. She's hiding something."

"Everyone is," Frank observed offhandedly.

Erin stiffened her spine to look up into Frank's eyes. "That's not an answer. What's going on?"

He stepped closer. "She's a Knowledge Keeper, and neither Gretchen nor I knew until she approached me this morning."

"I thought you had some sort of secret handshake, so you didn't have these misunderstandings."

"Well..." He brought his hands up near his head and let them fall to his side. "The Order apparently wanted an outsider's perspective. The irony is that she wasn't reporting anything different than Gretchen and I were."

"I hope you're holding back how the Bvindu live so long. The more who know, the greater the chance of disaster."

"Only the Committee knows, and that's the way it's staying—Lorah doesn't get that data."

"Why have her stay on then?" Erin asked. "She was spying on us."

"My issue is with the Order's regents, not Lorah. She did exactly what Knowledge Keepers do—observe and report. Had she broken in here, she'd be sitting beside James in Mars City, Knowledge Keeper or not. But with Shadow City holding Order members and allies, what's one more?"

"That's a good point."

Frank exhaled. "Before you ask, I'm running all Order matters on the up-and-up. Lorah knows that Gretchen's a Knowledge Keeper. You never came up, however, so she doesn't know you're an ally yet. And she still knows nothing about the Committee."

"I'll keep my mouth shut." Erin shoved her hands into her coverall pockets. "It's like the Order doesn't trust you."

"I *know*." He pointed to his head with both hands. "Isn't this the most trustworthy face ever?"

She rolled her eyes. "The ducking and dodging only works for so long. I can see why you allowed her to stay on. The question is, what's motivating the Order? Why did they spy on us when they're prepping for societal collapse?"

"That's one of many questions I sent via remora. We can get by without the Order, but I'd prefer receiving their food shipments until our farming gets up to speed. The more Knowledge Keepers and allies going to Shadow City, the better off we'll be long term. The Order's answers will determine our level of cooperation."

His explanation raised fresh concerns. "I don't have a problem with Lorah's presence—she's an asset. I hope you have a plan if the Order squirrels on us."

"Planning *is* what I bring to the table. We have some options, like approaching Fordham for help. I'd hate to have to trade tech, though. We're better positioned with the Order at our side."

Concern crossed her face. "With a Space Force destroyer on the way, this isn't the time to worry about our allies."

43 | Divergent Engineering

With the archaeologists gone, Frank had repurposed the Planning Huddle Area for Bvindu Dome's defense. He sat at the main table and grabbed a stylus. After pressing his hand to the surface to wake its touchboard, he opened a new document and drew a large oval, representing Bvindu Dome. He etched five tiny circles within. He made four Xs randomly on the dome and sketched a ring around everything.

This part of the defense plan, based on Red's suggestions, was ready. The completed work could mean the difference between victory and defeat. Frank would enthusiastically applaud if these measures were unnecessary, but an uneasy sensation in his gut suggested otherwise.

"Hi, Frank." Welles Decker, dressed in standard steel blue coveralls, strolled past several tables and chairs.

Frank stood. "Tell me some good news."

"My mining crew discussed the situation, and to a person, all want to stay with the Republic."

Frank smiled and shook Welles' hand. "That's good news." He pointed to the chair to his right, and they took their seats. "We have less than two weeks to prepare our defenses."

"How can we help?"

Frank waved his hand over the drawing. "I need these circles excavated. You'll find a half sphere about your height ten or twelve feet down on the dome. Dig out a thirty-five-yard diameter hole around each. More if you can manage it."

"What are they?"

"Protective enclosures for the Bvindu Asteroid Deflection System emitters."

Welles laughed. "Asteroid deflection. With a patented Brentford alternative use."

"Those four Xs are nothing, but plow them out just the same. I want the deflection system to look more involved. I'll provide dummy emitter enclosures." *Marsians can do PsyOps, too.*

"Got it." Welles examined the drawing closely. "What's this circle around everything?"

"We need a trench around the dome, no farther than a quarter mile from its edge."

"How wide and deep?"

"Ten to fifteen feet deep. No narrower than ten feet wide. The trench should be irregular—vary the depth and the width. I don't want Space Force driving up to our airlocks. Place the excavated sand on the dome side, but leave these lanes open." Frank marked swaths on the diagram. "Make the trench as wide as possible here."

Welles frowned. "That's a huge job without much time to do it."

"Eight more mining crews will arrive over the next couple of days. You're in charge. I'm not after pretty, and nothing has to be structurally sound."

Welles' expression changed, but it wasn't quite a smile. He tapped a finger against the planning table's side. "I suppose it's doable. I'll get my crew on one of the deflectors today. I need precise locations—we don't have time to play find-the-emitter."

"No problem. I'll send you this map with coordinates."

"Perfect. Once the emitters are excavated, we'll dredge the trench. Your decoys, the Xs, will be last."

"Agreed."

Welles scratched his chin. "This equipment must be ancient. It's buried, so you mustn't have tested it. When it's all said and done, do you think the system will work?"

"Clamshell enclosures protected the actual emitters. Diagnostics indicate all is well. Anyway, I don't want to tip our hand. Folks in Mars City could see a test and blab to Space Force. Severino's office has a conduit to the reporter." Frank ran his hand through his hair. "We have one more need. Our three excavated hatches— the Main Airlock, Raw Materials Entrance, and Waste Materials Exit—need their approaches turned into mazes. When you're done, all your equipment must be stored in the Raw Materials

Entrance and Waste Materials Exit. Anything left outside will become a target."

"No problem. We'll pile mounds of sand and blast some craters. Anyone coming faster than a cyclist in first gear would be foolhardy." After pushing away from the table, Welles angled his chair toward Frank. "What do you think of the media broadcasts?"

Frank swept the air with his hand. "The aggressive AIs are a fantasy."

"Earthers always loved the idea. Something else doing the work, so they don't have to. Twisting them against us was the next logical step."

"Pure propaganda. I haven't had much time and less stomach for their version of news these past few days."

"You missed it." Welles leaned in. "We are now biological warfare terrorists. Allegedly, we can develop and release a fatal disease, then hold everyone hostage, forcing them to buy the treatment from us."

A colossal lie wrapped around a kernel of truth—the cold cure. It was an excellent tactic, as fear was a powerful motivator and an even more efficient tool for manipulation. "It's all stage dressing for the public."

"Get me the map as soon as you can. We can start digging in an hour once my team eats and washes up."

"Will do."

Welles stood. "By the way, I'll send you contact info for my brother, Xavier, in the Belt."

"What's he working on there?"

"Mining survey. His company, a smaller one, is finally taking some initiative. Six months ago, they brought in a new CEO who's shaking things up."

"He wants to come to Mars?"

Welles shook his head. "You have more friends on Earth than I do, and I lived there until graduating college."

"And I've never so much as visited."

Welles flashed a full set of teeth. "I bet you'd love to chat with someone, perhaps someone on the inside or in the know. Create a message—encrypt it if you like—and send it to Xavier with delivery instructions. He'll pass along any reply he gets. No questions asked."

Welles was a stand-up guy, a bright and hard worker who'd proven himself multiple times. If he trusted his brother, then Frank could too. This way, Frank wouldn't have to endanger one of the satellite remoras to request a response from the Order about his Lorah inquiry. "That's generous, Welles. There *is* a message I'd like to send."

44 | Waiting at the Abyss

Frank sat in the kitchen of his quarters, elbows on the table, pondering upcoming events. The Asteroid Deflection System's sensors on Phobos and Deimos had confirmed the *USSF Baffin's* approach for the twelfth consecutive day. It would attain orbit the next day shortly after local sunrise. Then, who knew what would happen?

His datapad chimed, and he glanced at its screen. "Hon, Lorah's here."

"Got it."

A few seconds later, Gretchen and Lorah joined him around the table.

He pasted a smile on his face. "Gretchen and I have to meet Red soon, but I wanted to discuss the Order situation first. They finally responded to my inquiry after three reminders."

Lorah narrowed her eyes and knotted her arms over her chest. "About time."

He closed his datapad screen. "Your assignment was at the request of a significant minority of the regents. Its purpose was to judge the suitability of creating a society here while abandoning the United States."

Gretchen and Lorah spoke over one another, condemning the idea with words like cowardly, betrayal, and cold-hearted. They pointed out the utter chaos that would befall the people. Food would become the most pressing issue. Without the government resetting everyone's allocations monthly, deliveries would stop. Before they allowed themselves to starve, they'd loot food depositories and eventually riot.

When his fellow Knowledge Keepers quieted, he continued, "All that and more will happen when the government collapses.

We all heard about the water drugging experiment a few years back."

"Yeah," Lorah piped in. "It resulted in docile people unable to produce an ounce of work."

Frank sighed. "The government tried a different tactic by experimenting with brainwave modification, boosting certain behaviors, and interfering with carrying out unwanted practices. The Order took active steps to sabotage the pilot project."

"What does Washington want?" Gretchen asked. "Mindless drones?"

"A populous eager for direction from their betters," Lorah provided. "Public schooling no longer educates students to think critically. Instead, they're indoctrinated in the latest fashionable views. People are set up for compliance from the get-go."

Frank exhaled and looked Lorah in the eyes. "Regardless of recent government programs, the people are already followers and have been for centuries. The Order is undergoing an internal struggle. Some wish to thwart the government's ambitions, while others want to wash their hands of the entire mess and start again elsewhere. Right now, the interventionists are winning."

Lorah leaned back. "This explains why they're missing so much of the government's Mars ploy—they're too busy arguing among themselves. Regardless, I didn't join the Order to abandon hundreds of millions of people."

Gretchen looked at her. "Exactly."

"The Order's response was clear," Frank stated. "There will be no abandonment of their primary mission. However, they're broadening their range of actions. That includes investing more in Shadow City."

"Shadow City?" Lorah asked. "What's that?"

He explained how the Order had been sending people and resources to a buried city on the other side of Mars.

Lorah smacked the table. "That explains the missing people reports on the news lately."

"They're farming and doing manufacturing," Gretchen said, "not training to be a ground force to take over Washington."

"Back to the issue at hand." Frank redirected the conversation, preferring not to complain about what had already passed. "The

Order is currently searching for extreme government programs like the water drugging or the brainwave modification initiatives."

Gretchen said, "Nothing's in the Knowledge Keeper database about this."

"My reply covered that. Not only did I insist that this data tranche be made available to us, but I also insisted that Lorah's reports be opened to us." The weight on Frank's shoulders lifted slightly.

Lorah frowned. "You'll be disappointed. You know what I have access to. It isn't like I hacked anything."

Gretchen chuckled.

Frank acknowledged, "It's the principle. I also suggested that they consider how Mars resources could assist in a post-crash scenario, given a travel time of seconds instead of weeks and assuming we're well into self-sufficiency."

Lorah's eyes grew wide. "Mr. Fordham was right—you *are* hoarding Bvindu tech."

"Of course," Gretchen confirmed. "There's no way we're giving FTL tech to Washington. That'd be tantamount to handing it to Space Force to appear on our doorstep without warning."

"Once we get comms back, I'll send a message of my own. I should've been told what my efforts were supporting. And the Order should've been on top of Washington's moves against Mars instead of pursuing distractions." Lorah leaned toward Frank. "How *did* you get this message, anyway?"

He explained and offered to send Lorah's communique, which she accepted. He shifted in the chair, though his new position was as uncomfortable as his old. "As part of my inquiry, I posed two distinct questions and learned something that you'll find particularly interesting, Lorah."

"How so?"

"I asked how Shadow City is being supplied and what Fordham's overall strategy regarding the Bvindu is." *I got a surprising response—that's for sure.* "The answers are intertwined—Fordham transports are supplying Shadow City."

Lorah straightened in the chair. "Unbelievable! He's enduring a lot of upfront expense with no payback. What *does* he get?"

"Goodwill and, more importantly, a large say in post-collapse affairs." Frank placed both hands on the table on either side of his datapad.

"There it is." Recognition was painted across Lorah's face. "It all makes sense now."

Gretchen observed, "He's taking the long view."

"Given all of this, I suspect he isn't waiting for the government to collapse." Lorah sat back. "I bet he's helping it along."

"A destroy the country to save the country approach?" Frank laughed.

Lorah shrugged. "In the long run, everyone's better off. Before that, a lot of pain and suffering,"

Gretchen said, "The Order steps in to help the people, and he has a seat at the table in how things run going forward. It's all wrapped up in a nice, neat bow."

"And under my nose, no less." Lorah shook her head. "Regardless, Mr. Fordham won't send transports while Space Force is in orbit. How will he and the Order get supplies to us afterward? Surely, Washington will watch us closely and take regulatory, if not legal, action if his transports visit."

Frank shifted in the chair. "We said no Earth ships are welcome, and that remains unchanged. Yet, Order personnel will still want to join us, and we'll still want foodstuffs and other items... at least for a time. I'll suggest that Fordham begin a mining effort in the Belt. Our new scout ship can dock nearby with his ships, transfer people and cargo, and return. Give us some time, and we'll have more scout ships and pilots, too."

"Hell," Gretchen said with a disgusted look on her face, "Congress will probably subsidize his efforts since Mars ores won't be Earthbound anymore."

That insight was so annoying that she was probably correct. Frank ran his palm down his chin.

"You could also arrange with Mr. Fordham to transfer supplies at his orbital repair facility. He could send ships loaded with supplies for repairs." Lorah made air quotes around the word repairs. "Your ship transfers the supplies and comes back. Mr. Fordham's ship returns to service a day or two later."

"That's not bad, Lorah. Another means of resupply is prudent." Frank looked at his datapad. "Gretchen and I need to get to the Master Control Center."

They all departed the apartment, took the lift to the atrium, and Lorah bid them goodbye.

Once outside, Gretchen glanced over her shoulder toward the darkened area where the archaeologists had worked two weeks earlier. "After all this time, I can't believe we're still fighting to keep what we earned."

Frank took her hand and strolled toward the Master Control Center. "Hon, we either fight or surrender."

"It's not fair that we have to choose."

"The universe doesn't run on fairness. Everything about this is a shame. We lost good, experienced people."

Gretchen rubbed her eyes. "Everyone has their reasons for leaving. Some because we're forcing them. Others to embrace family and friends. And some, sadly, because of a lack of courage to live without the approval and validation from those in charge."

"Hon," Frank said, "We face a slew of unknowns, but I know two things. This fight won't be easy, and what we're fighting for is worth it."

45 | THE MARS REPUBLIC FIRST ARMY IRREGULARS

F rank entered the Planning Huddle Area with Gretchen at his side. Any peace of mind from resolving the Order situation was surely about to evaporate. He looked forward, not to Space Force's arrival, but to their departure.

They headed to empty chairs beside the other Committee members at the planning table, facing Red's team. Frank settled into the leftmost open seat, with Gretchen taking the one to his right.

"Space Force arrives tomorrow," Chuck announced. "Their goal is to stand in this spot. In the days ahead, we need Frank, Gretchen, and Red to lead us through the upcoming encounter. The rest of the Committee, including me, will fill in where needed. We can enlist more people as required."

Words caught in Frank's throat. With everything else occupying his attention, he'd never thought about who would give orders.

Red withdrew a large coin from his coveralls pocket and tossed it on the tabletop. When it hit, it produced a discordant clang.

The other four Space Force retirees did the same. Each coin was the same size but slightly different.

"Tradition, dating back centuries, dictates that soldiers carry their unit's challenge coin. If another soldier challenges and the coin isn't produced, the challengee must buy the challenger a drink." Red pointed to Hank.

She turned around and, a moment later, produced a wooden box about the size of one of Chuck's hardcover books. She passed it to Red.

He slid off the top, which produced a scraping sound, and pulled a coin from it. "*This* is our unit coin. We cast them in

Shadow City in anticipation of this day. Welcome to the Mars Republic First Army Irregulars. Take one and pass along the box."

He handed it over. In turn, each retired Space Force guardian took a coin. The box found its way to Chuck. He hesitated a moment before selecting his coin. It passed through Alan, June, Erin, and Gretchen's hands, finally reaching Frank.

He pulled the last coin. One side was engraved with 'Mars Republic First Army Irregulars' atop Mars, Phobos, and Deimos. The obverse displayed the Gadsden flag.

"Until you decide on a flag," Red related, "we'll use one my distant ancestor created. The words at the bottom—*'Don't Tread on Me'*—espouse the ideal we uphold."

After setting aside the empty box, Frank pocketed his coin as everyone else had. "Red, thank you. I appreciate you including us civies in the tradition."

"Once Space Force arrives tomorrow, no one'll be a civie. We fight side-by-side until we achieve victory... or until the last of us falls."

In unison, the four Space Force retirees said, "Damn right, Master Sergeant!"

Red gave a swift nod. "Hank, next item."

After standing, she lifted off the top of a cargo container and withdrew shock-tab guns. "Pass them down."

"Why are we getting weapons?" Gretchen asked. "The dome's defensive systems have proven themselves."

Red cast his gaze in her direction. "Space Force is capable of battering through the airlock with a ground transport and driving to the Master Control Center's doorway. Maybe the Bvindu security measures will stop it, maybe not. Ultimately, I'd rather have a weapon just in case."

Frank leaned forward and cinched the gun belt with two additional magazines around his waist like everyone else. Except for Gretchen. She laid her weapon on the table and placed her hands on her lap.

Red said, "A quick review. There are two safeties—one on the rear of the grip and another on the trigger. Each mag holds ten shock-tabs. If you're in a clash and need to reload, eject the mag and slam in a fresh one. Do it hard. Don't worry about the empty mag—let it fall. Lastly, please remember each shock-tab round extends its contacts when enough pressure is applied to the tip. *Don't* touch the tip."

Frank appreciated the reminder of their training session a couple of weeks ago. Rizzo had ably demonstrated activating a shock-tab. His seizure was still vivid. Afterward, he treated four nasty puncture marks as he'd noted the rounds were designed to penetrate clothes, spacesuits, and even air vests, though they only shorted them out.

"Thanks," Frank said. "Is there anything else?"

"One more item. Tomorrow, you and Erin will fly to Power Generator Three as Space Force makes orbit."

"Yes, the timing must be just so."

"It's a dangerous mission," Red pointed out, "since SF's intentions are unknown, and I'm assuming the worst. I recommend Baker flies, and I perform the extravehicular activities."

As Frank opened his mouth to object, Erin blurted out, "No one flies my shuttles but my team. I'm flying, and that's not negotiable. No offense, Baker."

She crossed her arms and leaned back in her chair. The hardness of her features dared anyone to argue.

Frank explained, "I need to handle the extravehicular activities, as you put it. They require some specialized expertise. Besides, if events go south, we'll need you and your team right here bailing us out."

Red looked around the table. No one raised an argument. "Very good. Hank, the last item."

Like a magician, she produced a pole from the floor and unfurled a Gadsden flag, showing a curled snake above the phrase "Don't Tread on Me" on a field of yellow.

"Hank, erect that outside the airlock." Red looked around the table as she departed. "We can use help organizing supplies. Meet me in the goods warehouse in fifteen. Thanks."

The others filed out except Gretchen, who stared at the shock-tab gun on the planning table.

Frank asked, "What's going on?"

She mumbled, "Nothing."

"Hey." He took her hand. "Share. What's on your mind?"

She pointed to her gun laying on the table in front of her. "*That* is the result of my relentless pursuit of knowledge. Everything I've done has led us here. Space Force arrives tomorrow. Red expects a fight, and I can't wrap my arms around it."

"None of us are to blame—the greedy political elite are pulling all of the strings. We're doing everything possible to avoid a confrontation, but if we must fight, then we'll fight to win."

46 | SCYLLA AND CHARYBDIS

Frank leaned on a shovel in a waist-deep crater-like hole to catch his breath. Sweat pooled at all of his spacesuit's joints. The rapid pulsing of the thermal fluid running through minute tubing in the suit regulated his body temperature. He was uncomfortable but not dangerously overheated.

The western range of the Maelstrom Mountains towered over him while the brightest stars rapidly dimmed in the nascent dawn. Time was running short.

About twenty minutes earlier, Erin had landed the shuttle half a mile away, where he'd slashed the cable connecting Bvindu Power Generator Three to Mars City. The seven domes' limited energy reserve would've activated immediately, enough to keep essential services running for a few days. Concern must be running through the loyalists living there. Soon, alarm would undoubtedly overtake them.

Afterward, Erin had flown them here, near the cave where Gretchen had originally deciphered the Bvindu symbols etched into a stone door. Behind that was the electricity-producing cavern filled with Marsium121 and water.

He'd severed the cable where it emerged from the ground near the cave and dug a couple of feet around the stub in the glare of a portable light until exposing the standard connector. Meanwhile, Erin reeled in a half-mile section of line into the shuttle's cargo bay.

"Hey, Frank. I'm full," Erin announced.

"Start up the third spool."

"We've got enough cable to thwart Space Force from quickly reconnecting the power. Once you quit leaning on the shovel like a supervisor and use it like a worker, we can get out of here before the *Baffin* docks with the OTP."

The spacesuit's control panel indicated he was using air ten percent faster than usual. At this rate, he had about eight and a half hours left. His power consumption was up twenty-five percent to handle cooling. He'd finish long before needing to swap for a fully charged air vest, though.

After tossing the shovel aside, he pushed sand away by hand from the connector and disconnected the arm span's length of cable, which he threw in the general direction of Erin. The empty socket lay there with sand seeping into its opening.

He grabbed the hole's edge and swung his leg up. The lip gave way, and his leg didn't reach ground level.

Erin said, "Sitting behind a desk is making you old."

For his second attempt, he pulled himself out by digging his left foot into the hole's side and flipping his right onto level ground. "Where's this desk you speak of?"

She laughed. "Face it. You lost a step since you quit crawling around conduits every day."

As he stood, he checked his control panel for suit integrity. "Are you gonna tell me I'm fat next?"

"You *have* put on a few pounds."

"Terrific."

A few paces away, a portable mixer rotated, thoroughly combining the nanoconcrete ingredients. The recipe had been used for centuries to build solid, durable structures on and off Earth, though those features weren't his concern today.

He switched the machine off and lugged the mixing drum to the hole's edge. Because Erin hadn't commented, she must've missed his awkward, uncoordinated lurch. He poured out the thick paste, irreparably fouling the empty connector socket.

When the drum emptied, the hole was nearly filled. He shoveled sand on top of the wet mixture. It wouldn't cure properly, but it'd be a pain to get to the now-useless connector.

Over the Bvindu comm, Red announced, "*Move out. SF is about ten minutes from the OTP.*"

"Got it," Frank said. "Is Chuck there?"

"*Right beside me. He's on his third coffee.*"

"He's up." Once Chuck sent the command, Frank's airlock programming change would be scheduled for immediate installation and execution.

"*Wilco. Wait one.*"

Frank turned off the portable light and brought it along with the shovel to the shuttle's cargo bay. On his second trip, he returned the mixer. "Halfway is good enough, Erin."

She stopped the spool's motor and squeezed the shears against the cable, allowing one end to fall to the ground and the other to smack soundlessly against the cargo deck. She retracted the ramp, closed the cargo bay hatch, and pressurized the shuttle.

Over the standard broadcast frequency, Chuck announced, "*Mars City is declaring an emergency. They lost main power and are running on emergency reserve. The airlocks have activated to the open position on six domes. Safeties failed. They're losing atmo and need assistance.*"

"It's going to get worse," Frank mumbled to himself.

As the garage bay hatches and emergency bulkheads had no manual override, the loyalists were sealing into spacesuits. Shortly, they'd transit through personnel airlocks and emergency hatches, which had manual overrides, to Dome 2.

An hour from now, Dome 2 would experience the same failure. At that point, the emergency would become a disaster. Unable to repair the problem, Space Force would have no choice but to evacuate all of the Mars City loyalists.

He followed Erin to the cockpit, taking his seat to her right. She shoved her gloves into her helmet and placed them in the netting on Frank's seatback. He did likewise to her seatback. After donning their headsets, she lifted off, heading for the eastern range of the Maelstrom Mountains.

"*Mars City, this is Colonel Elita Steele aboard the* USSF Baffin. *We'll dock with the OTP in minutes. However, assistance is on its way now.*"

On Bvindu comms, Red said, "*Heads up! SF deployed three gunships and a lander. Trajectory analysis indicates they're heading to Mars City. Wait one... A ship's breaking off.*"

"Where to, Red?" Erin asked.

"*Damn. It's a gunship on an intercept course.*"

"Can we make it to Bvindu Dome?" Erin asked.

"*Negative. The G7v4s are faster and more maneuverable than your shuttle. Intercept point is the eastern Maelstrom Mountain range.*"

"Acknowledged," Erin said evenly as she placed the Bvindu comm into monitor mode. She pulled back on the cyclic and applied full power with the collective. "We botched the timing."

"I never expected a launch *before* docking. My mistake."

Her easy-going demeanor, filled with friendly banter, became coolly professional. All her efforts were squarely focused on flying.

"How screwed are we?" Frank asked.

"On a scale of one to ten... eleven if we get boxed in between the ranges."

"*By order of President Dohbyn,*" came an announcement over standard comms, "*Mars is under martial law. All vehicular operations will halt immediately. Flights will land immediately. Report location and SF will transport you to Mars City.*"

Erin pushed the collective that was already at maximum.

Washington was covered legally by declaring martial law and issuing stand-down orders. *Not a surprising development.* The question was, how would Space Force react to defiance?

"*Mars City holds no rebels,*" an unfamiliar voice said. "*The traitors are in Bvindu Dome, and they sabotaged us. Mars City is unlivable. We need immediate evacuation.*"

Erin glanced Frank's way with a questioning look.

"Our former co-workers just did us a favor."

She scowled. "It doesn't feel like much of a favor."

"While Chuck's announcement could be ignored as propaganda, *their* declaration of an emergency ties Steele's hands via Stellar Law. Now she *must* render assistance. That means fewer resources can be devoted to us, especially in the short term."

Erin adjusted course toward a mountain peak. "Vessels must render assistance to anyone in need and not engaged in hostilities."

"Exactly. Someone in Mars City explicitly stated it held no rebels. Steele's trapped."

Erin soared past a jagged red-brown mountaintop, close enough to reach out and touch. Before them, in the distance, lay

Bvindu Dome, mostly buried. Welles and the miners had created fresh scars in the landscape. All five Asteroid Defense System emitters had been revealed, and the trench looked as imposing as he'd imagined. Several maintenance engineers lent the miners a hand to create six decoy emitters.

And none of that can change the fact they couldn't outrun the gunship.

"This is Captain Dennis 'Ghost' Casper. Rebel shuttle, you are ordered to land and be boarded."

"Ignore them," Frank ordered.

Erin pointed to her display. "They're nearly on top of us."

"And they're not firing. We're in good shape."

Red said, *"SF hasn't launched fighters or another gunship. They don't want to destroy an unarmed shuttle outright."*

Frank had heard better news, but he'd take what he could get.

The stern of the gunship descended into view at the top of the cockpit window.

"Rebel shuttle, I repeat, you are ordered to land and be boarded."

Erin reduced power and violently pushed the cyclic forward, sending the shuttle into a dive and Frank's stomach into his throat. After a heartbeat, she banked to starboard with a hard tug on the cyclic. "I'd hate to see what bad shape looks like. Take your motion sickness pills now. This ride's only going to get rougher."

We just needed five more minutes... Frank tore open a foil pill packet with his teeth that he'd snatched from his left sleeve pocket. He dry-swallowed the two small pills from within and stuffed the used packet back in the pocket. *Erin doesn't take kindly to litter.*

Meanwhile, Erin flipped the Bvindu comm switch. "Red, that crazy Space Force pilot almost rammed us."

"Standard combat maneuver. Our tac display says you lost three hundred feet. Still no reinforcements."

She applied power and pulled up. "They're not grounding me that easily."

"Gaining altitude is—"

Iridescent green tracers blazed past the port side of the cockpit as she banked to starboard.

Erin exclaimed, "Shit!"

"—*exactly what they want you to do.*"

Frank relayed, "Now they're firing on us."

"*And you evaded toward the mountains. SF's setting up a Scylla and Charybdis scenario.*"

"Speak English, dammit!" Erin exclaimed.

"*It's a no-win situation. They force you to the ground or fly you into the mountain. You either comply, or the crash will be written off as pilot error.*"

The gunship fired again. Tracers raced past overhead.

"Huh." She pushed the shuttle into a dive while doing half-rolls and throttling back. Instead of the mountain growing larger, it was the ground. "I don't care for either of those options."

She pulled out, now flying low and parallel to the mountain. Bullet impacts beside and in front of them produced dust plumes.

"*The gunship's maneuvering to your six.*"

Erin violently banked to starboard and applied more power by pushing the collective forward as far as it would go. Frank's seat harness dug in. However, his stomach felt as if it had left the cockpit.

"Don't barf on my ship."

At least she believes we're going to get out of this... He was about to say that was the least of their problems when she banked just as violently to port.

Captain Casper said, "*No more games. This is a no-fly zone by order of Space Force. Land, or we'll shoot you down.*"

Erin continued the banking, increasing and reducing speed randomly. Bullets landed more off-target against the nearby mountain. At least they weren't missiles. Space Force mustn't want the PR disaster that would accompany the obliteration of an unarmed shuttle.

"Hold on tight," Erin commanded.

She pulled back on the cyclic, sending the shuttle straight up. Then, she performed a half loop and rolled the shuttle upright.

A moment later, she dove toward a mountain peak, banking away at the last moment.

As red and black filled the cockpit, she flicked on standard comms. "Ghost, time to dance to my tune. Care to do a little mountain hopping?"

47 | END OF AN ERA

Gretchen stared at the tactical display. Her worst nightmare was unfolding in painfully slow motion.

Other Committee members huddled around. Red had ordered Rodriguez and Baker to the drone consoles but to remain grounded as drones were ineffective against a gunship.

The shuttle buzzed so close to the mountain peaks that they frequently merged on the display.

"Damn. They're not following. We're taking fire," Erin said over Bvindu comms. On Earth comms, she rebuked, *"I thought you military hotshots would be up to a little flying challenge. Firing guns isn't much of a skill."*

Whatever Erin's plan, Captain Casper wasn't taking the bait. The Space Force gunboat maneuvered high. An odd sound, like sleet striking an autocab roof, echoed over the speakers.

"They're kicking up a lot of rock fragments," Erin observed over Bvindu comms. On standard comms, she announced, *"Goodbye, Casper."*

For several seconds, the shuttle icon appeared to fly inside the mountain, gradually losing altitude but not speed.

On Bvindu comms, Erin said, *"Red, we're trying something... Do it now, Frank."*

Red ordered, "Erin, report!"

More sounds of rocks pinging against the shuttle's hull came over the comms.

A heartbeat later, the shuttle's icon disappeared from the tactical display. The gunboat's icon circled over that position.

The shuttle's icon refused to reappear...

Gretchen exclaimed, "Oh, God, no! What will I do now? My baby needs a father!"

48 | ENCOUNTER'S AFTERMATH

Gretchen scrutinized the tactical display. Frank's shuttle's icon refused to appear. Yet, the murderous gunship continued to circle.

Just like that, Space Force had stolen him. He'd never see their child's first steps. They'd never play catch. He'd never get to show off Mars and Bvindu Dome or help them accumulate Mars Scout badges.

All because of the elitists' insatiable lust for power...

Like a faraway echo, someone said, "Gretchen, come over here."

She brushed over her coverall leg until she came to her datapad, which held the trigger to the demexes positioned about her head. She held the trump card. Without Frank, any victory would be pale and hollow. Until that moment, she hadn't known if she could do it. Now, the answer was obvious. If the time came, she'd do it—for Frank.

June took her by the shoulder and guided her to a chair against the wall.

Chuck and Red spoke in hushed tones near the tactical display. Whatever they were discussing didn't matter. Frank was dead.

June handed her some water, wrapping an arm around her shoulders. Gretchen stared at a spot on the floor about ten feet away. After a couple of slow blinks, tears ran down her cheeks.

* * *

Chuck looked around and motioned to Alan. Frank dying was an unpreventable tragedy. Chuck's immediate concern was for Gretchen's baby.

When Alan arrived, Chuck asked, "Did you know Gretchen was pregnant?"

"Not a clue."

"Get a doctor here. In-person, don't use the comms."

"Right, boss." Alan scurried among the cabinets of the Master Control Center and exited.

In front of the tactical display, Red stood transfixed with a frown on his face. Chuck sidled up beside him. "What do you hope to see?"

"Not hoping. Just confused. If the shuttle is truly down, why is the gunship still circling? They should've proceeded to Mars City, returned to the *Baffin*, or landed and inspected the wreckage."

From outside the main airlock, Hank reported, "*The gunship is on station. I haven't seen any smoke plumes.*"

Rizzo, at the Raw Materials Entrance, concurred.

Red turned to the vidcomm. "Acknowledged. Remain and report any changes."

"*Ghost, this is* Baffin *Actual. Report the status of the insurrectionist shuttle,*" Colonel Steele ordered over Space Force frequencies.

"*Unknown. They dropped off tac, but we have no evidence they're down.*"

Chuck peeked over to Gretchen, who stared blankly at the floor. June looked up, her eyes pleading for good news.

Quietly, Chuck asked Red, "What does all this mean?"

"The gunship sees no signs of a crash or destruction—no smoke, dust plume, or wreckage. Another piece of good news—no one is asking for or sending reinforcements, so that means they're taking the Mars City evacuation seriously."

The Earth loyalists were the last thing on Chuck's mind. Right now, getting them off Mars fell in the "Good" column—Erin and Frank's status was more pressing. "Maybe they feel they don't need to waste more resources on a single unarmed shuttle."

"Good point."

Chuck leaned closer. "Until we know something concrete, don't say anything. I don't want Gretchen experiencing Frank dying twice if you're wrong."

"Wilco."

Gretchen wiped her cheeks with the palm of her hand.

Chuck looked back to Red. "How do we find out what's going on?"

"We're hamstrung during daytime. The gunship or the *Baffin* will see anything we do."

"Can we sneak another shuttle over there tonight?"

"No." Red tugged his ear. "We can mask or disable most of the electronics, but the engines are easily detected. It'll be another target, day or night."

"We'll have to use monoriders," Chuck suggested.

"That'll get people to the mountains, but Erin and Frank are on a slope or in a ravine." Red rubbed his forehead. "We can send our drones to perform a search. They're small enough and use Bvindu comms, so they'll probably go undetected."

"I like it," Chuck said. "Do Erin and Frank have until night?"

"Only if the shuttle's inner hull is intact and life support is functional. If both hulls are pierced or life support is down, they're relying on spacesuit air vests, which are partially expended. That's probably eight hours of air, give or take—it won't be enough. And if life support is down, air isn't their biggest issue."

Chuck glanced at Gretchen, numb in the throes of fresh grief, as Red continued, "It's the cold. They'll freeze to death."

49 | Picking Up the Pieces

Two hand-sized circuit boards lay on the deck in dim lighting beside Frank. His left forearm throbbed. As he reached for a board, a blinding pain commanded him to stop. He rolled onto his back and closed his eyes. He took slow, deep breaths while embracing the painless dark.

A couple of slaps to his face later, he reopened his eyes. The silhouette of Erin's head filled his view.

He asked, "What are you doing?"

"You passed out."

He stirred, which produced a wave of pain. "My left arm hurts."

She pressed his upper arm, working her way down to the elbow. She moved a little farther, and pain consumed his attention.

"Ow! Stop!"

She continued feeling and rubbing, causing waves of pain. "Okay, Frank. Your arm's broken."

"Terrific."

"The good news is, it's a simple fracture. I think. I'm pretty sure."

"You and I have different ideas of good news."

"Where are you?"

Is she kidding? "How am I supposed to know?"

"Frank, now's not the time for stubbornness. That gunship is probably trying to figure out what happened. We need to get moving before their patience gives out and they start firing randomly. And I need your help."

"You win. Catch me up."

"You were unconscious. I'm running the medical emergency checklist. We're in the concussion section." She waved a page before his face. "Now, cooperate."

"I passed out? Damn... Hey, I didn't vomit." He chuckled, which caused more pain. "I'm in a MarsVantage shuttle that has hopefully landed?"

"Yeah, we landed. It wasn't my best..." She flashed a light in his eyes, blinding him. He squinted and fought the urge to blink or turn away. "Your pupils are responsive. No concussion. Anything else hurt?"

"No, just the arm."

"Move your feet," she ordered.

He made kicking motions.

"Good." She affixed an immobilization cast to his forearm and gave him the inflation tube. "Blow."

"What's our status?"

As he blew into the tube, she recounted, "You yanked the transponder and Earth comm control boards. Space Force can't track our electronics. I suspect one of my maneuvers in this chasm caused your injury. Either that or the hard landing under this overhang."

He pinched the tube and pulled it from his mouth. "How did you know this was here?"

"I explore, too, though I never entered here so fast. The shuttle's outer hull is punctured, but the inner hull is intact. Talk less—inflate more. We're on the clock."

Again, he puffed into the tube. She squeezed the cast several times until she sealed the inflation port and took the tube from him. After unfolding another page, Erin read and arranged something out of view. She referred to the page once more.

"What're you doing there?"

She produced an injector. "I'm going to give you a painkiller so you don't pass out when I move you."

"You have a plan?"

"We're going to do something untried and unorthodox, but if I don't get the dose right, you'll conk out or die."

"I certainly want to be alive *and* awake to see this."

"You weigh two-twenty?"

"Two hundred."

"Standard Earth weight?" She raised an eyebrow as she twisted the injector's base for the dose. She pushed the left spacesuit sleeve an inch to the cast, eliciting a sharp pain.

"Sorry." She pushed the plunger.

A sharp pinch followed.

"That ought to take the edge off."

She jammed the supplies and instructions into the medpac and stowed it in the bulkhead outside the cockpit. After gathering the two circuit boards, she placed them atop a toolpac in a compartment near the cargo bay's hatch.

She returned and knelt. "How's the arm?"

"I can ignore the pain now."

With one hand, she held his elbow, and her other held his wrist. Slowly, she moved his arm. "Easy... Let me do it."

The pain edged up a notch, but it was manageable. Sweat gathered in the small of his back, and he finally inhaled with his arm against his chest.

"Give me a second." She slid his arm into a black sling. She fed a strap behind his neck and velcroed it to the sling near his wrist.

He sat upright with her guidance.

"Hold there." She secured the sling around his back and verified his arm was snug against the air vest. "Try to stand now."

He leveraged himself up against her until he was squarely on his feet. Between the injury and the painkillers, he needed help like he was a hundred years old. He didn't fight it—his father had always said the wise man accepts help when needed.

Now was the time to be wise. And it was humbling...

With Erin close behind, he made his way into the cockpit, one unsteady step after another. She eased him into the co-pilot's seat. Rock, bathed in shadows, filled the cockpit window. He took a couple of breaths.

She affixed his left glove to his spacesuit. Surprisingly, it didn't elicit more pain.

"What're you doing?" Frank asked.

"Safety precaution. My idea—"

"Idea? It was a plan a few minutes ago. Why do I think you're actually working with a notion?"

"*Anyway,* we're in danger if that gunship is still around." After she attached his gloves, she seated his helmet. She withdrew a handheld diagnostic unit from a storage pocket on her seat and plugged it into his air vest since the cast obstructed the suit's control panel. After several seconds, she unplugged and stowed it. "The air vest is functioning normally, and you have a seal."

"Now for the harness." She guided the two chest straps of the five-point harness between the sling and the air vest before inserting them into the buckle. She connected the other three straps with ease. Once she buckled in and completed her own spacesuit preps, she activated the shuttle's Bvindu comm, then synced the spacesuit comms to it.

"Bvindu Dome, this is Erin. Come in."

A few seconds later, Red said, "*Erin? We thought you were destroyed.*"

"*Why didn't you contact us immediately?*" Gretchen's voice was fainter, as if she were far from the vidcomm.

Frank said, "We're fine... but I'm injured. Nothing serious... We're ready to come home."

"*What's wrong? You're speaking a little slow,*" Gretchen said, her voice much clearer.

Erin gave a half-shrug.

At least I'm not slurring my words. He outlined his injury.

"If we're done playing long-distance doctor," Erin said with an annoyed tone, "I'd like to return so that a licensed doctor can *treat* Frank. Is the gunship still around?"

"*Affirmative,*" Red said. "*They've been circling where we lost your signal.*"

"I hoped disabling the transponder and Earth comms would be enough to fool them as we hid."

"*On the plus side, SF's not following tactical protocol and adding a wingman. It appears they're utilizing most of their flight capability in evacuating Mars City.*"

"That's something," Erin said.

"*They're stuck using radar to find you among the rocks. I'm guessing they have a mess for a tac display right now.*"

"At least that part worked." After a second's pause, Erin explained what she called a plan.

It *was* more like an idea.

After Red voiced several concerns, she looked toward Frank and frowned. "I'm open to other options."

Several seconds passed before Red admitted, "*We don't have a better idea here.*"

"Let me know when that gunship is above where you lost the transponder and heading east. I'll leave comms open. Frank, yank the access panel by your right knee. There's a connector, a large one, fifty pins. Do you see it?"

With his right hand, he undid four wingnuts and pulled off the cover. As he placed it on his lap, a blinking green flash reflected off components within. He shifted within the harness, reached in, and felt around. "Is it attached just below the opening?"

"Yeah. When I say to yank it, do it, not before. That's the Safety Systems connector, which, among other things, controls the engine's governor. Disabling it gives us extra speed until the engines overheat and burn out. Or explode."

She pushed the collective ever so much and pulled back on the cyclic a little. Outside, the rock face sank a foot or so. Then, she performed a flat 180-degree turn to port. Slower than he'd ever seen her fly, they traced a path toward where they'd entered the chasm.

"Whenever I wanted to test my reflexes, I flew this fissure and several others as fast as possible. I had no idea one would save my life someday."

"We're not saved yet," Frank pointed out.

"Can you switch to optimist mode?" Her eyes bore into him.

"You've done a great job. No question. What we're attempting is far from guaranteed. There are easily a half dozen ways for it to go south."

"When Severino, Dohbyn, and Space Force make their next move, you'll have more of a say. Right now, you need to have faith in Red and me."

She was right—he could only trust her flying skills and Red's aim.

"*Mars City signaled the* Baffin," Gretchen said. "*They lost airlocks on the last dome. They've declared a disaster.*"

Red added, *"Space Force launched another lander and three gunships toward Mars City."*

"Something's going right today," Frank said. A Mars City disaster declaration had always been the goal to force the evacuation of all the Earth loyalists to the destroyer. Now, it could help get them to safety.

"Get ready… a few more seconds…" Then Red ordered, *"Go, go, go!"*

Erin pushed the collective forward and maneuvered through the deep trench, avoiding landslides. Her maneuvers caused the harness to pull against various points of Frank's spacesuit. His arm didn't complain, either because the painkiller or the cast was doing its job. Finally, red sky appeared in the cockpit window.

"I'm beginning my upward spiral."

"The gunship performed a half-roll and is approaching your six," Red cautioned.

"Do we have enough altitude?" Erin asked.

Altitude was the key. The shuttle had to be high enough for an Asteroid Deflector System emitter to take a clear shot from the bottom of an excavated crater.

Green tracers zipped past the cockpit windows, farther away than before. Erin continued the spiral and made random, erratic movements with the cyclic every so often.

"They're closing," Red warned. *"They're expecting you to break off and flatten out."*

"Got it," Erin said as she pulled back on the collective a tick. "Yank the connector. Now!"

A few loud pings on the hull announced the gunship's presence. Though it had to be Frank's imagination, he felt each at the base of his spine.

He shoved his gloved hand into the access panel as Erin juked the shuttle. He lost his grip on the connector. He groped about. Once in hand, he yanked it from the socket.

"It's free."

Erin jammed the collective forward the entire way. Frank was sucked into the seat.

"That's all I have," Erin said. "Red, deploy the Lightning's Hand."

50 | COORDINATED TEAMWORK

Gretchen glanced over her shoulder at the tactical display. The gunship icon stopped closing but kept pace with the one representing the Republic shuttle icon.

"Acknowledged, wait one." Red sat beside her at the Bvindu console, deftly working the controls like an archaeologist works a brush around a delicate find.

Chuck observed, not saying anything but breathing hard.

I can't keep running the engines this hard," Erin said, worry creeping into her voice. *"They'll burn out. Deploy!"*

"Wait one," Red repeated evenly. Beads of sweat formed on his upper lip.

"For God's sake, shoot!" Gretchen implored.

"Almost..." Red worked the short-range targeting controls that aimed the emitter. He pressed one final button. "Firing."

An alert appeared across the display. "Emitter fault. Switching to another."

"You've got to be kidding me," Erin said.

Again, Red aimed and pressed the button. "Firing."

The lights dimmed ever so slightly for a split second.

From outside, Hank said, *"Whoa! That's a hit. No secondary explosions."*

Red moved to the tactical display. Baker and Rodriguez were watching intently.

"Baffin, *this is* Ghost," Casper said over Space Force frequencies. *"Unknown weapon took out starboard engine. Looking to make orbit."*

"Erin," Red said over Bvindu comms, "return before SF launches another gunship."

"On our way. Have a med team meet us at the landing pad."

"Perhaps we can avoid another gunship." Chuck sat and swiveled the vidcomm to show a nondescript bulkhead and processing cabinets. Then, he activated MarsVantage's frequency. "Space Force, you committed an act of war by firing on an unarmed shuttle. Mars is a no-fly zone for all non-Republic craft. We grant you temporary flight privileges to evacuate Mars City as they declared a disaster. Do not approach or overfly Bvindu Dome. Any violation will be viewed as a hostile act and met with force."

He closed the channel and returned to stand with Alan, June, and the doctor who'd remained. The latter quietly took everything in. Though never staring, he kept a constant eye on Gretchen. He wasn't the only one. They all seemed to be eyeing her like she'd spilled coffee on her coveralls.

I'm pregnant, not helpless.

She adjusted the Bvindu comms into monitor mode and faced her colleagues. "I'm fine. I suppose I should've told you sooner. Actually, I should've told Frank first. With everything going on, I didn't want anyone worrying."

"We're thrilled you're having a baby," Chuck said, "and not because our long-term future relies on Marsians having plenty of children. We're genuinely happy for you and Frank, though the timing's interesting. Now, go with the doctor and get a thorough checkup."

That's why I didn't say anything. "I feel fine, really."

"We have things covered here. Put our minds at ease, and get a checkup. Then see Frank."

She sighed. "Fine. And for the record, the timing surprised me, too, but not as much as it'll surprise Frank."

51 | Until Space Force's Next Move

E rin watched the medical team whisk Frank away to the Bvindu medical center. Hopefully, he wouldn't need surgery. She thought it odd that Gretchen wasn't there to greet her husband, but a lot was going on.

She scooted under the hull to the forward landing gear. From its control panel, she retracted the ramp and closed the cargo hatch. At the nearby Bvindu control panel, she manipulated the controls to relocate her shuttle to one side.

As she approached it, the bow looked pristine. She slid her hand over several rough scorch marks along the underside. The dimples were nothing, but the four holes, which were filled with sealant, were bothersome. Had a round hit a fuel cell, her shuttle would've been debris strewn across the landscape, along with her and Frank.

Nine more punctures lay around the engines. How bullets didn't destroy them was nothing short of a miracle. "Damn..."

She climbed topside using the hand and foot rails on the starboard hull. As she crawled, she counted a dozen holes and countless scorch marks and dimples. Upon reaching the deck, she surveyed the sides, finding two more holes on the port side and three starboard.

Hours of patching lay ahead. The shuttle would require a full diagnostic suite, which meant more downtime. That would have to wait—all of the parts and equipment were in Mars City. She tamped down the frustration of her ship being less than one hundred percent.

Erin mounted the cargo mover and drove to the Master Control Center. After parking, she played the tones. In response, the door descended. She strode inside, entered the security code, and traversed past the processing cabinets to the control console.

Everyone was there except for Gretchen. *Where is she?*

Red stood tall, his chest out. "Well done, Fire Rider. That was fine flying, in a civie shuttle, no less."

"Fire Rider?"

"Military pilots earn callsigns."

"I'm *not* a military pilot."

Red grinned ear to ear. "You're part of the First Army Irregulars, and you've taken fire. You earned the title and the callsign."

Her cheeks warmed. "Fire Rider, huh? Swiss Cheese may be more appropriate. There are thirty holes in my shuttle."

"You made it back under your own power. That's a huge win."

"We don't see winning alike."

"You're alive and accomplished your mission."

"I feel like we're tossing stones at people firing machine guns. Force only understands force. We need to defeat that destroyer above us, and that's a tall order."

Red stepped forward. "We can carve that destroyer up like a butcher. I used one emitter at ten percent power. It wouldn't stand a chance if we used full power and multiple emitters."

"But our co-workers and friends will be there," Erin pointed out.

"There's the monkey wrench. My take is that Frank won't indiscriminately fire on it, regardless."

"You're right." She placed her hands in her coverall pockets. "I can help. Can you outfit a shuttle with weapons?"

"We don't have standard 50mm machine guns or ammo. How about Bvindu weaponry?"

"Do they even have weapons?"

"Gretchen and Frank haven't said." His face beamed with anticipation. "Would you consider flying a drone? I have five, but only two pilots."

"Absolutely. I always wanted to."

"Excellent." Red gestured toward the door. "Let's grab a FieldMeal. We earned it."

"What if Space Force attacks again?"

"They will, but it'll be tonight," Red said evenly.

"How can you be sure?"

"They have to account for the Lightning's Hand in their plans. Plus, they'll attack when the sleep cycle makes people the least alert while using the psychological advantage of moving without being seen well."

He led her from the Master Control Center to the Planning Huddle Area. After making their choices, they settled at a table facing one another.

Red pulled the tab to activate the heating process as she opened her container and bit into a chicken salad sandwich. "How is it?"

"Good. This is one of the better options."

The readout tab on Red's FieldMeal turned green. He unsealed it and took a few bites of meatloaf.

Anxiety over Space Force's next move weighed on Erin's thoughts. She stopped her heel from bouncing against the floor. "I feel like we should be preparing for a Space Force move, or better yet, forcing their hand."

Red set his fork down. "We're as prepared as possible. SF is evacuating the loyalists, which is the priority. Afterward, we can push back."

"How long will the evacuation take?"

"A day, minimum." He looked up for a moment before returning his attention. "Probably, two."

Erin blinked slowly and exhaled. "It's going to be a long couple of nights."

"We have a choice." He ignored his meal and looked her squarely in the eye. "We can worry about what comes next—that's SF's preference. Or we can eat, rest, and face the next challenge with clear heads."

"That's easy for you to say," she said looking at her sandwich. "You're trained. We're civilians. We're not used to people trying to kill us."

"You never really get used to that." Red tapped the table near her sandwich to get her attention. "My team's here to keep us alive."

She gave a lackadaisical nod and picked up the sandwich.

Out of nowhere, Red announced, "Gretchen's pregnant."

Instead of taking a bite, Erin coughed as she set it down. "How'd that happen?"

Red gave a sliver of a smile.

"I *know* how it happened." Heat rose in her cheeks. "I mean, the timing's interesting... I dodged a bullet."

"How so?"

"Back in the day, I turned down Frank's marriage proposal. I knew he wanted kids."

Red's expression remained unchanged by her revelation. "And you don't?"

"I had pilots fly while pregnant, some very pregnant, but after giving birth, every single one transferred to different positions."

"Why?"

"The schedule conflicted with parenthood." She took a small bite of the sandwich and swallowed. "When a transport's in orbit, we take shifts transferring cargo. Four hours on, eight off until everything's at its destination. "One shift might be during the day while the next is at night."

"It's tough enough juggling kids with stable work hours." He chuckled and looked her in the eyes. "You haven't thought about SF, have you?"

"No."

"Mission accomplished."

Erin sat back, her lips slightly parted. "Okay, my turn. When we first met, you said you came to Shadow City to live how you choose. What'd you mean?"

He scooped up his fork and stabbed a potato chunk in one smooth motion. He ate it. "My fellow SF retirees and I are interested in farming, especially Baker, but found reg compliance so involved that actual farming was secondary. After discussing our challenges in an online forum, we were each anonymously contacted. Discussions occurred for several months until we ended up on Mars."

"The Knowledge Keepers played it carefully."

"Along the way," Red continued, "we discovered we have additional skills and interests. Rizzo's a decent software developer, and Hank's an excellent singer. She can drop you from a thousand yards away with a single shot, but her voice is heaven-sent."

"She'll have to perform at our monthly celebrations."

"Ah, we'll be a planet away."

She leaned in close. "I'll pop over and fly your whole team to Mars City. Perhaps you can get some ideas to bring the tradition to Shadow City if things return to normal."

"When."

"I'm sorry, what?"

Red swallowed his latest bit of the FieldMeal. "*When* things return to normal. Actually, *when* we create a Mars normal. This crisis will pass as all crises do."

Easy enough for you to say—you weren't just shot at. "When everything settles down, what'll you do? You don't strike me as the farmer type."

"No? Farming is a means to an end. I love to cook. I took culinary classes toward the end of my service."

"A chef? That wouldn't be my first guess."

Red sat straighter. "Cooking's full of infinite possibilities. How about you? What are your plans when you stop flying?"

"I don't plan on stopping." In response to his disbelieving expression, she added, "Okay. I've been thinking about teaching. I have to in the short term. We'll produce more scout ships, and they'll need pilots. We'll be flying food and personnel to and from Shadow City. And if I know Frank, he'll work out how to get cargo and more people from Earth. I'm sure scout ships will be involved somehow."

Red swallowed another bite of meatloaf. "No doubt."

"It'll be an ongoing effort. Eventually, I suppose I'll end up teaching full-time."

"Good." He looked her square in the eyes. "Guardians have a saying, 'People without plans for tomorrow plan on dying today.'"

52 | Breaking News

Propped up in a bed in a makeshift hospital room, Frank watched Chuck's latest broadcast to Earth on his datapad. He'd hit the critical point—firing unprovoked on a defenseless shuttle when civilians needed to be evacuated in the middle of a disaster.

In a perfect world, the *Baffin* would break orbit as soon as everyone from Mars City was aboard. Nothing about the circumstances was perfect. Space Force would surely move against them, probably once night fell.

His left arm lay on a table before him. The doctor had set the bone and applied a cast. He waited with growing impatience to be released.

I'm done waiting... He stood, pushing the table aside.

Gretchen entered, wearing her shock-tab gun. "You haven't been released. Back to bed."

Frank was about to argue when she put her hands on her hips and glared. His shoulders slumped, and he returned to idleness.

She hugged him tightly from the right side. "I'm glad you're okay. I thought you died."

He whispered, "I'm fine. Erin refused to get shot down. At least, tell me what's going on."

After releasing him, she grabbed a nearby chair and sat beside the bed. "Red will brief you when you're discharged. I have something else to share."

"Is it why you're wearing a shock-tab gun?"

Confusion crossed her face. "Well... Space Force isn't holding back. I'll protect myself. My friends. My husband—"

"We're aiming for a different outcome, hon."

"I know." She took his hand. Tension etched fine lines around her eyes. "There's more... We're pregnant."

"Pregnant?" They'd never discussed children. They had no plan. With everything happening and what was to come in the days and months ahead, intellect would put off having children. None of that mattered. *I'm going to be a dad!* "That's the best news ever. Come here and give me another hug."

This time, he returned the embrace with his right arm.

"How far along? When did you know?"

"Two months." She sat down. "I confirmed it with a doctor about a month ago."

What'd she been waiting on? Withholding the news from friends and family was natural, but not from the father. "Why didn't you tell me? Is there a problem with the baby?"

"The baby's fine. I just had a check-up." She wiped tears from her eyes. "I should've said something. You should've been the first to know, not the last."

"I'm last?"

"When I thought you crashed, I kinda blurted it out to everyone in the Master Control Center."

I can't blame you for that, but... "Why didn't you say anything sooner?"

"I should have... You were struggling with Washington's intentions. I didn't want to confuse matters more."

"A baby confuses nothing. It's a gift."

"Still, Frank... Washington and Space Force... I want our child to grow up with the choices and opportunities Mars can provide, not the limited options Washington allows." She straightened in the chair. "I didn't want to distract you."

Inwardly, he groaned. As much as he wanted to argue, she was correct that adding his child to the mix might've affected his preparations. "Hon, I understand. We make the best choice possible at the time. I want you to know—our child is a blessing. I couldn't be happier, and you're gonna be an amazing mom."

She rose and kissed him. Slowly, passionately. Thoughts of Space Force and his arm faded away. Nothing beyond their embrace existed...

A female voice said, "Okay, okay. We need to take another x-ray."

Gretchen broke the embrace.

The doctor stood at the foot of the bed with equipment in hand. She set up the imaging components on the table around his arm and took two pictures. After studying each for several seconds, she said, "The bone's set. The nurse will be in shortly with some instructions. Then you're free to go. Come back in two weeks for a progress assessment. Get as much rest as you can."

"Thank you, doctor. I'll do my best, but we both know that won't happen while Space Force is overhead."

53 | CHALLENGES AHEAD

With his cast snugged against his chest by a black sling, Frank's arm ached as he approached the Master Control Center. He didn't dare complain, otherwise Gretchen would insist he take the prescribed pain meds. He'd rather deal with the discomfort and have a clear head to make decisions.

She played the entry tones from her datapad, and the door descended. After she deactivated the trespasser protocol, he followed her to where the rest of the committee members and Red's team clapped and cheered. In turn, they shook Frank's hand and hugged Gretchen, congratulating them.

Frank's cheeks warmed and impatience welled up. "Thanks. We're very excited about the baby. We'll have a proper celebration soon, not only of our baby but also of our freedom. We need to plan our next move because Colonel Steele is certainly plotting hers."

"We had developments while you were being treated." Red guided them to the tactical alcove. "The gunship achieved orbit and docked with the *Baffin*. I obliterated their port engine."

That was good news. They didn't have to worry about Space Force casualties or prisoners. "How much power did you use?"

"Ten percent with one emitter."

Gretchen added, "We experienced a minor power drop-off."

"I suspected the power requirements were high. Did you start the other two power generators?" Frank asked.

"June and I already did it before I went to medical."

"Good. Is Mars City being evacuated?"

"They're rotating six landers escorted by gunships. While three offload personnel onto the *Baffin*, the others are picking up loyalists." Red switched the tactical screen's view to show three lander icons atop Dome 2's landing bays. "Logistics aboard the destroyer are stretched thin, I'm sure. Handling three landers' worth of people at a time is reasonable. Stripped of vehicles and supplies, each can transport close to a hundred people. They'll need several hours to get everyone aboard."

"Have they reported the airlock status?" Frank asked.

"SF has computer and control specialists working on-site," Red confirmed. "The lead tech reported that he eliminated hardware issues and grumbled loudly about no backups. He outright complained about no source code and having to debug executables."

Frank chuckled. "He doesn't realize we shouldn't have the source code. Otherwise, he's on his game, taking the steps I would've if I were tackling this problem."

"He's corrected the high-level executable," Red related, "and the hatches and airlocks still malfunction. He lamented that every file associated with the airlocks and their safety systems had been modified."

Gretchen inquired, "Can't he get the source code or new executables from the manufacturer?"

Red restored the tactical display to show the immediate area around Bvindu Dome. "I doubt the PAA companies will hand over their proprietary code to a foreign nation's military, or even help them without considerations."

Frank exhaled, thankful this part of the plan was working as designed. Plenty of approaches existed to fix the problem, like reverting to the last good version of the executables, which the backups would've provided. If the tech had the source code, he could've compiled it and reinstalled everything.

With those quick fix options removed, that left debugging the executables, which was why Frank ensured that they all looked as if they'd been changed. The specialist was left to prioritize dozens of files and debug them instruction by instruction.

Should Space Force manage to undo his changes, the Republic would be left with breaching the domes with demexes. That'd make the Republic's eventual return to Mars City much more difficult.

"Let me know if they fix the airlocks." Frank adjusted his arm and sling slightly. "We can't have our former co-workers remaining on Mars and certainly can't provide Space Force a foothold."

"Wilco. Next item, we deployed cyber-sentries."

On Earth, cyber-sentries were devices analogous to large breed dogs capable of rapid movement over uneven ground. The military, law enforcement, and many large corporations used them for security patrols. They were perfect for the Republic's needs.

"You have cyber-sentries?" Gretchen's eyes were wide. "I could never get them for digs, even government-sponsored ones."

"They were off-limits for us, too," Frank said.

"We have a lot of equipment that violates the former regs — like the guns we're wearing." Red pointed to hers. "Your inability to get cyber-sentries, which are easily configured for exploration, and surveying drones was meant to make MarsVantage expend manpower, bringing all associated regs into play."

"It's ironic that for the longest time of human exploration of Mars," Gretchen interjected, "either remote-controlled or semi-autonomous vehicles exclusively populated the planet, and once humans took up residence, we couldn't have them."

"Is there any way you can modify the cyber-sentries to use Bvindu comms?" Frank asked.

"Already done."

"Excellent, Red. We have too much area and too few people to watch our perimeter."

"That's right." Red rubbed the back of his neck. "Make no mistake, SF will come tonight. I scheduled watch shifts among the retirees—SF won't catch us off-guard."

54 | Regroup for Reward

After changing out of her smart, professional pantsuit, Maura pulled on slimming black slacks and a comfortable, flattering powder blue top. She pulled back the sheers on the floor-to-ceiling windows to take in the red-lined clouds of sunset over the DC skyline, and she did the same in the sitting room before igniting the gas fireplace.

She strolled to the kitchen, humming a tune she'd heard in the auto-cab on the way to her Georgetown condo. She pulled a walnut charcuterie board from the cupboard and placed mild cheddar and gouda cheese cubes from Barney's. She added several pieces of dark chocolate from another black market a few blocks away near Georgetown University, then placed the plate on the mahogany coffee table in the living room.

After transferring a Waterford decanter half-filled with cognac and two matching glasses from the wet bar in the corner to the coffee table, she sat in one of a pair of high-backed, overstuffed chairs and re-read the latest Mars briefs from the CIA and NSA. The Marsees were attacking rhetoric with rhetoric, taking advantage of their accumulated goodwill to arouse support for their rebellion. Many officials, including herself, would smother those assertions with their own interviews starting the next day. The pressing question was, how were the Marsees transmitting to Earth?

Whatever weapon the Marsees had deployed concerned everyone. Initial analysis of the gunship showed an engine had been destroyed beyond repair, and the nearby metal had been melted into a shapeless mess. Apparently, the Bvindu had high-energy weapons unlike any on Earth... and now they were in the hands of the Marsees.

Their hubris endangered themselves and threatened Earth's citizenry. Like all government officials, her charge was to keep everyone safe—even the ungrateful, rebellious Marsees.

A century earlier, the European Union of Socialist States allowed Geoffrey Bauln free reign to operate his colony, ending with every colonist perishing. Nothing like that would happen on her watch.

The building's front entrance chime rang, and Peter said via the intercom, "*Good evening, Maura.*"

"Come on up. Entrance Control, open."

A few minutes later, she welcomed him inside and showed him to a chair around the coffee table. He wore a stylish Italian blue suit but had removed his tie and unbuttoned the top button on his white shirt. He must've been working all day and hadn't taken a moment to change.

She poured a measure of the amber cognac into two snifters, handing him one before taking her seat. As she swirled the liquid with one hand in her palm, she said, "Thanks for coming by."

"Happy to do so."

With Peter's advice, she'd defeat the Marsees and return MarsVantage to his fold, where its personnel would follow experts with incontrovertible credentials and experience. "The Marsees caught Steele with her pants down."

Peter warmed his cognac and popped a gouda cube in his mouth. "Clearly, the Marsees haven't been bumbling around."

"Are you suggesting they planned to secede upon finding the Bvindu?"

"Step into their shoes for a moment. In the beginning, the regs worked in concert with their efforts. A person could only be in the wild for a limited time in ninety-day periods."

"Exactly. Overworked, sleep-deprived people make mistakes, for which Mars exacts a steep price. Instead of rebelling, they should be thanking me."

"No question, but Washington added rules, then inspections and audits for no reason other than to make Marsee life more difficult. No doubt, they saw the writing on the wall."

He'd painted an anti-government picture like an angry, distrustful Marsee.

"They're miners millions of miles away digging in the ground." She took a sip, not appreciating the cognac's intricacies. "Dozens of experts with advanced degrees from our best universities researched and evaluated the challenges posed by Mars. The regulators and legislators propose nothing without first receiving their council."

"Do you believe they need to be told how many days in a row any one miner can be on-site? This isn't the early 1900s with fourteen-year-olds digging for coal. Every interaction with Washington leaves the Marsees with the short end of the stick." He inhaled the cognac's nose and gave an approving nod before sipping. "I know—I helped to perpetuate it. We started the space microbe scare a few years back, suggesting the need for a customs quarantine on all Mars exports."

"What's your point, Peter?"

"Between Interplanetary and government actions over the last decade, the Marsees had two choices—surrender or strive for self-sufficiency. With Bvindu Dome in hand, they chose the latter. I'll bet my company they would've been satisfied with self-sufficiency and a hands-off approach from Washington.

"In the end, we backed them into a corner without any options."

"You're forgetting we suggested an NSM partnership," Maura pointed out.

Peter savored a piece of chocolate. "That *partnership* was a euphemism for takeover. I'm sure they saw through it like plastiglass."

"With the Bvindu tech, we can elevate humanity—cure the sick and feed the hungry worldwide. That's more important than the feelings of a handful of miners."

"You asked for my advice, so here it is. The Marsees are far from dumb—on Mars, that gets you killed. Accept that and reassess the situation. Don't, and you will lose everything. No Bvindu tech. No presidency. Perhaps even your current office."

"Lose? We can send the entire fleet."

"And do what?" Peter's jaw muscles flexed. "Bomb them back to the Stone Age? You and President Dohbyn can reign over the rubble that *was* priceless Bvindu tech and knowledge."

"We can starve them out. A few days of arguing with empty stomachs will change their minds. If not, what's a few dead Marsees compared to all the benefits humanity will receive?"

"You may gain Bvindu Dome, and in doing so, you'll be reviled by history. The few Marsee-friendly media outlets will take up their cause all day and night. That's not factoring in O'Donnell weaseling his way into our comms, broadcasting whatever he wants."

"Our best engineers are working on that little problem. Do you have any proposals?"

Peter sipped his cognac. "First off, evacuate Mars City to the *Baffin* ASAP. My sources say that about forty percent of the population remains."

"What good will that do?"

"Chuck won't shoot down the *Baffin* with all his former co-workers on it."

Maura coughed on her cognac. Peter was dreaming if he believed the Marsees could destroy the *Baffin*. "You're suggesting we use them as human shields."

"The same way Bvindu Dome is shielding O'Donnell and the other rebels."

"Then what?"

"That's the trick," he said. "You have to subdue the rebels somehow while leaving the dome intact."

"That's over three thousand people." With the Courvoisier near her nose, she inhaled deeply as an idea formed. A hint of orange with a trace of vanilla teased her. She sipped, allowing the aged fluid to sit on her tongue momentarily. She swallowed, appreciating the slight woody taste. "*But* if we can get the leaders, the insurrection will quickly implode."

Peter took a chocolate from the tray and sat back. "Marsees are an independent lot. The vast majority who went with the Republic weren't involved in the planning and decision-making."

"Exactly. The more people involved in a conspiracy, the greater the chance of their secret going public. No one heard a peep until O'Donnell ruined my hearing."

He tipped his glass to her. "Odds are, most of them don't know how to work the Bvindu equipment. The archaeologists were the primary occupants of Bvindu Dome—few MarsVantage employees spent any time there."

"According to intelligence reports," Maura recalled, "the archaeologists, to a person, say access to the Master Control Center was limited to Frank Brentford and Gretchen Blake."

Peter leaned forward and sat his snifter on the coffee table. He looked directly into Maura's eyes. "Without those two, the insurrection will fall apart. They need to be eliminated."

55 | OFFENSIVE

The Committee and Red were already standing around the tactical alcove when Frank entered the Master Control Center with Gretchen. Instead of being first on the scene, he'd been last, all thanks to needing help getting dressed because of his injury. *It is going to be six long weeks.*

Once she entered the security code, they walked through the rows of waist-high cabinets. Blueish-white sparks arced rapidly across their faces, faster than Frank had ever seen. "What's our status?"

"The cyber-sentries and stationary sentinels detected ground transports heading toward the Raw Materials Entrance and the Main Airlock. Rizzo is performing forward observation at the Raw Materials Entrance. Hank's at the Main Airlock." Red pointed to the tactical alcove. "Baker and Rodriguez are piloting drones."

Erin sat beside them, watching Baker.

Frank pointed to the tactical display. "The trench will slow down the ground transports. They can't traverse it. The sides are slanted and unstable."

Gretchen asked, "Why didn't they land on our side of it?"

"Landers aren't combat-rated. A well-placed demex or two would ground them," Red explained.

"The trench will buy us twenty to thirty minutes max." Rodriguez twisted to look at Red. "It's quicker to bridge it than fill it. The two ground transports are carrying spanning planks. Permission to activate scattershot?"

Red looked to Frank. "Troops will debark to lay the planks and supports for the ground transports to traverse the trench. Scattershot comprises pellets designed to penetrate spacesuits and air vests but not kill outright. Shall we proceed?"

Firing on people was different, but it had to be done. The ground transports would roll up to their airlocks if they did nothing, making every Marsian a target. "We don't have a choice."

Red shifted to Rodriguez and Baker and gave the order. Everyone gathered around them.

After Rodriguez touched a control, a light on the panel changed from red to green. In the upper right corner of the screen, the number ten-thousand appeared. He twisted a selector, and ten appeared directly below ten thousand. The night vision filter produced an image in shades of green with surprising detail, considering that the stars overhead provided the only light. The ground transport still had a way to reach the trench.

Rodriguez said, "Erin, ready your drone."

"Destination?"

"Nowhere, yet. I have ten thousand rounds, firing ten with each trigger pull. It sounds like a lot, but you can never have enough when the shit hits the fan. You'll take over while we reload."

"Or to swap fuel cells. Furballs," Baker looked around and shrugged, "ah, aerial combat, burns through power fast."

"On it," Erin replied, and she pressed buttons and verified the status on display.

"Heads up. SF stopped on the far side of the trench from the Raw Materials Entrance." Rodriguez's screen displayed the image from the drone's camera. The ground transport had stopped several yards before the trench, and seconds ticked off with no additional action. Baker's display showed the other ground transport still advancing toward the trench opposite the Main Airlock.

"*Confirmed,*" Rizzo said. "*No visible movement.*"

"*This is Attack Two. We are at our rally point. No resistance encountered,*" came over the vidcomm monitoring Space Force frequencies.

"That confirms it." Red snapped his fingers. "They botched the timing. Sound tactics are to advance on multiple fronts, arriving at their assigned destination simultaneously. Rodriguez, circle away and hover near ground level a fair distance behind the ground transport."

There was nothing to do but wait until Space Force proceeded.

Red leaned closer to Baker's display. The ground transport continued its approach to the trench opposite the main airlock.

The sling had pressed creases from the t-shirt and coveralls into Frank's side, and that annoyance demanded his attention. After scratching, he adjusted the sling's straps and tugged at the coveralls.

"Attack One here. We reached our rally point. No resistance encountered."

"Baffin *Actual here*," Colonel Steele said. *"Proceed with Phase Two. Attack any targets of opportunity."*

Each display screen showed four people emerge from the ground transport's rear hatch.

"Engage the guardians. Target area is the legs." Red glanced toward Frank. "That damage is the easiest to patch."

Rodriguez's screen showed the landscape speeding by as the guardians detached bridge planks from the sides of their ground transport. According to Red, standard bridge planks were eight feet. The trench before them was ten feet or more across, so the guardians had to join planks, which would expose them longer.

The on-screen target reticle turned green. Rodriguez fired, and the guardians crumpled to the ground and reported enemy action and injuries. His drone overflew the ground transport and circled back to fire a couple more bursts at the other pair. More guardians emerged from the ground transport, one holding a rifle.

A confused jumble of reports over Space Force frequencies erupted as Red exclaimed, "Bug out, Rodriguez!"

He pulled up and applied full power, heading toward the Maelstrom Mountains. After a wide, lazy circle, he slowed and hovered several yards above the ground. He zoomed in on the ground transport. Guardians were already patching their spacesuits. A couple of the bridging planks dangled half-attached to the ground transport's side, and others lay scattered across the sand.

"Fuel and ammo good. Awaiting next task," Rodriguez reported.

"Baffin *Actual here. Report.*"

"*Attack Two here. We have injuries. The Marsees have weapon-capable drones firing scattershot.*"

Colonel Steele said, "*Acknowledged. Attack two, deploy weapons. Fire on sight. I want all drones out of my sky.*"

Frank mumbled to no one in particular, "It's *my* sky."

Baker engaged the first duo, overflying the ground transport like Rodriguez had, and attacked the last two on the other side. A tracer cut across the drone path. Baker applied power with the collective and barrel-rolled toward the Maelstrom Mountains. "Bugging out. Fuel and ammo good."

Attack One reported casualties over Space Force frequencies. When Baker took up a stationary position, he zoomed in like Rodriguez. The bridging planks were scattered haphazardly on the ground.

"Hank, report in," Red ordered.

"*Four guardians are down and being tended to. They have a rifleman standing guard.*"

"Rizzo, whatcha got?" Seconds passed with no answer. Red glanced around, concern etched across his face. "Rizzo, report."

Alan raised his hand. "Probably a transmitter issue. June and I will go check it out."

"As quick as you can." Frank's stomach soured. Now wasn't the time for comm issues.

Behind them, the Bvindu control console shrieked. The sensors had detected an impact on the dome. After glancing at it, Red replayed the last minute of the tactical display. "We have a breacher."

Baker offered, "I can get there."

"Negative," Red ordered. "Fire Rider, you're on. Get me eyes on the breacher."

"On it." Erin manipulated the controls at her console.

"Hank, did you get all that?"

"*Yes, Master Sergeant. I didn't see the breacher. I've been watching the ground transport.*"

"Get in here and head toward the landing pad. The breacher's on your way."

"*Acknowledged.*"

Red rubbed his eyes. "Steele has me so distracted with her right hand that I ignored the left. The third lander must've launched the breacher."

Chuck stepped forward. "I can man tactical and speak up if there's movement."

"That's a huge help." Red gestured toward the chair. "Thanks."

Chuck took the seat and got a quick primer from Rodriguez.

"I have the breacher," Erin announced. "It looks like they attached to the dome beside an emitter decoy."

Red and Gretchen turned toward Erin's screen.

"Oh, hell." Frank snorted. "I had Welles do half the work for them by creating the decoy. I was too smart by half."

"Better beside a decoy," Gretchen said. "Look at that."

On Erin's screen, a guardian exited a hatch and stepped toward the phony emitter's protective clamshell. He placed something on it and returned to the breacher.

Erin said, "C'mon. Don't you want to look around a little? I only need a few more seconds to get in range."

Red touched her shoulder. "Bank away. Bank away, now."

She manipulated the controls, and the breacher moved off-screen, replaced with a view of the plain, which looked more like a big emptiness of dark green and black.

The Bvindu console alarm sounded again.

Gretchen checked it. "That was a seismic event."

Red said, "That was probably a standard demex to eliminate what they believe was an emitter. And the guardian wore an armored spacesuit. Scattershot can't penetrate it."

"*Armored spacesuit?*" Hank asked.

"They finally implemented the tech," Red pointed out.

"*My sharpshooter rifle won't penetrate it, either.*"

"Hank, get yourself a couple of blocks from the attachment point and take high ground. Provide a visual. Do not engage until ordered. Coordinates incoming." Red transmitted them from the tactical console.

"*Acknowledged. Give me a few minutes.*"

Red took everyone in. "SF accomplished their first milestone by placing guardians on our doorstep. Get ready for their next move."

56 | BREACHER

"Colonel Steele, this is Frank Brentford of the Mars Republic. Your breacher team is in danger. Withdraw immediately." Steele would certainly ignore his warning, but he had to try. He switched the vidcomm to monitor mode and glanced to his right. "Are you sure you shouldn't talk with Space Force?"

"Absolutely not." Red brought his hands up to chest level. "Steele is unaware you have military assistance. That works to our advantage."

"He's right." Gretchen placed a hand on her belly. "The less information Space Force has, the better off we are."

"Take credit for everything, Sow confusion. Foment frustration. Win victory." Red's eyes glinted with the rush of excitement.

Frank resisted the urge to say, "Yes, Master Sergeant." Assumptions led to error, and error on Space Force's part would work in the Republic's favor.

"No matter what she says, whatever she threatens, our goal is to get the *Baffin* to return to Earth," Red reminded.

And not get everyone killed in the process. "Hon, send a broadcast message to all datapads. Everyone needs to shelter in place. We have Space Force troops in the dome. Tell June and Alan to find a safe spot and hunker down."

"On it."

On-screen, Colonel Steele appeared. "Brentford, you're causing me an untold amount of difficulty. I dislike difficulty."

Frank unmuted. "Finish rescuing our former co-workers and depart Republic space."

"I have a mission, and a Marsee maintenance engineer, a disgraced archaeologist, and miners using illegal, weaponized drones won't stop me."

"In the Mars Republic, drones are perfectly legal. To my point, your breacher crew is in immediate danger. Withdraw them now. There's no need for deaths today."

"My guardians are well-trained. Your little rebellion is over."

"Space Force will never take Bvindu Dome."

"Civilians are going to keep it from me?"

"You will *never* get Bvindu Dome," Frank stated firmly. "The only question is, how much blood splashes across the deck before you accept that fact?"

"You have no idea what lengths I'll go to achieve my mission."

"Let history reflect that I warned you, Colonel." Frank disconnected the vidcomm.

Red announced, "She'll escalate until she achieves her objective. We need to go on the offensive."

Before Frank could respond, Hank reported, "*I've got breacher activity on the dome. I'm turning on the front camera. I'm three stories up, about a block and a half away.*"

The vidcomm display flickered to life with the picture zooming in on the open hatch. The image was bright and clear. Since Gretchen and June had activated the other two power generators, the entire dome was illuminated.

From within the breacher, a guardian shot a cable to the deck. He pulled it taut, emerged wearing an armored spacesuit with a rifle slung over his back, and descended. A second guardian appeared immediately afterward.

Hank said, "*They're using ascent/descent grips. Ten seconds to the deck.*"

Gretchen inspected the Bvindu control panel. "The intruder system detects unrecognized movement."

Frank activated the vidcomm. "Colonel Steele, withdraw your team. They're in immediate danger."

Hank panned her datapad to follow the guardian team as they touched down. The first guardian detached from the cable, and a handful of seconds later, the other mirrored the move. Side-by-side, they took one step and another. A crimson beam from above struck the leftmost guardian in the chest. Though his spacesuit was singed, he stumbled forward.

The other guardian looked up, searching for the origin of the blast. From a different location on the dome, another beam, glowing brighter than the first, struck the leftmost guardian again. He slumped to the ground like a marionette whose strings were cut. The other guardian knelt at his side.

A beam struck the second guardian, and he toppled over.

Frank closed his eyes for a long moment, inhaled, and exhaled. If Steele had heeded his warnings, those two guardians would still be alive.

"*I count two down,*" Hank said. "*Orders?*"

"Hold position. They may send another team. Do *not* engage."

The breacher commander requested status updates from his scout team three times before reporting to Colonel Steele. "*Sunspot to* Baffin."

"Baffin *Actual here.*"

"*Scout team is down. The Marsees deployed a high-intensity energy weapon that burned through the armor. I've never seen anything like it. Awaiting orders.*"

After a few seconds, Colonel Steele answered, "*All units, return to the* Baffin. *Repeat, bug out.*"

A collective sigh erupted from the committee members.

Red glanced around. "Don't celebrate yet. Steele learned vital information that she'll use for her next attack."

57 | Unwanted Consequences

Frank sat at the table closest to the street in the Planning Huddle Area with Gretchen at his side. Red sat across from them.

"You know Steele isn't giving up, right?" Red looked between Gretchen and Frank. "She only withdrew because infiltration won't work."

"Infiltration?" Gretchen asked.

"They observe who enters and leaves the Master Control Center, perhaps from a rooftop. Between James and the archaeologists, Steele knows its significance. After a day or so determining who's important, the guardians eliminate them. They weren't carrying shock-tab rifles but sniper rifles based on lethal two-hundred-year-old firearms' technology."

"How do you know that?" Frank asked.

"If I had this mission, it's how I'd approach it." Red leaned back in the chair. "Put the snipers in armored spacesuits to counter the defense system and bang, bang, bang... They couldn't know the armor would be ineffective against the Bvindu Intruder Defense System."

"Couldn't they just enter the Master Control Center?" Gretchen asked. "Surely, James told them how."

"Excellent point." Red gave her an approving nod. "Speeds up everything."

Welles rolled up on a cargo mover and sat beside Red. "What's the emergency?"

Frank summarized the situation, ending by saying, "And I never want Space Force to use that airlock again."

"There are a few things we need to do." Welles brought a hand to his mouth to cover a yawn. "I assume it has standard physical docking interlock and control connectors."

"Yes," Red confirmed.

For a moment, Welles looked like he was performing a few mental calculations. "We'll foul them with nanoconcrete like you did the electrical connector at the power generator yesterday. Then, we cement over the entire hatch. I can do it in twenty minutes. Inside, we add graphene supports to the dome across the hatch. It'll be good as new, and the hatch will be completely inoperable."

"I'll lead the outside crew at daybreak," Frank announced.

The rest immediately objected.

The loudest was Welles, who said, "You'll only be in the way with one good arm. Would you let anyone do this type of work—inside or out—with a broken arm? My crew will handle both jobs."

Gretchen's stony green eyes conveyed her opinion without another word.

"I agree that I can't perform the physical work. I can supervise, which leaves Welles to oversee the inside work. I can also keep a lookout for Space Force. If it's not me, then another member of the Committee should be present. Chuck's crewing the tactical console. Gretchen's focusing on the Bvindu control console. Erin's piloting a drone. Should we send Alan or June, who have zero construction experience? My presence makes sense."

"It sounds like you want to tractor to the breacher," Red interjected. "That'd leave you exposed for a long time. We can reassign Erin—a member of the Committee—to pilot a shuttle rapidly skimming across the ground. Do you still need to go?"

"Strictly speaking, no." This conversation wasn't heading in the direction he'd anticipated.

"Good. I had to help you dress this morning." Gretchen turned from Frank and looked hard at Red.

That minor fact dealt a critical blow to his chances. "I'd still like to oversee the work and get a lay of the land."

Welles slapped Frank on the shoulder. "Sit this one out. I'll lead the outside team."

"I'm not asking someone to do something I'm unwilling to do." That was his last reason, and it wouldn't be enough.

Red, his shoulders straight with authority, leaned in. "Look at it from the miners' perspective. If SF moves to enforce its No-Fly-

Zone, they'll have to bug out quickly, even with us providing cover fire using the Lightning's Hand. Worrying about you is just an unnecessary burden. Besides, the Republic needs you in the Master Control Center with Gretchen to monitor SF."

Frank pursed his lips, wanting to argue more.

Welles leaned forward, and Gretchen's jaw tensed.

After looking around the table, Frank sighed. "You win. I'll stay in the Master Control Center."

Gretchen relaxed and exhaled. She let her hands rest in her lap.

"Now that that's settled," Red said, "we have a pressing issue. What you just saw was only Steele's opening move."

Gretchen crossed her legs. "Surely, she realizes she's stalemated."

Red shook his head and closed his eyes for a moment. "The ground transports were a diversion, perhaps reinforcements, to the breacher team."

"I agree with Gretchen—stalemate," Frank said. "Just like we planned."

Red placed his hands palm down on the table. "You are mistaken. Let's take a variation of what we saw SF do. Instead of the lander setting down beyond the trench, it lands near the Main Airlock."

Gretchen interrupted, "You said they weren't combat-rated."

"We could destroy it easily with a demex or two. If they get a ground transport out beforehand, which is likely, they can ram the airlock and ride directly to the Master Control Center. Perhaps the intruder system disables it, perhaps not. Once they occupy the Master Control Center, we're toast—victory to SF. Steele wouldn't think twice about sacrificing a lander to gain Bvindu Dome. She's incentivized to win. With success in this high-profile mission, she'll be in line for admiral's stars, regardless of casualties or equipment losses."

Gretchen looked at Frank. She was surely pondering the demexes in the Master Control Center's ceiling. He patted her hand under the table.

Space Force will never claim its prize. That wasn't victory, though. It didn't advance the Marsians' interests—it merely kept the Bvindu tech from the hands of the greedy elitists who'd pervert it to accumulate more power.

"What's your point, Red?" Frank asked.

"Steele has options. You and the rest of the Committee have to take the fight to Space Force."

The possible tactical options Red outlined were messy and ugly. Whatever the Republic would do needed to be in response to a Space Force action. Frank said, "Let me think it over. Defense is our only option until the loyalists are aboard the Baffin. Afterward, we have to convince Steele to leave orbit."

If Steele realizes she can't win and goes scorched earth, I'll be forced to choose between my former co-workers and Republic citizens...

Before Red could reply, Alan and June pulled up to the Planning Huddle Area on a cargo mover. Alan dismounted, and June stepped down from its bed. Together, they approached with haunted eyes.

Frank stood. "What happened?"

The others at the table mirrored him.

Alan said, "I'm sorry... Rizzo's dead. He was shot through the helmet."

"He was holding binoculars. His rifle wasn't in hand. He wasn't a threat," June said with a pinched voice.

Frank exhaled and bowed his head. "Let's take a moment."

He didn't know what else to say. War meant that good people died, though those making the decisions were the most insulated. He suppressed the urge to point out to the Committee that *this* was why he'd hesitated in choosing independence and insisted on doing so only when Washington pushed them too far.

Who would be next? Gretchen and our baby?

Red folded his hands in front of himself. "Rizzo was an excellent guardian and an even better friend. I'll miss him. We all will."

Frank raised his head. "When this is all over, we'll have a proper ceremony and bury him with honor outside Dome 6. Right now, it's up to us to ensure he didn't die in vain."

* * *

Frank settled into a chair beside Chuck before the tactical console. It displayed nothing aside from an icon representing the destroyer overhead.

Because he wasn't participating in this mission, he'd given Erin instructions before she headed toward the landing pad. *"If we detect a hint of Space Force coming our way, we'll recall you. Leave the equipment behind. Get everyone in the shuttle and haul ass within thirty seconds."*

Red interrupted his memory by asking over Bvindu comms, "Fire Rider, are you ready?"

"Yes. The miners and equipment are in the cargo bay."

"Launch when ready," Red ordered.

For many long seconds, the display remained static. Erin had to activate the landing pad, rise to its airlock, and open the dome doors. Frank could only rub his sweaty right hand against his coveralls.

"Taking off... Applying full power... Time to landing zone is forty-five seconds."

The shuttle appeared on the tactical display as an unknown radar contact. She had pulled the transponder and vidcomm boards from it, like Frank had done to hers. Space Force hadn't responded. Yet.

Seconds ticked off. Undoubtedly, the shuttle showed on the *Baffin's* tactical display. Space Force frequencies remained quiet.

Steele isn't enforcing the No-Fly Zone.

Perhaps she wasn't willing to engage over Bvindu Dome. Or maybe it was something else.

"We're at the breacher hatch. Hank is outside on lookout. The miners are deploying now. I see no sign of activity on the landscape."

"Copy that," Red acknowledged. "Everyone, stay alert. SF may've landed troops that we overlooked."

Staying alert was great advice, though the odds of missing a launch from the *Baffin* were low. Everyone taking shifts at the tactical station understood what was at stake.

Over the next thirty minutes, Welles provided several updates. Everything was going as planned. Erin and Hank had seen nothing during that time.

The tactical display showed a lander and two gunship icons depart Mars City.

Erin said, "*Heads up. I see three ships to the west. They appear to be heading into orbit.*"

Red knelt beside Chuck and pressed a couple of controls. "Confirmed. Their trajectory is toward the *Baffin*."

Chuck pointed to three more icons appearing atop the *Baffin's* icon on the screen. "We have more ships in the air."

Red pressed the same control sequence again. "The new ships are heading to Mars City."

"*Acknowledged. We're stowing equipment. Estimate five minutes to lift-off.*"

Red wiped his forehead with his coveralls sleeve. "Make it two. We're watching closely. If their course deviates, we'll let you know. You have to be in the air before they go behind the horizon. We don't want them sneaking up on us."

"*I'm done with surprises,*" Erin said. "*You all heard Red. Let's pick up the pace, people.*"

Three minutes later, Erin lifted off. The Space Force ships didn't stray from their courses.

Red, frowning, looked to Frank. "Steele's let us operate with no response."

"We caught a break."

"For our people outside. It also means that hatch plays no role in her plans. She has something different up her sleeve."

58 | CHECK

C'mon, Frank. Wake up. SF's on the move," Red said.
Frank opened his eyes. The hastily hung black curtain against the long edge of a row of processing cabinets consumed his vision.

Frank propped himself up on his right elbow. "What time is it?"

"Three. The military loves nighttime offenses."

"Four hours sleep—more than I expected." He yawned and wiped his watering eyes. "Gretchen and I'll be there in a minute."

As Red slipped beyond the curtain, Frank shook Gretchen's shoulder as she lay on a cot beside his.

She sat up, also fully clothed. "Time to go?"

He covered a yawn with his right hand and followed her around the curtain to the tactical alcove. Red, Baker, and Rodriguez trailed behind June and Alan, walking from their curtained-off areas. Everyone huddled around Chuck, seated at the tactical console.

Chuck took a gulp of coffee. "We spotted three gunships departing the *Baffin*, heading over the horizon six minutes ago."

"They'll likely hug the ground and land on our doorstep," Red added.

What would Space Force do next? Gunships were too small to carry ground transports, so that scenario was out. Were they just going to hole the dome, hope they didn't destroy anything valuable, and force everyone into spacesuits, making it impossible to eat or drink anything?

"Red, target the *Baffin* as we discussed," Frank said. "June, notify Erin to be ready for liftoff on ten minutes' notice."

Red sat beside Gretchen at the Bvindu control console, and Rodriguez and Baker waited at the drone consoles behind them. Frank watched the tactical display, which showed no activity.

Hank, who was stationed in the supplies building, asked, "*Master Sergeant, should I observe outside?*"

"Negative. Deploy the demexes on the dome side of the Main Airlock and around the Master Control Center's entrance. Set them for remote detonation."

Frank focused on June, who'd taken a seat before the vidcomm. "Send an alert to everyone. I want them to be ready to seal spacesuits on thirty seconds' notice."

After June transmitted the vidcomm alert, she and Alan brought spacesuits for everyone. One at a time, they donned them, leaving their helmets and gloves beside their stations.

Frank was last. Gretchen helped him into his, finally securing his arm against the air vest with the sling.

Seated before the Bvindu control panel, Gretchen announced, "I have thermal signatures and movement at the Power Generator 3 cave. Bringing up a visual."

Frank swiveled his chair to look over her shoulder at the Bvindu console's holo display. Two guardians in standard camo spacesuits using helmet lights and hand lights pushed a hand truck to the rear cave wall. Their lights converged on the dashes and circles etched into the stone door. The left figure pocketed a hand light and unpacked a high-end scanner with handles on either side and a screen opposite the front emitter.

"*Upload link established. Beginning scans,*" one guardian, a male, said over the Space Force frequency.

"*Acknowledged.*" The voice wasn't Steele's. There was no way of knowing if it was coming from the *Baffin* or the gunship.

With the scanner in hand, the guardian ran it parallel to the door from the ground to as high as he could reach. He made several passes and examined the screen.

Because Frank and Gretchen had been in that position two years earlier, that scan would not have revealed anything beyond what they'd reported. The cavern was filled with Marsium121 stalactites and stalagmites.

Red asked, "What're they looking for?"

Frank tapped his forefinger against his chin. "Steele may be brighter than I gave her credit. She may've connected the dots that the caretaker's message we found in the cavern got there by the caretaker transiting underground from Bvindu Dome."

"But they have to get into the power-generating cavern first," Gretchen said, "which is tough without the access sounds."

This was precisely why Gretchen hadn't provided details on how she deciphered the door's symbols or that they translated into musical tones.

Red sighed. "Explosives have a way of solving problems."

"Damn!" Frank exclaimed. "June, open our broadcast frequency."

After pressing a few controls, she gave a thumbs up.

"Colonel Steele, withdraw your guardians from the cave. They're in imminent danger. Do not detonate explosives."

"Brentford, I'm done sparring. I repeat—your little rebellion is over."

"You're going to get more good people killed." Frank looked at June. "Cut transmission."

"What am I missing?" Red asked.

Gretchen explained, "Power is generated by the Marsium121 stalactites and stalagmites *submerged* in water. If the guardians blast through the door, that water rushes out, probably with a million Marsium121 splinters slicing and dicing everything in their path."

"So much for giving Steele too much credit." Frank shook his head. "The power-generating capacity would be ruined. If Steele destroys all three power generators, Bvindu Dome will only have minimal power from the backup generator beneath us."

Red squinted while puckering his lips. "Got it. We lose the Asteroid Defense System and the Intruder Defense System. After we're subdued, they can drop a nuclear reactor on our doorstep, never giving the power generators another thought."

"Even if the Marsium121 remains intact," Frank said, "they can sever the transmission line. Without power, we don't just lose our defenses. Environmental control, water purification, and air generation go offline, too. We'd be forced to surrender."

Gretchen shuddered. "Or die freezing, dehydrated, and gasping for air."

59 | ULTIMATUM

On the holo, Frank watched the two guardians pack the scanner and push the hand truck beyond the Bvindu visual pickup. They returned, each carrying a suitcase-sized container. One of them said, "*Proceeding to phase two. We should secure the objective within ten minutes. Prep the techs.*"

"Those are standard demo packs," Red warned.

"Gretchen, activate emergency shutdown," Frank said.

Red concentrated on Gretchen working the Bvindu console while he ordered, "Baker, get a drone to Power Generator 2. Rodriguez, Power Generator 1. Now! Open fire on anyone visible."

"Roger, Master Sergeant!" they said in unison.

Baker added, "The armored suits' protection is great, but mobility sucks. I'm not surprised SF reverted for this mission."

"*Shall we launch?*" Erin asked from the Bvindu Scout Ship.

"Hold for now," Frank said.

In the holo of the cave's interior, the guardians placed two demo packs at ground level on the door as Gretchen hit the last control. The door cracked at the top. Water blasted straight out, gaining in intensity as the door receded into the ground. The visual didn't show much more than whites and grays of warm, gushing water.

Over the Space Force frequency, the guardians shouted surprise, then grunts coupled with multiple expletives. Steele requested a status update.

A voice infused with tension said, "*Wait one.*"

Gretchen explained, "The cave is part of the emergency shutdown facility. Its purpose is to evacuate the water under pressure and can clear the cavern in a tick under a minute."

"Close the door." Frank leaned closer to Gretchen, his head almost on her shoulder. "Let's evaluate what we have."

Gretchen pressed a series of controls. "Emergency evacuation overridden. The door is back in position, and the cavern is sealed."

The cave's water level slowly receded beyond the visual pickup, leaving a lazy swirling mist.

"This is taking forever," Red said.

"The water's flowing at the speed of Mars gravity." Gretchen yawned into the back of her hand. "It's just a cave—no pumps to help."

Red rubbed the back of his neck. "So why didn't this happen to you and Frank when you explored the cavern?"

"At that time, Power Generator 3 was idle. My translation," Gretchen used air quotes around the word *translation*, "of the dashes and circles played aloud in Bvindu tone language what was carved into the door. Only after I had a better vocabulary did I understand the symbols. They warn that water under pressure is behind the door. Then, they provide the command to drain the water via normal means into holding tanks beneath the cavern. Last was the command to open the door. When I transmitted the entire sequence, the system ignored the warning and the drain command—that action had already been accomplished. It simply opened the door for us."

Frank harrumphed. "We got lucky. I never liked luck—it has a way of running out when most needed, getting you and everyone around you killed."

Colonel Steele requested status.

"*Spinner here, Colonel. Everything went pear-shaped. The cave just spewed a torrent of water like a dam bursting. The specialists' status is unknown.*"

"Refilling the generator," Gretchen announced. "Generator water level at sixty percent and filling. Once done, the generator's storage tank won't have enough to refill if we emergency vent again."

"Got it," Frank said.

After a few minutes, the Bvindu holo display showed the water draining to roughly knee level with fog hovering on its surface.

As no one had ever released that quantity of water on Mars, it was hard to know exactly what was happening science-wise. Some of the water would've sublimated—the fog showed as much. The rest would soak into the ground beyond the cave entrance and freeze into an ice layer.

The most important thing was what wasn't visible—lights from the guardians or demo packs.

"*Spinner, Giles here. Renfro and I are partially buried in water and ice at the bottom of the cave's slope. We need assistance. Renfro's spacesuit has visible breach sealant, and I'm almost sure my leg's broken.*"

"*Renfro here. I have suit integrity. I have broken ribs and a dislocated shoulder.*"

"*Acknowledged,*" Spinner said. "*Stay put. You may damage your suits further and lose integrity. We'll be there in five minutes.*"

Red took a few breaths. "Rodriguez, what do you have?"

"My drone's still in transit."

"Baker?"

"Mine just arrived. A gunship landed about thirty yards from the cave at the base of its slope. No activity."

Spinner said, "Baffin, *this is Team One. We are a no-go. Repeat, no-go. The demo packs and two specialists were flushed out of the cave.*"

Colonel Steele said, "*Say again, I did not copy.*"

"*The guardians were thrown from the cave by a pressurized stream of water. They're both alive but injured with spacesuit damage. We're retrieving them now.*"

"*This is Lunchbox. Shall we proceed?*"

"*Wait one,*" Steele said.

Frank ordered, "Deploy the Lightning's Hand on the first target."

"On it," Red acknowledged.

Gretchen slid to the left, allowing Red complete access to the Bvindu control console.

He manipulated the controls and fired the Lightning's Hand. "A *Baffin* cargo storage hold is open to space."

"Open the MarsVantage vidcomm frequency."

June touched a few controls and pointed to Frank.

"Colonel Steele, this is Frank Brentford. Please respond."

A few moments ticked by. *"Brentford, what the hell are you doing?"*

"What the hell I'm doing is putting an end to Washington's power and money grab. You aren't getting Bvindu Dome. Period. The Mars City evacuation is complete—no evacuation flights have occurred for over two hours. Your choice is to withdraw or have your ship destroyed. You have two hours to recall all your gunships and break orbit."

"Would you actually destroy a ship holding your former co-workers?"

There was a victory, not for the immediate battle, but for the long-term struggle for the Earthers' hearts and minds. "Colonel Steele, you're using our friends and former co-workers as human shields to continue an unwarranted aggression. That's a tactic only the most brutal and tyrannical regimes in history have used. It's contrary to the Law of War, not to mention human decency. You now have one hour and fifty-nine minutes. Cut transmission."

Red stood and shook Frank's hand. "Well done."

Gretchen hugged him tightly. His left arm protested the pressure.

Once she released him, he looked to everyone present. "We haven't won anything yet."

60 | FROM A POSITION OF STRENGTH

Frank settled into the co-pilot's seat of the Bvindu Scout Ship. Erin helped to strap him in.

Thirty minutes earlier, the last gunboat had returned to the *Baffin* after rescuing the two trapped guardians from the ice. No ships had departed, but the destroyer's engines remained in standby mode with fifteen minutes remaining on the deadline.

Erin said, "The miners in the cargo area with the emergency canisters filled with tranquilizer gas are ready to go."

The Committee's backup plan was to use the *Baffin*'s in-port atmo connectors to tranq the entire crew. According to Red, those connectors served another purpose—emergency atmo while the ship was underway. He'd also provided access codes to unlock those connectors.

If the Republic's primary plan failed, they'd try tranqing the crew despite murky logistics. He asked, "Are you sure you can pilot a destroyer?"

"I can get it underway. Probably. Most likely." She bit her lip. "How hard can it be? It's a spaceship."

"That's the Erin-patented can-do attitude I'm used to." Lately, everyone was doing something for the first time. Frank ran his hand through his hair. "This last attack was a complete surprise. I took the safety of the power generators for granted, assuming their physical presence would be preserved like the dome. I could kick myself for that oversight."

"Frank, your head needs to be here. Living in the past will get everyone killed in the present. Give yourself a break. Red didn't anticipate that move, either. You did the best you could."

"Point taken. We have to end this now. Should Steele counter our next move, the miners back there and your expertise will come

267

into play. Make no mistake. We won't be in control—there could be casualties."

"How do we stop Steele, so we don't endanger the ship and miners?"

"I will prove Red wrong and bluff Colonel Steele the entire way back to Earth. If our acting skills hold up..."

"There's a reason you've never been asked to perform in the plays at our monthly parties."

He laughed so hard his arm ached. "I thought it was because I was busy keeping everything running."

Erin glanced back to the cargo area. "Hold on. I'm taking off."

As the launch pad rose from the Bvindu Dome's deck, buildings beyond the Manufacturing Section came into view through the cockpit window. They stopped for the dome-side airlock doors to close. The Mars-side airlock doors opened, and they rose. The eastern range of the Maelstrom Mountains in the distance, with countless stars above, greeted them. She lifted off, staying close to the ground. When proximate to the mountain range, she banked to parallel it.

Erin flipped on the Bvindu comm frequency. "Red, has Space Force responded to my launch?"

"*Nothing yet. I'll alert you if anything changes.*"

"Appreciate it." She climbed, still heading away from the *Baffin* and the OTP. "Once we're not silhouetted against the planet, I'll change course to the *Baffin*."

Frank gave her the details of where he wanted to be positioned in relation to the destroyer. As Erin did her bit, he adjusted the strap on his sling.

The seat wasn't as comfortable as he remembered. Perhaps the excitement of the first flight had pushed the discomfort away. The annoying sling didn't help matters, that was for sure.

After ten minutes, they approached the *Baffin* from above. It was no bigger than his thumb. Erin slowly and precisely closed the distance and maneuvered off the *Baffin*'s port bow low, angling away from Mars and the destroyer still docked with the OTP.

Frank announced, "The deadline has passed."

61 | Seizing the Initiative

"**P**repare to shoot the next target, Red. Remember, I want the corner only destroyed," Frank said from the cockpit of the Bvindu Scout Ship. This move ought to impress upon Steele that the Republic was serious. If so, more people wouldn't have to die. *If not...*

"*Don't get between the* Baffin *and us. You don't register on our tactical display at all.*"

Frank asked, "Does that mean Steele doesn't know we're here?"

"*Most likely.*"

Frank breathed a sigh of relief. "Fire when ready."

A bright red beam struck the corner of the OTP. A white mist of atmosphere spewed into space. Once the atmosphere ceased gushing out, the hull was singed around the hole. Its edge shined from frozen water vapor. The decompression force must've strained the docking connectors, yet the *Baffin* stubbornly remained docked.

Steele hadn't undocked like a transport would have. Not only was that procedure but also common sense. She must not be easily dissuaded.

Frank ordered, "Carve it."

"*Acknowledged.*"

The red beam sliced lengthwise across the OTP. Then again and again.

Erin said, "It's like cutting cheese."

"I hate destroying it, but Steele needs to understand our resolve. Gretchen, patch me through on the *Space Force* frequency."

"*Hold, Gretchen,*" Red ordered. "*Say again, Frank.*"

"That's right. The Space Force frequency."

A few seconds passed before Gretchen said, *"You're patched in."*

Now was the time to sow uncertainty and doubt by using Space Force's own frequency, encryption and all. That ought to make them question their long-held assumptions, even if only on a subconscious level.

"Colonel Steele, our deadline has passed. You are violating Mars Republic space. You are ordered to depart immediately or face confiscation or destruction of your spacecraft."

"Brentford, I'm not intimidated by a group of miners whose ego is bigger than Mars. I'm curious—how do you know we didn't accommodate your friends on the OTP? You may have committed mass murder."

"The OTP is too small to house our former co-workers properly and lacks basic necessities for so many people."

"Quite shrewd. Still, you can't win. There's no one to help you. No supplies are coming."

"Your concern should be *your* supply lines. Any ship, civilian or military, US or foreign, will be destroyed when it gets within thirty light-seconds of Mars. Since you're using far more food than you planned, you'll need to be resupplied sooner rather than later."

Colonel Steele sighed. *"You expect me, Space Force, and the civilian leadership to believe you're willing to destroy ships and murder our crews? You don't have the cojones."*

"Next target," Frank said.

A red beam hit the destroyer amidships and, for a moment, proceeded beyond. Like the OTP, the atmosphere rushed out in a stream of mist. Flotsam, probably hand tools and spare parts, also drifted into space.

Frank added, "That was one of your port hangars. No more flight operations from there."

"Enough! We're taking off the gloves."

"Anything launched will be destroyed. Any offensive actions against Bvindu Dome will be met with devastating fire on the *Baffin*. Take a look off your bow around ten o'clock low."

"Great. Stars. Mars. Wreckage that was once the OTP."

"Partially disengage the phantom cloak now." That command was for Steele's benefit—Erin did nothing. Frank produced a hand light from his spacesuit. He shined it out the cockpit window toward the destroyer. "See anything else?"

Instead of a witty reply, silence reigned. He switched off the light. The *Baffin*'s bow cannons were swinging around. He winked at Erin. "Full phantom cloak and evasive maneuvers at variable speed."

As they'd agreed, Erin jumped the scout ship out of orbit, much like the test they'd performed a couple of weeks earlier. The *Baffin* ought to interpret what they saw as a ship having cloaked itself—it was more fuel to feed their uncertainty. As a good military leader, Steele would be rightfully concerned. Either that would prompt her departure or cause her to double down.

Erin adjusted the controls and jumped again. This time, they were about a mile from the *Baffin*'s engines on the starboard side.

"Fire on the next two targets," Frank said over Space Force's frequency.

Red followed the script, which was prearranged during the two-hour deadline. The first red energy beam hit along the port side just before amidships. A second hit closer to the bow.

"That's another hangar and a storage area. Pull out now."

Seconds ticked by. From a starboard hangar, a gunship emerged. Frank said over Space Force's frequency, "Heads up, everyone. Steele placed a new target on the board, and it looks like missiles are hanging from its underside."

"It's on the tactical," Gretchen announced.

"*They're probably bunker-busters,*" Red speculated. "*They can break through the cavern, and guardians can proceed with their original plan.*"

"Remove it from *my* sky," Frank said evenly.

"*Disabling now.*"

The gunship serpentined as a pale red beam slashed between it and the destroyer. A second shot hit an engine, which vaporized. A third shot eliminated the second engine. The gunship was adrift.

"Launch a rescue pod for your gunship. Anything else will be disabled or destroyed," Frank announced. "And then pull out."

Nothing happened. Steele didn't return banter, nor did she dispatch a rescue pod. The gunship's momentum drove it away from the destroyer.

Then, it adjusted course in a slow, wide arc using maneuvering thrusters. When the thrusters' exhaust stopped, the gunship moved on a trajectory toward the destroyer. The pilot reported they'd intercept within ten minutes.

Impatience urged Frank to continue as planned. His better judgment insisted on allowing Steele time to make the right decision. Ten minutes would tell.

"It's just us—we're not broadcasting," Erin said. "I've been thinking about tranqing the *Baffin*. It's a loser. We have no weapons. Their cannons will blow us out of the sky once they spot us."

Frank agreed with her assessment, but it was better than obliterating the destroyer, the crew, and their friends. "It's a last resort and risky, I know. If Steele sees reason, no one's leaving the comfort of this ship."

Erin pointed toward the cockpit window. Figures exited the disabled gunship. Three wore EVA propulsion modules, each trailing three others by a cable. They headed directly toward a starboard hangar. The gunship's trajectory would take it over the destroyer's topside, heading planetward, far away from Mars City.

"*We're approaching starboard, Beta Hangar.*"

Someone on the *Baffin* said, "*Acknowledged. Hangar opening.*"

Erin cocked her head left, then right, looking out the cockpit window. After consulting the navigational screen, she slumped into the seat. "We're creating a navigational mess here. We have chunks of the OTP and the *Baffin* floating about. The gunship ought to crash soon enough, though."

"Add it to the growing list of messes."

"Now's not the time to slip into cynical mode." Erin's face was expectant. "We have to let the *Baffin* recover the gunship crew. Tell me what you're thinking."

"Shortly, we'll disable all their hangar bays. Will Colonel Steele force a choice between our friends destined for Earth and our Mars Republic citizens? She can still bombard Bvindu Dome."

"Isn't that cutting off her nose to spite her face?"

"As much as the corrupt Washington elitists want the Bvindu tech, they want to retain power more. They're worried about losing elections, power, and status." He rubbed his eyes with his right hand. "Regardless, Steele may go scorched earth."

Erin blinked a few times. "The elites rarely lose offices, but their reputations could be damaged."

"Ego... I hadn't considered that much. Whatever the motivation, it's feeding their fear and driving the entire conflict."

"What'll you do?"

"Whatever I have to." He set his jaw.

Red could try reducing power to disable the cannons without destroying the ship. With too little power, the *Baffin* would continue a bombardment. Too much, it'd be sliced apart like the OTP. The margin of error was slim.

"There's the *after* to consider, too." Frank sighed. "People won't like living in Bvindu Dome for long. Taking an elevator to the showers permanently is a bridge too far. I already heard grumbling."

"Wait. You *can* fix Mars City, right? You only have to get control over the hatches and airlocks and then repressurize."

"I backed up the original programs to my datapad. We'll get Mars City livable and get our people back there. It's too far away to commute by a tractor and too expensive to fly. We have to figure out how to make Bvindu Dome more livable."

"Huh. Wouldn't a high-speed train work?"

No reason it wouldn't. The power generators would have enough leftover for a maglev train. "That's a brilliant idea. Given a reasonable speed, we could do the trip in thirty to forty minutes."

Erin nodded and switched on Bvindu comms. "That gunship crew should be out of the hangar by now."

Frank shifted against the harness. "Okay, Red, disable the remaining hangars."

63 | CHECKMATE

Seconds later, Red fired three beams, one after the other, to find their targets on the *Baffin*. From the cockpit of the Bvindu Scout Ship, Frank cringed at the amount of damage the destroyer suffered. None of that compared to the lives that hung in the balance, depending on Steele's next move.

"Colonel Steele," Frank said on Space Force frequencies, "all hangars are inoperable. You cannot accomplish your primary mission. Your best move is to withdraw."

"I don't take orders from the enemy, nor do I take advice from miners."

"I agree about the enemy. But I'm open-minded about advice, regardless of the adviser's position. However, I'm only offering information. Our conversation, like all of our conversations, is being recorded. We've had your comms since you made orbit, and we've recorded them. Friends on Earth have copies already. Shutting down the M-T wormholes hasn't hindered us."

"That means nothing. Some cubicle-bound geek will figure out your little tricks, and we'll plug the holes soon enough. I still have a mission."

That poor analyst would learn the meaning of futility. Perhaps they'd eventually recommend improvements around the margins, but the root issue would go unresolved.

Before getting any answers, Space Force would change the encryption keys. It was quick and easy but wouldn't safeguard the comms for long. A Knowledge Keeper would provide new ones whenever needed. The task Space Force would find more difficult, if not impossible, was locating the person or people passing along the encryption keys.

"Your options are few. I suspect every ship within the *Baffin* is damaged. Perhaps you can repair a few, but you lack time. We're prepared to destroy your engines and tow a derelict *Baffin* beyond our territorial space."

Erin looked his way with horror etched into her face.

He met her gaze and shook his head. "As I mentioned earlier, we're recording these conversations. You're on notice that bombarding a civilian population from orbit will not be tolerated. We will take whatever action is needed. Also, a record will be provided to the International Criminal Court for prosecution. You can leave now of your own volition or be towed. You can leave without further hostility or answer war crimes charges. Our patience is exhausted. You have five minutes until your engines are targeted. End Space Force transmission."

Gretchen confirmed the channel was closed.

Erin also placed the scout ship's comms in monitor mode. "We can't tow that ship, and I have no idea what'll happen if I attempt a jump beside it."

"Remember what I said earlier? I'm bluffing so hard it hurts. If Steele buys it, we're golden. If not... we'll have to make a high-risk move."

Erin twisted, looking aft into the cargo bay. "Be prepared to move out on two minutes notice."

Welles confirmed before he had the other miners don helmets and gloves.

"Can you position us to get a better view of the *Baffin*'s underside?" Frank asked. "I want a good look at those cannons."

After regripping the collective and cyclic, Erin performed the maneuver. Slowly. "I'm being careful not to draw attention to us. This phantom cloak exists in your imagination and Space Force's collective mind. And before you ask, I won't allow Mars to silhouette us."

"You're reading my mind."

"It's good *you* can't read *mine* right now."

He laughed. She'd never witnessed him telling such a gigantic lie.

The underside came into view. As the scout ship continued toward the destroyer's aft, Frank craned his head to get a better look. *Are the port side cannons moving?*

A few seconds later, Erin announced, "I can't be certain, but the port side cannons appear to be moving."

"Damn. I thought it was an illusion. Enable Bvindu comms."

She pressed the proper controls.

Frank explained the situation to Red.

"*Steele could hole Bvindu Dome, or she could bombard the power-generating caverns. Either way, we surrender or die. I recommend firing on the cannons.*"

Their choices were that or trying to tranq the destroyer. The latter could kill the miners before they deployed the sleeping gas while the former could destroy the cannon and hole the hull in critical areas, killing his former co-workers.

Steele will only leave when that's her only option...

"Red, fire on the port side aft cannon, one emitter at one percent power for five seconds."

"*Acknowledged.*"

A maroon blast hit the cannon. When it ended, the cannon glowed a dull red but still appeared intact. "Up it to five percent and try again."

When the beam finished, the cannon looked like a melted candlestick. The hull nearby seemed intact, though crepe-like.

"Perfect. Take out all the cannons on the underside, port side first."

"*Firing now.*" The beams flared to life. Red's impressive marksmanship completed the task in seconds.

"Open Space Force frequency."

"You're on," Erin said.

"Colonel Steele, you have no launch capability, and your underside cannons are non-functional. Do you wish to try with your topside cannons? We can destroy those as well. Do you want us to destroy your engines next? We can tow you. Or would you prefer to withdraw on your own? Decide. Now."

"*Brentford, our engines are warming. We'll break orbit within fifteen minutes.*"

"We're watching very closely, Colonel. Any funny business and your engines will be atoms adrift on the solar wind," Frank warned. "Disconnect Space Force frequencies—enable Bvindu comms."

Erin adjusted the controls. "Done."

"Good shooting, Red," Frank announced.

"Remind me never to play poker with you."

"Can you get us a view of the *Baffin*'s engines?" Frank asked. "It's not that I don't trust Steele—it's that I *really* don't trust her."

The destroyer's hull passed by, allowing the engines to come into view. They glowed a brownish red. Steele had spoken the truth. So far. Activated engines didn't equate to leaving Mars space, though.

"Let's sit tight and ensure Steele doesn't pull a fast one. Red, prepare to fire on anything departing the *Baffin,* assuming Steele can get something in the air."

"Wilco, Frank."

A rational person would evaluate the situation, accept it, and withdraw. Was Steele sensible? Besides withdrawal, she could roll the *Baffin* and try with the topside cannons, or she could perform a suicide run. Red could take out cannons, but...

"Check that out." Erin pointed out the cockpit window. The engines transitioned from glowing yellow to blue-white.

"Tactical shows movement," Chuck announced.

"We see it, too," Erin said.

Frank asked, "Which direction? To break orbit or de-orbit?"

"What are you thinking, Frank?"

"Suicide run." Frank glanced toward Erin. "Take us to an atmo connector on the underside."

"On our way. Miners prepare to deploy."

"That's extreme," Red said, disbelief infused in his voice. *"Nothing in SF doctrine dictates such a maneuver."*

"Firing on civilians isn't standard procedure... Better safe than sorry."

Seconds ticked by. A group of four atmo connectors passed above the cockpit. Erin brought the scout ship to a stop relative to the *Baffin.*

Red announced, *"The* Baffin *is pulling away from Mars. They're withdrawing, Frank."*

"Erin, follow the *Baffin* at a discreet distance. I'm not letting my guard down yet." While circumstances were looking up, Frank wouldn't breathe easily until the destroyer was far away from Mars. "Open Space Force frequency."

"Opened," Erin responded.

"Colonel Steele, we're watching your withdrawal closely. Mars' territorial space extends thirty light-seconds. Any ship violating it will be met with deadly force. These rules remain in effect until the United States formally recognizes the Mars Republic."

"*We're withdrawing,*" Colonel Steele admitted. *"You win—for now."*

64 | UNEXPECTED HELP

With the *Baffin* Earthbound, Gretchen sat on the couch in her quarters, wishing Frank were by her side. He'd insisted on following the destroyer for a time to ensure Steele didn't attempt a trick. The Asteroid Monitoring System on Phobos and Deimos also tracked the *Baffin*, but he wouldn't be satisfied unless he saw its withdrawal with his own eyes.

She placed her hand on her belly, relishing the tranquility. "Little Jelly Bean, we averted catastrophe. Our former co-workers aboard the destroyer are out of harm's way, heading to Earth. Our fellow Republic citizens are safe. We achieved the freedom to choose our path. I can only imagine the future that you'll see."

With everything happening recently, she hadn't had time or energy to play the guitar. She retrieved it from the case and returned.

Playing would help her unwind. She exhaled and closed her eyes as she cradled the instrument against her body. "By the time you meet Daddy and me, you'll want to play, too."

She strummed her guitar, lazily changing chords. Under her skilled touch, the cold steel strings bent to provide a calming atmosphere, washing away the past few days of tension.

The issues going forward were formidable, though. Food remained the biggest. They needed the Order's help. Yet, the Knowledge Keepers' recent machinations gave the Marsian Order members pause.

Morale among the employees was low. Living in Bvindu Dome was more spartan than they were used to—traveling several floors to use communal shower pods had a way of doing that. With Space Force's retreat, morale would crater unless Frank could undo what he had broken in Mars City.

Though pleased with the battle's outcome, the Committee members doubted Washington would simply give up. They were already aiming to avoid another confrontation, starting with an unconventional move that Frank had advocated. Chuck was preparing a broadcast package to capture the hearts and minds of the US public. Otherwise, all Committee members disengaged from backchannel diplomatic communications.

Assuming no more confrontations, self-sufficiency was their immediate goal. It was no longer aspirational—it meant survival.

Her stomach growled. Several hours had passed since awakening, and she was finally hungry. After setting her guitar aside on the couch, she grabbed a Scrambled Egg Sandwich FieldMeal and water from the kitchen before sitting in front of the vidcomm. She pulled the container's heating tab and browsed her messages.

The FieldMeal's indicator turned green. She took a bite—it was a good lot, or perhaps it tasted better because Space Force no longer orbited overhead. She continued reading messages, coming to the end with nothing pressing as she finished breakfast.

Gretchen yawned and looked to the bedroom. Her datapad chimed with a vidcomm. *What could she possibly need?*

* * *

A few minutes after disconnecting, Gretchen sat across from Lorah in her living room. Curiosity drove away the desire to crawl into bed.

"It's been a long day." Gretchen fought the urge to yawn. "What do you need?"

"We've all been up for hours in spacesuits, waiting to seal in and fight." Lorah exhaled. "I'm glad we avoided that."

"We all are. Odds are, Washington will test for weaknesses eventually."

Lorah frowned. "A wise guess. We'll have to remain vigilant."

"It's another item on a long task list. Anyway, what brings you by?"

Lorah pulled a datacard from her coverall's inner chest pocket and laid it on the coffee table. "In many ways, the aftermath will be more difficult than the past few days. Mr. Fordham planned ahead. During one of our last conversations, he sent a file intended for Frank or Chuck."

Gretchen picked up the datacard and turned it in hand. "And you're giving it to me?"

"He wanted someone in authority to have this data. Mr. Fordham launched a communications satellite to orbit an Earth Lagrange point. The file contains connection parameters to use it. We can connect Mars City comms and then vidcomm anyone on Earth. A cursory inspection of the calls will appear internal to Fordham Industries."

Taking this meeting had been the right decision. The Committee wouldn't have to worry about the military detecting and destroying the remoras attached to the satellites. "This is welcome news. You've been sitting on this for at least two weeks. Why'd you wait till now?"

Lorah looked like she ate bad fish. "You'll see when you read the file. For one, Mr. Fordham needed time to position his satellite."

"And..."

"He didn't want Space Force getting the info, so they had to depart or be destroyed." Lorah shook her head. "Before you ask, I don't know how he predicted what we just survived."

Gretchen leaned back into the chair. "As hard as we tried to avoid it, conflict was inevitable."

"I suspect Mr. Fordham expects the Republic to reestablish communication with the Order."

"I'll give this to Frank when he returns. He's already contemplating next steps and has talked the Committee into authorizing a trip to Earth."

Lorah drew her eyebrows together. "Earth? I thought he'd focus on getting Mars City habitable. Surely, he's heard the grumbling about Bvindu Dome's inconveniences."

"A maintenance team has to restore power to Mars City before Frank can address the airlocks."

Curiosity filled Lorah's eyes. "Why visit Earth?"

65 | SCIAMACHY

The sun had climbed halfway up the sky on an unseasonably cool August day in Washington, DC, as Maura walked through the Upper Senate Park a block from her office. Several others, in ones and twos, enjoyed the low humidity and temperatures in the low seventies. Who could blame them? They had an unexpectedly beautiful day without a care in the world. Her responsibilities, though, inhibited her appreciation.

The president had already vidcommed for advice to salvage the situation. Her recommendation had been to classify the engagement and claim the need to bring the civilians home. An asteroid strike could explain the *Baffin*'s heading to dry dock for repairs. That subterfuge would satisfy the public, but the Marsees had done the impossible and remained a threat.

The wooden bench Peter had specified lay ahead and empty. He was late. Instead of solving the Marsee problem, she was having a clandestine meeting in an out-of-way location.

The recriminations among Space Force, intelligence agencies, and the president looked more like a circular firing squad than adults solving a serious problem. She refused to listen to Peter complain or to soothe his bruised ego.

Perhaps Peter had an insight—it was the only reason she'd agreed to meet. *There still must be a way to end this rebellion.*

She sat on the steel and wooden bench, trying and failing to find a comfortable position. In a ploy to force that annoyance from mind, she pulled her datapad from her purse and browsed the latest report from Colonel Steele. All hangar bays were inoperable. Three-quarters of all spacecraft had been damaged beyond repair. Worse, Marsee operations in Bvindu Dome remained functional. Space Force had accomplished nothing except leaving the *Baffin* combat ineffective.

What remained to be seen was the status of Mars City. Clearly, the Marsees had sabotaged it. Officials argued over whether the damage was permanent.

Her bet was that it was repairable. Frugality and resourcefulness were synonymous with Marsee—destroying such a valuable asset was unthinkable.

Peter walked at a brisk pace toward her. He wore a fashionable tan Italian suit, a red tie with thin white stripes, and dark sunglasses. He sat to her right and glanced about casually. "We have a problem."

"*I* have a problem. The All News Network is resisting the direction we want to move in."

"Which is?"

"The destroyer disengaged to bring the civilians out of harm's way."

He scratched his forehead with his thumb. "What aren't they buying?"

"That damn reporter, Wagoner, figured out the Marsees severely damaged the *Baffin*. And he knows that Space Force attempted and failed to take Bvindu Dome."

While he took in the scenery, Peter nodded nonchalantly. "I'm sure you can find the proper mix of incentives and threats to get the story you need. How are you planning to regain control of Mars?"

"There's talk, which is gaining momentum, of sending multiple destroyers. They'll orbit out of sight of Bvindu Dome and destroy the power caverns. Then, SF takes Bvindu Dome—their weapons are useless without power. Mars City, if the Marsees get it habitable again, will eventually run out of fuel cells. We simply wait them out."

Peter placed his sunglasses into the inside pocket of his suit coat, then leaned forward, placing his elbows on his knees. "Maura, doing the same thing over and over and expecting different results is the definition of insanity."

"The destroyers will fly a route outside the normal travel lanes, more in a parabolic arc above and below the galactic plane. SF feels approaching the poles will allow for surprise."

"It's thinking like this that made me want an unofficial meeting. The wizards of smart at the White House aren't listening to reason and experience. Everyone is thinking about tactics and maneuvers instead of considering personalities. Worst of all, no one wants to give credence to our not seeing all of the Bvindu surprises." He rubbed his eyes. "Once we're done with this little talk, I'm taking the next hop to New York and releasing a statement separating myself from Washington's actions. I need to salvage my credibility. I'm looking at opportunities in the Belt and need bankers to take me seriously."

She gripped the bench seat like it was a lifeline. "That's a chickenshit move. You want MarsVantage back into the Interplanetary fold. Step back now, and you'll never get it."

Konklin tilted his head to one side like he wanted something to slide off. "Maura, when Brentford and Blake discovered Bvindu Dome, the odds were stacked against me ever regaining MarsVantage. That's the reason I tried so hard to prevent it. Whether they're a self-sufficient company or a nation-state, MarsVantage will never be mine again. Your scheme was my last hope, and it died hours ago in Mars orbit."

"Funny, it seemed like we were partners. Now that the path gets a little rough, you bail."

"Our options are exhausted." Konklin leaned back. "You're going to send good men and women off to slaughter using variations of tactics that already failed. There is only so much you can cover up. You realize the only reason the *Baffin* isn't twisted pieces of metal is that the Marsees' former co-workers were aboard. Remain on this course and you'll have nothing but wreckage and dead guardians. The next election cycle or two will send plenty of representatives and senators packing. Perhaps the president will be impeached and convicted by those same politicians in an attempt to salvage their careers."

He's right, damn it. All of the tried and true solutions had never worked with the Marsees. Regulate them, no. Tax them, no. Even force, under one of the best line officers, had failed. "Give me your take then."

"Really? I'm surprised."

"Hell, Peter. Other than Marsees physically attacking Washington, the only worse position we could be in is if they obliterate more destroyers."

"Finally, a spark of sense. Keep in mind that I reviewed all available information on the Bvindu—facts, reasonable speculation, and some conspiracy theories—while ignoring most of the news, punditry, and entertainment. I suspect the Bvindu were proactive and careful, much like the Marsees themselves."

"We've been working with *facts* and reasonable extrapolation of them."

He interlaced his fingers and placed his hands in his lap. "Perhaps my analysis contains some insights. For instance, their beam weapon resembles a defense system. It targets with the precision of our best weapons. It could be benign, designed to handle dangerous asteroids and comets, or a defense against aggressive aliens."

She glanced around to confirm no one was in earshot. "You should keep talk like that to yourself. We don't need a panic on our hands."

He smacked a mosquito that landed on his hand. "Such a system needs a detection component. It's somewhere other than at the dome or the energy caverns. Remember, until two years ago, everything Bvindu was underground. If you're careful and proactive, do you allow your defenses to become buried? I wouldn't."

"There's another component somewhere that *isn't* buried." She exhaled hard enough that it almost sounded like a snort. "I'm not liking where this line of thought leads."

"I don't want to say, 'I told you so,' but I did try to alert you. Notice the Marsees' warnings aren't about entering orbit. They claim five and a half million miles out. Whatever they have can reach that far. Maybe it's that beam weapon... It could be something else."

"You actually believe they can project that kind of power?"

"Guaranteed. If they can't, when you send automated probes—you will do that, right?—you'll discover they're bluffing and attack again. The Marsees know that. They don't kick the can down the road—they address an issue and move forward."

Ascertaining—not guessing—whether the Marsees were bluffing would provide valuable data. She opened her datapad and made a note. "That's a great idea. Anything else?"

He shifted to look her in the eye. "Understand that O'Donnell and his team thought through the practical considerations of their independence. They already have water and power. They have a solution to the food issue. I don't know how, but they aren't going to starve. Waiting out their failure isn't the road to victory."

"They *don't* have the capability. You designed Mars City to rely on Earth's resources, especially for food. The auditors and inspectors verified no farming was underway in Bvindu Dome. Mars City has minor capabilities, but it's a far cry from supporting their population."

He shook his head. "That's the problem. You and the others make decisions based on data—great—but it's incomplete, and you refuse to acknowledge it."

"Fine. They magically have food."

"No, not magic. *This* is an even bigger problem—you don't understand Marsee psychology. For years, they had to plan *months* in advance for their necessities. I have a notion for sushi— I visit my favorite black market. I want an apple—I go to the pantry, which is automatically restocked weekly. The Marsees can't even get decent apples. They've proven your assumptions wrong time and again. Give them the benefit of the doubt in everything, then reevaluate."

"C'mon—"

"Or don't. I'm sure you can arrange a soft landing once you're voted out of office in disgrace. Perhaps a teaching position or endless discussions in a think tank."

She crossed her legs and smoothed out her skirt. "Why the hard sale?"

"You're captaining the *Titanic* here. This is my last time yelling 'iceberg.' Right now, a presidential address to the country acknowledging Marsee independence with a path to rejoin us can keep you and your colleagues' heads above water. All you have to do is eat a little crow."

Peter pulled at his collar and tie. "Attack the Marsees again and lose, and it's all over. Nothing the president, you, or the pundits can say will save you."

"We could win."

"You haven't heard a word I said." He slowly shook his head. "I expect any win would equate to mass civilian casualties. Hear me—*how* you win matters. What's your real concern? What's driving this push so hard to bring the Marsees to heel?"

"What if people rebel here?"

"Seriously? The only people who had the slightest independent streak *moved* to Mars. Everyone else lacks the will to implement change."

How true. Most troublemakers had self-exiled. The few who were left could fill a single prison facility. If they stepped an inch out of line, that was precisely where they'd land. For life, and then some.

"Fine. We can handle any immediate problem. What happens when the Marsees, armed with Bvindu tech, set their sights on us?"

"There it is. This isn't about the Marsees breaking away." He placed his hands on his thighs. "Before Interplanetary lost MarsVantage, how many employees who held positions on Mars returned and became involved in state or federal politics?"

"No one comes to mind."

"Since my father forged the foundation block on Dome 1 five decades ago, no one who held a position more than five years on Mars ran for office when they returned home. Four others with short-term stints attempted a run, with one who held office for two terms as a state representative before moving on to other endeavors."

Only Konklin would know such trivialities. "How does that relate to the Marsee situation?"

"Look at the bigger picture, Maura. Marsees aren't interested in our politics. They grudgingly hired lobbyists who only engaged in matters directly affecting them. Marsees are the inheritors of the long-defunct libertarian movement. They see no prize in governance."

"If you're wrong, we're screwed."

"If Marsees attack Washington, the public would condone any weapon and tactic." He stood and she matched him. "I'm still taking the hop to New York City, but I'll hold off on a statement. If you continue recklessly attacking, I'll distance myself from this misadventure. Should you pull off humble contrition, saying your primary concern was their safety, I'll be evenhanded in my comments. People will forgive the misjudgment if you fake sincerity well enough. One last bit of advice—let go of the missing people attacking Washington talking point. No sane person is taking that seriously."

He put on his sunglasses and turned.

"Peter—"

He looked back.

"I'll talk with the president and his advisers."

66 | Verbum Sap

Earth replaced the rainbow Frank and Erin flew through. He blinked a few times, and his stomach settled quickly. "That will take a few more trips to get used to."

Erin maneuvered the scout ship level with the horizon. "Getting here in seconds is worth it."

"Uh-huh." The view beyond the cockpit was the planet's nightside. A faint blue and green aurora played against the starry sky. "Where are we?"

"Northern Canada. It's the safest insertion point. Everything below us is forest or snow plains."

She pulled back on the collective to descend. "We're between the Satellite Zone and Flight Zone used for intra-planet hops. It's smooth sailing to our destination."

"How smooth do you think sailing will be for Mars?" Frank asked. The previous night, Erin had been uncharacteristically quiet during the Committee strategy meeting.

"We're fortunate Space Force didn't sabotage Mars City or have a strike team waiting when you went to repair the airlocks and emergency bulkheads. But Washington hasn't forgotten us. As I see things, Space Force will appear on our doorstep within a decade if we do nothing."

"The two Space Force destroyers stationed on the shipping routes *outside* our territorial space are doing more than enforcing a blockade, don't you think?"

"They're spying on us, looking for weaknesses." After consulting the instruments, she adjusted course. "Alan summed it up best—they'll gather intelligence for a few years while politicians and pundits paint us as just short of evil incarnate. With changed perceptions, Washington can initiate a broader range of actions acceptable to the public."

"Why didn't you speak up last night?"

"It's easier to see the big picture with my mouth shut," she said.

"This trip is our opportunity to convince Severino to change course... If she listens to reason."

"I hope so. I don't want to see another attack."

"I'm willing to disable Space Force ships and bases in orbit and on the Moon if they attack again," Frank assured her. "Let's hope good sense comes from tonight."

"Normal relations should be the goal."

"I agree in principle, but that road must be traveled step by step."

The view outside had changed—no more auroras illuminated the sky. Concentrations of city lights dotted the landscape.

Erin banked to port, heading east. "We're approaching Washington now. It's 2:30 A.M. Where exactly do you want us?"

After pulling the datapad from his spacesuit thigh pocket, Frank extended the screen and held it with both hands close to his chest. A few more days and the sling would be out of his life forever. It couldn't come soon enough.

He duplicated his display to Erin's console. He annotated a path with a finger. "Pick up the Potomac River and follow it to this condo building. Orient the ship so I can see in."

"On it." She manipulated the controls. "I take it the Order provided this information?"

He chuckled. "Yes. Though I've been suspicious of Fordham from the beginning, the truth is he positioned a communication satellite to orbit the L2 Lagrange Point. After we're done here, I'll open up all the vid channels. We'll be able to see the news the people are seeing, not just the propaganda they're transmitting to us now."

"It'll still be propaganda, maybe with a smidge more truth mixed in." She adjusted course and speed, then pointed out the cockpit window. "That's our target, the building low to port. I'll come about."

With the simultaneous manipulation of the cyclic, collective, and pedals, she slowed the scout ship and guided it into a gentle turn. The streets and sidewalks below were vacant, at least what was visible in the streetlights. The ship maneuvered directly over the Potomac River. Forward motion slowed, and they descended.

"The building's coming up. What floor do you want?"

"Top floor. North corner."

When they reached the destination, Erin adjusted the controls for station-keeping. "I'll connect you to civilian comms, then I'll monitor military frequencies for any response."

* * *

The chiming datapad woke Maura. She reached for it on her nightstand, finding it on the third attempt. The front display showed the caller as *Out of Area*. She sat up and pulled open the screen. Strangely, no video displayed.

"*Senator Maura Severino, it'd be fruitful if we spoke.*"

"I have office hours and an assistant who schedules my meetings."

"*It's the only time I can speak with you in person. I'm outside your window. My name is Frank Brentford.*"

For a prank to be funny, it had to be plausible. "I'm not amused. That insurrectionist lives on Mars."

Light played across the drapes of her bedroom window. She crossed and pulled them apart. A ship hovered impossibly close to the building. Its surface glistened like thousands of irregularly shaped, gray patches brightening and dimming randomly. The steady beam stopped.

"Senator, nice to meet you."

Nice wasn't the word that sprang to mind. Unexpected and alarming were more like it. "What's on your mind for you to travel all this way?"

"It's best for everyone that we clear the air. A friend suggested that Washington and other ruling elites fear we Marsians will come here to take over. You see serving in Congress or sitting in the White House as the pinnacle of power and glory, the ultimate prize to the ultimate game.

"The Bvindu technology opens vast realms, which we're eager to explore. We've always viewed your political machinations as a childish game yielding dubious rewards. Now, it's never been truer. Earth, in general, and governing, specifically, is meaningless. Now, should you care to enter into trade treaties as peers and equals, we'll discuss it."

When Hell freezes over.

"I'm a senator. I don't negotiate treaties. You ought to speak to President Dohbyn or the State Department." Brentford broaching the subject suggested their position was shaky.

The insurrectionist actually chuckled. "Senator, there's no need for modesty. Everyone knows you have the president's ear in Mars matters."

"I won't confirm any such thing. We're willing to wait until your little experiment fails and return to pick up the pieces. Time and practical considerations are on our side."

After a few seconds, Brentford said, "We expected as much. Here's the thing—should you get impatient, our response to another attack will not be as measured as the last. We consider your spaceports as well as your warships fair targets. We refuse to live under the threat of force."

"How dare you threaten us, you silly miner."

"Senator, I intended no threat. I'm providing valuable information as to the consequences of certain actions. We are content to trade with the US and the other Earth nations. Or not. Beyond that, we wish to go about our business on Mars, in the Belt, and the outer planets without interference."

"Yet, I don't believe you."

"Unfortunately, I can't help that. We won't initiate violence. But if provoked, we'll meet violence with violence. Goodbye, Senator."

The spaceship followed the Potomac and rose rapidly until it disappeared in a burst of colors, which Steele had described as the Marsees' Phantom Cloak.

Senator Maura Severino wanted answers. How had Brentford reached Earth in mere days? Why hadn't the defense networks detected his ship while still in space? It was unconscionable that it reached the capital. She vidcommed the authorities—several workers would have to provide explanations to difficult questions.

67 | FORGING THE FUTURE

" I 'm on my way." Frank closed the datapad's screen and stowed it in his coveralls' thigh pocket. He turned his back on a Bvindu Scout Ship under construction. Progress was smooth. The Bvindu construction monitor reported the ship was nearing the halfway mark. A dozen semi-autonomous drones, each the size of a football, were installing and configuring circuits. In another two or three months, the ship would be ready. Erin should have a pilot or two trained to fly it by then, too.

He mounted the cargo mover and headed toward the Master Control Center. The natural light overhead had been a welcome change. Since the *Baffin* departed two months earlier, Welles had directed crews to plow away bands of sand covering the dome. The Bvindu surroundings had taken on an entirely new and pleasant appearance in the natural light. The buildings' exteriors were shades of tan, brown, and green.

After arriving, he entered and joined the rest of the Committee at the Bvindu control console. Red sat next to Gretchen. Frank looked over their shoulders.

Red turned. "The probe on a parabolic arc crossed the thirty-light-second demarcation. Its speed and trajectory are unchanged."

"You're sure it's uncrewed?" Chuck asked.

"Yes. It's a standard recon probe, twenty feet long."

Frank inspected the holo display. "How far into our space is it?"

"About a hundred thousand miles."

"And we agree it must be destroyed?" Frank asked.

June nodded while Chuck and Red said in unison, "Yes."

"Absolutely," Alan confirmed. "This is clearly a test of our will. If we fail to live up to our word, Washington could fire a barrage of missiles that we may or may not intercept. They may have the mindset that if they can't have the Bvindu tech, no one should. Bvindu Dome protected us when we knew Steele intended to capture it. That may not be the case anymore."

Chuck added, "We have to enforce the line we drew, or Washington will see it as weakness and send a full invasion force."

Frank straightened and ran his hand through his hair. "Phobos is out of position, but Deimos can eliminate the probe."

"But we'd reveal another capability," Chuck stated, though everyone present who knew him took it as a question.

Red offered, "We have a clear shot at the probe with the Lightning's Hand. I can hit it if it doesn't change course or speed."

"What's the monkey wrench?" Erin asked.

"It's at the targeting's outer range. I'd have to aim and shoot manually. Should I miss, we'd provide SF data on our capabilities." Red waved his hand at the controls. "I've been clearing the orbital debris. I can destroy it within five to seven shots. Probably."

Everyone chattered for several moments.

Gretchen turned to her co-workers, hovering behind her. Her face held equal measures of determination and annoyance. "Really? We're worried about *how many* shots it takes to destroy the probe? If it takes ten shots, Washington could interpret that as the edge of our range, and we aren't a threat. But the probe will be *destroyed,* and that's the point."

That's my wife. The others just stared at her. Frank struggled to suppress a grin. "Unless there's a strenuous objection, Red will take the shot."

"We're worrying about minor considerations and losing sight of the big picture." Chuck gave Gretchen a quick nod. "If it doesn't work, we can always use Deimos' capabilities. Washington is testing us. We absolutely must follow through on our word now. Otherwise, Washington will send more destroyers that we'll be forced to engage, killing untold numbers."

Gretchen faced the console while Red manually adjusted the targeting. The probe grew until it filled the holo display. He touched several controls, and an energy beam fired.

They had to wait thirty seconds to learn the results. No one dared speak. Frank barely breathed, waiting for the beam to obey the laws of physics.

The beam intercepted the probe, winging it.

"Factoring in the result. Wait one." After a couple of adjustments, Red fired again.

Frank swallowed, but his mouth was as dry as the sand outside.

Thirty seconds later, only chunks of varying sizes remained.

Frank shoved his hands in his pockets and breathed easy. "Two shots. Great work."

"I'll monitor the debris as it approaches," Red said, "and eliminate any hazardous pieces."

"That'll work. I've got a lot to get done before the Steering Committee meeting this afternoon." Frank strolled among the data cabinets toward the exit.

After centuries of near inactivity, those cabinets were overseeing dozens of tasks. Besides manufacturing scout ship components, the factories created supports, ties, and rails for the maglev rail line that'd connect them to Mars City. The detection portion of the Asteroid Defense System on Phobos and Deimos, updated with a lower mass detection threshold, transmitted its data here for analysis. The now-destroyed probe was a testament to its capabilities.

Near the door on the floor lay the keypad to his makeshift security system. The Committee agreed that it needed to be mounted waist-high near the door. Everyone was annoyed at bending over to enter the code. *If this is our most pressing problem, we're in great shape.*

Outside, he stopped and peered toward the farmland district under the red skies shining through the dome. He couldn't make out any details, but that didn't matter. Knowing work was underway was gratifying.

A handful of farmers from Shadow City were preparing scores of acres for planting using Bvindu techniques, including the perfection of vertical planting for many crops. Once everything was set in motion, they'd upgrade Mars City's planting areas on the upper levels of the domes.

Upgrading farmland was a euphemism. When he'd exposed the domes to below-freezing temperatures, he'd killed everything being grown and rendered the soil useless. The farmers' task in the domes would be closer to starting from scratch like they'd done in Bvindu Dome.

Within a year, the farmers estimated they'd have more variety and better quality crops than anything grown in Mars City thus far. Until then, everyone relied on rationed portions from the food produced by Shadow City and whatever foodstuffs Fordham shipped. Shortly, Erin should land the scout ship that had docked with a Fordham transport *en route* to the Belt.

That morning's Steering Committee agenda centered around Shadow City. The psychological benefits of rotating people among the three cities were overwhelming—complexity lay in formalizing guidelines and schedules. Complicating matters was that they couldn't agree on excavating it like Bvindu Dome.

Each side had excellent points. He'd been against excavation until Gretchen privately pointed out he'd been making decisions based on fear of what Washington might do or be able to do in the future. Washington would eventually discover that they had a base at Shadow City's location—there was no hiding the shuttle traffic. Transferring so much more cargo to and from the surface via the sole elevator was becoming impractical.

Many would drown in all of these details and a hundred more. For him and the other Committee members, their spirits were buoyant. They were forging the future, free of pointless restrictions. No longer were they pawns in the elitists' quest for power, wealth, and reputation.

His daughter, Freedom, and all the Marsian children would grow up surrounded by limitless opportunities that had last existed centuries ago. They'd go to the outer planets and their moons. With what they'd find, combined with the Bvindu knowledge, they'd live in a future their parents could barely imagine, leading humanity to new heights.

The End

About the Author

George G. Moore worked on the International Space Station project in the late 1980s. Since then, he created computer systems and managed projects for BoatU.S., a recreational boaters' association, and Geico, from which he retired in 2021.

He co-chairs elections for Pennwriters, an organization that helps writers of all levels to improve and succeed in their craft. Also, he participates in several writing critique groups.

While he primarily writes science fiction and speculative fiction, he's working on a contemporary mystery.

He currently lives in northern Virginia and relaxes by swimming, golfing, reading, and attending concerts.

He previously published the novel, *The Music of Mars* and the following short stories:

- Forging Freedom Anthology, Freedom Forge Press
  (Short story: The Shape of Things to Come)
- Forging Freedom II, Freedom Forge Press
  (Short story: Unintended Lesson)
- Spies & Heroes: An International Anthology, S&H Publishing, Inc
  (Short story: Spying Isn't Easy)
- Restless Spirits: An Hourlings Anthology
  (Short story: The Curse of Rachael's Crest)

For updates on more Mars stories and future projects, check out:

www.GeorgeGMoore.com

Instagram @GeorgeGMoore

@George.G.Moore.Author

@GMoore_Author

**Visit georgegmoore.com/the-music-of-mars/freemiums/
If asked for a password, enter Gretchen.**

If you enjoyed this book,

please review it on Amazon and Goodreads.

www.ingramcontent.com/pod-product-compliance
Lightning Source LLC
Chambersburg PA
CBHW021505110726
47899CB00001BA/307